PROPHECY AWAKENED

BOOK 1 PRIME PROPHECY SERIES

TAMAR SLOAN

JESS CONNORS
PUBLISHING

To Sean, Jesse and Connor.
You teach me the power of connection every day.

1

EDEN

Finish it and run.

That's all I need to do.

Finish it and run. Seems easy, fairly straightforward. I pull in a breath, needing some calm, but it doesn't work. Anxiety is still cartwheeling in my stomach.

It'll be just like the others. The nervousness spikes, growing, amplifying, and I realize that's not what I need to be thinking right now.

Standing alone as students mill about in groups, some chatting, the odd one laughing, others glancing, I shut the metal door of my locker with an unavoidable clang, wishing I'd finally figured out how to be invisible. The locker, the looks, are just like Boston High, and Chicago High, and Pittsburgh before that.

The cartwheeling sensation grows to Ferris wheel proportions. *Please don't let it be like some of the others*.

I clench every muscle I can find, clamping down on the fear like I have every other time. If I don't get this under control, I'm going to run out the wooden door I came in only a few moments ago. The last time I did that I was eight, and my mother was so annoyed, she actually grabbed my hand when bringing me back in. I'd been so surprised by the sensation, she'd dragged me right back in before I realized what was happening.

Thank goodness she didn't come to this one.

Which straight away makes Jacksonville High different. I'm glad she decided seventeen is old enough to do this alone. I glance around, managing to avoid any risk of eye contact with the students moving up and down the hall. Actually, Jacksonville High is pretty different to the multi-story monsters that I've called schools. I doubt it has a second floor to anything; one needs a school population above four hundred to justify stairs to anywhere.

But most importantly, it's the last one. The last move. The last school. The road is clear; the dream that's sustained me is within reach—finish what's left of my senior year and escape to college. All I need to do is keep my head down and fly under the radar for a few short months. *Please, please let that happen at this school.*

I stare at the piece of paper in my hand, conscious of lockers banging, the hallway emptying of sneakered feet. The smooth, white slip is supposed to enlighten me on where to go next, but it appears someone with a sense of humor has given me a timetable written in hieroglyphics.

"Hi!" a cheerful voice interrupts my reverie. I glance up from the blurry slip.

A petite girl with deep red hair, falling in stylish waves around her hazel eyes, stands in front of me. My hand clenches around my timetable; little people always make me feel like Godzilla. She's wearing tight jeans, a cute grey cardigan over a matching top, and a hint of mischief in her wide smile.

I glance over my shoulder, confused as to whom this bright, pretty girl is speaking to.

"Yes you, silly! You're the new girl, aren't you? Well, of course you are. There's no such thing as an unknown face in Jacksonville, now is there? Do you need a hand with your timetable? Nobody figures those things out on their own, but still, once you get the hang of it, you'll be all over it like hair on a gorilla."

I pause for a moment, considering whether there was a question that I actually needed to answer in that one-sided conversation, although I've discerned she's definitely speaking to me.

I shift my weight to my left foot, casually creating a little more distance between us. "Ummm, I think I'm getting the hang of it."

"Oh, where are my manners? My name is Tara Channon, long-time resident of the area, recently elected as your personal guide for the day." Tara executes a small curtsy, pinching and pulling her skinny jeans at the seams. The material remains determinedly moulded to her legs.

My lips twitch as I glance around her. "It appears to be a unanimous decision."

Tara giggles—a bright, tinkling sound. "Yep, we all voted!"

The generous offer is tempting. It does save me standing outside the reception office, trying to decipher the slip of paper in front of me, which could take the remainder of the day, maybe the week. But I feel uneasy being the focus of this girl's attention.

I take a deep breath. "Well, I suppose it's majority rules. Thanks. I'm Eden St. James." I pass her my timetable and the map of the school.

She glances down and promptly turns the map ninety degrees. *Well, there's my first problem.* Tara holds out her hand, and I pass her a pen, feeling a little like a nurse in an operating room. She efficiently marks several rooms on the map, writing the names of my classes. English, math, biology, chemistry... A group of seniors wanders past and a few call out to Tara. She smiles and waves at them absentmindedly. *Great, she's perky and popular.* The earlier uneasiness slithers further up my chest. I question whether aligning myself with this girl constitutes flying under the radar.

"The good news is we have math together second period; the bad news is you have old Mr Dough-e-rty for bio." Tara says Dougherty so slowly I almost fall asleep waiting for her to finish.

"Old Mr Dougherty?" I ask tentatively.

"Yep, I'm pretty sure he took his driver's test on a T-rex."

I burst out laughing, then quickly glance around. No one seems to have noticed my noisy outburst.

Tara leads the way down the corridor. "So, what do you think of Jacksonville, Wyoming, so far?"

"Well, the reserves are spectacular. On the other hand, I've discovered small town democracy is a little backwards." The minute I say it, I worry I may have offended her. An image of Tara frowning and turning away flashes through my mind, leaving me to navigate the school alone.

Tara giggles again, and I inwardly sigh. "Come on. We have a few minutes so I'll give you the grand tour. We'll start with the west wing."

Tara walks me through the handful of buildings that make up Jacksonville High. As we walk, she educates me about important school information. Don't drink from the bubbler on the left, Gavin sneezed there once. There's Beth, she sewed her finger on to a pair of jeans in Fashion Design last year. I learn Doug's acne is much better than it used to be (not wanting to be rude, I quickly glance away from his pimple-ridden face). Tara's voice drops to a conspiratory whisper as she informs me his third cousin, Mark, whose mother is the school librarian, is dating Beth's older sister. And I discover Tara's parents have a taste for themes as she points out her younger siblings: Dana and Gemma—their signature red hair peeking through the throngs of students—while commenting that Erika, Christa,

Breanna, and Flora will eventually go here. I have a sinking feeling it may be difficult to remain incognito in a Polly-Pocket-sized school.

"And that's Mitch." I glance at Tara. *Did her tone just get all breathy?*

I turn in the direction where Tara is staring. Walking toward us is a tall, broad-shouldered guy. Dark hair flops over bright blue eyes and a huge grin splits his good-looking face, his eyes focused on Tara. Tara has good taste in guys. She clutches her bag and beams in return.

Suddenly, Mitch pitches forward. From behind him appears a slighter guy, trying to wrestle Mitch into a headlock. The two laugh, and strong arms tangle as they push and shove. The milling students divide around them, some smiling and shaking their heads, some playfully jostling them back.

Tara groans. "And that's his twin, Noah."

Now that my attention has been caught by Mitch's brother, I can't tear it away. He's leaner than his brother, and a little shorter. I register tousled, dark blond hair, and an equally broad grin, but at this angle I can't see his eyes. For some reason I want to know what color they are. The brothers right themselves, giving one last shove. He turns his head to me as they stride closer. As his eyes settle on mine, the breath leaves my body in a rush, and just like that...*my world stops.*

And has a pulsing new focal point.

Brilliant blue eyes, the color of a seamless summer sky, brand me with the intensity of the sun. I feel my heart strike up a rapid new rhythm, my body temperature rising with each flutter of its hummingbird beat. My attention slowly branches out to register dark lashes, sensual lips, sculptured features. And something else. This boy radiates warmth, security, the promise of something more. I have a compelling urge to step forward into the welcoming glow. But a sense of undeniable, indefinable connection roots me to the spot. It coils and loops around me; all I can do is stare.

The smile fades from his finely chiseled face, his blue eyes widening. The blatant change from laughing and carefree to wordless shock thrusts me back to reality. I suck in the breath I'd forgotten to take. *I've been standing and gawking like I have the IQ of a watermelon!* I blush, the heat splashing across my skin like an exploding volcano. My eyes shoot to the floor.

Thank goodness Tara is unaware of my faux pas. I suspect only a split second has passed, rather than an eternity. She squeals and jumps into Mitch's arms. He chuckles as he spins her around. I watch the two, feeling even more uncomfortable ogling their public display of affection, but it's preferable to the azure gaze I can feel focused my way. I realize my timetable is slowly being mangled in my clenched hands.

"Guys, this is Eden. The new kid on the block." Tara says as she nestles below Mitch's arm.

"Hey, Eden, welcome to Jacksonville." The warm reception comes from Mitch. I give him a small smile. Noah hasn't said a word.

I avoid looking at him again. I don't need my GPA to translate the look on his face. No one wants someone staring at them like they're a freak. Believe me, I know.

"Hi, Eden." Noah's voice is like warm chocolate, viscous, dark heat that trickles down my spine. I long to look at him again, but I keep my eyes glued to the blue-and-brown patterned carpet.

"Nice to meet you both." I mumble, my hands thrust into the front pockets of my jeans. I wish I had bangs to hide behind, rather than my boring brown hair in its usual loose knot. Anything to take the spotlight off me. Maybe a natural disaster of some sort? I appreciate a tsunami is unlikely so far above sea level, but surely someone could rustle up a minor earthquake?

"I have to show Eden the labs. I'll see you later?" Tara's voice ends on a coy note, she's obviously addressing Mitch.

"Cafeteria at lunch. It's a date!" He grins.

Relief washes over me. I swiftly turn to my left.

"Not that way, goose. The labs are this way." Tara grabs my arm and propels me in the opposite direction. I take my flaming cheeks and stumble along with her, hyperaware that Noah hasn't twitched a muscle beside Mitch. I remind myself I'm used to staring. I ignore the strange fact that it bothers me so much.

Whatever just happened was a figment of my anxious, addled brain.

Tara drops me off at my first class—behavioral science— with a quick smile and a promise to see me in math. I pause at the entry, my books clenched tightly against my chest. My teacher, Mrs Dougal, spies me standing at the doorway. She heaves her considerable bulk from behind her desk and waddles over to me. She opens her arms, inviting me in, and I know instinctively she won't force me through the indignity of being introduced to the class.

"Ah, you must be Eden." *Wow, word travels fast in these parts.* "Come on in, dear. We're doing group work for the next few lessons. Let me see..." Mrs Dougal looks around the room, where the largely female class are sitting around groups of desks. Most eyes are turned my way. I wait out the front, feeling like an unwilling bacteria under the glare of a microscope. "I think I'll put you with Bailey, Bianca, and Brandon." She points to a table to the left.

I walk over and sit in the spare seat, putting down the books that had provided some measure of protection. The three *B*'s look at me, openly curious. No one makes an effort to engage me in conversation. Despite the revolving door of schools that has been my life, I still struggle with these first day introductions. I suck in a fortifying breath.

"Hi." I extend an olive branch, albeit a spindly one, with just a handful of leaves clinging to its twiggy bough.

Brandon smiles. "Hey, Eden right? Hi, I'm Brandon." I figured the guy with the spiked, brown hair and cheeky dimple was unlikely to be Bailey or Bianca. "I'll show you where we're at."

For our current topic, we're completing a survey on sensation-seeking behaviors. Brandon pulls his chair around so he can lean over and talk me through the task at hand. I don't need to complete Zuckerman's thirteen questions to tell you the outcome of my questionnaire. Peace and Quiet are the two attributes at the top of my list for a good night. Bianca, who repeatedly uses her fingers to comb her blond hair, is loudly extolling the virtues of abseiling, which she indulged in last weekend. I don't want to be seen as too much of a foreigner so I keep quiet about my reclusive tendencies.

"What about you, Eden? What do you do for kicks?" Brandon's dimples flash at me.

"Well, I haven't abseiled for quite some time." *Well, ever actually.* "I haven't seen much of Jacksonville though. What else is there to do around here?" I deflect like a pro fencer. Brandon smiles as he launches into the limited activities a small town has to offer—bowling, movies, and a local art gallery.

We complete the exercise, then collate and compare results with the rest of the class. With my low scores, I conclude I'm definitely old before my time.

Just as the bell rings, Brandon casually offers to walk me to my next class. I freeze, my muscles locked in surprise. More small-town hospitality? I'm saved from responding when Tara waltzes into the room. Without a word she propels me toward the door. I throw Brandon a smile, hoping it's both grateful and apologetic, rather than the confusion I'm really feeling. Brandon shrugs, giving me a small wave as I go.

Tara chats without pause as we walk to math. In the class, she leads us to two seats at the back of the classroom. Unfortunately, I'm not as invisible as I had hoped. Mr. Rosenberg calls out to me by name, apparently there are banners around the school advertising my arrival. There appears to be nowhere to hide, so I return to the front of the class.

Mr. Rosenberg looks like math has aged him before his time; sparse hair circles his balding head, whilst outdated clothes hang on his thin frame. He provides me with several handouts, I barely glance at them before I thank him, spin on my heel and aim for a hasty retreat. But Mr. Rosenberg stands and clears his throat. I cringe, my shoulders hunching up around my ears, knowing what's coming. He formally introduces me, following the same standard recipe I've endured before. *This is Eden, she's moved here from Boston. I hope you'll make her welcome.* I pretend to smile, my eyes scanning the room, seeing nothing but the faded posters on the walls. The now-crumpled pieces of paper bear witness to the awkwardness and agitation that clench and tangle my muscles.

I return to Tara, avoiding the gazes of my peers around me. I can just imagine their curious faces, judging my social status on the basis of my plain clothes, unstyled hair, and makeup-free face.

We're covering algebra, and rehashing the turning points of polynomials doesn't keep me engaged for very long. Apparently, it doesn't inspire attentiveness in Tara either. She holds her phone under the desk and types, her fingers flying across the keypad. I wonder if she's texting Mitch. My thoughts instantly turn to Noah. I try to rationalize my earlier irrational response. Of course, there are countless reasons for my thunderstruck reaction. He is pretty hot after all; any girl with a pulse would be a little flustered. Although I don't usually get worked up about compelling blue eyes framed by strong brows...or full lips that would look effeminate on a guy if they weren't resting above a sculpted firm chin...

I give myself a mental slap and return to my inner checklist. There is my first-day jitters. Oh, and I forgot to take my multivitamins this morning. Didn't I hear somewhere that the moon is in Sagittarius...

Tara elbows me in the ribs, saving me from my spiralling lame excuses. "I just updated my status. Look." She holds up her phone for me to see. *Scored a sweet gig, escorting the hot new notable around JH. eden st james is in da house!* Why would she call me hot? I draw in a sharp breath as I register that *my name is on Facebook*! I withdrew myself from social networking back in Boston. The lancing comments that were flung at me, particularly when people had the protection of anonymity, had cut deep. I feel the blood drain from my face as I stare at the screen. So much for flying under the radar. Right now I'm a great big bleep on the screen!

Tara notices my pale complexion. "What's wrong?"

"Ms. Channon!" Mr. Rosenberg's gravelly voice calls across the room. His bald head bobs over on matchstick legs. "Are you aware of our cell phone policy?"

"Oh, I'm so sorry, sir. My mother sent me a text about my sister's cello lesson this afternoon. I should have waited to look at it. I didn't mean to interrupt." Tara bats her long lashes, looking contrite.

Surely he's not going to get sucked in by that blatant buttering up. Mr. Rosenberg puffs out his pigeon chest. "Put it away. I don't want to see it again." I blink once, twice. Apparently Mr. Rosenberg doesn't mind being Tara's piece of toast.

"Of course not, Mr. Rosenberg."

Mr. Rosenberg returns to the front of the class. Tara waits a few moments before turning to me.

"You just went albino on me there for a second. What happened?"

Thankfully, those few moments have allowed me to pull myself together. "Just saw the next question." I shrug. "I really don't believe that it's 'interesting' that polynomials behave differently depending on whether they have odd or even exponentials." I wonder absently if Jacksonville High has a fencing team, because I could qualify for the Olympics.

"Gee, you take your math seriously!" Tara doesn't look convinced, but she lets it slide. "Unlike Luke over there." I follow the direction of Tara's finger. A dark-haired boy has his elbow resting on the table, his head in his palm, eyes closed. I'm pretty sure he's asleep. Mr Rosenberg is focused passionately on the board, his arms gesticulating wildly as they trace the wavelike graphs. Tara and I cup our hands over our mouths, suppressing our giggles.

I take a moment to realize that I don't recall having this much fun in math since we measured flour to make play dough with Mrs. Moore. Actually, I had forgotten what it's like to talk to someone whilst in a classroom. Or a school.

Once the bell goes, my stomach sinks at the thought of recess. Scrutinizing eyes. Gossiping lips. Expectations fortified or vanquished. Not the most appetizing of fare. My new knight in shining armor saves me again when she offers for me to accompany her to the art room.

"I get the place to myself every Monday recess and some days after school. It's too hard to work on stuff at home." I imagine Tara's brood of younger siblings may make that a little difficult.

"Sounds good to me." I try not to sound too enthusiastic.

In the art room, it's apparent Tara is in her element. She hurries over to an easel, where a large painting is resting. She removes the cover and steps back, eyeing it critically.

"I'm making it for Mitch's birthday." She glances at me nervously. "What do you think?" she asks, biting her fingernails.

My muesli bar stops midair. This effervescent girl is asking for my opinion? I hope it's good, I'm not a very good liar and I don't want to offend the first person to show me some measure of hospitality for some time.

I step cautiously toward the painting. It's a detailed and vibrant depiction of two wolves dominating a snowy landscape. The sweeping paints outline a reddish-brown wolf standing in front of a larger black wolf. The darker wolf is affectionately licking the muzzle of the red wolf, whose ears are back, eyes closed, mouth slightly parted. Tara has captured its look of blissful contentment with soft, fuzzy strokes. The black wolf's blue eyes gaze reverently as it strokes the red wolf with its tongue. I stare at the painting for long seconds. The expressions are virtually human, the connection unmistakable. I almost feel like I'm intruding on a private moment. In the corner is a small backwards *r*, which I figure is Tara's signature.

"It's amazing. How could he not love it?"

Tara is watching my face with a keen intensity. She nods, apparently satisfied with my reaction.

"It's almost finished..." She picks up a paintbrush, instantly absorbed in the precise finishing touches only a creator can divine.

I'm not bothered. Actually, I'm relieved. It's nice to relax away from prying eyes. So far I've met my three requirements for a first day. One, maintain my grades. I've already spent the weekend scanning the subject outlines and making notes on upcoming assignments. This one I can do. Two, not get irreversibly lost. So far so good. Admittedly, there are only a few scattered buildings and I've had a guide, but I'll take what I can get. Finally, not set off anyone's freak-o-meter. At this stage of the proceedings, I'm feeling hopeful.

Then I remember Noah's stunned expression. I scowl and my mood drops several notches. I use the remainder of recess to munch on my muesli bar, trying to translate my rumpled timetable.

The ringing of the bell breaks the companionable silence. Tara jumps, and knocks over a small pot of paint.

"Sneezing hotpockets! Not again. Sorry, Eden, I'm going to have to clean this up before Mrs. Malibu gets back. Are you okay to get to biology?"

"Sure, I remember where the labs are." I think. Tara showed me the labs just after I met...*him*.

I offer her a hand, but Tara shoos me off, so I head to the labs on my own. Biology with the infamous Mr. Dougherty. Surely he can't be that old, could he?

I promptly break my second new-school-rule, and manage to get a little lost. It means I'm a couple of minutes late. Now I have to enter after everyone else, meaning, once again, I'll be the focus of attention. I don't want to know if Mr. Dougherty leans toward kindly Mrs. Dougal or merciless Mr. Rosenberg when it comes to introductions. I enter with my head down, wearing my books like a shield, and quickly walk to the back of the room where I find a lone bench. I sit down with a small sigh. Crisis avoided.

Mr. Dougherty, a small, gnarled man, is sitting at the front bench, deeply immersed in a textbook open in front of him. I look closely at him. He's very still. Deathly still. Deep wrinkles line his leathered face, reminding me of an ancient ridged mountain that has been eroded by time. His sparse, grey hair seems to spring from the top of his serene head like a fountain. I can almost hear his joints creak as he slowly and deliberately turns a page. Tara was right; I think he could be older than Yoda. Curiously, one would expect that the classroom would be loud and jostling as the students wait for the teacher to reign in order.

But the students talk quietly amongst themselves, their books out and ready.

I remove my text and shiny new writing pad, prepared to wait. I sneak a peek around the room from beneath my lashes. And that's when I see him. Noah. He's sitting on his own several rows up, leaning forward on his elbows as he speaks to the students at the bench in front of him. The position bunches his shoulders, showing defined muscles beneath a loose-fitting tee. Even across a room I feel the urge to look longer, deeper. My breath hitches, and my eyes make the small leap back to my book.

Sneezing hotpockets, all right! Why did he have to be in my favorite class? Correction, what used to be my favorite class. I keep my head down, pen up. The less I look at this guy, the better. I refuse to make any more of a spectacle of myself. I just walked straight past him, and he never said a word.

It's obvious what he thinks of me.

2

NOAH

Wow.
    And I mean W. O. W!
    With feet rooted to the spot, jaw possibly sitting beside them, I stand and stare.

    The girl in front of me is tall, almost as tall as me, and lean. I know I'm not meant to notice, let alone appreciate the curves in all the right places. But I do. My eyes flicker past mahogany hair tied back in a loose knot, flushed skin, slightly parted lips, but it's her eyes that draw my attention. As I connect with eyes as deep and green as the forest I've grown up in, every muscle fiber locks on impact. My lungs freeze, and my heart pumps hard inside my suddenly tight chest. Who was it that said eyes are the windows to the soul? Because that wise, old mortal certainly knew what they were talking about. Those mysterious forest green pools are profound. Kindred. And soul deep.

    In a heart beat I know that something just changed. Deeply and irrevocably. That in the space of a few thundering heart beats something got rearranged...no realigned.

    And I want in.

    Amazingly, she's gazing wide-eyed right back

Suddenly, she drops her gaze to the floor, blushing. That amazing feeling that had sparked is abruptly severed, and I let out the breath that had been captured in my too-small lungs. Tara introduces us. Eden. Her name swirls in my mind, and I savor it. I duck my head, willing her to look at me again, but even when I say "hi," she just mumbles, staring at the floor.

Did I imagine what just happened? I'd frown if my face wasn't still slack with shock. I'm left trying to grasp the feelings that had felt so real just a few moments ago.

All of a sudden, Tara pulls Eden away. I have an overwhelming impulse to call them back, follow her, anything. Questions are flying through my mind, and they all start with 'What the...?' Mitch grabs my arm before I get the chance to do something completely crazy and stupid, and we continue down the hallway. Mitch has that skip in his step he always gets after seeing Tara.

While I'm left dazed and disorientated, and I wonder if I'm swaying like a drunk.

All through first and second period, my mind replays the scene from this morning. Those wide, green eyes. The flash of attraction that grabbed me — hard. I realize it's a good thing no major disasters had headed our way, because my feet had turned to lead and welded to the ground. And it felt like she was just as floored as I was. But then she shut down like the Millennium Falcon about to be assailed by storm troopers.

In biology, I'm still mulling over the puzzle, and what to do about it when she shoots past, head down, clutching her books to her chest. She's in biology. And I know opportunity has just been served to me on a shiny silver platter. I shift a little in my seat, turning to watch her walk to the back of the room. Her scent, wildflowers warmed by the sun, hangs in the space she leaves behind. I breathe it in, stretching my lungs to capacity.

She sits at a back bench, and busies herself with her books.

Mr. Dougherty is doing his usual beginning-of-class ritual. 'Centering' he calls it. I know I have a few more minutes. Now that I have a few uninterrupted seconds, I notice the unique almond shape of her eyes, tipping slightly up at the corners. I almost expect to see elven ears poking through the dark hair framing her cheeks, contrasting against her clear, pale skin. It's like Snow White and that elven chick from *Lord of the Rings* had a love child. Not physically possible, seeing as they are both female, or realistically possible, seeing as they are both fictional characters. And the girl in the back row is definitely, alluringly alive and breathing.

I try to channel The Force to get her to look at me. But apparently you have to actually train to be a Jedi, because she just stares down at her book. I know I need to talk to her—a proper introduction. Try to get to know this girl. I push my stool back.

"Hey, Noah." Jordan moves from the bench in front of me and holds up a fist, white teeth gleaming in his ebony face. I fist pump him back, my shoulders admitting defeat as I drop back onto my seat. "So, we've got a new girl, huh?"

"Yeah, I noticed." Jordan is half off his stool, looking over my shoulder, not even trying to be discreet. I resist the urge to turn.

"Nice bit of eye candy." Jordan's black brows wiggle beneath his curly mop. I bristle, although it's nothing I haven't heard from him before.

"Yeah, I noticed."

"Boys are so shallow." Darlene groans from beside Jordan, rolling her eyes. She turns and leans skinny arms on my bench, her freckled face leaning forward. "Noah, would you look over my assignment for me?"

I lift an eyebrow. "The one that was due two days ago?"

"Yeah." She hunches her shoulders, wrinkling her freckled nose. "That one."

I sigh. "Sure, email it through."

"Thanks, you're awesome." She beams, brown eyes winking merrily. She returns to her laptop. I suspect that's the assignment on her screen.

Mr. Dougherty finally joins the land of the living, rising from his chair, his movements slow and deliberate. I turn squarely to the front, knowing the window of opportunity just shut. He lifts the textbook from the desk, slowly running his finger down the open page. I almost want to go and give him a hand.

"Ecosystems." The word hangs in the classroom for several seconds. "A community of living organisms working in conjunction with the abiotic components of their environment." Mr. Dougherty speaks slowly and thoughtfully, each word calculated and purposeful. Seeing as he's too ancient for PowerPoint, we all know to take notes or miss out. He walks up and down the aisles between benches, scratching his papery chin, keen grey eyes, assessing how engaged his class is.

"Mr. Brand, what do I mean by abiotic?" he addresses Jordan beside him. He calls everyone by their formal title, something about affording the same respect given him.

"Non-living components sir, like air or water," Jordan responds promptly. Mr. Dougherty is known for his pop questions, and no one wants to be caught out in front of his peers. Smart kids come prepared for Mr. Dougherty's classes.

"Excellent, Mr. Brand. All linked together through fascinating nutrient cycles and complex energy flows. The ultimate circuit of conversion and succession." He's really getting warmed up now. He's almost speaking at normal rhythm.

I glance back at Eden. Unlike the rest of the class, she's staring out the window. I turn to see what's caught her attention. A blue jay is perched on a branch not far from the window. A smile tips up the corner of her lips. She touches a finger to the window. Expecting to see the bird flit away, my eyebrows leap up when it takes two hops toward her. Eden's smile widens, and she presses closer. The bird, unafraid, jumps to the window sill, flitting its brilliant blue wings and twitching its tail. I think it's flirting with her! Am I allowed to get jealous of a girl I just met, with a bird that could bath in my breakfast bowl?

"Ms. St. James." Mr. Dougherty heads to the back of the class. I cringe; not even the new kid is safe from Dougherty's perpetual quiz.

"Mr. Dougherty," I call out, but he sails past. I don't know if he didn't hear me, or ignored me.

Oh no. Eden is about to find out that spacing out in old Dougherty's class holds the natural consequence of social embarrassment. The blue jay flits away in alarm. He knows what's coming.

Eden turns to Mr. Dougherty, her hand quickly picking up her pen. "What is the primary energy flow of any ecosystem?"

A slow blush creeps up Eden's creamy skin. So it's not just me that has that effect.

I've just opened my mouth to jump in with the answer when she says in a quiet, clear voice, "Solar energy, sir. Energy from the sun generally enters through the process of photosynthesis, providing the continuous input of energy necessary to sustain ecosystems." My jaw drops open an inch.

Not just a pretty face, huh? Eden St. James has a brain between her non-elven ears.

"Exactly!" says Mr. Dougherty, waving his textbook like a preacher holding a Bible. He continues his monologue, spurred on by Eden's stellar response. Jordan flicks me a quick thumbs up, eyebrows raised. I stare as Eden, not bothering to see how the class responds to her answer, returns to her book. Why does it feel like the turtle just withdrew back into its shell? I scrape my stool back as I shuffle my books, attracting puzzled frowns from those around me. Eden's head remains firmly buried in her shell.

It's almost the end of the class before I get on old Dougherty's radar. He's waxing slow lyrical about the differences between food webs and chains, when he comes to stand beside me.

"Mr. Phelan, can you name a food chain close to home?"

As I'm asked the question, an idea forms in my mind. "McDonalds?"

Jordan chuckles quietly, whilst Darlene frowns at me. The rest of the class is silent. The furrows above Mr. Dougherty's eyes defy gravity as his eyebrows shoot up amongst the wrinkles, making him look like a shocked shar pei. From the corner of my eye I see Eden's head shoot up. Finally! I hadn't thought as far ahead as what to do with her attention, so all I end up doing is staring back. Beside me, old Dougherty takes a deep breath. Uh oh.

"Mr. Phelan." I reluctantly raise my eyes to his. "My classroom is not a place to gain social distinction, and it's certainly not a behavior I expected to see from you. As said by the great Martin Luther King, 'nothing in the world is more dangerous than sincere ignorance and conscientious stupidity'." His wiry brows drop low. "We don't need to corroborate that statement. Please review chapter six."

My gaze lowers to the hands clasped on my book. He turns to the remainder of the class. "The national park on our back doorstep is known as one of the few remaining, nearly intact, temperate ecosystems on Earth. As was uploaded last night, it will be your next major assessment task."

Phew. I survived. I feel a little bad for letting Dougherty down. Wow, that mutual respect thing really does work. I'll make it up to him, once I put my plan in motion. I glance back at Eden. Her tilted, emerald eyes are still on me, but the moment I turn, she darts back to her book. Definitely turtle-like.

As Mr. Dougherty finishes outlining our upcoming assignment, Eden doesn't glance up from her furious note-taking. At the end of the lesson she leaves the same way she entered, head down, books clutched tightly. I watch her leave, but she doesn't glance up.

It's time for phase two.

3

EDEN

Next lesson is physical education. I don't mind gym. I enjoy the release only physical exercise can bring. As I enter the gymnasium I feel like a popcorn machine has malfunctioned in my stomach. In the change room I notice Jacksonville High has followed the educational trend of gender specific classes as I'm surrounded by a small group of chattering girls. They're all throwing surreptitious glances my way. The all-girls class reminds me of West Boston High. But there the girls threw other things my way.

At least I know Noah won't be here. That guy is not good for my fragile equilibrium. Even though he barely noticed I was in biology, I'd been hyperaware of his presence. Luckily ecosystems are a favorite topic and I've already started the major assessment task. I'm pretty sure the notes I took are going to be in the same hieroglyphics as my timetable.

I've come in partway through soccer, and, for a little while, I don't mind being tall. By halftime I've scored two goals. When one of the girls goes to high-five me, I flinch as I see the hand approach. She stops it midair and, for a split second, I'm unsure how to respond. Thankfully, I manage to kick-start my brain and return the universal gesture of good sportsmanship.

"Great goal." The girl smiles and jogs over to her position on the field. A warm glow radiates in my chest. Then I realize she's probably pleased I've actually been useful to the team.

I'm still a little hot and sweaty as I head to the cafeteria for lunch. Tara, bless her, meets me in the corridor, and I smile at her gratefully. Entering the room with the majority of the school body will be easier with a friendly face by my side. My other good friend, Daunted, is clinging tightly to me. She's brought Apprehensive and Intimidated to join the party. Scared Witless is tugging on my sleeve, asking if she could come too. I hope I can get through this without giving myself a heart attack.

We join the line, heading toward the dubious smell emanating from the serving area. Tall, narrow windows line the external wall, providing fragmented frames of the grassy oval on the other side. Rectangular tables fill the room in regimented lines, the disciplined look broken by haphazard chairs, strewn paper, and milling students.

Tara chats to students in front of her, and those walking past to join the line. She introduces me to all of them. My brain is too consumed with keeping the extra friends I brought under control to remember their names. I paste a polite smile on my face, hoping I won't have to shake hands with my damp palms. Their faces pass in a blur of white, smiling teeth, and all I can manage are repeated mumbled 'nice to meet you too's.'

As we reach the source of the aroma, I reluctantly look through the heated glass. The view is dominated by a huge pan of grey meat, defying gravity as it floats in an expanse of blubbery gravy. A handful of potatoes and pumpkin pieces lean to the side, their oily surface gleaming under the heated lights. Seeing as there are no other options, I go for the roasted vegetables. I think they may have been deep-fried.

Tara leads the way, weaving through the rectangular tables. I kind of wish that someone a little taller and wider had befriended me. A human shield would have concealed me a little better. Instead, I have someone that can probably see up my nose.

Despite her slight frame, Tara is sizeable enough to eclipse where we're heading. It's only once she sits down and I'm left standing that I see there are three people seated around one of the tables. Tara, Mitch. *And Noah.* Once again, the undeniable magnetism pulls at me and my eyes fasten on him. His sky-blue eyes are centred on me and I feel that dynamic jolt. I instantly look down at the tray in my hand.

Tara sits beside Mitch, leaving me the only other space adjacent to Noah. I slide onto the plastic seat, hoping it can hold the truckload of nervousness that just spawned in every cell of my body. My tray clatters to the table, having slipped out of wobbly fingers. The fork bounces once on the table when Noah's hand flicks out, catching it midair.

"Thanks," I mumble, my cheeks going infrared.

Noah looks almost as surprised at his lightning reflexes as I am. He recovers nicely with a smile. "No problems."

He leans in a little to place it on my tray. A warm, masculine scent spills over me. Spiced sandalwood teases my nostrils, encouraging me to breathe deeper, longer. Leaving me to wonder if there is any sense that is safe from this guy.

My eyes return to the greasy food on my plate, my mind whirling with feelings I've never experienced before. Feelings that are overwhelming and confusing.

Mitch lazily puts his arm around Tara and drops a light kiss on her nose. "So, how's your day been?"

"Well, did some important status updating in math, managed to wrangle my way out of gym, worked in the art room, and I'm pretty sure I attended history and English." Tara ticks each period off on her fingers. At the mention of art, Mitch narrows his eyes at her, then turns to me.

"Eden, what do you think of the color choices Tara has chosen for her masterpiece?" He looks at me expectantly, apparently well-versed with his birthday present.

Tara's eyes go wide and she opens her mouth to speak.

Fortunately my mother determinedly hammered naiveté out of me long before I understood what it was. "Oh, the pinks are lovely".

Mitch looks a little stunned. "Pink?" he asks incredulously.

"Oh yes. They contrast beautifully with the purple polka dots on her sculpture."

"Sculpture?" Mitch has been reduced to an echo.

I look at him in wide-eyed innocence. "Although I figure she's using artistic license as I'm not sure how the color scheme relates to Justin Bieber."

Tara grins at me while Noah roars with laughter and slaps Mitch on the back. "You can't fool this one, bro!"

As is my perpetual tendency around this guy, I blush. Tara turns to Mitch, eyes shooting hazel-colored nuclear missiles.

Noah turns those mesmerizing eyes on me. "So, Eden, how has day one been at Jacksonville High?" Hmmm, I quite like the sound of my name being dipped in that chocolaty voice.

"So far, so good." My voice sounds like I've just been for a hard run around the oval. I quickly jam a piece of greasy potato in my dry mouth, and discover my mistake when it struggles to make it to my throat.

Noah turns his body to face me squarely. The sounds of the other students talking, laughing, walking past, fade as my view is dominated by him. "What did you think of old Dougherty?" So, he noticed I was there. Apparently my skin had finally cooled, because I blush again.

"He certainly knows his stuff, and likes to keep his students on their toes."

Noah chuckles. His smile lights up his face; up close it leaves me a little breathless. "Well, I think he builds biospheres in his spare time. Have you had a look at the first assignment?"

I'm not sure why he continues to make conversation. Maybe he feels sorry for the girl who obviously is sight impaired as she can't look anywhere but at him, and has some dermatological problem as she keeps flushing crimson.

"Yeah, I've checked it out," I hedge. If having the preliminary research and initial outline done could be considered 'checking it out'.

"It looks like a toughie."

Really? I thought it looked fairly straightforward. But I don't want to seem rude. "Yeah, just a matter of getting your head around some of the terminology, I suppose."

"Urgh, you guys are so boring!" Tara has obviously finished berating Mitch, because her elbows slide across the table toward us, her chin in her hands. "So, Eden, where were you before you came to this two-bit town?"

I look up at their expectant faces. My stomach drops a little. I'm the central focus of three pairs of eyes, one bright hazel and two sets of blues. One blue pair a little more distracting than the other. I trace a fake marble line on the tabletop with my finger.

"Boston." I shrug.

"Wow, you're slumming it now," Mitch states.

Actually, so far it's been a huge step up. "Everyone has been very welcoming." I glance at Tara gratefully. I don't look anywhere else.

Tara, who seemed so friendly and amenable, decides it's time to burst that bubble. Within minutes, despite minimalist answers, the three people in front of me know I moved with my mother.

"Wow, you must have such a close relationship with just the two of you!"

"Ah, yeah, you couldn't measure the distance between us."

That I live at the Clear Creek Inn, where my mother is the new executive manager. "That must be cool! You should totally invite me over." Have company? At my house? That would involve an alternate universe.

"Well, it's close to the Reserve." It has some lovely hiking trails, I've already investigated a few of them.

"It has some amazing wildlife," says Tara with a quirk of her lips.

That yes, I do have Coldplay's latest album. "Oooh, I knew I liked you for a reason!"

That I plan on studying veterinary science at college. Tara giggles at that one. I'm not sure why that is amusing, and I wonder why she's laughing at me. Anxious thoughts quickly provide a few likely reasons.

That I'm vegetarian. "Are you on some calorie control diet? There are like, three things on your plate."

"No...I'm vegetarian."

"Oh." Tara's first single word answer is telling. I really didn't think it was that big a deal.

Throughout, Mitch looks on amused. Noah is watching me with a quiet intensity, stroking his bottom lip with his index finger. It's a little unnerving. I have to work really hard to stop my eyes straying to that full bottom lip. I shift a little in the hard plastic seat.

The moment Tara takes a breath, I divert the focus from me. "What about you guys? You all from around here?"

Noah answers the question. "We were born and bred in Jacksonville. Our family is one of the originals around here." He tilts his head toward Tara. "Tara lives in nearby Wilmot, a fellow founding family."

Tara splays her hands on the table. "What else did you want to know?"

I'm debating whether I'm brave enough to actually ask anything. Maybe something that will give me an idea about how to disconnect the direct line to my blush reflex before I get permanent sunburn, when the bell goes. *Well, that doesn't seem fair.*

We all get up with our trays, and I dump most of the vegetables into the rubbish. I hate waste, but my anxious stomach had too much to deal with. Tara steps up on tippy-toes to give Mitch a quick kiss, and my gracious guide walks with me toward the cafeteria doors.

I have English next; satire and comedy I believe. I don't see a lot of humor in that. I pretend not to notice Noah and Mitch leaving for the side door. I think I'm feeling relieved.

"See you later, Eden." Noah is walking backward out the door. He flashes me a grin before turning and leaving.

I sag a little now that his cobalt eyes are no longer providing the structural support for my spine. I don't like this exhilarating quickening that occurs when I'm in close proximity with this boy. One I only just met. One whose behavior is fascinating and bewildering. One who could never be interested in me.

Every instinct tells me to fortify my defenses.

Well, not every instinct. A small part of me is curious, and delights in these feelings. It wants to spend time analyzing his reactions, looking for glimmers of hope.

It's this reaction that contravenes all my intentions of remaining detached and safe.

And I'm not the gambling type.

4

NOAH

"**N**oah, where's that brother of yours?"

I glance up from the application in front of me and flex my shoulders. Every time I complete one page, two more seem to spawn. The kitchen bench is littered with pages, looking like a printer vomited all over its smooth Formica surface.

"I think I saw him in the garage."

Our father, a giant of a man, growls under his breath. Confirming my statement, the shrill whine of a power tool spills from the east side of the house. Dad stomps to the garage, his police-issue boots echoing down the hallway. From beside me, Stash jumps up and follows, as if to provide canine corroboration for Mitch's misdemeanor. After a couple of minutes of muffled voices, Dad returns, his massive chest rumbling like distant thunder. He runs a hand through his dark blond hair.

"I should remind him of the last Precept," he mumbles to himself.

I hide a smile. Maybe I could poke the bear a bit.

"How's it going in there?" I inquire, eyebrows raised in innocent curiosity.

"Said he's making something for Tara." My father's bushy brows shoot down to meet above the bridge of his nose. "He should be looking at those applications like you." His tone reverberates with censure.

I sigh. There's a reason Mitch is avoiding these tortuous documents.

Mitch steps into the kitchen, wiping his hands down stained jeans. Sawdust clings to his dark hair, dusting him like icing sugar. "I'll just go clean up." He drags his boots up the stairs and my father's blue eyes follow his ascent. Those identically colored eyes turn to me, clouded with concern.

"Just give him time." Isn't it supposed to heal all wounds? Actually, personal experience has taught me all we do is camouflage the scar tissue in lame clichés. And, although the pain dulls and the nerve-damaged edges go numb, nobody acknowledges that the weakened, puckered skin is never the same.

I guess it depends on how much fate likes to pick at it.

Dad turns his solid body away from the staircase, I suspect signaling that particular well-worn conversation is over. "How's school going?" Yep, over.

"Fine, getting warmed up for midterms." I begin to tidy up the spewed paper.

"Mitch said a new girl started." Dad moves about the kitchen, making himself a coffee. He pulls down a ceramic mug, one I made in elementary school. It's supposed to look like Kung Fu Panda, but the googly eyes protruding from the chunky, black-and-white clay look more like a disfigured badger.

I barely miss a beat. "Yeah, Tara took her under her wing." The paper is stacked neatly, and I've run out of things to occupy my hands.

Dad's cup pauses on its journey to his mouth. His eyes narrow, measuring my response. Unfortunately, spending my early life preparing me for my supposed birthright entailed long periods of time with this man. Entire days spent hiking and training and learning. My father's voice rumbling through the history of our family, startling flighty sage grouse from the bushes. Moose lazily raising their racked heads to watch Dad kneeling in the tall grass, translating tracks into an animal's diet, age, habits. His great big mountain of a body, always there, apprenticing me with the skills and knowledge I needed to take on my future role. Thanks to him the Precepts are carved into my cerebral cortex.

Although that all stopped two years ago, it's meant he knows my nuances well.

"If she's with Tara, then she's not far from you guys." Doggone perceptive police skills. "She nice?" He takes a cautious sip of his hot brew.

I raise one shoulder, my head leaning as if to meet it midair. "I think so, kinda quiet."

Dad continues to regard me over the rim of that darned cup. I'm determined not to squirm like I'm eight and Mitch and I just got caught offering Uncle Joe Oreos with toothpaste for icing.

Mitch thwumping down the stairs saves me. I quickly grab the stack of paper and head over to the nearby desk. Mitch grabs a travel mug and fills it up from the coffeepot.

"Ready?" he asks Dad.

The censure is back in my father's glare. "I was ready twenty minutes ago." Mitch rolls his eyes, conveniently behind Dad's back.

Dad squeezes my shoulder as he walks past. He used to say 'next time' each occasion we endured this routine. Now he is silent. I stay by the desk, just as soundless.

He grabs the car keys from the hook, calling out, "Back after dark, love."

Mom calls her assent from the lounge. Tonight is scrapbooking night. We all keep clear of the room littered with baby photos and the guaranteed ride down memory lane.

I head to my room. I want to avoid the awkwardness that would be inevitable if I were to stay and watch their departure.

"Bye, Noah." Mitch calls out, his voice flat, weighed down by unanswered prayers. I don't know who wishes I was there more.

"Get one for me," I call out. At least I try for buoyant. I sense rather than hear Mitch's heavy sigh. Every time they go out, I feel that wound splinter a little. A bit like a zipper that can never quite do up and quickly unravels under the pressure of two years of disappointment and disillusionment.

I don't begrudge them; it's who we are.

Correction, it's who they are.

Once the truck has rumbled down the driveway, I return to the kitchen. I'm hungry again. I make myself a ham and cheese sandwich. On second thoughts, I make two. And just for good measure, I add an extra helping of ham on both. As I head upstairs to my room, I think back to my conversation with Dad. Eden. A bite of sandwich has a little difficulty descending as those forest-green eyes hover before me. Framed by dark hair swept back in a loose knot, pale skin contrasting against parted red lips. I wonder if she ever wears its unknown length down. I rub a palm on my chest as my mark becomes oddly warm.

With a jolt I realize these feelings are the realest I've felt in almost two years. For so long I've been wandering, drifting, purposeless. Now electric attraction is coursing through my veins; intriguing potential has me curious. I pause on the steps. It's like one look from this girl has charged new energy into my life. Who is she? And how do I get to know her?

In my room I head to the wall. I pull down my guitar, slowly brushing the dust off its curved body. I sit on my bed, fingers picking and strumming like I was doing this yesterday. I've just finished tuning it when a melody begins to form. I smile, recognizing it—an oldie but a goody—James Blunt's *High*.

There, surrounded by the memories of a childhood that had very different plans, I smile a little as I plot a new course.

One that involves a dark-haired, green-eyed enigma.

5

EDEN

As I step out my back door, I take a moment to absorb my surroundings. Clear Creek Inn is a luxury resort, providing affluent visitors designer décor and lavish spa facilities. The whole place screams Angelina Jolie perfection, where Mother Nature's canvas has been polished, manicured, and plucked into a stunning panorama. Lush lawns surround voluptuous flower beds in flawless lines, while duplicate rows of cabins parade through with angular precision. Elegant beauty that is designed to look natural and easy and effortless. Like countless landscape artists haven't put endless hours into creating the exquisite facade before you.

Tucked at the back of the cabins, I'm glad our timber cottage is situated far enough away to mute the tourist hustle and bustle. With the added advantage of being close enough for my mother to have difficulty clocking off. I turn my back on the resort; it's the spectacular surroundings beyond Clear Creek that have me wide-eyed and dazzled. I haul in a deep, purifying breath. The afternoon wind nips at my cheeks as I take the barely decipherable trail that heads away from the cultured resort grounds, toward a pure evergreen wonderland.

I leave the warmth of the cabin, my thick jacket retaining just a fraction of what I left behind. I don't think I'm going to like winter here. Caesar, the bounding German shepherd by my side, reminds me why I'm out here, despite the biting breeze. "You wanna go for a walk, boy?" I ruffle the thick fur of his shoulders. Caesar barks excitedly, pulling on his lead.

Once I'm amongst the towering pines, I lean down and release Caesar, wrapping up the leash and shoving it in the depths of my pocket. Caesar barks again, leaping like a puppy, and sets off. I smile a little; no one would guess this dog is the same broken mess I met over two years ago. I'm transported to that day I walked into Safe Haven Veterinary Center, leaving the world of school and home at the door, enveloped by the smell of domesticated animals and disinfectant.

"Thank goodness, Eden. Dr. Adams needs you in the back." Shirley, the receptionist who has a wonderful mother-hen persona, greets me in a rush. A few strands of her bright blue hair have begun to escape the elaborate knot perched on her head. What started as a work experience placement has become a voluntary part-time job. Animals are something I know, something I can do. And Jack Adams, the resident vet of this small practice, leapt at the opportunity for me to spend some more hours here. Probably the free cage cleaning.

I head out the back, and when I open the door, wailing and howling hits me like a wave. Jack is studiously ignoring the cacophony as he fills a syringe with clear liquid. His spectacled grey eyes glance at a large crate sitting to one side of the room. Ominous growling emanates from the dim interior. He scratches his disheveled grey hair, hair that would give Einstein a run for his money. Jack's frazzled expression dissolves into relief when he sees me at the door.

"Ah, Eden. The big guy here was involved in a hit and run. He was brought in unconscious, but now that he's with the land of the living, he won't let anyone near him. I can't get to him to assess the

damage, and he's upsetting the rest of the troops. Could you see what you can do?"

I walk slowly over to the cage, and squat down a few feet away. Inside sits a dirty and emaciated German shepherd. His muzzle wrinkles as he bares his teeth; another round of deep growling rumbles from within. He's not happy to see me.

"Shhh," I say soothingly. The menacing growling grows louder in response, exposing more bloodied canine teeth and pale gums. I absently note the telltale sign of anaemia.

"He almost took my fingers off when I tried to give him the piece of meat with the sedative in it," Jack volunteers from behind me.

I sit on the floor, not going any nearer. The noise level in the room is already decreasing, but the beast in front of me remains guarded. He doesn't relax his aggressive stance, nor does the growling abate. I glance at Jack, who remains still in the back corner of the room. He smiles at me encouragingly, the crinkles around his eyes deepening. This part is always embarrassing. I would much prefer to be alone, but Jack wouldn't leave me alone with a potentially dangerous, and rather large, animal.

I fill my lungs with air and begin to hum gently under my breath —a soothing tune, almost a lullaby. I don't know where I know this song; it has no words. My mother certainly never sang it to me. The dog doesn't take his eyes off me, but pauses his growling to listen to the melody. Ignoring my audience, the song gains momentum, and I sing a little louder. I gently move forward, testing. The dog simply stares, eyes wide and wary. A couple more shuffles along the ground and I'm at the cage door. He whines softly, unsure whether he wants me in his personal space. I continue the soft tune as I incrementally raise my hand for the door latch. I can almost feel Jack holding his breath behind me.

I cautiously open the latch and the door pops open a crack. I continue the song, not missing a beat, as the hound's ears dart forward. He leans closer to cautiously sniff my hand. I hold it there, *wanting to be as non-threatening as possible. He moves to shuffle forward, but whimpers quietly. He's hurt, and my heart aches for this proud dog.*

Jack passes me the syringe he filled earlier. I didn't hear him take those few steps, and the dog instantly stiffens. Jack gently moves back. What am I supposed to do with this? *I wonder incredulously.*

"Straight into his shoulder muscles will be fine," whispers Jack.

Panic flares brightly in my chest. Humming becomes a little difficult as my mouth dries; I've never administered an intramuscular injection. But I know the dog needs to be sedated so we can help him. The tune doesn't miss a beat as I reach into the cage and gently touch the furry paw at the entrance of the cage. I move my hand with gentle pressure up to his shoulder. He watches me cautiously, but his teeth remain concealed. I try to recall the countless procedures I've observed in my time here, and mimic Dr. Jack's movements. I administer the sedative as efficiently as I can, considering my absence of any prior experience with a hypodermic, and the confines of the crate. Despite my fumbling, the dog doesn't even acknowledge the sting. He must be in a great deal of pain, poor animal. I continue humming as he slowly drops his front legs and rests his broad head on his paws. A few moments later, his eyes close. The melody ends on a shaky breath.

"Great work, Eden. That voice of yours is magic. Who knows how we would have sedated him without you here." Jack is beaming. I blush under his praise as I reach in and run my hand through the dog's matted, crusted fur. I feel his bones jutting sharply into his skin. This stray has had a tough past, I notice sadly. A veterinary nurse bustles in and they take him away for an x-ray.

Caesar jumps up, placing his muddy paws on my jeans, jolting me back to the present. I smile down at him. "A few broken ribs, a punctured lung, and look at you now." I squat down, hugging his body to me. His tail wags so hard his whole body jackknifes like a pendulum on speed. He suddenly tenses and his ears prick up, and I release him as he sets off after whatever poor squirrel has grabbed his attention. His enthusiasm is contagious, and I breathe in the fall air through my smiling lips.

It's almost dark by the time I get home. I let myself in and the warmth of the décor and heating envelops me at the door. My mother curled her lip at the honey-colored wood and earthy-hued furnishings. I love it. It's the first time I've lived somewhere that resembles a home, rather than an institutionalized show-case. My mother was unable to change the décor seeing as it had been part of the multimillion dollar upgrade undertaken not long before we arrived. Caesar takes himself to a handmade rug by the gas fire, circles twice, and settles himself with a contented canine sigh.

I have my hands wrapped around a mug of hot chocolate when my mother comes through the door a short while later. She removes her wool jacket, revealing the black cashmere dress beneath. The chromatic shade contrasts against her claret-red nails and knee-high boots. Her heels rap across the timber floor as she strides across the open-plan lounge to the kitchen. I sip my drink, pretending to be reading the textbook in front of me. I infinitesimally hunch my shoulders, trying to be as conspicuous as a fly on a log. A camouflaged piece of lint on a couch. A sloughed-off dead skin cell on a sleeve.

My mother pours herself a wine and moves over to the lounge. She picks up the remote and the sound of the local news ruptures the silent air. This is my cue to leave. With my eyes focused on the hallway that will frame my escape, I silently call to Caesar. He gets up and follows me to my room.

"We'll head down to the dining room in twenty minutes," she calls out after me.

I sigh inwardly. The resort restaurant provides fine dining delivered within understated elegance. And Tony, the chef, can cook a mean asparagus risotto. But that interminable hour with my mother can spoil the finest cuisine.

It's under the scrutiny of her staff and beloved guests that she will make small talk. Pretending to know what's happening in my quiet life, and worse, to care. She'll ask me inane questions, like how my first day at school was. She won't notice my eyes spending more time regarding my plate than her. She won't see the way I eat as quickly as possible, barely tasting food that deserves to be treated with more respect and be savored. She'll be unaware that my monosyllabic answers are less than the average non-verbal teenager shares with their parents.

She won't notice those questions trigger a waterfall of emotion as I stagger under a deluge of feelings I've determinedly buried. *Noah*. I shift a little on my bed. Just his name is enough to make me uncomfortable. I don't understand these unbalancing emotions, and I know I don't like them. His image as he walked away this afternoon, glinting grin, sparking blue eyes, swims before me. But I stopped believing in dreams long ago.

I begin to make a mental note of things I need to avoid. Not sharing the same atmosphere would be ideal, but unfortunately the colonization of Mars is still some years away. I definitely don't want to be close enough to share the margins of my personal space bubble. It's more of a balloon actually. Maybe a blimp. Eye contact is certainly out of the question. All this seems possible, feasible even, except for our mutual class and lunch partners. The seating plan in biology has been a fortuitous fluke, and for lunches I have the buffer of the intractable Tara.

As I wait to go to dreaded dinner, I plot and plan the intricacies of avoiding Noah within the confines of the school, deciding my new alter ego is going to be a mole. Mostly solitary, definitely invisible.

6

NOAH

For an entire week Eden has shown no interest in spending time with me, or anyone apart from Tara actually. Biology is a study in frustration. Eden sits behind her protective back bench, entering and leaving with eyes glued to her shoes. I feel I could graduate magna cum laude from the school of dissatisfaction, discouragement and disappointment. Where setbacks, obstacles and stumbling blocks are the foundations of the curriculum.

Sometimes, as I sit there pretending to take notes, hyper-aware of her distracting presence, my chest warms and I feel like there's a green laser burning a hole through my back. But when I turn, even slightly, all I see is mahogany hair firmly entrenched in books. My runaway imagination is not helping the storehouse of frustration.

Lunchtimes are the exception. She still looks a little like a fish out of water, but appears to be happy to let the conversation flow around her. From time to time, I get to hear her soft, melodic voice. Occasionally she makes eye contact. The brief times our gazes meet, that electrical charge pulses. I'm starting to seek it like an addict.

But my fixes are few and far between.

Today, Eden is nibbling on the soggy vegetables on offer at the cafeteria. Head down, permanently tied hair falling forward to cover her cheeks. Eyes downcast.

I take a deep breath. Phase two is about to become operational.

"So, how are you doing with the ecosystems assignment?" I lean forward, my head facing toward her, resting my elbow on the table. Mitch and Tara are debating whether they'd send their child to Hogwarts if they received a letter of offer.

Eden turns to me slowly. Almost reluctantly. Her eyes creep up, but don't quite connect with mine. "I haven't really looked at it. I've been focusing on my English essay."

"Yeah, I'm a bit stuck myself..." I throw out a line.

Eden's eyes return to her lifeless vegetables. "Maybe you should reread chapter six?"

Hmm, the fish doesn't take the bait.

"I already have." I lie. "It just doesn't seem to stick."

"Oh."

I puff my cheeks out on a pent-up breath. I think this fish is either not interested or stubborn.

"I'm wondering if a study buddy would be helpful. I don't want my marks dropping."

"That sounds like a good idea."

Please let it be stubborn.

"You seem to have a good hang of it." I grin. Isn't there supposed to be a higher catch rate with sweetener?

Eden's eyes turn to mine. Finally. I'm hoping this is a good sign. But her next sentence crushes that optimistic interpretation. "Well, we already started ecosystems in Boston."

I finally concede defeat and haul my line in. I sit up straight. It's time for a more direct approach.

"How about you?"

"Me?" Eden's eyes widen a little. For a second, I get a little lost in those bewildered, surprised pools. Okay, maybe three or four seconds.

"Yeah. I could sure use the help. I need to keep my GPA up." I try for puppy dog eyes, although that's a little ironic for me.

"I'm not sure. I'm pretty busy."

"We'll study when you study. That way it's not a waste of your time. And explaining concepts can really deepen your understanding." I'm talking fast, like a salesman that's about to have the door slammed in his face. She doesn't look convinced, hunching her shoulders a little.

Eden considers this for long moments; her eyes are back to regarding her petrified vegetable matter. Wow, that reluctance wasn't my imagination. I try not to take it personally that she prefers to converse with her three-times-tortured greens than me.

"I don't think that's a great idea." What? Why? I'm scrambling for a winning argument, wondering if begging would be too desperate, when Tara pipes up.

"Hey, girlfriend, join me for a trip to the little girls' room?"

I turn to Mitch and Tara. They're both watching us: Tara is grinning like a loon; Mitch's face is quite the opposite. I notice Eden blush. I love watching that rosy glow creep up her porcelain skin.

I glare at Tara. She sticks her tongue out at me. "What? It's practically a commandment, always in pairs."

Eden agrees, and I watch them walk away. I deflate faster than a punctured lung. I'd imagined us walking to biology, planning our joint study schedule. Smiling. Chatting. Eden actually acknowledging my presence. But phase two has been a resounding failure. And I haven't thought as far ahead as a plan C. Frustration is no longer a problem. Defeat has taken its place.

As I collect my tray, Mitch grabs my arm. I turn to my brother. His brows are pulled low over his eyes.

"I don't think that's a good idea." Unfortunately, not much gets past someone you share a birthday with, and a significant part of your genetic makeup to boot.

I decide to act dumb. "I don't know what you're talking about."

Mitch's dark brows sink deeper, almost meeting at the bridge of his nose. He's not fooled. "She's not one of us."

Heat flashes across my skin, and I jerk my arm from his grasp. "Neither am I."

7

EDEN

"**T**hanks," I say to Tara.

"He can be so dense sometimes!" Tara is chattering as we head to the toilets. Confusion is roiling around in my head, giving me a headache. *Why would Noah want to study with me?* Surely pity wouldn't extend that far. What's worse, I was so close to caving. That grin had left me defenseless. Thankfully, Tara's shining armor is almost blinding, having been buffed to a mirror finish.

Tara seems to share my confusion. "I wonder what that was about. Noah's never shown any interest in anyone before." She's tapping her top lip as she considers this. She mumbles something about Noah certainly not lacking in offers.

Shown an interest? That doesn't make sense. A betraying sense of hope balloons deep in my belly. I quickly burst it with the tapered point of reality. Good-looking, in-demand, funny, intriguing boys like him don't become interested in awkward, plain, freaky girls like me.

"You didn't want to study with him, did you?" Tara is looking at me closely.

"No!" I realize I almost shouted the denial, and I hurry to

modulate both my tone and my horrified expression. "No. I'm just focusing on my English essay at the moment." My voice peters lamely away. I pick at a piece of lint on my jeans. Tara watches me for a few more uncomfortable seconds.

She shrugs delicate shoulders. "Oh well, hopefully he got the message." We head into our individual stalls, and I breathe a sigh of relief that the conversation is over.

As I wait outside the girls' toilets for Tara to join me, I study the laces of my Converse. My one concession to individuality, they're purple with white polka dots.

"Hi, Eden." I glance up, and see the girl that high-fived me in P.E. coming down the hall. She smiles, highlighting her sparkling brown eyes. I scramble amongst the filing cabinets in my mind for her name. Felicity? Fiona? It takes me a split second to realize I was thinking phonetically. I find the right file triumphantly.

"Hey, Phoebe," I reply casually, like I have these hallway conversations all the time.

"See you in P.E." She walks past, her ponytail swishing like a perky pendulum.

"Yeah, see you then."

What just happened there? Did I just have a casual conversation with a peer? At school? Tara interrupts my stunned musings when she skips up beside me.

"Ready for last period?" she asks. "I've got history." The pitch of her voice drops with her enthusiasm.

Oh, biology.

A whole hour spent trying *not* to stare at Noah's back. Not noticing defined muscles that seem to fill out those paper-thin T-shirts more and more each day. Not appreciating broad shoulders that taper down to fitted jeans. Not wondering if those shirts are getting smaller every time I sit here, once again not writing anything legible. Every lesson wondering whether he's doing this on purpose just to torture my firmly held resolve.

In class I head toward my standard back bench. Noah is already at his seat, but I keep my head down as I walk past. I absentmindedly rub the warm spot behind my right ear as I pass. Once seated I sneak a quick peek and find that cobalt gaze on me. I quickly return my glance back to my books before that sense of affinity can reach out and grab me with its compelling tendrils. Why does Mr. Dougherty have to take so long to get started?

He finally rouses himself from his Buddha-like state and stands before the class. When he remains at the front, hand clasped behind his back, grey eyes contemplative, I get a sense that he's about to make an announcement.

"The executive teaching team has decided that each subject will require one oral presentation in preparation for college requirements. After perusing—" Only someone as old as Mr. Dougherty would use the word 'peruse' with a straight face. "—upcoming assessments, the ecosystems essay is the most amenable to conversion." Add 'amenable' to the list of literary terminology no longer used in popular culture.

Then I process his statement. The next assignment—an oral presentation! My stomach contracts painfully. *An oral presentation!* Every scrap of my anatomy is freaking out, right down to the drop of sweat that's running a frantic line down my spine. Garish images of me standing up the front of the class are streaking through my mind. Someone asks a question. My scrambled mind can't form a coherent response. Soft snickers flow around me, morphing to soft laughter, and in no time people are holding themselves up so they don't roll amongst the aisles. Noah's beautiful smile is there amongst them. I stand up the front, feet frozen to the floor, and I can do nothing but endure it.

"Due to time constraints, you will be presenting in pairs." Muffled voices drift around the room as my peers glance at respective friends, mentally choosing their partners. Noah's gaze is lasered at me. My heart trips an uneven beat. *Oh no, oh no, oh no.* "I shall be selecting the lucky dyads." Groaning erupts from the class as hopes are trampled by Mr. Dougherty's eloquent statement. I breathe a sigh of relief.

As Mr. Dougherty starts to read out the list of names, students grudgingly move amongst the desks to their allotted partner. I wait, breath still, for mine to be called. Noah gets paired with a guy called Gordon, a name I haven't really heard. This is noticeable, seeing as Mr. Dougherty likes to call on his students so regularly.

As Dougherty looks up, I realize it signifies he's finished and I haven't been named. I glance around; all the names have an even split of pairs. Dougherty catches my eye and he realizes the error.

"Ms. St. James, it appears your late enrollment has put a snag in my machinations." I'm not sure I like feeling like a wrench. "Let's see..."

He glances around the room, and my eyes follow his. Our gazes fall onto Noah simultaneously. All that accompanies him is his signature grin. As Dougherty's furrowed eyes light up, my heart takes an elevator ride to my shoes. *Oh no, oh no, oh no.* Dougherty glances at his list. "Ah, Mr. Phelan. I see your partner is the perpetually absent Mr. Gordon. I think we can accommodate your allocation to include Ms. St. James."

Noah's splitting grin rivals the equator. "I'd say we can manage that." He cocks a single brow at me, I guess inviting me to join him at his desk. I sit in shocked stillness; the denim threads of my jeans have woven themselves securely to my seat. *How did this happen?* After a beat, Noah shrugs and joins me at my back bench.

"Howdy, partner." Noah drops himself on the adjacent stool. He flashes me a smile. I want to bury my head in my hands. Make that a giant pile of sand. Actually, what I'd really like is some quicksand to swallow me whole.

"Splendid," calls out Mr. Dougherty. I almost glare at him. That is not my definition of the current situation. "Now, there will be some class time allocated to this project, but you will be well-served to spend time on this outside of class." I glower at the book in front of me. I have no one to aim this feeling of helpless frustration at, so it bears the full brunt.

"Where's your partner?" I don't mean it to sound accusing. But it does.

Noah shrugs. "He has better things to smoke." *Great.* "So... your place or mine?" Over my dead, buried, and fossilised body. Unchaperoned time with Noah is the last thing I want.

"Don't you guys have a public library or something?"

"Shuts at five p.m." He holds his hands out, palms up, shoulders hunched up. "Not a lot of reading types here about," he says in a drawling accent. I almost smile, but I refuse to let our relationship reach that level of familiarity.

"What about a café?"

"Why, Eden, wouldn't that resemble a date?" Noah schools his face in an expression of innocent astonishment, although mischief is twinkling in those blue pools. I snap my mouth shut.

"Ah, maybe not a café then." *Definitely not.* Noah's grin amps up a few lumens.

I rack my brain, looking for a solution to this intractable situation. The answer—my ticket to salvation—comes to me in a blinding flash of ingenuity. "What about a walk in the reserve? The information will literally be at our fingertips."

Noah's eyebrows have hiked into the blond locks falling wantonly over his forehead. Hah, that wiped the distracting smile off his dial. "Sure, sounds great."

"Tomorrow afternoon? The visitor's parking lot?"

Noah's distracting, hypnotizing grin is back. I pull a fortifying breath into the depths of my lungs. I'm going to have to avoid looking at that smile too much; it's kind of like looking at the sun. If you look too long, you have to blink a few times before you can see again. And when you do, that blinding image is burned onto the back of your eyelids.

Noah's fingers rap out a cheery drum roll on the bench. "Biology is ramping up to a whole new level of fun."

Mr. Dougherty calls the class to attention. He starts another of his slow-paced soliloquies. Noah turns to the front and I pretend I'm not insanely aware of his scent wrapping around me. As Dougherty continues his literary diatribe, I start to comprehend what's ahead of me. I have to withstand more time with Noah. Unaccompanied by Tara. No diversions. No distractions.

Excited little butterflies dance around my stomach. Then any anticipation dies as I realize what it'll really be like. Me socially awkward, Noah finally realizing what a misfit he's been lumped with. Noah making lame excuses that he needs to get home. Maybe he forgot to put the lid on a shampoo bottle or something. The butterflies sense the impending scene and huddle together, uniting to form jagged, punishing lumps.

At least we won't exactly be alone...

8

NOAH

So this is what Stash feels like on a sting. He can sense something big is coming, that maybe that jackpot is just around the corner, every muscle straining against the lead that is holding him back, anticipation pounding through his muscles. It makes my nerves twitchy, zinging little electrical impulses down my arms and legs. I wonder if I look like I've got the tremors.

I wait at the agreed parking lot, shifting my weight from foot to foot as I lean against my truck. I'm early, which counterproductively gives me more time to build the edgy tension. A chunk of time alone with Eden. Unrivalled and uninterrupted. The thought, once again, has me pushing away from the car and taking several steps forward only to turn around and return. I wonder what we'll talk about. I'm looking forward to learning more about this mysterious girl.

A sporty Saab pulls in a few spaces away and that million dollar haul steps out. I'm surprised; it's not a car choice I would have imagined her in. Eden is dressed warmly in jeans and a jacket. It reminds me I forgot to pack a jumper, but I don't mind the cool air. Actually, I think I just got a few degrees warmer.

Eden approaches me, pulling a backpack onto her shoulders. She's looking everywhere but me.

"Hi, Eden. Nice ride."

She glances back at the car, frowning at its smooth lines. "It's my mother's." She turns back, and I find myself waiting, breath frozen in my expanded lungs for her to look at me. Her gaze slides right past me, to a point past my left shoulder. She's looking preoccupied, a small frown creasing her brow. It tilts the corners of her lips down ever so slightly.

"Ready to go?"

"Almost." She continues to stare at that point beyond me. I turn, and see a minibus pull into a park closer to the visitors' centre. A group of tourists clamber out and congregate near the trail signpost. There's about ten of them, toting children, cameras, and disordered eagerness. I don't relish the thought of the rowdy babbling that would accompany this group. Judging by Eden's face, neither does she.

"Yeah, I see what you mean." I turn back to see the furrows wash away, leaving relieved smoothness in its wake. Instead the baffled feelings leap over to me, corrugating my brow in confusion. A prickling sense of dread tingles the base of my scalp.

"Yep, all set," she states, and purposefully strides over to the group. She glances over her shoulder to check I'm following. The image of just the two of us, hiking serenely through picturesque terrain, is crushed by the cementing knowledge that we're joining the milling tourists.

Maybe I'm assuming incorrectly. "We're going with them?" I try to modulate my tone but it still hikes up slightly on the final word.

"Yeah. Todd runs a great wildlife tour. What better way to see everything we need to check out?" She looks at me expectantly.

I could think of several actually. "Ah...yeah...sure." So this is how Stash feels when the anticipated haul turns out to be nothing but sawdust.

"Hi, Eden, glad you could make it again." Todd is a fit-looking guy wearing a Clear Creek Inn logo on his shirt; artificially whitened teeth flash in a blinding smile as Eden approaches.

"Hi, Todd." I don't get to see if Eden is going to introduce me, because Todd is already waving his arms to the tourists.

"Okay, everyone, gather round," he calls out enthusiastically. Easy for him...his plans are right on track. I shuffle along with Eden and we stand on the outskirts of the group.

I jam my hands in my pockets. I'm officially moping. Todd starts a standard blurb about the national park, its tectonic birth, the diversity of its flora and fauna, all the fun things you can do...while staying at the Inn. I fade out his educational-information-that-is-really-Inn-advertising.

A young girl beside me in a pink, frilly number much more suited to a teddy bears' picnic smiles shyly up at me. Not wanting to scare her with my sulking, I grin back. Her mother glances over, and when she sees the exchange, frowns ferociously. She gathers her daughter protectively to her side. The edges of my mouth return to their downward position. I'm not sure what I just got tried and sentenced for, but I don't think I like it.

"Okay, everyone, let's move out."

Everyone follows Todd as we head for the hiking trail. There's a slight jaunt in Eden's stride as she walks along with the group, her thumbs looped in the straps of her backpack. The group is slowly spreading out as people pause periodically to view their surroundings. The trail winds through open woodland, the trees opening at opportune moments to provide unhindered vistas of open meadows. Their green expanse reaches out to the massive mountain range breaching the horizon. We seem to reach an unspoken agreement that we'll remain at the rear. Despite Eden's glowing reference of Todd, she doesn't seem to be paying attention to his animated, albeit scripted, narration. I decide I might as well make the most of my thwarted situation.

I start with something safe and mundane. "So, we need to look at ecosystems."

"Yep, I checked out the worksheet."

I pull the said worksheet from my back pocket and scan its rumpled surface. "Okay then, we need to identify the various habitats of the ecosystem."

Eden rolls her eyes, and ticks her fingers off as she lists them. "Alpine in higher altitudes, from the tree line to valley floor there are coniferous forest and open woodland, moving down to the marshes and meadows before we hit aquatic habitats in the rivers and lakes."

I raise my eyebrows as I look back to the sheet. "Okay, smarty pants, what about the energy transfer through the food chain?"

She glances at me, unimpressed. "Well, it starts with autotrophs like grasses photosynthesising and finishes with carnivores like bears eating just about everything below." Or wolves.

I pick a flower nearby, a fragile columbine that modestly hangs its pale yellow head beside the trail. I hold it out to Eden. "So flowers are down the bottom?"

She frowns at the slender bloom. "You're not meant to pick flowers in the reserve." I continue to hold the flower out, seeing if she'll leave me hanging. When she reaches out to take it, my breath halts as I wait to see if our hands will brush. Eden grasps the flower just below its delicate petals, neatly avoiding any physical contact. She tucks the flower into the side pocket of her backpack.

"You know you can eat them," I offer, trying for a spot of humor.

"Thanks, but I've had lunch." She moves forward again; her unsmiling mouth remains firmly entrenched in the land of serious.

Undaunted, I use the cue to move onto more personal topics. "So, how long have you been vegetarian?"

"Since I was eleven." Eden remains focused on the trail ahead of us.

Taking her cue, I stare straight ahead, hands shoved in my pockets "Why the change?" Eden opens her mouth, hopefully with more than a four word answer.

I don't get to find out.

"What's yaw name?" I glance down to see a blond boy, maybe five years old, looking up at me, thumb firmly planted in his mouth. His forefinger curls around the tip of his nose. Frustration clenches like a concertina between my shoulder blades.

"Ah, Noah." The boy looks at me expectantly, cheeks drawing in rhythmically around his thumb. My irritation drops with each steady pulse. I've just learned you can't stay frustrated with a precocious blond thumb-sucker. "What's yours?"

"Dewemiah." Taking into account the thumb, I think that translates to Jeremiah.

"Hey, Jeremiah, nice to meet you. Shouldn't you be with your mom or dad?" I don't want a repeat of the accusing mother lioness from earlier.

The thumb comes out with a pop, and Jeremiah uses the soggy digit to point over his shoulder. "Nah, she's over there wif my little brothers." Eden and I look over to a slim woman, hair wisping from a crooked bun, one toddler wailing on her hip as another darts away. "My dad couldn't come. He's on doody." His tone drops on the final word, as if it bears the weight of great importance.

"On duty, you say?" Jeremiah nods solemnly, thumb securely back in his mouth. I glance over at Eden. Her lips are pulled in between her teeth, holding in a smile.

Jeremiah tugs on my hand, pulling me down. I squat, and he leans in, and asks in a loud whisper. "What's her name?"

"Eden." I stage whisper back as I grin up at her. Eden is pretending she can't hear the not-so-hushed conversation happening right beside her.

He glances at her, an assessing glint in his eye. "She seems nice."

I pause for a second. "Well, I certainly think so." Eden's pretty blush creeps up her cheeks, her hand rubbing behind her ear.

Jeremiah considers this. "I'm gonna walk wif you." He announces with the confident nod of a child that has yet to learn stranger danger. He doesn't wait for confirmation, before taking my hand and starting forward. I send a helpless shrug to Eden, but she's looking at Jeremiah with a gentle expression. I mentally catalogue the softened lips, relaxed muscles around her eyes, pearly skin painted with a tender glow. This girl gets more beautiful by the minute.

"What's dat?" Jeremiah points toward a bright yellow and black bird.

"That's a Western Tanager." Jeremiah watches it in fascination as it darts about the tree branches, its bright red head standing out against the green foliage.

"Yeah, each male and female travel together all winter, to get to know one another, before they settle down to hatch their eggs in spring." This added detail comes from Eden. I look at her in surprise. She shrugs, as if to say its common knowledge, and quickly walks on.

By the time we arrive at the clearing that signifies the halfway break, I've reached the conclusion that the term 'what's dat' should be struck from the English language. And all other languages for that matter; it would be discriminatory not to. Jeremiah's insatiable curiosity started as cute and charming, but with the passage of time deteriorated into exasperating and exhausting.

On the upside, there's a softness to Eden that I've enjoyed walking alongside. Her patient explanations, although probably highly reinforcing for young Jeremiah, were the most I've ever heard her talk. It's quite possible that Jeremiah has created a chink in that armor of hers. One that I fully intend on exploiting and expanding.

We're sitting on a log, slightly apart from the others, when I try to strike up another conversation. "You've been around kids a bit then?"

She looks surprised, and for a split second, her eyes fly to mine. Against the coniferous background, her evergreen eyes are luminescent. They widen slightly, and I drink in the heated sense of awareness that invariably begins in my chest and steadily spreads to every corner of my being. I suspect if this girl looked at me for long enough, my body temperature would reach thermonuclear. She returns to studying the blades of grass between her shoes, shrugging a one-shoulder shrug. "No, not really."

"You were great with Jeremiah. I just thought..."

She contemplates this as she watches Jeremiah chase his younger brothers, squealing and giggling. Their mother sits across the clearing, watching in contented exhaustion. I wonder if Eden's going to answer, expecting this conversation to mirror the short, monosyllabic exchanges we've had up until now. "They're much like animals, I suppose. A little patience and understanding can open just about any door."

I have a feeling those two words are significant. Patience. Understanding. I wonder if that's the key for this mystifying girl.

For Eden, I'm willing to invest a truckload of patience. Although it appears that getting to the understanding bit could take an entire convoy.

I almost fall off the log in delighted astonishment when she contributes a question of her own. "What about you? You obviously know kids."

I roll my eyes. "I have a lot of cousins." I place hefty emphasis on the understatement 'a lot'.

Eden doesn't miss the significance. "How many is a lot?"

"Like you wouldn't believe. I have more extended family than Jeremiah has questions."

Eden's lip twitches. An almost smile! I resist the urge to jump up, fist pump, and totally overreact.

"Okay, people, let's start the walk back." Tour-guide-Todd maintains the theme of this little expedition: Mission Interruptus. We get up and dust ourselves off, once again forming the tail of the group as we start the family-friendly walk back.

As we walk, I try to pick up the thread of our conversation. "So, you should check out one of our family barbeques. We have to serve up half an antelope just to feed the immediate Phelans."

There's no response. Oh no, did I just offend her vegetarian sensibilities? I turn to see if I can judge her reaction. The girl can be hard to read, especially with her eyes glued to her shoes. But Eden's not there. I stop, and turn one way and then the other.

Eden is nowhere to be seen.

She couldn't have gone far; we were talking just a minute ago. But she's obviously left the trail. The group continues up ahead, unaware of her disappearing act. My eyebrows sink over my eyes. Where did she go?

I take a deep breath, in through my nose, and let it flow out of my mouth. In that brief pause I decide to go left. Within a few steps I'm amongst the trees, instantly enveloped by their shadowy coolness. I continue walking, looking for signs that she may have passed. Nothing signals Eden took this route: no broken branches, kicked stones or trampled moss. I continue doggedly, unsure why I'm continuing. Like a wild goose chase, I have a target and not much else.

It's only a short minute before I hear the soft gurgling and bubbling of water. The trees open around a small creek running through a grassy clearing. The last blue camas of the season dot the picturesque meadow. I pause, because Eden is kneeling beside the water; her dark hair drapes over her cheek, obscuring her face. I'm about to ask her what in the heck she's doing when she shifts, and I see the graceful outline of a trumpeter swan besides her.

It's then that the haunting melody reaches me, the luminous notes carried on the fluttering breeze. Shocked awareness registers that it's flowing from Eden, that she's humming to the bird. I squint, and see her fingers deftly moving around the bird's left foot. I realize with a jolt, she's unwinding fishing line. The bird remains still, neck arched toward her, wings tucked passively into its sides. It calmly allows her to twist and unwind the cutting braid. Twice Eden reaches around in the process of unravelling the line, circling the bird with her arms. The swan patiently and calmly remains still.

The whole time the earthy, wordless tune ebbs and flows around the landscape. A sense of serenity and peace is being artfully woven, note by haunting note. I stand in stunned silence. This is the second time this girl has left me slack-jawed and mute.

Eden finishes, and sits back on her heels. She slides her hand down the swan's sleek, white neck. The swan arches, and I feel myself mimicking its stretched pose as it seeks more of the gentle caress. She stands, takes a step back, and the melody fades from her lips. The swan stretches and ruffles its feathers before waddling to the creek edge. It's then that I notice its mate, gliding gently by the shore. With a splash, the swans reunite and paddle away.

Eden turns; a soft, satisfied smile tilts her rose lips. She angles to head back and sees me at the edge of the trees, and the smile falls like a puppeteer has cut its strings.

"What are you doing here?" Her tone is sharp with disapproval.

I hold out my hands, palm up. "Looking for you?" She frowns. "You did a Houdini on me, so I went searching." She takes a few steps toward me, closing the distance between us.

"How did you find me?"

I shrug again. Seeing as I don't really have an answer for that one, I decide to ask a question of my own. "What just—?"

"We'd better get back to the group." Eden rapidly covers the remaining distance and sails past me, leaving flurries of her wildflower scent swirling around me. She quickly steps amongst the trees. The ridges on my forehead rival those of the giant mountain that juts in the distance. Did she just brush me off? I don't think so.

As I stomp after her, I notice only one set of footsteps can be heard. Eden's light footed tread gracefully sidesteps understory bushes, agilely ducks branches, deftly avoids rocks. Barely a blade of grass is out of place. That's why I couldn't track her. The girl is like a nimble ghost. My irritation doesn't afford the forest the same respect as I trample behind her. I call out, but Eden continues toward the trail. With an unerring sense of direction she doesn't head toward where we left, but meets the trail farther up. It's not long before the noise of the group can be heard up ahead. Eden only slows down once we are at the back of the chattering, snap-happy group.

I try again. "Did you want to tell me—?"

"Noah!" Jeremiah throws his stubby arms around my leg. I

stare at the sky, shoulders deflated, wondering why the universe hates me so much. "Where did you go?"

"Hey, bud. I was just checking something out." Eden stiffens beside me. I concede defeat, knowing an explanation won't be forthcoming for the moment. I'm willing to wait.

On the return walk I discover there are worse torture mechanisms than the dreaded 'what's dat' question. Jeremiah ramps it up with the agonizing and tedious 'why'. Eden impresses me once again with her knowledge as she answers the ceaseless questions. Why don't fish drown when they go to sleep? Why don't spiders get caught in their own webs? And why is that deer doing that? A bull elk, resplendent in his daunting headwear is bugling, the eerie sound piercing the late afternoon air. Even informative Eden glosses over the mating rituals of an elk in rut, blushing delicately.

On the upside, the walk goes quickly. This is good, because the casual, easy air that had developed on the walk in has evaporated. Although Eden chats openly with Jeremiah, she casts me guarded looks from the corner of her eye.

As I walk, I have time to think. Until I came across Eden and the swan, she had slowly relaxed and started talking. Jeremiah and the scenic surroundings had loosened her tenacious armor. She obviously doesn't want to talk about whatever went on in the glade and as perplexing as it was, I know better than anyone there's more to this world than meets the eye. And I don't want to make her uncomfortable. I decide to let the topic slide. For now.

As we return to the visitors' centre, Jeremiah flings himself at us, endowing us each with a soggy hug, before running up ahead to his mother. She throws us a grateful wave before climbing onto the bus, one child asleep on her shoulder. Once we're again standing beside Eden's apparently offensive sedan, I lean on it, hands back in my pockets. Eden stands beside me, upright, arms crossed across her chest, lips stretched tight like a bow. I'm not sure if it's an offensive or defensive stance.

"Nice kid," I comment.

Her mouth softens, now just an archer watching, waiting warily. "Yeah. Do they usually ask that many questions?"

I chuckle. "I think Jeremiah took a child's natural curiosity and dialed it up to insatiable."

Eden shifts her weight to her other foot.

I turn to face her, my hip resting on the car. "Well, I had a great time, and we've got half of the assignment done."

Confusion tangles the fine muscles of her face. "Yeah." I'm not sure which half of the statement she's referring to.

I pause for a second, but she doesn't elaborate. "Well, I'll see you at school tomorrow, and we can come up with a game plan for the rest of it." I push away from the car. "Bye, Eden."

Eden takes a cautious step away from the car, uncrossing her arms. Although a moment ago she looked like she was about to single-handedly defend a fort, one whose battlements were compromised...and contained vulnerable women and children, now she almost looks disappointed. She pauses, like she's waiting for something else. I simply stand and wait, unsure what she's expecting of me. After a confused moment she takes two more backward steps toward the driver's side.

Her eyes meet mine briefly, her lips gently tipping up at the corners. "Bye, Noah."

Something strikes me, making me pause. Eden continues to her car. I watch her climb in, noting her ability to make even that look graceful and eye-catching. And I realize what caught my attention. Eden just said my name. The beautiful, meaningful sound sings through my veins. For the first time since my gaze collided with this girl, I have something to pin hope on. With a chuckle I refuse to acknowledge how little it takes to fuel that optimistic emotion.

As I clamber into my truck I realize something else. I never reached my goal for today. Despite the past couple of hours with Eden, I haven't learned anything I didn't know before.

I already figured there was more to this girl than meets the eye.

9

EDEN

I'm pacing the confines of my room, queen-size bed to flat screen TV, and back. Queen-size bed to flat screen TV, and back. But the few marching steps it takes my lanky legs to traverse the room are not helping my tense muscles or tangled mind. I'm tired of spending time in that convoluted, chaotic maze, where all I keep finding are dead ends.

Needing time, I once again avoided Noah at school. The undecipherable timetable was actually on my side today—no biology. But despite endless hours spent considering, deliberating, and speculating, I haven't made any progress. I consider taking Caesar for a walk, but decide that something more strenuous may be in order. Besides, my monotonous pacing appears to have lulled him to sleep. He's curled up on the bed, snoring softly. I glance at the clock. I should have time if I don't go too far from home. I briefly consult the map for somewhere close and convenient.

Luckily, living on site means my mother doesn't need the use of her car. Unluckily, it means there's no reason for me to have my own wheels. Ones that don't say, "I have a pretentious amount of money." Although I hate what the sleek sedan represents, I jump into my only form of transportation and head to the reserve. The drive is short and sweet, leaving me plenty of time for hiking. I quickly grab my backpack and head for the trail.

Within seconds, as the sun pierces the clouds to warm my face, I know that it was a good choice to go hiking in this picturesque valley. The trail beneath my feet is a well-worn path through the skeletal soil. An arresting kaleidoscope of green blankets the expanse before me. Glades of wildflowers, brilliant red paintbrushes, and bright blue alpine forget-me-nots sprinkle the basin floor. The walls of the valley are all variegated angles, sheer faces through to gently sloping embankments, rising to frame the dramatic snowcapped mountains in the distance. As the altitude increases, harsh rock juts amongst the striking greenery, extending until the highest peaks are nothing but naked grey ridges. The breathtaking grandeur is a balm for my agitated mind.

There are a few fellow visitors sharing the walking trail with me. One mother's face is drawn in tight lines as her daughter aims rapid-fire questions with the speed of an assault rifle. Farther up, a teen lags behind his father, feet scuffing the ground, a frown on his pimpled face. His father is peering through binoculars, impervious to his son's scowling. At one particularly scenic area a young couple, shoulders brushing intimately, are taking a gazillion photos — mostly selfies, their cameras sounding like a family of crickets.

I fade them out of awareness as I continue up the trail. The visitors thin along with the oxygen the farther I climb. Here, I don't dwell on Tara's motivation to befriend me. I have a few theories, and they are all predicated on pity, or maybe curiosity for the new freak in town. I don't dwell on the confusing feelings I have for Noah—the breathless impact his blue-eyed grin has on me, the little part of me that wants to see that grin again and again. The seductive hope that keeps trickling from invisible cracks in my tightly held control. I stumble on a barely protruding stone. Okay, maybe I haven't banished these feelings completely.

I turn a bend and, to the left, a rocky outcropping in the distance glows under spears of light breaching the pale clouds. The secluded little space calls to me. I glance over my shoulder and, seeing the trail empty, head toward it. I slip in amongst the tall trees, walking for a several minutes until I'm surrounded by the pungent scent of sage and pine. There, alone, I sit down cross-legged and allow my surroundings to seep into my consciousness, stillness descending on me. Slowly, the warm mantle of nature's chorus envelops me in the singing and warbling of birds, the welcome whispers of the leaves, and the subtle promise of serenity.

As I sit there, a marmot, scrambling through the bushes, catches my attention. The plump ground squirrel nimbly navigates through the thicket, his speckled grey fur mimicking the shades of the surrounding rocky outcrop. He pauses in alarm a few feet in front of me when he notices my presence. My lips tip up in delight, and almost unconsciously my melody flows from my lips. The rock chuck stands up on his hind legs, nose twitching, the soft fur of his belly the color of mellowed honey.

My smile widens. I slowly pull my hands from my pocket, extracting the biscuit I'd packed earlier. Its nose twitches again. The humming continues as I slowly hold the treat out and wait patiently. He sniffs cautiously, then starts up a rhythm of taking two or three tentative steps followed by a pause. I simply hum and wait. A few moments later he reaches out its neck and nibbles the barest edge of the cracker. When I don't move, he steps closer and takes a braver bite. Another minute and he's eating the biscuit with enthusiasm, nose twitching, rabbit-like teeth flashing.

From the corner of my eye I notice a furry head pop up from a burrow hidden amongst the rocks. Three more marmots bustle from the tunnel opening. The larger marmot makes a few clicking sounds, and his harem of females cautiously approach. It doesn't take long for them to register the food, and they join their mate. I break the remainder in two and hold the pieces out. Delight courses through me as one rests its little paw on my finger to eat the remaining crumbs. It's always a high when a small, wild animal puts such trust in you. Then again, there's little I wouldn't do for a sugar fix either.

A sharp gust of wind breaks the reverie, and the male marmot twitches his nose again. He sounds a high-pitched whistle before darting away, the females hot on his heels. Another icy blast returns me to my immediate surroundings. I glance up, and notice for the first time, the dark grey clouds obscuring the once-blue sky. I stand up, tension tightening my brows. In the shaded copse I didn't notice the accumulating hazard overhead. I begin walking toward the direction of the trail when a flash of light splits the darkening sky. Ominous rumbling echoes across the valley. Shoot, I don't think I have long before—

A fat, cold drop falls on my face. A frisson of alarm streaks down my spine. Belatedly, the safety warnings I read on the map run through my mind: *DO NOT leave the walking trail*. Ah yes, and the warning about rapid changes in weather being common in the fall months. I quickly take my plastic poncho from my backpack and put it on. An edgy nervousness is crawling around in my stomach, like spiders have spawned in there and aren't appreciating the confined space. I need to head back to the trail and get back to the car. Noah's concerned blue eyes flash before me, although why he would cross my mind now, I don't know.

Another crack of lightning heralds the onslaught of rain as the tap upstairs goes from drip to deluge in the space of a few seconds. This would certainly be the definition of a freak weather change. The poncho offers little protection and I'm drenched almost instantaneously. Small shivers run through my body as I wrap my arms around myself. *Okay, I really need to find the trail.*

I walk toward the direction I entered. I trudge through the muddy soil for several minutes before I realize the trees should have opened up by now. Rivers of rain run down my face and below the neckline of my shirt, trickling icy tracks down my torso in random lines. I push my sodden hair from my face and bite my lip. It's starting to feel like I'm running out of room for the ballooning anxiety in my tightening chest.

I have no choice but to continue. I trudge for another few minutes before relief sweeps over me when the dense vegetation thins and I'm out in the open. Out from the protection of the trees, the rain hammers with unobstructed ferocity.

Now, rather than green landscape, I'm greeted by a granite curtain of rain. I can't see more than a few feet in front of me. My shoulders sink. I'm unlikely to find the trail with the grey shroud obscuring my vision. Alarm begins to morph into fear as I realize that night is impending and I'm wet, cold, and isolated, my mother won't be home 'til late, and there's no guarantee she will notice my absence.

I curl up at the base of a large aspen tree. Wandering aimlessly is likely to get me even more disorientated, but sitting here with no concrete plan feels fruitless. I can almost feel the lengthening shadows reach their gnarled fingers across the sodden earth, seeking each other, wanting to blend and make night. Desolation wraps cold arms around my shivering shoulders.

Just as my teeth start clattering, a large shape materializes from the curtain of rain. I scramble backward like a crab, painfully scraping my shoulder on grey bark. I shoot to my feet when I see it's a black wolf. At least I think it's a wolf. It's bigger than any wolf I've ever pictured. Its head could easily reach my shoulders, its mammoth shoulders intimidating. Dark fur surrounds its muzzled face. Every molecule of air vaporizes from my lungs. My heart has shot up to my throat, hammering violently.

I have two options—fight or flight. Flight—this giant creature would own me in a millisecond. I could hum, but I can't hear my own teeth chattering over the pounding rain, let alone hope that it would help me right now. *That leaves fight.* I squat slowly, my hand reaching out blindly for something, anything. My fingers wrap around a short, fat branch. I stand up, avoiding any sharp movements. I glance down at my weapon of choice— the bark is peeling from my partially decomposed piece of wood.

Great.

The wolf cocks his head to the side, and sits back on his haunches. Piercing blue eyes regard me from his broad head. If it were human, he'd be saying *'Are you kidding me?'* His behavior doesn't fit the definition of threatening or aggressive. My heart rate slows from that of an out of control train to just an express during peak hour. He barks once then turns and walks a few feet away, before glancing over his shoulder at me.

I think it wants me to follow it! My confusion feels like it's been buffeted by the gusts of wind swirling around us. My limited options are being pounded and thrashed until all that's left is indecision. The wolf takes a few more steps before stopping, waiting expectantly.

I can't be considering walking toward gigantor, can I? My shoulders hit an all-time low—I don't really have a choice. I suppose if I was going to be dinner, I would have been carved and served as human sushi by now. I drop the useless piece of wood and take a few hesitant steps forward. The wolf's tongue lolls out, his gums pulling back.

Did he just smile at me? I take a few more steps, and the wolf turns and continues walking in the direction he arrived.

As we walk through the rain, I watch the giant beast warily. Since when did wolves grow to the size of a pony? On steroids. His towering frame is black from his intimidating, imperious head, across daunting, proud shoulders, down to his humungous, furry feet. Despite his size, he walks with the grace of a wild animal, muscles bunching and releasing beneath midnight fur. He's not bothered by the sleeting ice, unlike my pathetically shuddering human form. He periodically checks that I'm following, before continuing to lead me to who knows where. Straight to my own death, for all I know.

After twenty minutes of miserable hiking, the wolf stops. I look up from my hunched shoulders, unsure of what's coming next. The wolf merely looks at me, blue eyes blinking, and sits. I glance around again, and notice the compacted ground of the trail beneath my sodden boots. *He brought me back to the trail!* I let out a relieved breath I hadn't noticed I'd been holding. I turn east, and start trudging with a renewed burst of energy.

I turn toward the wolf, wondering how to express my gratitude, only to find he's disappeared behind the granite curtain, vanishing into the wild, grey twilight. I send him a silent "thank you" before wading back to my car.

10

NOAH

I stand behind a tree as I watch Eden get out of her car. Her shoulders are slumped and, even from a distance, I can see the shivers racking her body. I notice, with a frown, that her house is dark. Despite the late hour, her mother isn't home. Eden lets herself in and I release a sigh.

I head back to my car parked at the Inn parking lot. Mitch meets me there, leaning against its metal body.

"She got in all right?" He wipes at the water streaming down his face.

"Yeah. She looked cold and tired, but home safe."

Mitch's eyes squint as he regards me. "How did you know?"

I shift uncomfortably, shrugging. Sitting with Mitch in his room, I didn't understand the uneasiness that morphed in my stomach. It's not what you usually feel when enduring Mitch's brand of heavy metal. Techno metal— whatever that is— certainly gets you on edge. But not scared. When it steadily grew, I rushed around the house, checking on Mom and even Stash. I phoned Dad; his confused tone reassured me that he was indeed safely driving home. I don't understand the sense of urgency that rushed me here. It only grew into alarm when I saw Eden wasn't home. As it grew later and the rain started, I felt her fear. Yes, felt the clenching pit in my stomach, the helpless despair.

"I felt a disturbance in the Force." I try to make the joke a statement, but my tone hikes up at the end, making it sound more like a question.

Mitch purses his lips, the pouty-purse that shows he's not impressed. And waiting.

"I don't know, okay? I just felt it."

Mitch impatiently pushes back the wet hair that has flopped down into his eyes, his cheeks deflating on a baffled puff. He opens the door of the truck. "Come on. We have to come up with a good reason why we rushed off like lunatics or Mom is going to give us the Phelan inquisition."

I shudder. No one wants to endure my mother's single minded cross-examination. She doesn't take prisoners.

"See you at lunch." Mitch thumps me in the arm before turning to go down the hallway. Having your brother with you during Gothic Lit's a blessing. It means you're less likely to die of boredom.

He pauses, turning back. "Hey, is that my T-shirt?" Mitch pinches the sleeve of my light blue shirt.

"Yep." My grin lacks any skerrick of apology. "I need to lay off mom's brownies. Mine don't fit anymore." Mitch arches a brow at my flat stomach. "Besides, I think this one looks better on me." Mitch grunts, an uncanny imitation of our father, and punches my shoulder again, this time with a bit more oomph. I laugh as we head in opposite directions. "See you at lunch, little bro!"

Mitch stops again, in the middle of the almost-empty corridor. "You haven't called me that in a long time."

I'd guess almost two years. "You'd like the title reinstated?"

He rolls his eyes. "Ah, no."

"We may have a problem then, little bro."

I'm pretty sure he wouldn't mind punching me a third time, but then we'd both be late for class.

Biology next. My heart jumps a smidgen, moving up in my chest. I haven't seen Eden since our jaunt two days ago. Will things be different? A little more thawed? Eden's micro smile flashes in my mind, and my chest warms. It felt like progress.

Eden is already sitting at her back bench, head buried deep in her textbook. I bet she already has that thing memorized. Dougherty doesn't stir from his Zen-like contemplation as I walk past.

"Hey, Eden." I sit on the stool beside her.

"Hi." Eden doesn't glance up from her busy note taking. Although there's no outward sign, it feels like she hunkers down. Back to square one. Maybe even in the negatives, seeing as she didn't use my name. I really want to hear it colored by her soft, musical voice.

I glance over at the textbook that holds her rapt attention. *Chapter Six Ecosystems.* "Working on the assignment?"

"Yep. It's almost done." Mostly monosyllabic answers. Way down in the negatives.

"Did you want me to do the presentation?"

Eden's gaze flies to mine. Now I have her attention. "Would you?" I had a feeling this reclusive girl wouldn't be keen on public speaking.

"It only seems fair, seeing as you've done so much of the research." I shrug. "And had to answer endless Jeremiah questions."

Eden turns a little more toward me, her lips softening. "Yes, I wouldn't want you to feel like you haven't contributed." Clever girl knows I'm giving her a get-out-of-jail-free pass.

"Gotta do my share." I smile. For long seconds we sit in suspended animation. Her—delicate lips parted, eyes green and unwavering. Me—mute and barely breathing.

A slap on the back crashes me back to reality. Eden's eyes widen before darting back to her book.

"Hey, dude, we've moved!" Dale, my phantom lab partner, stands beside me. He's wearing his standard shirt with too long sleeves, beanie, jeans and fingerless gloves. All in faded black, no matter the season. He holds out a hand to shake mine. I return his hearty pumping reluctantly. I'd much rather be swimming in the forest-green pools beside me.

Dale scrapes a stool across and sits down beside me. I shuffle closer to Eden to make room. Her scent—those elusive wildflowers, wraps around me. Maybe I don't resent him being here so much after all. Eden shuffles her stool closer to the wall.

Dale turns to Eden beside me, and his eyes widen. I bristle, although I expect she has this effect on all guys. I wonder if I looked like that when we met. No way. Definitely not.

I was far more dumbfounded. Dazed. Disorientated.

"Hey, I'm Dale. I'm the dude who usually sits next to Noah." Eden glances up from her book and mumbles a hello. I half expect her to rub behind her ear, what I thought was Eden's gesture of shyness. But she doesn't.

Undaunted, Dale holds out his hand for a second handshake. I don't move, knowing Eden will have to reach across. She's going to have to get into my personal space or leave Dale hanging. She pauses, looking at those pilled-black gloves, and good manners win out. She leans over and her shoulder brushes my chest. I hear her sharp intake of breath and I wonder if she feels it too. The slow burn that starts from that single point of contact. The tiny sparks of heat shooting outwards.

Eden quickly retracts her hand. Dale draws his hand back and I notice, inwardly frowning, that he slowly brushes his half-naked fingers across her palm. My frown never sees the light of day though, as Eden's doing that for me. She surreptitiously wipes her hand on her leg. Hah. The jealous streak that I have no right to feel fizzes out.

Mr. Dougherty approaches us at the bench. "Ah, Mr. Gordon. You're present." He pointedly glances at Dale's beanie. Dale sighs, and unwillingly removes it. Freed from the faded black wool, his dark hair springs outward in rebellious spikes.

"Yeah, my mother was sick."

"Oh, I'm sorry to hear that. She has recovered, I hope?" Old Dougherty is pulling concerned teacher like a pro.

"Yeah, much better."

"And your sister, she's better now too?" One white, wiry eyebrow rises into Dougherty's wrinkled forehead.

"Yep, made a full recovery."

"And your grandmother?"

"Getting there. You know how oldies take longer to bounce back from these things."

"Indeed." Dougherty folds his arms across his chest. I think his mask is beginning to slip.

Dale continues, oblivious to the frostiness in Dougherty's tone. "Such are the responsibilities of being the man of the house." Now it's Dale's smile that turns a little brittle. It's common knowledge that Dale's father left when he was ten. His mother works at the local café by day, and Tyrell's movie theater by night; making her the sole supporter of Dale, his two sisters, and her ailing mother.

Dougherty takes a deep breath. I'm guessing he's had to center again. "Well, your team members have been industriously working on the current assessment piece. It's in your best interest to discuss with them your role and responsibilities."

Dale gives him a thumbs up. "Sure thing Mr. D." Dougherty closes his eyes and takes a second, longer, deeper breath before returning to the front of the class.

Dale promptly pulls his knitted beanie down over his ears. "So Eden, where are we at?"

Eden looks up from her book, eyebrows raised. Although her voice is quiet, she doesn't hesitate in answering. "Well, Noah and I had just decided that he would be the one presenting." *She said my name! Noah and I. The phrase repeats its beautiful sound in my head.*

Eden passes Dale the page of notes she'd been scrawling on. "Ah yes. Phelan would be the ideal choice for that one." *Of course I would. I actually attend the class.* Dale barely glances at the page before passing it to me. "Well everything seems to be in order. Keep up the awesome work, dudes." Dale's fisted glove once again thumps me in between my shoulder blades.

Eden blinks a couple of times. I doubt Dale even knows what the topic of our presentation is.

"Ladies and gentlemen." Mr. Dougherty's age-old voice brings our attention to the front again. He begins outlining key points for the presentations in a week's time. Eden once again begins taking notes. Dale starts flicking a lighter in his pocket. Again and again. I block out the annoying noise and the tiny hope that the flint might catch, setting those stained-black jeans smoldering.

It's not hard, as my attention gravitates toward the girl sitting next to me. My chest has stored the electrifying heat from our earlier contact, maintaining a slightly higher than comfortable body temperature. As I pretend to listen to what-ever Dougherty is explaining, I try to take deep cooling breaths. Instead, wildflower scent fills my nostrils, and they flare reflexively. I feel Eden pause in her note-taking beside me, before dropping her head farther into her book and writing again. The remainder of the lesson passes in agonizing awareness.

When the bell goes, Dale jumps up with split-second timing, his stool screeching his rush. "See you, dudes." I think Dale just spent an hour being reminded of all the reasons he doesn't attend biology.

We wait until the other students leave, then stand and walk to the front of the class. I'm acutely aware of Eden following behind. As we leave the room, we fall into step down the hallway, heading to the cafeteria for lunch.

"Well, it's good to see that Dale approves of our efforts," I say wryly.

Eden gives me a thumbs up. "Dude, we're doing awesome!"

I chuckle. Eden smiles. And I realize we're walking and talking, like any guy and girl would, on the way to lunch. It's a heady feeling.

"Hi, Noah." I turn my head and straighten; I hadn't realized I'd been leaning in. Bianca is walking toward us. She combs her hair back with her fingers. I feel Eden stiffen beside me.

"Hey, Bianca." I turn back to Eden, not wanting to lose the connection we'd been building. But Eden has taken a step to the side. The distance between us is small, considering the flowing mass of students around us, but it's significant.

"Are you heading to lunch?" Bianca is now directly in front of me. Well, obviously. I throw her a smile, but turn back to Eden, hoping Bianca will take the hint.

"You guys go. I'll catch up." Eden is smiling. A full-blown, teeth-glinting smile. But it's not the smile I've been waiting for. It has the warmth of a fridge and the sincerity of Dougherty's concern for Dale.

"Sorry, Bianca, we're catching up with Tara and Mitch." I smile and keep moving forward.

Bianca flicks her hair over her shoulder; her smile matches Eden's. "That's cool. I'll see you in math."

"Sure. See you then." And she heads down the hall.

Eden is quiet, the artificial smile nowhere to be seen. "You could have caught up with her. I wouldn't have minded."

I frown again. "I didn't want to." I stop and turn toward Eden. She pauses besides me. I wait for her to turn and face me. "This is where I want to be."

Eden's eyes widen, evergreen oceans which tilt delicately up. Her mouth forms a silent "Oh." How could she not know? I hold myself there, slowly dissolving in her bottomless eyes. I want her to see my sincerity. I want her to know. And greedily, I want her to reciprocate. The curling feeling is swiftly wrapping us in its magical cocoon, the noise of the masses falling away.

And I know I'm telling the truth. There's nowhere else I want to be.

Our bubble is burst by the bright, tinkling giggle that has followed me since childhood. Tara skips up between us and loops her arms in each of ours. Oblivious to her interruption, she starts leading us toward the cafeteria doors.

"How was bio?" she asks as her head swivels from Eden to me and back again.

I playfully jab her in the ribs with my elbow. This is what an annoying little sister feels like. "Interesting." I shoot a glance over Tara's head. Eden's soft smile is back and she shyly returns my expression. "Dale put in an appearance."

Tara drops her voice, doing a poor imitation of a guy. "Dude! No way!"

Eden's face goes serious. "Dude. Way."

Tara peals into laughter as we head into the lunch room. Mitch is already sitting at our table. His smile mirrors ours as we approach. Tara and I head over to the line, but Eden pulls up a seat at the table.

Tara looks at her questioningly. "Not eating today?"

Eden pulls out a paper bag from her backpack. She wrinkles her nose in the direction of the serving area. "Brought my own."

Tara nods. "Good choice. Those vegetables will probably shorten your lifespan."

Mitch already has his lunch in front of him, so Tara and I head to the line.

While we wait, Tara shoves me with her shoulder. At her height, its bony point gets me in the ribs. "So..." She leaves that one little word hanging.

I look at her, letting it dangle there.

Tara rolls her eyes. "So...Eden?"

I roll my eyes back. "What about her?"

We move down the line, our equally greasy-looking cafeteria lady drops a ladleful of browny-grey sludge onto each of our plates. Maybe Eden has the right idea.

"You two seem to be getting along nicely."

I grin. "So do you two. You've made a friend outside of the Channon and Phelans."

Tara shrugs, smiling. "There's just something about her."

Yes, there is.

We leave the line and head back to the table. Mitch and Eden are chatting easily; Mitch is pointing in various directions as he talks. Eden doesn't seem to have any issues opening up with him. What does that mean, I wonder? How come she can't give me that easy eye contact, relaxed posture? Is her discomfort with me a good or a bad sign?

Are these questions actually getting me anywhere but confused?

Tara and I slide into our seats. Tara is just about sitting in Mitch's lap, but judging by his tender look, that's just where he wants her. I sit next to Eden, but as much as I would like the equivalent proximity, I maintain a more socially appropriate distance. Mitch and Eden seemed to have finished whatever they were talking about, and have returned to eating. Eden is focused on what looks like a peanut butter sandwich.

"I can't believe how much homework I have!" Tara is dejectedly poking at her sludgy lunch. Her plastic fork disappears into the rat-colored lump.

Mitch groans in agreement. "Yep, the buildup for midterms is in full swing."

This is the perfect lead-up for where I wanted the conversation to go. I turn to Eden. "So, we need to finish this assignment."

Mitch looks outside the window at the autumn rain that is pouring down the cafeteria windows. "You won't be walking in the reserve today." I quickly glance at Eden to see if she's surprised by Mitch's knowledge of her walk. She follows his eyes to the grey world outside, unconcerned.

One delicate shoulder lifts then drops. "That's fine, I can work on it this afternoon and show you what I've done tomorrow."

Not exactly what I had in mind. I take an imaginary deep breath. Here goes nothing. Well, hopefully it will be something. Anything. "We could study at my place?"

Eden freezes. I have a sinking feeling that is not a good sign. She opens her mouth, in what I already know will be another rejection. I steel myself to pretend it doesn't matter.

"That's a great idea!" The enthusiasm comes from Tara. We all turn to her. "We can have a study sesh!"

Mitch shrugs. "Well, I'm already on the premises, so I should be able to make it. And maybe it will get that Tech Design assignment finished."

"Come on, Eden. I'll bring the popcorn. It'll be fun." Tara has that wingy-whiny tone that always gets people to cave, just because it's so annoying.

Eden looks at the expectant faces surrounding her. Her eyes rest briefly on mine, and in that unreadable moment, I have no idea whether she wants to spend this time with me.

"Pleeeease?" Tara's pitch is progressively getting toward the excruciating range.

Now it's Eden's turn to roll her eyes. "Fine, but the popcorn had better be butter flavored."

"Done!" Tara sounds like an auctioneer closing a sale. She even slaps the table for emphasis. Although I don't think auctioneers bounce up and down in their seat with anticipation. Over a study session.

Excitement bubbles in the pit of my stomach. Not exactly time alone with Eden, but time with Eden is a gift I'm starting to treasure. If I'm going to be totally honest, I'll take anything I can get.

The jaunty sounds of Smurfs singing fills the air and Tara dives into her bag for her phone. She glances at the screen, groaning that it's her dad. Giving Mitch a quick kiss on the head, she leaves the noisy cafeteria to take the call.

We have only a couple of minutes before next class, so I consider trying to make some conversation with Eden, maybe try and copy the easy camaraderie that she had with Mitch. That we almost had walking in. But Eden glances at her watch, the universal sign of someone wanting to make a hasty retreat. She smiles briefly in our direction, mumbling something about talking to her chemistry teacher before class and disappears through the cafeteria doors.

I turn to Mitch, wondering if he's going to give me another pseudo-lecture that'll just tick me off. But Mitch is staring out the rain-soaked windows. His index finger is rubbing back and forth along his lower lip.

"What?"

He glances at me, surprised out of his musings.

"Nothing really." But he continues to stare out toward the soggy oval beyond the school walls.

"What?"

"I don't think it means anything."

"What doesn't mean anything?" Frustration hikes my voice up a few decibels.

He frowns slightly. "When I was talking to Eden, I asked if she's checked out the reserve yet."

So that's how he would have known she was out yesterday.

"She said she went for a walk yesterday and got caught in the rain."

"Oh." I'm not sure where he was going with that line of conversation. I wait for him to continue. But the silence stretches out, becoming taut. "And?"

"She said she had to trample back, in the dark—sopping wet."

My stomach sinks. This time I draw out my question. "And?"

"That was it. She said she got home, had a hot shower, and learned to time her walks better."

"Huh."

Neither of us says another thing. Call it the twin bond if you want. But we both know that Eden never mentioned the overwhelming danger she was in stranded in that sleeting storm, or her overwhelming fear at being lost.

Or the overwhelming black wolf that lead her back to the trail.

11

EDEN

As I drive to Noah's house, my mother's white Saab slicing through the sleeting rain, I notice a dangerous emotion bubbling up. A feeling that's been buried deep, smothered, practically made extinct by ruthless reality. It effervesces up my spine, warm and vibrant and full of promise, expanding my chest, making me light-headed. I imagine this is what a caged bird feels like set free for the first time. Unrestrained, buoyant, facing a clear sky crowded with possibilities. The temptation to soar on those wings is undeniable.

I think it's called hope.

And it's all due to one guy. A guy that's far too good-looking. A guy that's much too magnetic. A guy that's way too appealing, inviting, tempting.

But I know hope is dangerous. I remember what happened when I hoped my mother would chase away the Bogey man that was under my bed. When I hoped a 'fresh start' would be a promise of something good. When I hoped that I would be a normal kid like Janey next door. I know what follows hope is crushing disappointment, shattering disillusionment, pulverizing defeat.

As I continue driving, greenery thrives as suburbia thins. Down the unbroken secluded road, without the disembodied voice of google-maps-lady, the only sound is rain pummeling the car. We certainly couldn't have gone for a walk in this weather. I shudder as I recollect my last foray in the rain. Besides, Todd doesn't work Thursdays. And time alone with Noah is out of the question.

His presence is too closely linked with hope.

According to my phone, I'm almost at my destination. The rain picks up, hammering down like it wants to be a waterfall when it grows up. I switch the wiper blades to warp speed as it gushes across my windshield. The frantic swishing matches my frenzied pulse, pounding the knowledge that I'll soon be seeing Noah through every fiber of my body.

"Your destination will be on the right." I shut off the annoying woman. I drive up the short driveway to a two-story house. A broad veranda hugs the front of the old timber and stone home. Through the rain I see a lawn, made up of a patch-work of greens and yellows, surrounded by a medley of garden beds. I can't distinguish the plants, but they rise up in a mish mash of heights and shapes. Not a manicured, landscaped piece of vegetation to be seen. The charming scene is nestled within a small clearing, enveloped by ancient pines, like giant protectors of old.

I dart up the paved path to the front door. Despite the three-second dash, rain soaks my hair and jacket. *Great.* Nothing like the drowned-rat look. If I hadn't been so full of nervous anticipation, I would have remembered to bring an umbrella. To the right of the softly lit doorway is a rough-hewn timber seat, sanded and oiled to a rich, warm honey. I look a little more closely at its chunky craftsmanship. Underneath one of the legs is a tightly folded piece of cardboard.

I knock on the door, armed against this warm, inviting home

with my shield-like books and a fortifying breath. Heavy foot-steps can be heard walking swiftly to the door. My already mad pulse escalates to crazy. The door opens and there's Noah. I take in the sculpted lips stretched wide over straight teeth, the brilliant blue eyes focused on mine. The dangerous temptation that no one else has ever posed.

"Hi, Eden."

"Hi, Noah." The beaming grin amps up to blazing. My lungs stutter for breath and my cheeks flame. *Here we go*. Another couple of hours of looking like a malfunctioning stoplight.

"Come on in, it's bucketing out there. Good thing we didn't go for a walk again."

He opens the door wide and I walk past, holding my breath so I don't absorb his warm, masculine scent. The stuff infiltrates my system and it takes hours, days, for it to stop tripping memories of his magnetic blue eyes.

The short hallway opens to an open-plan lounge room. I stand awkwardly as timber furniture built from every wood known to man checkers the room; CD racks and shelves and coffee, side and end tables. And jammed on any flat surface, in a tangle of mismatching frames, are a multitude of photos—each capturing a birthday, a holiday, an inconsequential everyday moment. It looks like any day is a reason for a photo opportunity in the Phelan house.

A series of thumps sound down the hallway and a brown Labrador, ears flapping, tail wagging furiously, catapults toward me. I smile in delight—finally something I'm comfortable relating to. I kneel down and rub my hand through the folds of skin along his neck. The dog sits, his tail thumping out his welcome. "Hello to you too."

"Well, you're either a dog lover or you just came from a drug lab."

I stand and face a mountain of a man, obviously Noah's dad

by his dark blond hair and intelligent blue eyes, and blush the brightest red so far. *Enough,* I tell the capillaries beneath my cheeks.

"Dad." Noah says in that universal parents-are-so-embarrassing tone. "Eden, this is my dad, Adam Phelan, and this is Stash." He stands beside me to pat the Lab. "He's a police dog, drug detection, and search and rescue."

"Nice to meet you, Mr. Phelan."

"Adam, please. That's the most excited I've ever seen Stash with a stranger."

"Eden has a way with animals."

I pretend I don't hear that one as I bend down to pat Stash, who's leaning his chocolaty weight against my leg.

A dark-haired woman enters from the doorway on the left, I'm guessing the kitchen judging by the apron. She's tall, with soft, kind eyes and a welcoming smile.

"Hi, I'm Beth." She looks meaningfully at both Noah and Adam. She leans forward, one hand cupping her mouth. "I find the best way to handle the Phelan men is to completely ignore everything they say."

Adam wanders over to slip an arm around his wife. "Which she does astoundingly well."

Beth looks up at him, grinning shamelessly. She doesn't look old enough to be the mother of two teenage sons. She pats his chest. "Years of dedicated training."

I notice that, for once in my life, I'm not the tallest person in the room. It's a novel feeling, one I don't want to admit I like. As I look into their open, welcoming faces I begin to relax.

But in the silent pause I finally notice the absence of Mitch and Tara. Then I belatedly register the deserted car space in the driveway when I arrived. Apprehension is gently lapping at the edges of my consciousness. Did I actually think for a second that this would be a safe and straightforward endeavor?

Noah notices me looking around. "Tara got a call from her dad. He needed her to babysit. Something about a doctor's appointment for her mom." He rubs the back of his neck. "And Mitch decided to go with her."

How does this keep happening? Alone with Noah. Twice in one week! I take a very Dougherty-like deep breath. Apparently I haven't mastered its calming effect, because my nervousness continues to gain momentum. I consider looking for exit signs as I try to calm my racing heart. It'll be fine. I'll spend an hour going over the presentation then hightail it home. *Please let it be fine.*

Noah breaks the silence by telling his parents we'll study in his room. Anxiety is now crashing in roiling waves, spraying icy droplets down my spine. Maybe his parents will suggest the much more open, safe, and populated lounge room. But they accept his statement easily and, after gifting me with another kind smile, head back to whatever my arrival interrupted.

I follow Noah across the lounge room I don't want to leave and up a set of stairs. More photos are strung along the wall heading up to the second floor. They seem to be a timeline, starting with twin babies in matching prams, up to a diapered Noah grinning on a trike; the next sees Mitch sitting on the floor with a toy drill. Each milestone celebrated with a step up the stairway.

Noah glances back and notices my scrutiny. He scratches above his ear. "Nothing like having every second of your childhood as a permanent art exhibition, huh? We joke that Mom's pointer finger is permanently bent thanks to repeated photographer's strain."

"It's sweet. There doesn't seem to be anything too embarrassing." Until, halfway up the stairs, the school photos start. From the toothless smiles and flattened comb-overs of elementary school, through to the spotted acne and outdated hair of junior high.

"Oh." Now it's Noah's turn to blush.

Interestingly, Noah and Mitch appeared evenly sized until the last couple of pictures. Then Mitch becomes the burly young man he is now, while Noah stayed the lanky teen. Although, looking at Noah's broad back—thankfully in a looser T-shirt—he's had a growth spurt as he no longer seems to match his senior year photo.

At the top of the stairs Noah leads me to a room situated on the right of the hallway. He stands back, bowing slightly at the waist, sweeping his arm out in a gentlemanly flourish. I step through the door into what I imagine is a standard senior's room. A double bed, covered in a navy comforter, sits against the far wall. A window on the external wall looks out to the ubiquitous mountain range that can be seen from any point in Jacksonville. A small desk, crowded with books and papers, sits below the window. The opposite wall is dominated by shelves holding a myriad books and DVDs and what looks like built-in cupboards.

It seems unthreatening enough. Until Noah enters and the room shrinks with his no-longer-lanky presence. Then he takes the only chair in the room. I stand awkwardly, once again holding my breath in the confined space.

"Just put your stuff on the bed." Noah grabs a laptop and powers it up, all business. I take two shaky steps to the bed and place my backpack on it. I perch on the edge, pretending to look through my alphabetically organized backpack for the relevant book.

"Your parents seem nice." I say to break the lengthening silence.

"Yeah, I don't think I'll trade them in this week." He wheels the desk chair toward me, laptop in hand. I'm stuck between the summer-blue eyes that I'm desperately trying to escape and sitting farther back on the bed. But settling in on that dark blue comforter represents an intimacy I'm equally trying to escape.

Stash grabs that moment with all four paws and dashes into the room. He leaps up on to the bed beside me, tongue lolling. I smile, my hand naturally sinking into his thick fur. I move back slightly on the bed. I feel a little better with a police escort.

Noah reaches over to ruffle his ears. "And if Stash likes you, then Dad likes you. He's like his canine barometer for people."

Eden has a way with animals.

He never says the words but I know they're there in his summer-sky eyes. And I know he's thinking of the swan. His brows form questioning arches as he waits. I can feel defensiveness climb up. Brick by oppositional brick. I consider saying something acidic, going on the attack to get him off track.

"I don't understand it." I tell this to the quilt in front of me, bunching the dark blue cotton in my fist.

Noah pauses then nods once. "Okay."

And for some reason I want him to know. "I can't explain it."

"Okay."

I look up. Straight into warm cerulean pools of acceptance. Directly into acknowledgement and understanding. Conclusively into the knowledge that I want to dive and revel in this feeling before it dries up. Noah remains there, and I take the time to study his sculptured features, soft lips, unblinking eyes. A small part of me is taking the time to look for subtle signs of dishonesty. She comes up empty-handed. While I come away full and overflowing. Full of...*hope.*

Banging and clanging sounds waft up from the kitchen, breaching the breathless moment. I can feel my cheeks warm, but this time it's not from embarrassment. I straighten and mentally shake myself. My imagination is blazing out of control.

My eyes slide back to my bag. It's time to step back into reality. "Right. The...ummm...PowerPoint."

Thankfully Noah takes my cue. "Let's check out what you think of my efforts so far."

The assignment sheet is in my hand, although I have no memory of how it got there. I really need to get a grip. I use all my willpower to focus on the paper in front of me. "We need to cover the definition and example of a parasite."

Noah reads from the screen in front of him. "Where one species benefits at the expense of the other." He tilts his chin up as he scratches it. "Dale?"

I snort, a very unladylike sound, and look up quickly to find Noah grinning, right there with me.

I return to the sheet. My finger quickly runs down the dot points. Back in the realm of hard science, I feel like I'm regaining some equilibrium. "We've covered predator prey relationships in the food web?"

Noah hits the keyboard with a flourish. "Slide three." He announces like he gave birth to it himself.

"Okay, what about symbiosis?"

"Symbiosis." I glance up at Noah's echo. Something in his rich voice reaches out and grasps my attention. "A close, and often long-term, relationship where both individuals benefit." Somehow he manages to make the scientific term sound appealing...*seductive*. I feel my blood start to pulse in an infinite number of places. My cheeks. My fingertips. My lips.

And just like that I'm catapulted off center again. I swallow. My throat feels raspy and thick. I try to muster up some saliva to soothe its parched surface before I make an attempt at a verbal response.

The realm of hard science. The realm of hard science. A quick ahem and I'm under control. I think. "For the example, I think we should go with the relationship between the conifers, pine drops, and fungi. It's a fairly recent research project undertaken in the reserve." I sound a little hoarse and I hope it isn't noticeable.

Noah coughs a little. "Yeah, the pine drops..." He blinks at the screen, then quickly types in a few words.

We spend some time sorting out the definitions and examples, with no more serious distractions. We discuss and debate the order, key points, and best images for the presentation. Noah is sitting back, feet propped up on the bed, computer on his lap. The passage of time sees me slowly relax until I'm sitting cross-legged almost, but not quite, in the center of the bed. Books and sheets are spread around me like a papery pinafore. Probably the closest I'll ever get to that feminine apparel.

I'm feeling so relaxed that I decide to venture a little further than the safe margins of hard science. "So why do you need to keep your GPA up?" Although, seeing Noah in action, his obvious knowledge of the reserve, his ability to assimilate our research into a coherent whole, shows an intelligent, capable guy. I doubt he's ever struggled in biology.

My comment seems to spur another of those moments where he blinds me with his smile. I almost want to rub my eyes. "I'm applying to do criminal justice at Wyoming State." He leans back, his arms folded behind his head. "It's a family tradition."

My mind briefly flashes to the application for early entry into veterinary science that slid into the postbox this morning — at Wyoming State. It's not my first choice, but my mother insisted. Ironic, because it's thanks to her that I would never consider it. One hour away is too close.

"So Mitch will too?"

Noah's smile dims a little, his lips moving down infinitesimally, his eyes losing a little of their pride. He returns to his earlier position, leaning forward, long fingers on his keyboard. "Yeah, probably." It's the first guarded, indirect answer I've had from Noah. "What about you? You always wanted to be a vet?" As a deflector from way back, I recognize the strategy. But I'm too insecure to dig deeper.

"Yeah. That whole natural ability with animals thing."

Noah grunts, acknowledging my understatement. He types a few more words. "Ah, that should be a good one."

He moves from his chair to perch on the edge of the bed. I scoot over, under the pretense of making some room, when my real aim is to gain some necessary distance. He passes me the laptop, pointing at an image he's had pasted on the slide. It's a picture of me, smiling slightly, squatting besides Jeremiah. I'm pointing at something in the distance as he stares at the mountainous vista with rapt attention. Noah must have taken it on our walk. That photo is not going in the presentation. Beside me Stash sits up, folded ears perked up. I open my mouth to object.

Downstairs the front door opens and closes, and Mitch's voice skips up the stairs. Stash lets out an excited bark and launches off the bed in a single leap. His jet-propelled body vaults through Noah as if he doesn't pose a barrier. And he doesn't, he's unceremoniously bowled backwards from the bed. Stash streaks from the room without a second glance.

Noah is nowhere to be seen.

I scramble to the edge of the bed, heedless of the paper crinkling beneath my knees, and peer over. Noah is lying on the ground, eyes staring at the ceiling in shock. He blinks several times. The humor of the situation hits me like a seventy-pound Lab and a giggle slips through my lips. The sound draws Noah's bemused gaze to mine. And I can't help it. The laughter bursts through like...like a seventy-pound Lab. It bounds and bounces around the room, the sound welcome but alien. Noah joins me, our laughter merging and mushrooming. Stash's enthusiastic disregard for human safety, Noah's involuntary gymnastics down to the floor, and his comically stunned expression has me laughing hard. So hard my sides hurt, my eyes water and my joints go weak.

Suddenly their crumbling strength gives out and the next moment I'm falling. Falling over the edge of the bed, straight toward Noah. Noah's eyes widen as he registers my trajectory. With split-second reflexes, his arms shoot out and grasp my waist as I gracelessly tumble, straight on top of him.

My head bumps his chin as my chest crashes into his. My legs follow in a tangled mess. His strong arms break the fall, then still just above my hips. In a moment of klutzy weakness I've gone from avoiding all and any physical contact, to undiluted and absolute full-frame collision. My body, with the aid of gravity and its own treacherous yearning, molds every inch to the hard muscle beneath me. It's overwhelming.

And amazing.

I raise my head and look down at Noah, and I know his face matches mine. Wide eyes, warm cheeks, bewildered lips. That connecting attraction no longer coils and loops, instead it snaps taut, like two pieces of a puzzle have just clicked into place. Beneath my hands his chest is blazing hot. It matches the heat starting behind my ear, spreading across my scalp and sprinting down my spine. My eyes travel to his eyes. Nose. Lips. Curiosity and longing, feelings I've never experienced before, blossom. I'm torn between the desire to explore those soft-firm ridges and the urge to snuggle into the comforting sense of belonging that radiates with the force of the sun. And the urge to run for the hills, as fast as my long-legged stride can take me.

Because I'm scared. I know with a certainty born of self-preservation that Noah is penetrating the impenetrable... breaching the unbreachable...accessing the inaccessible. It's paralyzing, petrifying, and downright exhilarating. And therein lies the problem. There's a part of me that's standing on the other side, aiding and abetting in the destruction of my own protective armor. She's not heeding the alarm bells, tolling the dangers of being left exposed and vulnerable.

Heavy footsteps echo up the stairs, thrusting me back to reality. There's no time to sort through the confused jumble in my head. I scramble off Noah and back onto the bed. I look up to see Mitch standing at the door, mouth snapping shut like he was about to say something and has just changed his mind, the remnants of a smile falling from his face. He looks from me to Noah, who is picking himself up from the floor.

Noah dusts himself off. "Stash just knocked me off the bed because you came home." He points at Mitch as he makes the statement.

Mitch shrugs, not deigning to defend himself. He once again glances between the two of us. I feel like I've been judged by a disapproving parent. Although it's a familiar feeling, Mitch had seemed so open and welcoming. Quick as a flash, a succinct list of my most obvious flaws scrolls through my head. They easily explain why Mitch would veto whatever it is he just saw.

"How's the study going?" Mitch's arms come up to cross his chest.

Noah narrows his eyes at him. "Great."

A strained silence begins to stretch out as matching blue eyes engage in some sort of battle of wills. But this game of tug-of-war appears well matched. As the seconds draw out, I wonder who will win, or whether the taut stillness will simply snap under the weight of their silent communication. I shift uncomfortably, desperately hoping I'm not the reason for the unspoken argument. Mitch sighs, almost sounding resigned. "I'm gonna head into the garage. I'll see you at dinner. Bye, Eden."

I want to sigh myself. "Seeya, Mitch." At least this time around it took a couple of weeks before I inadvertently got on someone's bad side.

"Right, where were we?" I like Noah's train of thought. Back to business. And just like that we focus again on my reason for being here. Not to experience unfamiliar stirring emotions. Not to cause conflict between twin brothers. Not to laugh like no one is watching. Certainly not to feel hope.

We throw ourselves into the virtual world of the reserve's food webs and chains. We debate and discuss the structure of each sentence, the best font and format, the placement of commas. Progressively we boil down information to dot points; headings are diced and shaped; a garnish of images are strategically placed— excluding any that feature me. Together we create a darned fine presentation.

Our creative flow is interrupted by Beth's voice as she comes up the stairs. "Noah, dinner will be ready soon."

Oh my goodness, it's that time already. I glance at my watch and realize we've been so absorbed in the assignment I'd lost track of time. I sit back; our heads had almost been touching as we leant over the laptop, creating the PowerPoint slide by slide.

Beth stands at the door, a tea towel in her hands. "Eden, great, you're still here. You'll be staying for dinner?" The question-that's-more-of-a-statement takes me off guard.

"Oh, that's not necessary."

"Great idea, Mom." Noah sits back, looking satisfied. I'm not sure whether it's with the PowerPoint or his mother's suggestion.

"I couldn't." I'm blushing again. It was nice to have had a break for a little while.

"Nonsense. I always make extra with a house full of hungry males to feed."

"Eden's a vegetarian, Mom."

Beth's eyes widen slightly, the edges becoming imperceptibly rounder. "Oh." Why do I keep getting this reaction to the vegetarianism thing? Luckily I'm still blushing, otherwise I would have gone again.

"Really, I have dinner waiting for me at home." By this time it will be the old faithful peanut butter sandwich.

"I won't hear of it. I'll just whip up something on the side." And she's gone.

"I really don't want to be a bother." I place one-tonne emphasis on the second word.

Noah doesn't look fazed in the least. "Humor her. She loves to nurture." A flash of frown streaks across his brow. "Just keep that in mind when she serves up." And the smile is back.

I throw my hands over my face and groan. "Aren't I supposed to ignore Phelans?" I groan again; I doubt Mitch is going to be pleased to see me at the dinner table.

"Only the men." He reminds me. "Do you need to call your mom?"

And tell her what? That I won't be in our empty house this evening? "I'll just text her." I pull my phone out and pretend to type.

Mitch's broad shoulders and dark hair fills the doorway. He glances at the open laptop and papers strewn about. "You guys done?" There's only a hairsbreadth pause as he waits for a response. "Excellent." He comes in and perches on the edge of the bed. I shuffle across, unsure of this friendly demeanor.

Noah leans back in his chair, linking his fingers across his abdomen. I studiously avoid glancing at his biceps, the long fingers resting on his flat stomach. "How's the present going?"

Mitch huffs. "Stupid timber split. I'm going to have to start that whole section again."

"Bummer."

Mitch shrugs and turns to me. "Eden, Tara said to say, and I quote, 'Soz about the popcorn. Raincheck?'"

Sounds like Tara. Although it's her fault I'm trapped in this uncomfortable, strangely invigorating situation. "Tell her it's fine."

Mitch gives me a small salute. "The good news is, I've down-loaded a new track!"

Noah groans, and it's a drawn out, long-suffering sound. It couldn't be that bad, could it?

Mitch takes himself over to the small stereo sitting on a shelf above Noah's desk. He plugs in his MP3 player. Within seconds techno beats thump through the bedroom, followed by hoarse harsh screams. It sounds like someone is violently vomiting on a microphone.

"That's horrible." The truth escapes before I have a second to think. Then cringe, expecting the worst.

Noah bursts out laughing. Mitch turns down the awful, beat-driven screaming, shrugging. "No one appreciates true art nowadays."

"Mitch, turn off that hideous excuse for music and come down to dinner." Adam's voice booms up the stairway.

Mitch huffs again, but complies. Noah breathes a sigh of relief, sending me a conspiratorial look. I can't help but smile back.

I quickly pack up my books and follow Mitch and Noah out the door and down the stairs. Partway down Mitch stops and spins back to Noah. We all halt. I instantly pull myself backward, having almost collided with Noah. I'm still reeling, tingling from our earlier contact.

"Have you told her?" Mitch is looking at Noah, eyebrows raised.

"Ah...no." Another meaningful glance passes between the two. *What now?* I shift from one foot to another. Should I ask? Do I want to know?

Mitch shrugs. "Well, it's the ultimate Phelan test..." I don't like the sound of that. I already feel like I've run multiple gauntlets. He throws me a smile from his place several steps below me. I think it's meant to be reassuring.

In the dining room that adjoins the lounge room, five plates wait around a large wooden table, this one made from a dark brown timber. I hold back, unsure of what I do here. Adam sits at the head, with Beth on his right and Mitch beside her. Noah takes the seat on the left, leaving me the seat next to his. I pull out the matching timber chair and sit. Noah flashes me a grin. I'm too nervous to smile back.

I look down at the plate in front of me where a meal is already waiting. And pause for long seconds.

12

NOAH

Most of my mother's meals look like a hiking boot has been dismembered, tortured then burned to destroy the evidence. Today, the laces have been arranged to look like greyish beans, the leather upper has been battered to make an odd-colored potato mash, and the sole has been brutalized into a steak. Eden is extra lucky as she got eggplant, its previously thick chunks reduced to a charred carcass.

Eden takes long moments to comprehend the carnage served on my grandmother's delicate china. I cringe. I should have warned her. What's worse, my mother is looking at her, hands clasped hopefully.

She looks up, eyes wide and honest. Uh-oh. "It's been a long time since anyone has cooked me eggplant, Mrs. Phelan. I really appreciate the effort you've gone to."

My mother blushes at the sincerity in Eden's clear voice. "Beth, please. I'm glad you like it. I haven't cooked it before, so I wasn't sure if it was overdone."

I glance at Mitch, and he shrugs. She meant it. A few more threads weave together, slowly winding to form the rich tapestry that is Eden. Eden's dark, front porch, the absent reply to the text, the perpetual peanut butter sandwiches. I suspect Eden's mom may not be up for any mother-of-the-year awards. And here I was thinking I had to unravel the mysteries of this girl.

"It looks just right." Her warm smile barely trips when she crunches into the eggplant's blistered remains.

And she just scored more brownie points with my dad. According to him, anyone that survives my mother's cooking is praiseworthy. Anyone that appreciates its unique contribution to the culinary world is extraordinary, and deserves a special place at the Phelan table.

Mum puts down her fork, looking at everyone around the table. "Now, Eden. We have a Phelan dinner tradition we do every week."

I groan, and Mitch echoes the sound. I lean over to Eden and stage whisper, "I'm so sorry."

"Thank you, Noah." Mom's eyebrows are fitted in a stern line. Eden smiles politely, but has that guarded look of hers I'm getting to know. I want to assure her that what's coming next is not nearly as bad as the meal she's having to consume.

"So, I throw out a conversation starter, and everyone has to contribute. It's always a bit of fun." My mother's eyebrows shoot back up now that she's smiling happily again.

This one I should have warned Eden about. I swear my mother trawls the net for ideas on this. We've been doing it since Mitch and I could barely speak. Then again, Eden wasn't real keen to be here in the first place. If she'd known about the quality of the food, or the prompted dinner conversation, she would have hightailed it for the hills before I could give Stash the command to search.

"Okay. If animals could talk, which would be the most fun to talk to and why?" My mother throws out the line like a consummate fisherman.

Dad looks thoughtful, rubbing his forefinger across his

bottom lip. "Good one, love." I roll my eyes; that's one interpretation. He clicks his fingers triumphantly. "The fly on the wall!"

Okay, I'll give him that one. Eden's lips twitch in that almost-smile of hers. I keep waiting for it to breach its shackles and finally break free again. Her laughter from earlier is still singing in my ears.

I come up with one of my own. "A kangaroo, purely for the accent." My mother's tinkling laugh glitters across the table. Eden's smile is slowly blossoming. It's an amazing sight.

Mitch arches a brow. "A fox." We all turn to him quizzically. "Then I'd know what the fox says." The younger generation chuckle at the reference to the popular song. The two oldies at the table maintain their confused expressions.

All eyes turn to Eden. She looks a little cornered for a second, and I wonder if I should rescue her. But, as she always seems to do, she steps up to the challenge, calmly and quietly. "A chicken, so we finally know who came first." That one is universal, and everyone joins in the chuckles and confirmation nods.

"Okay, now you get to be an animal for a week." Mom manages to nicely sidestep providing an answer of her own. No one bothers to point it out. My mother's saint status is undisputed.

"A grizzly bear." Dad is looking wistfully at the ceiling. "A hibernating one."

I stage whisper to Eden again. "Dad just came off night shift." She passes him a sympathetic glance.

Mitch leans back, his hands behind his head, like a tycoon addressing his board of directors. He picks up a crispy-grey bean, holding it like a cigar. "I'd be a marmot."

"A marmot?" Not what I was expecting.

"With my harem of gorgeous marmot babes." Mitch has a cat-got-the-cream look. Until he bites into the bean.

I snort. "Like that would ever happen. If Tara wasn't *the*

marmot matron who scares all the others off, then she would be a fox feasting on every last one."

Mitch's shoulders droop. The mighty mogul has been defeated. "That's true."

"Well, seeing as we've got a reserve theme going, I would be a golden eagle," my mother chimes in. "That razor-sharp sight, cruising around, never missing a thing." Which is exactly what my mother does, in human form.

"I'd be a wolf." Eden's musical voice contributes this time with no prompting. All eyes turn to her.

My mother barely skips a blink. "That's a good one. Why a wolf?"

Eden glances down at her meal, and I wonder if she will converse with her vegetables again. But her eyes return to us, and she smiles lightly, shrugging. "Well, the freedom of roaming the reserve, everyone knows their place in the pack, the protection of family."

"We've all had those moments," I say, trying to keep it light. Although neither of my parents crack a smile.

"Would you be an alpha?" This comes from Mitch. I'm tempted to kick him under the table.

Eden wrinkles her nose. "I don't think so. I'd be happy to be one of the betas."

Huh, Eden knows her wolves. Most people think the beta is the alpha's mate, but the label actually relates to the other mature wolves in the pack that are subordinate to the alpha pair.

Mitch nods. "Not everyone wants to be an alpha." I cross my legs so I don't reach out a sneakered toe and connect with his shin. Hard.

Dad clears his throat. "So, Eden, your mother works at the Inn?"

"Yes, she does."

"Lovely spot there. And your father?"

Eden's fork pauses on its way to her mouth. "I'm not really sure what he does..." Eden is once again looking uncomfortable.

I open my mouth to jump in, but Mitch beats me to it. "Hey, Noah. Do you remember that time when we were five?"

Uh-oh.

Mitch is already chuckling before he tells the punch line. "And you called 911 to speak to Dad?"

Two can play at that game. "Wasn't that about the same time you asked Mom if old Mrs. Harris was pregnant?"

Mitch's smile fades a little now that he's on the receiving end. "Well, she's certainly...big-boned."

"As we stood behind her at the supermarket."

And Eden's smile is back, crystallizing across her face like a rare and magnificent gem.

Mom sighs. "And all we can learn from those little stories is that it's a miracle I haven't gone grey before my time." And it's my mother's turn for a sympathetic glance from Eden.

The conversation flows around the table as we crunch through dinner. Thankfully, Dad doesn't put his foot in it again. And luckily Mom doesn't notice that even Stash won't eat the titbits that Mitch sneaks under the table. I certainly notice that Eden doesn't stop smiling. And I don't stop glancing at the captivating sight from the corner of my eye.

As we finish up, Eden offers to help with the cleanup, but Mom won't hear of it. Eden thanks her again for the lovely meal. Without blinking once. My mother blushes a little, while my father beams. This girl entrances everyone. Even Mitch is looking relaxed. I suspect Eden will leave now that we're finished, so I'm not surprised when she heads upstairs for her bag.

I meet her at the door. Both of her hands grip the strap of her bag resting on her shoulder. I stand by the door, one arm leaning against its edge. As is the case around this breathtaking girl, I'm a little unsure of what to say. Mitch would think that's hilarious. And unbelievable.

"So...we got the assignment done." Which means I have no more excuses to spend time with her outside of school.

"Yeah. It looks really good." Eden's eyes are on me. It feels like, since the moment she fell on me, that sense of connection has gotten undeniably stronger. I wish I could reach out and touch her. I shove my free hand in the back pocket of my jeans.

"Thanks for being so good with my mother's cooking." I lean in a little so I can speak in hushed tones. I breathe in her untamed floral scent.

Eden grins at that one. An actual full-fledged grin. My breath vaporizes in my lungs. "She was very sweet to cook me eggplant."

"I have to say, that was the best time I've ever had working on a presentation." I rub my chin where her head collided. A gentle glow rises up Eden's cheeks. Not quite a blush, but a definite slow spread of heat. It holds me transfixed.

Her eyes never leave mine. "Me too."

Long seconds pass. She doesn't move back. She doesn't break eye contact.

"Seeya Eden!" A chorus chimes from my family in the kitchen.

She smiles, standing on tiptoe so she can call good-bye past my shoulder. When did she get that short? And with a whispered 'Bye Noah', she turns and leaves.

I shut the door, taking a quiet feeling of joy up the stairs to my room, my fingers doing an air guitar impersonation. Imagine Dragons *I'm on Top of The World* coming right up.

13

EDEN

I don't think I can do this.

I've spent all of Saturday cleaning my clean room, completing completed assignments, consuming too much of Tony's white chocolate cheesecake. Now it's Sunday, I'm sitting at my too tidy desk, a veterinary science textbook in front of me. My dried-out highlighter drops to the desk. None of it has stopped Noah dominating my every thought. And with each remembered scent, each enduring glance, each unforgettable touch, the fear continues to grow.

I don't think I can do this.

I don't even know what 'this' is, but I do know it's too tempting. These merry-go-round thoughts wouldn't have momentum if it wasn't for the magnetic pull Noah presents. He's kind, funny, and intelligent. And much too good-looking.

It's too complicated. And I avoid complications. The one person to befriend me is practically his sister-in-law. And I need to focus on my studies; I can't afford for my grades to drop. My saving grace has always been to leave for a college that is far, far away.

And it's too scary. Risky. What do I have to offer Noah? When he finally realizes the truth, I'll be a shell. Hollowed out, echoing with pathetic dreams of what was never going to be. This is already hard enough, let alone if I let my defenses down.

It feels like I'm standing at a threshold, looking out into an uncharted, unfamiliar unknown. And no matter how hard I try, I can't see ahead. There's no path. I don't have a map. I don't know where this goes.

And I know I can't do this.

Because there will be no turning back. No safety net. All I can see is all the ways this doesn't end well. I take a step back from the dangerous, seductive ledge.

Instead of relief, all I feel is sadness. Painful, heavy sadness. Like everything has given up the fight with gravity, and sunk. My mouth, my shoulders, my heart. This isn't a sadness I've felt before. Kind of like I've lost something. Something very precious. I frown. Something I never had.

I push away from my desk. I need to go for a walk. A strenuous one. One that will leave me exhausted, body and mind.

I pull out my map, unfolding it on my desk. It flops open, its folds now well-worn and tired. I survey the topography, looking for the closely knit lines that will mean a hard climb. One walk, this one starting at the ranger's station, parallels the park border and the neighboring hunting reserve. It's just what I'm looking for. I quickly pack my trusty backpack, and head out the door. Caesar thumps a tired tail from his mat. Thanks to our early morning power walk, he's had his exercise for the day. I pat him on the way out.

The drive is eclipsed by loud music, obliterating any sound, distraction, or thought. I start with Coldplay, then promptly change it to the local radio station when it reminds me of my first day. Plus I don't need to hear about a girl escaping her sorry life, trying to find paradise.

I park at the ranger's station, grabbing my backpack and

jacket. Despite the bright midday sun, the breeze carries the coolness of autumn. There are a handful of tourists milling around. I head for the walking trail at the far right of the parking lot, gratefully noticing that no one appears to be joining me. A place called Break Back Ridge isn't for the fainthearted.

As is always the case, the scenery is breathtaking and, for a short while, it's all that consumes me. At this altitude, the pines dwindle out, leaving craggy rocks sprinkled with mat-like vegetation. I admire the plants' ability to adapt to these harsh alpine conditions. Strong tap roots anchoring them to the rocky soil, small evergreen leaves harnessing every glean of sunshine they can get. They aren't scared to face a little adversity. Actually, they thrive on it.

This area is different to my other walks. The terrain is wilder, the area more isolated. These walks are only for the fit and committed. Or those running from something.

The hiking trail begins a predictable pattern through the foothills: hike up, contour across, hike up, contour across. My muscles strain as I continue the steady climb, my breath coming in labored puffs. It's not long before I've removed my jacket, the cool air now welcome on my heated body.

Within the isolation of the reserve, I once again find some peace. Not enough to allow me to sort through my jumbled emotions. But enough for the fear, the inexplicable sadness, the creeping uncertainty, to take a back seat.

As I reach a plateau, I take a moment to catch my breath. I take a few steps away from the trail, climbing onto a rocky outcropping. In the shade of a giant boulder, I take out my canteen for a thirsty gulp. My throat is a testament to the fact I've been hiking for two hours straight. Its parched surface revels in the cool water.

From my protected lookout I'm afforded an expansive view of the park and its adjoining reserve, the man-made boundary indistinguishable, completely disregarded by nature. A mosaic of coniferous greens, rocky greys, and autumn yellows make up the magnificent vista. In the distance the mountain range juts proudly into the sky, the snow on its white-capped ridges patiently waiting for cooler temperatures so it can start its steady climb down.

From the shaded granite perch, something catches my eye. To my right, something is moving. I pause, curious. In slow, deliberate movements, I put down my drink bottle and creep forward ever so slightly. On a fellow rocky outcropping, about twenty yards away, a mountain lion has dropped into a crouch. I exhale in a rush, delighted surprise contracting my lungs. *A cougar!* The elusive, secretive cat of the park. The tawny giant takes a few stealthy steps forward, then gracefully drops his sleek body. I follow his line of sight.

Farther down is a group of elk, grazing in a small clearing, unknowingly providing a moving smorgasbord for the cougar. With the cougar downwind, the elk are oblivious to his predatory intent. My eyes move from stalking predator to unsuspecting prey and back again.

It pauses, erect ears twitching. I freeze, not even my eyelids fluttering. The cougar slowly turns its feline eyes to me, his yellow gaze reaching across the distance. I don't move a muscle as fascinated awe suddenly steps up to cautious fear. Amber eyes rimmed in black blink once. Twice. His broad head arches, his sensitive nose testing the air. The tip of his tail twitches from side to side. I stare back, my wide eyes getting sore with their need to blink.

His tawny head returns to its prey, unconcerned by my presence. Air flows back into my starving lungs; my eyelids blink rapidly over dry eyes. Every other muscle remains transfixed.

Once again focused on his lunch, the cougar takes three, four measured steps forward. This is nature at its most wild, most captivating. The whole world seems to freeze as it waits for this moment to unfold. The air is still—even Mother Nature seems to hold her breath.

The perfect ambush.

I'm so focused on the unfolding Attenborough moment, that it takes long seconds for a flash of light to register as odd. Sunlight just glanced off something shiny, somewhere on my left. I turn my head slowly, and my mouth slackens in shock. Lying commando-style behind low-lying sage brush are three men in triangular formation. Two are holding rifles. The stock against their cheeks, the butt against their shoulders. Their sights on the elk.

Oh no.

From my right I see the mountain lion take several more crouched steps forward, moving into the line of sight of the camouflaged hunters on my left. Their rifles drop as the men signal, a closed fist held up, then a short, sharp point. They've seen it. I look back at the cougar. It continues its trajectory, focused on the elk, unaware it's sharing its prey.

I turn back, and my eyes widen until they hurt. One of the hunters, the dark-haired man forming the apex of the triangle, has his rifle back up. And this time the barrel is pointing at the cougar. My heart screams an objection.

Nooo!

The cougar stands up, alarmed. Its eyes fly to mine.

Run!

Although the words never gain voice the cougar turns in one fluid leap and sprints toward me. My heart jackknifes into my throat, and I scramble, crablike, until my back painfully hits rough rock. The cougar covers the distance in long fluid strides, its sleek muscles contracting and extending in rapid rhythm. The cat's powerful haunches bunch, and with graceful precision, it leaps high onto the boulder towering behind me. In a split second it's gone; a handful of pebbles skipping down the boulder to rain on my head, the only testament of its flight.

A breeze caresses my cheeks.

I smile slightly. Mother Nature's sigh of relief.

I see the hunters point again, this time in repeated, sharp movements. Angry voices carry on the breeze. And I realize I'm far from safe. The men shoulder their rifles and start to head up the mountain. Toward the boulder. Toward me.

I grab my backpack and streak behind the rock. I lean against its cool surface, knowing it no longer provides sufficient protection. I need to get to the trees. Leaving the trail that would lead straight into their angry, armed company, I head over the low rise. My heart thumps wildly as I stumble and skid down the opposite side. I plot a course for a wide arc, heading for the protection of the forest. I'll parallel the walking trail and hightail it back to the car.

I turn, glancing up at the rocky outcropping. The hunters are nowhere to be seen.

But I don't slow my pace. I set up a jogging rate back in the direction I came. I don't use the trail, and shelter in stands of trees wherever possible. Open areas are unavoidable, and I pick up my momentum when exposed and vulnerable.

Once in the protection of dense trees, I pause again, chest heaving. Fed by my fear and the jogging run, adrenalin is pumping through my veins. I struggle to listen over my panting breaths. In the dim silence I don't hear tell-tale boots, heavy breaths, or low voices.

After what feels like hours, I slow down. The strenuous hike up and frantic run down has taken its toll. Sweat has pooled beneath my backpack, sticking my shirt to my skin. Tense muscles have formed intricate knots I'm not sure will ever undo. My trembling lungs beg for a break.

I haven't seen or heard the hunters. And according to my

calculations, it's only another twenty minutes or so to the parking lot. Less if I hurry. Feeling a little safer, I step back onto the trail. My shoes crunch along the narrow track as I stride away from the park, toward the security of my car.

I come to a stand of quaking aspens, who with the sweep of autumn, are starting to lose their golden glow. I know these trees open out around the bend, heralding the last few minutes before the parking lot. Their autumn leaves shiver in the breeze, a handful raining down on me like tears. In their dim coolness I pause once again. All I can hear is their gentle whispers.

I round the corner and stop dead in my tracks. The three men are lounging on a low lying rock. Waiting. The dark-haired hunter elbows another when they see me. He juts his chin toward me. All three of them smile. My shoulders drop. They knew I would return this way. Taking the scenic route merely gave them more time to head down. And wait.

The perfect ambush.

The fear that had receded is back, with the force of a tidal wave. It amplifies with each step the men take. They fan out, forming a trident as they come toward me. Their thick boots crush the pebbles beneath them as they stalk forward. The guy directly in front has dark hair contrasting against pale skin, dark brows framing dark eyes. His smooth face smiles, showing pale, even teeth. He'd probably be considered good-looking. His bloodless features remind me of a snake.

The three men all wear matching camouflage gear. Knives hang from their woven belts; two of their rifles lean against the abandoned rock. The guy on the right has a skinny angular face that lacks a chin. The third, the brawn of the group, is short and stocky. Built like a fridge.

I take a half-step back. But there's nowhere to go. We're too far from the parking lot for screams of help to be heard. And my exhausted muscles would never outrun these three.

"Hey, pretty lady. We were hoping you would come this way," says Snake, his smile getting bigger. His two comrades snigger. Chinless steps farther out to the side, while Fridge holds back a little, his rifle tapping his palm.

"What's your name?"

I keep my head down as my eyes dart left, right. The men's formation is wide enough to form a threatening semi-circle but close enough that there are no openings. A sense of claustrophobia closes in.

Snake shrugs. "It doesn't really matter."

He steps up, close. His dark eyes are calculating; his pale tongue flicks across his smiling bottom lip. My eyes settle on the top button of his army-colored shirt.

"Excuse me, I need to get back to my friends." *Yes, pretend there are others. Waiting for me.*

"Friends?" Snake seems to think this is humorous.

"Yes. If you can just let me pass, I won't bother you."

"Well, sweetness." He draws out the words, the final sound hissing along his pale lips. "I don't think I can do that. You see, my friends are pretty upset that you ruined our shot."

I consider denying it. I never said a word. But then anger shoots through my veins, settling in the fingertips clenched in my palms. "You were shooting in the park!" That proud animal did not deserve to be shot, unsuspecting, mid-hunt.

Snake's smile dips a little as his eyes narrow, like the muscles can't keep up the pretense.

Chinless steps up closer. "I like the way she smells." He wipes his hand across his mouth.

"I like the way she sounds." Fridge is bouncing on his toes, his rifle jiggling in his pudgy palms.

And I know I'm in danger. Desperate danger.

"I don't want any trouble."

Snake's hand comes up with measured slowness, then picks

a leaf from my shoulder, brushing my throat. I swallow; my nonexistent saliva does nothing for my dry mouth.

Snake's eyes follow the pointless process, fastened on my neck. "Too late."

Fear is peaking, pounding through my body. Spiking along nerve endings, tightening muscles, running in rivulets down my sides. I hope it'll provide the strength and stamina I'll need.

I'm going to make a run for it. Knowing it will be useless. Knowing they will catch me within seconds.

And horrible things are going to happen.

My weight eases back onto my left foot, ready.

The silence is ruptured by a powerful growling thundering through the clearing. The sound slams through me, reverberating among the trees. Snake's head shoots up from where he was leaning over me. He looks behind me, the white around his dark eyes growing, multiplying exponentially.

I turn to see a giant wolf breach the trees and enter the clearing. Even larger than the last, this one is white. Snowy, blindingly white. Except for pink gums that gleam dangerously over razor-sharp teeth.

The wolf leaps toward us, fierce muscles coiling and releasing. Teeth snapping, it roars out its rage, head shaking with fury. I stand frozen, any thought of flight obliterated by shock. It slows and menacingly dips its head, ears flattening across his massive head, white muzzle corrugated to expose intimidating canines. It stalks forward, terrifying in its size, power, and ferocity. The three men stagger backward.

Leaving me in the middle of the path. Alone.

The wolf continues to walk forward. Powerful muscles bunch as it glides toward me. I'm rooted to the spot as it stalks closer and closer. It's not physically possible for my eyes to go any wider. My heart to beat any faster.

The wolf is now beside me. He's practically eye to eye, and

I've never felt so small in my life. Intense blue eyes assess me from his white, furred face. His lips dip for a second, his head coming up a fraction. An almost familiar sense of connection reaches out to me.

The crunching of gravel captures the wolf's attention, and we both turn to see Snake steadily walking backward, his hands patting the air in a conciliatory gesture. Once close to the tree line, he turns and runs. He doesn't look back.

Fridge is the next to react. Sausage fingers grapple with his rifle, the muzzle rattling. He fumbles with the bolt. Before he can grasp it enough to hold, the wolf leaps forward, another terrifying roar filling the clearing. Fridge jumps, the rifle flying from his hands. He turns and flees.

Chinless is wobbling, from his concave face down to his army-issue boots, chanting incoherently under his breath. He spins on the spot, and promptly trips on his lanky legs. On all fours, his boots grapple for purchase as his torso strains to move forward. They finally grip and he stumbles after Fridge. Snake is long gone.

Silence descends amongst the trees.

It's just me and the wolf. I stand in the center of the narrow trail, chest heaving. The wolf turns and his massive head slowly lifts. His whole body unwinds as he straightens; his teeth disappear as his face relaxes. His wild blue eyes connect with mine. There's something about them that pulls at me. Without thinking, I take a step forward. This animal just saved my life.

The wolf's eyes widen, and he takes a step backward. *He's scared of me?* I consider humming, but sense it's not needed right now. I pause. How do I tell him 'thank you'? The wolf turns and walks toward the trees. He pauses, looking over his shoulder. His piercing blue eyes transfix me. Then he turns and leaps, disappearing into the dim shade.

Disappears just like his black counterpart.

Except this time I'm not willing to let him go. I leap into action and sprint forward after him, a renewed burst of energy pumping through my veins. I don't know what I'm going to do if I find him, but I can't just let him disappear again.

I break through the trees and come to a skidding halt. Not far within the forest edge I see him, glowing white in the dappled shade. Surprisingly, he hasn't gotten far. I frown when I see his back haunches sink to the ground. He was hurt? But the hunters never got near him. I stand, torn. I want to help, but even I'm not stupid enough to approach an injured wild animal. Particularly a mutant-sized one.

His front legs give out and he sinks to the ground. Without a second thought, I rush forward. And stop.

Because the great beast is changing. Altering. Shrinking. He writhes and arches; an anguished sound begins as a growl and ends as a groan. Muscles tremble as they tear and reform, bones morph and realign, fur converts to skin. A final shimmer of light, a flash of naked skin...

And a fully dressed Noah lies before me.

14

NOAH

The first thing I register is how much my exhausted body aches, from throbbing limbs that refuse to move, to burning eyelids that are too heavy to lift. Have I been hit by a car? It feels more like a semi-trailer. Scents trickle into my consciousness: conifers above me, the earth beneath me, and wildflowers beside me. The twigs digging into my back are the final piece of evidence telling me that I'm lying on the forest floor. What in the heck just happened?

My mind tries to process what, where, why... I remember going for a drive to get a burger, to try and silence my constantly rumbling stomach. When I was hit with that same gut-clenching fear from before. This time I didn't question it. With white-knuckled force I swerved the truck around and drove blindly, guided by instinct.

I'd ended up at the ranger's station. Without another thought, I leapt out of the car and into the forest. And ran, desperately hoping I could get to wherever I was going in time.

I remember stumbling, slowing as intense pain constricted my chest, my back arching, my torso twisting in agony. It felt like my heart was swelling, like everything within me was rearranging. I regained my balance, knowing I couldn't stop. I had to get to her.

Another stumble, as I felt like my bones were breaking. The torment of grinding and crunching screamed through my body, the sounds of cracking and snapping crashing across my eardrums. And, in what felt like slow mo, I pitched forward as dislocated joints gave out.

My hands shot out to break my fall.

By the time they hit the ground, limbs and joints had painfully reformed. And it was four paws that regained the frantic forward momentum.

New sensations were hitting me all at once: the feel of the wind coursing through fur; the sensation of fangs resting on gums; the strength of claws gripping the soil as I was propelled forward faster and faster.

Keener senses than I've ever imagined assailed me. I maneuver around obstacles as reflexes instantly react, leap, deflect. Scents assaulted me: resinous pine, mossy bark, a rotting log. I could hear the wind coursing past me, birds calling in alarm, prey scampering away.

But I didn't have time to understand or grasp the significance. All that consumed me was the ice-cold fear that was not my own. I powered through the forest, one word chanting through my mind.

Eden.

I remember seeing those three scumbags surrounding her, that slimy guy's hand touching her. Ice-cold fear was replaced with the fiery blaze of anger. The animal I am wanted to rip them apart. To sink teeth into fleshy stomachs, stomp on sunken faces. To claw off creepy grins. But I held back, because of Eden...she was so scared.

I remember them running away. Cowards.

And I remember Eden's wide-eyed shock. Her standing

deathly still in the middle of the trail. But the feeling of fear had gone. There was no trace in her tilted eyes. No frozen fingers gripping my altered insides.

And then she took a step forward.

But I didn't feel steady anymore. I remember knowing I had to get away. Things were shifting again. Changing. I ran into the forest. I don't think my unsteady paws got me very far.

Then I remember more pain. As once again bones rearranged, muscle and ligaments realigned, and hair receded. Although this change felt quicker, as my body returned to its familiar form.

"Noah?" I don't think any more shock, confusion, or astonishment could be injected into one word.

And I register. I shifted! For that period of time when those lowlife's were threatening Eden, I was a wolf. A wolf!

"Noah?" Eden's voice picks up a notch, sounding panicky. I hear her move, and the scent of wildflowers sprinkles down on me.

I groan as I cautiously open my eyes. Through the narrowed slits, I see a world that looks less sharp, less defined. Ah, the loss of wolf senses.

Eden lets out a breath, and it puffs across my cheeks. I turn my head slowly. She's crouching besides me, a cautious hand stretched out, but not touching.

"Are you okay?"

Despite feeling like Thor dropped his hammer on my face, a train has rammed through my body, and a hurricane has reorganized my brains, I grin. I *shifted!*

"Never better."

She looks at me like I've lost something vital. Like my mind.

"I shifted!" As if saying it out loud makes this more real. Just as real as the pain tingling along my nerve endings, as the petrified faces of those men, as the pale face next to me.

"But how...?"

I sit up, and Eden falls back with a soft thump. Like her legs have given out.

"I don't know. I was running here, the next thing I know —bam!"

"I mean, how is this possible?"

And through my euphoric haze I realize Eden is assimilating far more than me. Although I never thought this was possible, at least I knew Werewolves existed.

"I think I need to explain a few things."

Eden's eyebrows shoot up. Okay, understatement.

I take a deep breath, and say the words I've never said to anyone before, forbidden words. "My family are Werewolves."

"You're a Werewolf?"

"Well, I wasn't until about half an hour ago."

Eden pulls farther back, her brow furrowing. And I realize what the catalyst was.

"Until I met you." Eden instantly begins shaking her head. I start explaining, fast.

"My family are all Werewolves, my dad is Alpha. Mitch shifted at 16, like we're meant to. Like all Werewolves do." I swallow. "I didn't."

"Why not?"

"No one knows. It's never happened before." I move forward to rest my wrists on my knees. "I'm an anomaly."

Eden sits still, watching me. Most likely wondering how much to believe. I'd be skeptical too, unless I'd seen a massive white wolf change into me.

Her eyes widen. "Mitch is the black wolf. The one that rescued me."

I nod slowly, seeing how much she will figure out.

"And Tara, she's one too?"

I nod again, smiling. "Yep. Both our families. Everyone except me. But you were the reason I changed."

Eden is still again, wide-eyed.

"It was you in danger that triggered it."

Eden is back to shaking her head, now with more energy. "No, it's not possible."

This time I go silent.

"I don't believe you."

"You can believe Werewolves exist, but not this?" I wave my hand to encompass the two of us.

Eden's head dips, her hands twisting in her lap. "So, you've never changed before?"

I roll with the fact she's ignored my statement. "Nope."

"How do you feel?"

"Like I just got taken down by Godzilla. Totally amazing."

She nods, gaze back in her lap. "We'd better get you back." Her eyes settle on the rifles, two abandoned by the rock, one lying on the ground.

"I'll take those to my dad. He can dispose of them."

We both stand. But there's one thing I want Eden to understand before we leave. To believe.

"Wait."

She stands still; I step closer.

"It was you, Eden."

Her hands come up to cover her face. I close the last of the distance between us. Peel back the hands that try to create a barrier. My hands stay to frame her face.

Her eyes lift to mine. They are wide open, so vulnerable.

"It was you."

She takes a shaky breath. "Noah, you are the one person that can hurt me the most."

I stroke one thumb across her soft cheek. "I'm the one person you can trust to keep you safe."

She looks at me for long moments, eyes searching mine. I remain there, just as still, just as vulnerable.

"I don't know how to do this."

"Let's figure it out together."

Her head, resting in my palms, slowly nods her agreement. Her hands slowly, ever so slowly, creep up to rest on my chest. Her warm, soft palm cups the mark I spent the past two years believing was a farce.

A beautiful smile spreads across her beautiful face. I feel my lips tip up in response.

Actually, a grin splits my face with such ferocity that I doubt it will ever be the same again.

15

EDEN

I wake to a wet nose nuzzling my face. I smile, stretching out a hand to ruffle Caesar's fur.

"Need to go out, huh, boy?" Caesar's tail thumps the bed, and the nuzzling intensifies. "Okay, okay." I pull back the covers, swinging my feet onto the heated floor.

And it hits me.

Noah...is...a...Werewolf.

By the time I'd arrived home yesterday, it had been late afternoon. I'd climbed into bed, drained and done. Despite a mind full of images that defied belief, I must have fallen into an exhausted sleep.

Now, under the light of a new day, I try to process it all. I feel shell-shocked. Like someone has detonated an explosive, disintegrating the world as I know it. I'm left standing with thoughts fragmented, beliefs demolished, and emotions tangled.

I blink at the floor. The world I thought I knew no longer exists. Gone. Kaput. Creatures that I thought belonged in the realm of fiction are undeniably real. They are huge, fearsome, intimidating and...friendly and welcoming and warm. I bring my fingers to my temples, pressing in as my mind struggles to accommodate the evolution, the confusing contradictions, the implications...

Caesar barks, jolting me from my stunned musings. "Sorry, boy." We pad to the back door and he disappears into the trees. I cross my arms as I stand in the doorway, the early morning light making the mist glow.

For all intents and purposes, just another day.

But everything is different.

Noah is a Werewolf.

And I said I would give this thing between us a chance.

And I thought this was scary before. The one and only boy who I've felt attracted to. Who moves me in ways I didn't know possible. Who transformed only when I was in danger. Is the one who asked me to take the leap of faith...and I agreed.

I breathe in the morning air. It smells of conifers, the brisk morning fog, and something else. Possibilities? Promise?

Caesar comes bounding back, exhilarated by the cool air. I squat down to bury my face in his neck, wondering what this new world will hold for me.

I suppose there's only one way to find out.

I shower, put my hair up, and pack my bag. My stomach grumbles, grouching about its missed dinner. I throw some cereal in a bowl and gulp it down. I'm rinsing my bowl in the sink when my mother walks in, pulling on her suit jacket as she enters. The matching pinstriped slacks flare above her spiked heels. She must have a big meeting today.

She pauses mid-stretch, one hand slowing its travel down the sleeve. "Off to school already?"

I turn back to the sink, stacking the bowl in the dish drainer. "Yes."

"Since when did you get to school early?"

I shrug, drying my hands on the towel hanging next to the oven.

"Anything in particular happening?"

"Not really."

"I can't remember you ever getting to school early."

I return the towel to its hook, carefully arranging the folds.

"Unless there was something happening." I turn to find her grey eyes watching me.

I shrug again, and start heading to my room. "I have a presentation I need to work on."

When she doesn't answer, I look over my shoulder. She's adjusting her jacket, tugging on the lapels so it sits just right. Her eyes narrow a little. "Okay."

Once back in my bedroom, I sigh. Caesar looks at me, his brown eyes questioning. I sit beside him on the bed, resting my hand on his head. "Why is she so interested all of a sudden?" I whisper. He whines, burying his head into my shoulder.

I shrug; I've never understood my mother. I grab my bag and head out to the car. To school. To Noah.

As I pull into the school parking lot, the hastily eaten cereal does a flip flop in my stomach. Will I see Noah before first period? Or will I have to wait until lunch? The bright excitement dims a little now that I'm here, uncertainty casting its gloom. What do you say to a guy you just found out is a Werewolf? Anxiety starts to gnaw at the edges of my stomach.

It takes a great big bite when I see the Phelan truck pull in two spaces down from me. Noah is driving, with Mitch beside him. I hover by my car as I watch them climb out. Mitch yawns and scratches his head, saying something to Noah. Noah grins, and jumps out, a spring in his step. Figuring I can't stand here like an awkward giraffe, I start to walk over.

Noah seems to know exactly where I am, because he turns and starts striding toward me. When his gaze settle on mine they light up. I feel a corresponding fireworks display ignite. It stops me dead in my tracks. Noah keeps coming.

In a few short steps, he's in front of me, eyes alive with some-thing I can't decipher. Searching mine, questioning. The nervousness melts away.

I smile. "Good morning."

And he grins back. "Yes, it is."

I consider staying here indefinitely. Smiling. Staring. Not a fear in the world. Noah seems content to spend forever with me, here in the school parking lot.

"Ahem." It's with great effort that I haul my gaze away from those summer-sky pools.

Mitch has come up to stand beside Noah. "Morning, Mitch."

He yawns again. "Hi, Eden."

"You look tired."

"Yeah, a bit more sleep would have been nice." He slaps Noah on the back. "Someone came home last night with news." His blue eyes return to me.

"Yeah." I shift my weight to the side, Mitch's cool welcome at his house flashing through my mind. Who knows what he thinks of me now.

"The talks went way into the night."

"Oh."

"And then someone got me up at the crack of dawn. Like there was some big rush to get to school. I only got one bowl of cereal for breakfast."

A splash of pleasure flows over me, and my eyes return to Noah. He's smiling, but a tinge of pink has colored his cheeks. "It wasn't that early, drama queen." He shoves Mitch. "And you forgot the four pieces of toast."

Mitch turns, a big happy smile on his face. I shift a little awkwardly. The next thing I know I'm engulfed in a hug, my chin over his shoulder. I pat his back a little awkwardly. I'm not really sure what to do with a hug.

As quickly as it started, he pulls back, still smiling. "It was good news. Really good news."

I try to smile, but an uncomfortable lump has lodged in my chest, throat, and stomach.

Tara skips up behind Mitch and reaching up on tippy-toes, puts her hands over his eyes. "Guess who?"

"Hmmm." His hands reach back to glide up and down her arms. "Obviously someone gorgeous."

"Smart boy."

His hands flutter across her fingers. "And a talented artist."

Tara giggles. "Correct."

Mitch's hands dart behind him. "And ticklish!" Tara hunches over with a squeal. Mitch spins and continues his merciless torture. Tara dissolves in peals of laughter. I step up beside Noah, and we both smile at their antics.

"He seems to have woken up now," Noah comments.

With a playful shove, Tara pushes Mitch away. She turns to me. "Hi, Eden."

"Hey." I feel a little awkward, not knowing if Tara knows that I know.

Tara claps her hands. "This is going to be awesome. It will be nice to have a friend on the inside." She tilts her head toward Noah and Mitch. "That isn't a Phelan or a Channon."

"A mere human."

"There's nothing mere about you."

"Agreed." This comes from Noah, and I blush.

"Come on, Tara, let's head up." Mitch takes Tara's hand and they start walking toward the school.

Noah holds out his hand. "Ready?"

I glance down at the palm waiting for me. *Am I?* I try to take a deep breath, without expanding my ribcage so it's not too obvious. It doesn't work. All it does is hit my tight chest and shoot back out in a rush. But I know I want to take that hand. The one that is patiently waiting.

I move my hand forward, and glide my fingers over his palm before wrapping them around. As our palms connect, fitting together like two halves of a whole, that delectable warmth starts spreading. It sprints up my arm, into my chest, squeezing my heart. Noah catches his breath, and my gaze shoots up. He's looking at me, a little wide-eyed.

As we walk toward the front doors of the school, I wonder if this feeling will ever get old. I hope not. I hope Noah stays around long enough for me to find out.

Mitch and Tara walk on ahead, hands also clasped, heads close together as they talk. No one pays them any attention. Noah and I are not afforded the same anonymity. We're surrounded by surreptitious glances, followed by the odd raised eyebrow when they register the clasped hand surrounding mine. Noah appears oblivious, smiling broadly, saying "hi" to those he walks past. I don't know if I should hunch my shoulders or puff my chest out in pride. I opt for pretending I don't notice.

"So, psych first?"

"Yep, you?"

"Gothic lit."

At the other end of the school. "Okay." I figure he'll drop me off at our lockers, but he waits for me to get my stuff, before grabbing my hand again and heading to my classroom.

Noah cocks his head. "Why so quiet?"

I consider giving him some lame lie, but I've already figured out nothing much gets past Noah. And although it makes me feel vulnerable, I would prefer to be honest.

"Everyone is staring. Because of this." I glance down at our held hands and Noah's fingers tighten. It's unnecessary, because although the staring makes me uncomfortable, I don't intend on letting go.

"That's because of me."

"You?" I say incredulously. Can't he see people are wondering what in the world he's doing with someone like me?

"Yeah. They haven't seen me with a girlfriend before."

Pleasure at the word 'girlfriend' washes over me. I have to make a conscious effort to analyze why his statement confuses me. "They haven't?"

Noah rubs the back of his head with his free hand. "Yeah. We don't usually date, you know..." His voice drops to a whisper. "...you guys."

Humans? "But you weren't...until a little while ago." Like, yesterday.

He shrugs. "Wasn't interested back then."

I frown. "But now you're a..."

"This is different." He scowls, and his hand tightens mine in a squeeze. Sparks of warmth shoot up my arm, and I instinctively grip back.

Noah's grin is back. "Maybe they all thought I was gay."

I snort. Unlikely. Or if they did, the girls would have all worn black in mourning.

We arrive at my classroom, and we both stop. We stand there, as if neither of us wants to let go.

"Hi, Eden." Brandon comes up behind me. His eyes inevitably slide down, as everyone else's have, to register my hand in Noah's. His smile dips a little. "Hey, Noah." Noah nods, giving Brandon a small smile.

I pretend everything is normal. "Hi Brandon. See you in there."

Noah watches Brandon go in. "He's in your group?"

"Yeah. Why?"

"Just curious. I'll see you at lunch?"

"Sure."

I release Noah's hand, my fingers tingling as they fall

through the air to rest at my side. I lean against the doorjamb, my body a little limp. I admire those broad shoulders and long lean legs as he walks away. After a few steps, Noah turns to give me a wave. I smile, shaking my head as I enter the classroom.

For all intents and purposes, just another day.

But everything is different.

I sit at my desk with my allocated group, and Mrs. Dougal begins outlining how humans respond to emotional stimulus. I reflect back to yesterday, when a giant, white wolf changed before my eyes. My mind a whirl of denial, disbelief, shock. Before coming back to denial. I suspect I stood there, eyes wide, mouth slack, hands gripped with uncertainty. I remember the desire to run coming up against concern for an unconscious Noah. It all fits neatly onto the flow chart she's projected on the screen.

The minute Mrs. Dougal instructs us to work on the assigned task, Brandon leans forward on his elbows. "So, I didn't know you and Noah were an item." Across from me I can almost see Bianca's ears twitching, her head down as she pretends to write notes.

I fiddle with my pen, blushing. "It's a fairly recent thing."

Bianca ditches feigning disinterest, and turns toward us. "Kind of quick, isn't it?"

I blink. "Yes, I guess it is." In my surprise, the truth is all that I have to respond with.

Brandon frowns at Bianca. He turns back to me, and his dimples appear again. "Phelan is a smart guy."

I blush again, with a little more blaze, and muster up a small smile. It's sweet that he would say something like that just to get Bianca off my back. "Thanks."

Bianca flicks her hair over her shoulder, returning to her notes. She doesn't say anything for the remainder of the lesson.

At the end of the lesson, I meet Tara in the hallway, picking up the rhythm we've established over the weeks as we head to math. I notice Phoebe as we're about to head in and wave. She smiles back as she jogs to whatever class she doesn't want to be late for.

In math we take our back table and wait for Mr. Rosenberg to hand out today's sheets. I only had to be in his class three times to discover the routine. It's as predictable and unchanging as times tables. Hand out worksheets, circle the room as students work, whole class discussion in the last seven minutes —not five, not ten, but seven. And as long as you look like you know what you're doing, he leaves you alone.

More algebra greets me from the white piece of paper. The letters and numbers looking like they cohabit happily, despite their differences. Like every other math lesson, we spend a significant part of the lesson scrawling through our books, rubbing out mistakes. We ask each other questions, point out where we went wrong, and start all over again. It's at the end of the lesson that the ordinary bubble bursts.

Tara leans over, whispering. "Sorry I couldn't make the study sesh." She puts so much innuendo into the word 'study sesh', I wonder why she didn't use her fingers as bunny ears to emphasize it.

Don't blush. Don't blush. "That's cool. We finished the presentation."

"Great. And?"

"We present it next week."

Tara sighs. "And?"

I duck my head. "I stayed for dinner."

"I heard." So Mitch has already filled her in.

"It was really sweet of Beth to cook me eggplant."

Tara frowns, erasing the last line she wrote. "Although I've read that charcoal is carcinogenic."

I smile. "Yes, it was...well done."

Tara looks up from the paper before her, her hazel eyes studying mine. "Do you like him?"

I stare at Tara. *Can I say it out loud?*

But I don't have to say a word; Tara reads between the lines of my mute response. "I knew it! You could power Texas with the electricity that crackles between you two."

Mr. Rosenberg claps his hands, saving me from responding. He pushes his glasses up when the jolt makes them slip down. "Okay, class, let's review the sheet." I glance at the clock. Yep, seven minutes.

Afterwards we head for the art room. I take my usual seat by the window as Tara heads over to her easel. The painting looked perfect to me two weeks ago, but she always finds some small touch-up that needs tweaking.

She picks up her paintbrush. "So, how many questions do you have?"

"I lost count at a gazillion."

"What do you want to know?"

My hands go out wide. "Everything, I don't even know where to start." And I realize I don't know anything about Werewolves. I might have to spend some time on Google...

"I wouldn't bother with Google. You'll just end up deciding whether you're on Team Edward or Team Jacob."

Scratch that then.

"There are two packs in this area, covering most of the state. Adam is the Phelan Alpha, my dad is the Channon Alpha. Both are old, and fairly big." I wonder if that corresponds to nature—the bigger the pack, the more powerful.

"And there are a heap of myths. The whole dramatic clothes tearing Hollywood images? Doesn't happen. It's not really helpful to be left naked in the middle of a forest."

I blush as I recollect the flash of skin that's branded in my mind.

"Clothes have always been part of shifting, as long as they're touching our body, they come along for the ride. And the full moon thing? Certainly part of our traditions, but not necessary for shifting."

"Anything else?"

Tara taps the end of her paintbrush against her lips. "The silver bullet—hogwash. Any old bullet would do."

Right. Before I can change my mind, I ask the most pressing question, the one that is clamoring the loudest. "Why didn't Noah change?"

Tara pauses in her dabbing, and her hand drops to rest on the easel. "No one knows. He spent his whole life preparing to be Alpha. And then...nothing."

"Nothing?"

"We shift for the first time at sixteen. They all went to the Glade. Mitch turned. Noah didn't."

I try to imagine what that must have been like. Mitch going through the pain of the first change. I remember Noah's confusion, his pale face, his slow, achy movements. It didn't look pleasant, or easy. But then Noah, standing there. Waiting as the minutes dragged out. Waiting.

"He must have been devastated."

Tara's shoulders drop a little; her eyes unfocus out the window. "So was Mitch. And Adam and Beth." I picture the beautiful family I met, confused, grieving. It's a sad image.

I shake off the melancholy. "So, you guys grew up together?"

"Yeah, we've been hanging out since diapers." I feel a pang of envy that she has been in one place long enough to grow those roots. "I spent more time with Mitch though. Some days Noah had alpha training with his dad."

"And you and Mitch...?" I'm not sure what it would be called —dating?

Tara goes all dreamy on me. "Yeah, we were friends through childhood, and it grew from there."

"You two have something really special."

Tara shrugs. "I love him." Envy twinges again—Tara's ability to be so honest and open about her feelings. Her faith that the universe will work out the way she plans. That I would like.

"We're bonding at the end of the year."

"Bonding?"

"Weres mate relatively early, and for life."

"Like wolves." I say the words quietly, under my breath.

But Tara hears me anyway. "That's it."

I stare down at my muesli bar. So much to digest, and I'm not talking about the oats.

"Sorry I couldn't make it, to the study sesh."

"That's okay."

"My dad phoned. And when an Alpha asks, you obey." Her shoulders droop a little. "Especially when that Alpha is my dad."

I nod, wondering what it is she's trying to tell me.

She shakes her head, and the Tara smile is back. "Anyway, I owe you some popcorn."

"Don't worry about it."

"What about Wednesday?"

My eyebrows shoot up. "Sure."

She gives me a mischievous grin. "At yours?"

"Mine?" My eyebrows are sitting somewhere in the stratosphere.

"Yeah. Oh, is that a problem? I keep meaning to install a filter between my brain and my mouth."

"No, no. It sounds like a great idea. I'll have the microwave ready."

Tara beams. "Excellent." Something in the painting grabs her eye, and she dabs her paintbrush, eyes squinting. "We'll tell the guys at lunch."

Oh. Mitch too. And Noah.

Anticipation thrums through my veins. More time with Noah.

I look up at Tara. "Yes, I like him." *More than is safe.*

Tara grins. "I know."

The ringing of the bell pierces through the room.

"Fudge berries! And I'm late again." She picks up her painting supplies and rushes over to the sink.

As I always do, I offer Tara a hand, but she shoos me off to next period.

Biology.

I walk quickly down the hallway. It could probably be considered more of a skip, really. Another glaring difference from previous weeks. I haven't allowed myself to feel the tingling excitement of seeing Noah, to revel in the close proximity, to look into those beautiful blue eyes for more than a safe second. To allow myself to feel.

I'm there before him, and take my usual seat. I pull out my books, and place them on the bench. Now what? I open my textbook; the familiar pages I've studied in minute detail over the past weeks look up at me. I start to get nervous. I fiddle with my pen and turn pages when I already know what the next one will say.

I sense something, and look up. He's walking toward me, a wide grin splitting his face. My breath congeals in my lungs. It's as if Father Time has realized I can now look uninterrupted, and the seconds slow down. I take in the tousled hair—darker strands highlighted with blonde. The sparkling blue eyes framed by sculpted features. The soft grey shirt hanging on broad shoulders, the worn material contouring over ridged muscles. The lean width spearing down to narrow hips encased in denim. I feel my face heat; I think a vegetarian just made a meal of a hot red-blooded guy.

"Hey." Noah's eyes are scanning, roaming my face. My cheeks heat up a few more degrees.

"Hey." I realize my voice has taken on a breathless-Tara quality.

Feeling a little stunned, my eyes slide down to my book.

"It's pretty overwhelming, isn't it?" I look back up, my eyes connecting with his. "This feeling."

And I don't look away. "Yeah. It is."

So he feels it too. Although these feelings don't have him running scared.

He pulls in his stool, closer than we've been before, and I breathe in his sandalwood scent. Feel his warmth reach out to me with compelling fingers. Noah is a delight for all the senses.

Mr. Dougherty stands up at the front and silence descends on the class. I feel Noah's hand move closer beside me; I reach out and we clasp beneath the bench. The warmth that is almost familiar now, sparks and spreads. From the corner of my eye, I see Noah's lips tip up. My whole body smiles in response.

"Today is the last day you will be able to work on your oral presentation. I have posted a schedule on the notice board. Make sure you use this time productively." Books shuffle and stools scrape as students walk over to the notice board, and a low hum begins around the class.

"I'll go check it out." Noah releases my hand and heads to the front of the class. I clasp my hand, my palm tingling.

I watch as Noah scans the sheet, his finger running down, the muscles of his back bunching. Two students join him, a dark-skinned, dark-haired boy and the red-haired girl that sits beside him. They chat, and I see the boy glance over at me. I duck my head back to my books, but continue to watch from lowered lashes. I see Noah nod, and the boy holds his fist up, teeth flashing. Noah shakes his head, but when the boy's fist remains high, he returns the fist pump. The girl slaps the boy on the arm. Noah laughs, and turns to come back. I pretend to be writing something in my book.

"We're third on the list."

Urgh. "Yay."

"It'll be fine, I'll do the talking. You just stand there and look beautiful."

My response dies on my lips. He called me beautiful? Noah busies himself getting out his laptop and powering it up, unaware he's said anything of significance. *He thinks I'm beautiful?* Stunned pleasure creeps up my cheeks.

"So, I think this is pretty much done...?" He turns to me, eyebrows up in question.

"You think I'm..." I blush the brightest so far, and quickly return to my books. I've managed to simultaneously show too much, and look like I'm fishing for compliments.

A finger hooks under my chin, pulling me back. "How can you not know?" There's a tinge of something in Noah's voice. Wonder?

He scans my face, and heat seems to follow his gaze. Across my eyes, cheeks, nose, lips, chin. Before returning to my eyes. "All I can say is," he pauses for a moment, holding me in breathless limbo, "wow."

Oh. Heat stains my stunned face, for once a pleasant, warm feeling.

"Okay?" He looks at me closely, like this is important.

"Okay," I say quietly. This guy sure knows how to get his point across.

I struggle to find my equilibrium. "We should probably go over it, just to make sure."

Noah looks at me for a second longer, before turning back to the desk. He tilts the laptop to face the two of us. "I do have a couple of questions."

"Oh?"

"What's your favorite dessert?" Huh? I look at him quizzically. He shrugs. "It's time to get to know Eden St. James."

I shift a little in my seat. "Cheesecake. It should be a sixth food group."

"Favorite fruit?"

"Tomato."

"Drink?"

I roll my eyes; there's a definite trend here. "Lunch is next, huh?"

Noah rubs his stomach sheepishly. He looks thoughtful for a second. "Okay then, what superpower would you most like to have?"

I tap my pencil on my lip, considering. "To be able to speak to unicorns. You?"

Noah grins. "To fly like a penguin."

He rubs his finger along his bottom lip. "Are you addicted to anything?"

"Cheesecake. You?"

"No."

I narrow my eyes at him. "Have you ever lied?"

Innocent blue eyes blink at me. "Never." I snort. His family guards one of the biggest secrets of all.

He turns a little more toward me. "Do you believe in vampires?"

"No," I respond automatically. Noah's eyebrows rise a little. Oh, until yesterday I didn't think any supernatural beings existed. Today that world no longer remains. "Do they....?"

Noah wiggles his brows, and they brush his blond locks.

"Very well, students. I shall see you next period." And with impeccable timing, the bell goes.

We pack up and follow the stream of students. I follow Noah, and his hand reaches behind. I slip my hand into his. I could get used to this.

As we walk toward the cafeteria, Bianca comes toward us. Her eyes flicker down and back up. I think I see her jaw tighten, but I can't be sure.

Bianca stretches a smile across her face. "Hi, Noah. Eden."

"Hey, Bianca." Noah's hand tightens around mine.

"Hi." I step a little closer to Noah. He turns a blinding smile down to me, and as I tend to do, I lose myself in his gorgeous features. When I look back up, Bianca is gone. I can just imagine the hair flounce this would have brought on.

We head to the cafeteria, where Tara and Mitch are already seated. I pull out my jelly sandwich. When I look up, Noah is watching me.

"No peanut butter today?"

Does he notice everything? "All out." I shrug. "But I brought cookies."

I pass around a brown paper bag full of chocolate chip cookies. I know, from previous experience, they are phenomenal. Tara pulls up her shoulders, closing her eyes as she savors hers. I don't think Mitch chews his. I pretend not to notice the crumbs sprinkling across Noah's lower lip.

"Tell your Mom these are sensational."

I don't bother to correct Mitch. Most mothers would bake cookies for their kids.

Tara taps the table to get everyone's attention. "So peeps, Eden and I have spoken, and it's study sesh take two at hers on Wednesday."

"I'm up for that." Mitch leans back in his chair.

I look to see what Noah thinks of the idea. He's grinning widely. "Sounds like a great idea."

So lunch passes, as it always has. I listen to the three of them joke and talk, ribbing each other about childhood moments, discussing upcoming events and assignments. I laugh, and occasionally contribute. But everything is different. Now I know I'm sitting at a table with three Werewolves. The life they lead is far from normal. And, beside me, my hand is tightly clasped by one of them. One that I fought so hard to avoid. One that I'm now recklessly opening to.

At the end of lunch, Noah once again walks me to my class, hands joined. I'm quite liking this new world. Time moves slowly in English, and I spend most of it looking at the clock rather than at the novel in front of me. I realize there's a fine line between nervousness and anticipation.

At the end of last period, I find Noah standing at the door, waiting. Definitely liking this new world. We walk out to the parking lot and stop in front of my mother's car. I don't want this day to end.

Noah turns to stand in front of me, our held hands between us.

"See you tomorrow." I have that breathless tone again.

His hand comes up to gently, slowly brush across my cheek. His gaze follows its path. Heat blazes from that soft graze, igniting behind my ear, down my spine.

He steps away, taking two backward steps. "Looking forward to it." He turns and heads to his truck.

To all intents and purposes, an ordinary day.

But so, so much better.

16

NOAH

I indicate left off the highway, fingers drumming on the steering wheel in time to the Black Eyed Peas as they tell me tonight's going to be a good night. Mitch leans his elbow on the door, head tilted in boredom, roaming on his cell phone. He's not loving the Phelan rule— He Who Drives Picks the Tunes. Although admittedly, the decree doesn't work for either of us when Dad's driving.

The phone beeps in his palm and Mitch scans the lit screen. "Tara's going to be ten minutes late."

"Wonder what her dad needed now."

Mitch's mouth turns down a smidgen. "It must suck to be the eldest."

"Tell me about it."

Mitch snorts and a napkin hits me on the cheek, before fluttering down to my thigh. I flick it back at him.

But Mitch is already looking out his window, staring at the real estate that is progressively getting newer and bigger.

He turns to me. "Does this mean you're gonna be Alpha?

It had occurred to me. Sixteen years of preparation. "It's possible," I say slowly, cautiously. "We need to talk to Dad."

We exchange a glance, the memory of a few nights ago when I told Dad, passing between us. His disbelief. Then he registered the slow, pained movements that made me look like I'm eighty. He comprehended Mitch's huge grin. He recognized the metallic scent only a Were can sense, that only happens after a shift. I remember his ear-splitting whoop that had Stash leap up in guard mode. His spine-snapping hug.

And imprinted in my memory is the sight of my mother, holding Mitch with one hand, the other covering her smiling lips as tears ran down to meet it.

"Thank goodness." Mitch's voice rushes out.

"You never wanted it."

"Not even a little. Not the role, or everything that goes with it."

I cock an eyebrow at him. "Well, you never did complete those application forms."

"I was waiting for a miracle."

Well, I found one.

A large, timber sign indicates the turn off to Clear Creek Inn. A road takes us up through the pines, meandering beside a river. We turn a bend and find ourselves driving up to a sprawling building, an elegant 'Clear Creek Inn Reception' sign on the front.

Mitch lets out a low whistle. "This place is something."

I silently agree. If you have a shiny gold credit card, this is the place to be.

A huge, timbered entryway is supported by four massive posts, each one rising from a small, evergreen garden bed. Antlered chandeliers highlight the raked ceilings. All around are matching gardens, lush lawns, and well-dressed people. Behind it is another building with 'Luxury Spa' written in curved writing, while its identical twin on the other side says 'Big Game Hunting' in bold stamp.

I point it out to Mitch. "His and hers."

He looks at the 'His' section. "Mr. Channon would be in heaven."

"Eden said to head around the back."

We follow the gravel road as it snakes through more landscaped lawns, the gurgling river never far away. Rows of log cabins look out over its crystal cascade. The last of the cabins ends as we pass a 'No Admittance' sign. Another cabin comes into view, a little larger than the others, but with the same pimped-up gardens. A white Saab is parked out the front.

I feel my chest expand with anticipation. I've watched Mitch go through these feelings over the past two years. And now I see why they are so compelling. Why people go to great lengths to experience them. To never let them go.

The last few days with Eden have been amazing. Who knew that the simple act of putting her hand in mine would have my whole body igniting? That those smiles that are becoming more and more common are directly connected to my happy bone. That her fragile trust would have my heart doing victory laps. I can't get enough of it.

"You're thinking of Eden again, aren't you?"

I flush a little, keeping my eyes on the road. Stupid twin bond.

"And it's not the twin bond. You just get this look on your face..." Mitch goes wide-eyed and slack-jawed.

I shove his shoulder. "Zip it. You and Tara weren't much better."

We park the car behind the Saab and grab our bags. A gardener, his old, faded body looking odd in pristine coveralls, comes up the path, pushing a wheelbarrow full of pots. He pauses when he sees us at the front door.

I knock, the hammering of my heart doing its own battering within my chest. The door opens, and she stands there. My thirsty gaze takes in the mahogany hair, tilted green eyes, those smiling lips. How can this girl not know she's drop-dead gorgeous? Runway model beautiful.

She glances to her right. "Hi, Mitch."

Then turns to me. "Hi, Noah." Her tone holds something else, a hitch that pulls at something deep and primitive within me. I think I forget to respond.

Mitch clears his throat, shifting slightly to his left. "Tara said she'd be ten minutes late."

Eden turns her head; her eyes take a split second to follow. "That's fine."

Another throat-clearing rumbles over to us. Eden steps farther out and sees the gardener standing near the front fence, his wheelbarrow resting besides him. She smiles and waves.

"Hi, Stan."

He nods, his gaze scanning the two of us top to toe, and back. If he were a cop, he'd be patting us down.

"Tell Jenny the cookies were great. These guys demolished them."

The cookies came from the gardener?

Stan nods again. "Will do, Eden."

His stooped shoulders lift the wheelbarrow and move on.

Eden glances at us apologetically. "He doesn't say much."

I don't think she realizes how much he did say.

Another wave of grumbling comes from the path, and I turn, thinking Stan has changed his mind. A mammoth German shepherd comes pounding up the path. He stops in front of us, his tail high, body tense. I wouldn't say he's threatening, but he isn't happy to see us standing between him and Eden. He sniffs the air, registering that we're not normal visitors. His head drops, erect ears pointing straight at us. He's unsure of how to proceed, aware of our dominant status, but wanting to get to Eden. I step aside, giving him space to dart through.

The dog instantly sits by Eden's side, his shoulder resting against her thigh. Tension is apparent in his taut frame. Eden's hand comes down to rest on his head. He looks up, and she smiles down at him. And the dog relaxes, without Eden having said a word.

"Sorry, I think it's because you guys are..." She looks down the path to see if Stan is still around.

Mitch shrugs. "We get it all the time."

Well, I haven't. I've never been a threat to dogs before. I crouch down, holding my hand out.

"His name is Caesar."

"Hey, Caesar." He glances at Eden, and appears to gain her permission because he steps forward. He sniffs my hand and I slowly reach out to pat him. Caesar watches me as I rub his head, then slide my hand down behind his ear. His tail drops to level with his shoulders. Not a wag, but for this proud, protective dog, it's a start.

Eden has a soft smile on her lips. Her evergreen eyes meet mine, and the smile grows. I wish I could capture it. For the first time, I get an inkling of my mother's photo-taking obsession.

"Come on in, guys."

Eden and Caesar lead us into a large open-plan living area, featuring the same raked ceilings from the main entrance. The place is decked out. Complete with leather lounges, large fireplace, and paintings of the mountain range which are artfully highlighted by angled lights. It's homey in an expensive kind of way. Actually, the place screams 'we don't want to flaunt our money, but secretly want you to know we're loaded'.

Eden looks to me; I think she's trying to judge my reaction. I keep my face deliberately neutral. I'm not sure if I should be intimidated or not.

Mitch lets out another of his low whistles.

Eden looks around, like she's taking it in for the first time. "I love the color scheme. Actually looks like a home."

Mitch snorts. "What did you live in before, a glass penthouse?"

Eden grins. "Not the last place." She walks over toward one of the leather lounges, and Caesar leaps onto it, effectively vetoing my sitting next to her. "I figured we could study in the lounge. There's plenty of room."

In front of her is a giant flat-screen TV. The thing looks like an adolescent movie screen. Give it a couple of years and it will be all grown up.

Mitch walks over to stand in front of it. "What size is this sucker?"

Eden rolls her eyes. "I have no idea." She sits down on the sofa next to Caesar. "Did you want a ruler?"

Mitch snorts. "I should have brought my tape measure."

I take the single sofa seat, pretending I'm not disappointed. I'd imagined something a little different. I duck my head, getting my books out of my bag. Get yourself together, Phelan.

Another knock sounds at the door, and Eden gets up to let Tara in. Once in the lounge room, Tara does a small circle. I'm surprised she hasn't whistled like my brother.

"Holy shibblets, Eden, this place is something!"

Eden rolls her eyes. "We don't own it, you know."

Tara walks over to the drive-in-sized TV. She twirls to face us. "Do you know what I'm seeing?"

"Uh-oh."

Tara continues as if I haven't spoken. "Movie night!"

Mitch groans, saying two words that would scare even the most besotted guy. "Chick flick."

But apparently I'm more besotted than most. Because the idea of sitting here with Eden, lights dimmed, curled on that sofa, has me wiping damp palms on my jeans.

Eden looks contemplative, her hand rubbing that spot behind her ear. "That sounds nice." Her thoughtful eyes reach over to mine, and I wonder if she's thinking the same thing. I hope so.

Tara and Mitch settle themselves on an adjacent two-seater. I glance at the taken seat besides Eden, wishing I could do the same. Eden is biting her lip beside Caesar.

Tara passes her the popcorn packet. "I believe you ordered butter-flavored?"

"Thanks." She heads across the lounge to the kitchen. "I'll get everyone a drink."

I practically jump out of my seat. "I'll help you."

Tara giggles from besides Mitch and I throw her a mock glare. She covers her mouth with her hand, but another burst escapes from between her fingers.

I follow Eden across the timbered floor, knowing Mitch and Tara are watching us.

"Er, I'll just put the popcorn in."

She puts the bag in the stainless steel contraption that's hidden behind a cupboard door. Without the hustle and bustle of school, it feels a little too quiet, more intimate. I step out of the way when she moves over to the fridge, getting four cans of soda. I step forward again, feeling a little empty-handed. She turns from the fridge and we bump and brush, bumbling and blushing. I clear my throat. From the corner of my eye, I notice the glasses hanging above the bench, so I grab four. I turn to find Eden, the popcorn now in a bowl, trapped between me and the counter. We're not quite touching, but her warmth and scent pulls me in. Her eyes, wide with surprise, call to me.

"Do you think we were like that in the beginning?" Tara whispers to Mitch, knowing full well my sensitive new ears can hear.

I scowl at her; I can just feel Mitch trying to contain his

laughter. Eden notices the exchange and blushes. Good thing she couldn't hear the peanut gallery. She slips past, grabbing the popcorn and two of the drinks.

I follow Eden back to the seating area, juggling the remaining drinks and glasses. Eden comes to the couch and looks down at Caesar. He drops his head onto his paws, canine eyes sliding to the floor. She quirks her brows, and after a moment, he jumps off the sofa. I realize Eden just cleared a space for me. She sits on one side, Caesar curled at her feet, and looks up at me, once again biting her lip. How can she doubt that I want to be near her?

I plonk myself beside her, with a smile that would make the Cheshire cat very, very jealous. I watch in fascination as her bottom lip slips from the hold of her teeth, and along with its upper half, tips up in a smile. Once again, her warmth and scent envelop me. I've lost count of the things that I love about being around this girl.

"Right, that Design Tech assignment." Mitch pulls his laptop out of his bag, looking like he's about to eat our mother's cooking. He's been avoiding this one for days.

We all take his cue and retrieve our own. I open mine up, looking for the document I've started for English.

Tara opens hers. "Could someone proof my lit review for history?"

"Sure." Eden reaches over, and Tara passes her laptop. When she returns, she sits back, crossing her legs. Her knee comes to rest on my thigh. Her fingers stall on the keyboard and I see her look at me from the corner of my eye. I feel my lips twitch, wondering what she'll do, silently daring her to keep it there. I practically feel her chest rise and fall, and the knee relaxes, its heat flowing into my leg. A little burst of joy jolts through my chest. I resist the urge to reach over and give it a squeeze.

I don't know why, but I sense each of these touches are a

milestone for Eden. A micro-step forward. An expression of trust. Maybe I'm just looking to justify the feeling of elation and significance I experience every single time we touch. Every. Single. Time.

Admittedly, it does make it a little difficult to concentrate. That pinpoint of heat rapidly spreads up my leg, reaching my chest in no time. It ramps up my breathing. Accelerates my heart rate. Amps up my senses.

But I have my twin, a childhood friend, and Edgar Allan Poe to keep me grounded. It's not long before Tara is wishing she had the ability to know exactly when to use a semicolon and Mitch curses loudly when his computer freezes. Even Eden joins in the lively debate about whether eyebrows are considered facial hair.

So we plow through upcoming assignments. It's only when my stomach grumbles that I realize a good couple of hours have been spent studying, laughing, touching. Time seems to do weird quantum physics when I'm with Eden. Some seconds lasting a breathless lifetime, while other times, hours pass without my awareness. Mitch's stomach joins in symphony.

Eden and Tara look at each other, rolling their eyes in tandem. Eden gets up, my leg feeling the coolness of her absence. "I'll order something."

"Oh, don't do that!" Tara exclaims.

"It's no problem. There's not much in our cupboards anyway."

I stop myself from frowning. What family has no food in their cupboards? Especially one that's quite obviously well off. I picture a large, immaculately clean pantry, a lonely jar of peanut butter sitting on the shelf. With nothing but a fellow jar of jelly to keep it company.

"We eat down at the restaurant most days. I'll see if Tony can do us a couple of pizzas."

Tara looks impressed. "You eat out most days?"

Eden's face is the polar opposite. "Believe me, it's not as cool as it sounds."

She heads over to the phone, a sleek digital one, and dials a single number.

"Hi, Tony. I was just seeing if you could do some pizzas for me." She smiles, turning her back a little. "Yes, more than one. Just the usual for me, then a selection for the other guys."

She blushes, completely turning her back. "Three—two guys, one girl. Two more should be enough?" A male voice can be heard laughing over the line, followed by a few words I can't decipher.

"Fine then, four more." She glances over at me, green eyes questioning. I give her a thumbs up.

"That would be great, Tony. I appreciate it."

Why do I get the feeling Tony doesn't mind one bit? I imagine a young up-and-coming chef, a guy who gets to cook for Eden every night. Knowing 'her usual'.

Eden hangs up the phone but, before she can sit, Tara pipes up.

"So, where's the little girls' room?"

"Right this way." And they disappear down the hallway leading from the kitchen.

Mitch leans back, two arms stretched out across the back of the leather lounge. "So, your girlfriend is loaded, huh?"

I shrug. "Who knew?" It's surprising, considering Eden's complete lack of pretentiousness. But I don't see how it makes a difference.

Tara's voice carries down the hallway. "Eden, how many people can you fit in this spa?"

"Ah, six I think."

"Do you know what I'm thinking?"

"No. And I don't want to." I can just imagine Eden's crimson blush.

Tara huffs as she comes down the corridor. "Spoilsport."

They return, and we go about clearing the coffee table of empty cans, bowls, and laptops. Within a few minutes the doorbell rings.

Eden opens the door and it's filled by a large, middle-aged man, his white shirt stretched around a belly that hangs over chef pants. He enters, swaying on a slight limp.

"You didn't have to bring them Tony. It's getting cold out."

"I don't mind doing it for you, Eden."

She peers at him. "How's the leg?"

"Aw, Eden, no need to fuss over me. You got company." He glances into the lounge, where we're all sitting, his gaze passing over each one of us. Eden introduces us and we wave, calling out a chorus of hello's. Tony hands her a stack of pizza boxes, two wrapped packages sitting on top. He leans in to whisper, unaware we can hear every word.

"I packed a couple of extra treats."

"You didn't need to do that, Tony." But Eden is smiling broadly.

"It's nice to see you relaxed, having fun, sweetheart." Sweetheart?

Eden thanks him again and sees him out the door. She spreads the pizzas on the coffee table, and we pile around. She reads the lids, "Philly steak, Middle Eastern lamb, prawn and pesto, duck ragu, and, if you're feeling adventurous, mine is the sweet potato, feta, and pine nut."

Mitch peers at it. "It's got green bits on it."

"That would be the garnish of baby spinach."

"Right." Mitch heads to the lamb pizza. He takes a bite and lets out a low groan.

Tara goes for the duck. "Son-of-a-biscuit-eater, this is really good."

Eden ducks her head. "Tony is an amazing chef."

Feeling like I should, I take a piece of the vegetarian. Eden's eyes go wide. "You don't have to—"

I bite into the meatless slice. And my own eyes widen. "It's really good."

She nods her head smugly. "Told you."

We all hoe in, exclaiming about each and every pizza. Tara jokes that she may have to marry Tony. Mitch doesn't laugh.

Mitch grabs another slice. "So have you talked to Eden about the Phelan barbeque this weekend?"

Eden's slice of pizza stills on the way to her mouth. I duck my head. I was working up to it. "Not yet."

She picks at a piece of feta on her slice. "That's okay, I have stuff on."

She thinks I haven't asked because I don't want her there? I throw a split second scowl at Mitch. He grins around his pizza slice.

"I was going to ask you tomorrow." I look meaningfully at the other two. "When we were alone."

"Oh."

Tara pipes up. "It's great fun. All the Phelans get together, and us Channons gate-crash every year."

Eden looks at me, not looking terribly convinced.

"It's not bad, despite all of the oldies." I pause. "And I'd love for you to come."

She nibbles her lower lip for a moment. I wait, breath held. "I'd like that."

I resist pulling her in for a victory dance. Just. "Great."

Tara claps her hands, doing a little jump on the spot. "We'll talk deets tomorrow!"

Eden looks at the empty pizza boxes, even the vegetarian one. "Wow, you guys really wolfed that down!"

Eden's hand flies to her mouth, her eyes wide and round above it. There's a short pause of silence as I register her shock, and growing discomfort. Puzzled, her statement goes through my mind again.

I burst out laughing, with Mitch and Tara not far behind. Eden's lips twitch, then she's laughing along with us.

Mitch flops back into the sofa. "Why, I'm practically howling with laughter." Tara elbows him in the ribs.

"What? You always said you loved my wolfish grin." Just when I thought the puns couldn't get any worse.

Tara is holding her sides, rolling on the sofa next to Mitch. "I'm going to get a stomachache."

And I can't help myself. "Must've been someone you ate!"

Eden's laughter sings through the lounge room, through my body. She's laughing so hard she collapses against me, her soft curves melding against my side. I can feel the laughter shake her lean frame. Almost unconsciously, my arm goes around her shoulders. She looks up at me, happiness sparkling in her eyes. I lean forward, drawn to those twinkling green oceans.

We're so caught up in the ridiculous moment that we don't immediately notice the extra person in the room. It's only once heels rap, rap, rap across the lounge room that we all pause.

Eden immediately sit ups, ramrod straight. My arm falls beside me. I turn to see a woman standing by a chair. Black hair brushes her chin, which has jutted to the side ever so slightly. She's slim, like Eden, but not as tall. She's wearing some sort of wrap dress, in black and red. Jewelry sparkles from her neck, ears, wrists. I'm guessing this is Eden's mother.

"I didn't know we were having company."

Eden's smile is gone. "Guys, this is my mother, Alexis St.

James. This is Mitch, Tara." Her gaze brushes over to me, but doesn't quite meet mine. "And Noah."

Alexis smiles. "Nice to meet you all. You're all from Jacksonville High?"

Huh, Eden hasn't mentioned us? Or me? I'm not sure what to make of that. "Yes ma'am. We were just working on assignments."

"Great to see. Keeping grades up for college applications?"

"That's the plan. I'm applying for Criminal Justice at Wyoming State."

Alexis nods. "Wyoming State has an excellent reputation." She's looking at Eden as she says this.

Beside me, Eden shifts a little, the movement moving her toward the other side of the lounge. I sit up a little straighter.

"I'm looking at elementary teaching, while Mitch plans on doing an apprenticeship in carpentry," Tara volunteers.

Alexis smiles again. "What a great idea to study together. It's so...refreshing to see she has made some friends."

Eden gets up from the sofa, her usual grace gone as she stiffly stands.

Alexis glances at the pizza boxes stacked on the coffee table. "Ah, I see you've been introduced to my chef's cooking."

"Thank you, it was amazing."

Another smile stretches across Alexis's face. "My pleasure. I could order dessert? He's been experimenting with some wonderful cheesecakes."

Tara stands up, Mitch along with her. "Thank you Mrs. St. James, but we'd better get going. We've still got school tomorrow."

I join them. "It was lovely meeting you Mrs. St. James."

We pack up our belongings and head for the door. Eden follows us, still practically mute.

"Come again anytime," Mrs. St. James calls from the lounge.

Tara is the only one that's brought a jacket, keeping up the pretense that we feel the cold.

"Thanks for the food, Eden. It was great." Tara gives her an impulsive hug. Eden never gets a chance to reciprocate before Tara releases her and heads for the door.

"Thank you for the popcorn," she says in a small voice.

"Seeya, Eden." Mitch looks at me, holding his hand out. "My turn to drive?"

I fish the keys out of my pocket and hand them over.

I turn to Eden, countless questions running through my mind. She looks at me, eyes troubled, mouth firm and flat.

I lean in to whisper, ever so quietly, in her ear. "What's the difference between a Werewolf and a swallow?"

Her mouth relaxes around the edges. "What?"

"Swallows don't Werewolf people."

And her shoulders quiver, a smile splitting across her face, as she gives me a little shove. "That's terrible."

I wiggle my brows. "I've got worse."

She rolls her eyes, but she's smiling again. "I'll see you at school tomorrow."

During the drive home, it's my turn to stare out the window, head resting on the cool glass. I can see where Eden gets her beauty from. Although Alexis's matches that of the Inn, cultured and costly, as opposed to Eden's natural, earthy looks. Her mother had been polite, gracious. But something is niggling me, and I'm not sure what. It wasn't the makeup or the bling. Or Eden's shut down.

I push my head away from the window, sitting up straight, realizing what it was.

Alexis never once said Eden's name.

17

EDEN

W hy in the world did I agree to this?

A family barbeque. I've never been to a family barbeque. Let alone with a pack of Werewolves.

I don't know what to say, do, bring. What to wear!

I scan my wardrobe. It has two distinct sections. A smaller, modest part with clothes I've bought myself, using my over-inflated weekly allowance. It boasts sensible denims and comfortable cottons. Safe, practical, and unobtrusive.

The larger portion on my right, my mother has bought for me. Bags subtly embossed with designer labels left on my bed for me to find. The ones I had to wear if she held dinner parties, cocktail parties, tea parties. Although I stopped attending them as soon as I was old enough to consider defiance, it hasn't deterred her from keeping up the pretence that she provides for me. It's crammed with blouses, skirts, and dresses. In cashmere, angora, the odd slip of silk. Pretty, impractical, and impersonal.

I stand there, feet growing roots into the floor. I want to look my best, keep up Noah's misconception that I'm pretty as long as possible. But I don't want to look like I'm trying too hard, or get it irrevocably wrong.

I decide on jeans—warm and comfortable, but a dark blue pair that I bought on a whim because I liked the way they fitted, then never wore. They were too different from my usual faded familiarity. I never did anything that would get me noticed at Boston High.

I take a cautious step to the right. To my mother's purchases. I nibble on my lower lip as my hand comes up to brush over the jewel colors. *Should I?*

A soft cashmere blouse in emerald green catches my eye, and I lift the hanger out. The material falling from a scoop neckline is so fine it would be sheer if it didn't crisscross over the front. A designer tag hangs from the sleeve, a name I've always rejected. Just because it's so important to my mother. *Could I?*

I slip it on before I slide back into dithering uncertainty and step before the mirror. The green blouse flows over the dark blue denim, the intersecting hem framing my hips. My fingers brush over my exposed collarbones, the hint of shoulder. I pull at the material softly molding to my chest and waist. It's a little... clingy. But I think I like what I see.

I briefly consider braiding my hair. But I've had enough of stepping outside my comfort zone for one day, and default to my usual knot. I take one last look in the mirror, trying to see what Noah might see. A plain girl trying to be something she's not stares back at me.

Caesar thumps his tail from the bed, barking once. I lean over to pat him. "Thanks, boy, I need any vote of confidence I can get." He licks my hand, his head nuzzling my palm.

In the kitchen I grab the bowl of salad from the fridge. Tony's amazing quinoa, feta, and pomegranate mix. I have my hand on the door when it opens. I jump back, surprised. My mother's equally surprised face halts its momentum through the doorway. I quickly step back, uncomfortable with the close proximity.

My mother steps through, briefcase in tow. Her eyes scan me from head to toe. "Where are you off to?" Her tone is as sharp as her gaze.

"Family barbecue." I hold the bowl a little tighter. "The guys you met the other night."

"With Noah?"

"Yes."

"Do you think this is a good idea?"

"Yes." Although I'm not totally convinced of that.

My mother gradually straightens from putting down her briefcase; she even seems to be breathing slowly. "I don't."

I briefly consider asking why, but I'm not sure I want to know. I take the car keys from the hook, continuing out the door, letting my actions say all that's needed.

Her parting words manage to slip through the door as I shut it, "That top would have looked better with the skirt it came with."

In the car the local radio station forecasts a cool evening, and I'm glad I wore jeans. I scrunch up my nose as they announce the latest one-hit wonder, but I pump up the volume, silencing my mother's parting comment ringing in my ears.

I sail down the winding road to the solitary house in the trees. It's amazing how little things fall into place now that I know the truth. The concealed out of the way house, giving this unique family privacy. Tara's painting, depicting two wolves in love, the two friends that will bond once we graduate. Even I smile at my chosen career path.

As the Saab purrs around the last bend, I see there are cars parked in the driveway, then nose to bumper up the road. *How many of them are there?* I pull in behind the last, several yards from the house. Voices carry across the distance, shouting and calling and laughing. A baby's cry wails over the top of it all.

And I'm hit by a rock hard truth—I'm out of my depth.

Wobbly legs take small steps away from the car, toward the house. I clutch the bowl of salad, grateful to Tony for insisting I bring it. I bet he didn't realize it would double as a Perspex shield. A few more steps and the house and yard are in full view. People covering the full span of ages mill about. Bald babies and roaming children, chatting men and women, hairless middle-aged men and their greying wives.

Noah is nowhere to be seen.

With a pounding heart, I consider my options. Drop the salad, somehow break the indestructible plastic picnic bowl, and head home. Fake a migraine and head home. Trip, break my femur, and head home.

As I stand there deciding which would be the best plan of attack, a minivan pulls up, having bypassed the snake line of cars. It parks behind Noah and Mitch's truck. The sliding door glides open and a red-haired girl skips out. And another, and another. As I stand there, salad bowl warming in my palms, a total of four bright-haired girls file out, each a little taller than the last.

A voice calls from the van's belly. "For sanitation's sake, Christa, Mr. Puddles is not a tissue."

The smallest of the red-haired bunch jumps out, a stuffed duck hanging limply from her hand, and skips after her sisters. Tara is not far behind, wearing a white summer dress and a yellow, short-sleeved shrug complimenting the big sunflowers adorning its hem. She's cupping the hand of a boy, only about a year old, in a crisp white shirt and slacks, and matching red hair.

"Thanks, Tara, just bring Kurt Jr. over here." A pale woman, a light summer dress hanging on thin shoulders, comes around to Tara. Fine blond hair is tied up in a bun, some strands having already slipped from its confines. She kneels in front of little Kurt, adjusting his already straight collar.

"Hey, Edes! Great timing." Tara skips to stand beside me. "This is my Mom, Lara."

"Nice to meet you, Mrs. Channon."

"You too, Eden. We've heard a lot about you. Please call me Lara." She reaches into the minivan and pulls out a giant platter of bread rolls. "I already feel old enough as it is."

A massive man comes from around the driver's side, tree-trunk legs supporting a barrel-sized torso. His face is covered in a big, red beard, surrounding his face like a mane. Bushy brows form a straight line over hazel eyes. I pull the poor tortured salad bowl a little closer to my stomach.

"Dad, this is Eden, the girl from school I told you about."

Kurt Channon grunts, his massive head turning to me. He looks down at my salad bowl, then back up.

"Hello."

"Nice to meet you, Mr. Channon."

His gaze shifts to Tara beside me, what-is-she-doing-here plastered on his face.

I shift on my feet, instantly uncomfortable.

Tara frowns, shifting her weight toward me. "Remember Dad? I told you about the..." she pauses to raise her eyebrows, "thing with Noah?"

Mr. Channon grunts again, then holds his hand out. Little Kurt takes it, liquid-hazel eyes looking up at his father as they walk toward the front entry. Lara smiles a pale smile before following, balancing the platter.

As they walk away, I hear Kurt's voice filter back. "I thought this was a family get-together."

Tara slips her arm through mine and starts walking around the side of the house. "Ignore him. He likes to define sour puss." She peeks over my shoulder, looking down. "Besides, girl, your booty looks amazing in those jeans!"

I blush, giving her a little shove with my hip. "It does not!"

Tara snorts. "I can't wait to see Noah's face."

My lip returns to its position beneath my gnawing teeth. What will he think? I glance back at Tara's light dress, arms and legs exposed. I didn't have to worry about being overdressed, but without a Werewolf's increased body temperature, I'm certainly wearing more than anyone else here. My lower lip hurts a little as I realize Kurt was right to notice I'm the odd one out.

"Tara, Eden, great to see you girls." Beth comes toward us, carrying a fruit platter. Her willowy frame is wrapped in a blue dress, strappy heels showing she's not afraid of her height.

"Hi, Beth."

"Hi, Beth."

"Wonderful, Eden, you brought a salad. You can't have too much food with the gigantic appetites that come to this event."

I'm doubly grateful to Tony for his thoughtfulness. I make a mental note to groom little Mitsy, his hyperactive shih tzu, tomorrow. "Our chef made his famous quinoa, feta, and pomegranate salad. Can we help with anything?"

"Sounds delish. If you girls could take this through to the back and put them on the tables, that would be wonderful. Noah and Mitch are there. I got them to get some more chairs from the garage."

"No probs." Tara slips her arm out to grab the platter.

We take the food and head to the tables. We round the side of the house, and a lawn opens up, reaching out toward the tall pines that surround it in a crescent shape. Tables line the back, colorful lanterns strung up above them. Each weighed down with plates of bread and bowls of salad and platters of meat. The owners of the voices I heard on arrival are milling about, wine glasses and beers in hand. Conversation flows as easily as the music that streams from the speakers under the veranda.

My eyes scan the crowd, but I can't find what I'm looking for.

We traverse the lawn, weaving through the people dressed as

if they're at a summer tea party. Not a fall barbeque in Wyoming. My green top and jeans weigh me down like snow gear. We come to the tables that form a dotted line between the milling crowd and the age-old conifers. I've just placed the salad bowl down when wailing breaks through the chatting and laughing.

Tara groans. "That's Christa. No matter how many times she does it, she hasn't learned that Mr. Puddles sinks in punch bowls. I'll be back in a second." She passes me the fruit platter, and her sunflower-dotted form is quickly swallowed by the multiplying crowd.

I'm left standing by the table, the lonesome fruit platter in my hands, awkward and alone. I'm considering what I do now, when a different kind of chattering reaches out behind me. I turn toward the trees, peering into the gloom. A ground squirrel leaps onto a low branch and stands on its hind legs.

I smile, delighted. I glance over my shoulder, then slip between the tables and into the protective shadows of the trees. The squirrel scampers between the close-knit branches around me, chattering excitedly. I glance down to realize the fruit platter is still in my hands. I carefully pull back the clear film, and pulling out a few grapes, I hold them up.

The squirrel sits up again, whiskers twitching. I don't even have to hum, before it shimmies down to a nearby branch. It's obviously used to being fed by humans. With lightning speed, it grabs two grapes and shoves them in its mouth, giving it over-inflated chipmunk cheeks. It chews rapidly and they're gone, sounding a raspy coo.

"My pleasure."

In a blur of motion, it leaps to my shoulder and spreads its tail lavishly, creating a protective umbrella around my head. Its teeth flash as it sounds a series of raspy clucks.

"I know, I know. Winter's coming." I fish out a couple of

strawberries. One disappears where the grapes were posted, and it grips the other in its leathery paws.

The next moment, the squirrel stills, his little body turning into a furry statue. With a last chirp, he spins and disappears up and across the trees. The voices that it registered before me filter through the trees. I freeze in the shadowy coolness. How do I explain my presence in the trees, with a fruit platter that's not my own?

"I just don't think it's right," says one male voice.

And I realize that, thanks to my indecisive pause, I'm now eavesdropping. How can I move now?

"We don't get a choice. It's already happened." I recognize Adam's deep rumble. "What does it matter?"

"It's not the way it's supposed to be."

"Some things happen in ways we don't understand. It doesn't mean they're wrong." The voices begin to fade, moving farther down the line of tables.

"It's just not right."

"We're Alphas, we say what is..." and the voices disappear.

We're Alphas. My heart sinks as I realize Adam was talking to Kurt. I stand between the conifers, my smile fallen amongst the pine needles at my feet. Why do I get the sense that I was somehow involved in that conversation?

"She was just here a second ago," says a voice I recognize.

I step through the trees to find Tara back at the table; Noah and Mitch are with her.

Tara peers into the trees behind me. "What were you doing in there?"

But my eyes gravitate to a new focal point. Noah is wearing a white shirt, muscled biceps peeking from short sleeves. A black pin-stripe streaks across his chest, emphasizing its width. A swirling tribal pattern down its side matches his dark slacks. His blond hair has been combed into submission, with a few unruly locks that refused to be tamed, resting on his forehead.

Right above simmering, sky eyes that are scanning me from head to toe.

He steps up toward me. "Wow."

I blush, ducking my head between my shoulders. His finger comes up beneath my chin, and my eyes go back to where they want to be. Losing themselves in blue. Blue pools that are smoldering hotter and hotter with the passage of long seconds.

And I no longer feel overdressed or out of place. I feel...*beautiful.*

I take a breath, wanting to venture a little past my silent walls. "Look who's talking."

I'm rewarded with a dazzling grin. One of my own involuntarily spans across my face.

"Let's not start a forest fire." Mitch has his arm around Tara, his dark shirt a sharp contrast against her bright dress. I blush again.

Noah tucks my palm into his. "Worried you'll need the material for your project?"

"Pfft. It's made of better stuff than pine."

"Oh?" Tara asks, eyes alight.

Mitch glares at Noah. "It's for a bird house."

Tara's eyebrows shoot up. "For around here?"

Mitch goes silent, making me smile. Apparently his lame lie didn't fool Tara either. Noah chuckles and turns toward the house; Tara and Mitch fall behind us.

"What were you doing in the trees?"

"A squirrel was hungry." Noah gives me a perplexed look. "You guys must have a feeder around here."

"Nope. Prey animals tend to avoid the area. Even though they aren't exactly a food source, just a whiff of us is enough to make themselves scarce."

"Huh? Well, he was quite happy to have some of your mother's fruit platter."

I don't have time to analyze the unusual behavior because we're walking toward the crowd. Noah didn't exaggerate when he said he had a big family. With my hand held fast in his, Noah pulls me around, introducing me to uncles who pump his hand enthusiastically, aunts who envelop him into their welcoming bosoms, and cousins, cousins, and more cousins. They dart between the people and tables like they're obstacles on a slalom run. When they do stop to say "hello," the boys high five Noah and Mitch, the girls squeal their names and cling to their legs.

Meeting Grandpa Ben is given its own reverent moment. The patriarch of the pack has a full head of speckled grey hair, making me wonder whether Mitch got his dark looks from his paternal side. Age hasn't dimmed his size, or presence. He sits at the head of the crescent-shaped tables, family flowing about him.

"Grandpa, this is Eden." Those four words showing me that Noah's already spoken to him about me.

"Ah, Eden." Ben pats the seat next to him. "Come and tell me what you think of my family."

I sit on the seat, perching a little on the edge. "They've been very welcoming Mr. Phelan."

Ben grunts, nodding. Then a mischievous glint appears in his blue eyes, one that's all too familiar. "Please, call me Ben. And what do you think of my grandson?"

So that's his game. "Well, he's very good looking, has the Phelan sparkle, but terrible taste in music."

Noah has gone from looking pleasantly surprised to thoroughly confused.

"And he'll make Tara a wonderful mate."

Mitch joins in with Ben's laughter. "We learned early on you can't fool this one, Grandpa."

Grandpa Ben leans over to me, speaking quietly. "I think you'll do just fine in this pack, Eden."

"I hope so," I whisper back.

As we continue through the throng of people, with Noah's warm palm cupping mine, his warmer body beside me, I think I can do this. Tense shoulders expecting the welcome I received from Mr. Channon slowly relax as smiling teeth and welcoming faces pass me in a continuous stream. I answer the polite questions, discuss the weather, I even contribute to a debate between Grandpa Ben and Uncle Joe about when wolves were reintroduced to the park. Joe, a younger, darker version of Adam, is arguing pointedly that his memory is obviously not tainted by age. Grandpa Ben slaps his thigh when I agree it was in 1995.

There are no raised eyebrows at my solitary human status. My long sleeves. The absence of meat on my plate. Actually, the only sign that I'm surrounded by a large pack of Werewolves is the large rotisserie in the centre of the lawn, an entire animal glistening over the coals.

"Does it bother you?"

My eyes shoot to Noah's in surprise. "What?"

"All the meat."

I shake my head. "Unnecessary waste of life bothers me. I don't need to eat meat." I tilt my head. "Some animals do."

Noah is rubbing his lower lip with his finger again. "The cycle of life, huh?"

"Exactly."

We continue heading down the tables laden with a spectacular amount of food, filling up our plates as we go.

"Everyone insists that my mother doesn't need to cook." Noah cocks a wry brow. "But she still does." Beside him is a bowl of charred remains; I think they're meatballs.

"Luckily Dad cooked these." In the corner of the table is a white plate with six sausages on it. Veggie sausages.

I stare at the thoughtful meat alternative. "That was very sweet of them."

Noah shrugs. "They wanted you to enjoy yourself."

I don't know what to say to that, so I quietly take one, eyes blinking a little rapidly.

As we come to the next table, the eldest of Tara's sisters, Dana, stands beside us, plate in hand. When she glances up and notices Noah, she goes beet red, and the plate tips precariously in her hand. Noah's hand shoots out to steady it. A pang of empathy shoots through me.

"Thanks, Noah." Dana's voice rushes out on a breath.

From the corner of my eye, I see Tara roll her eyes; Mitch's shoulders hunch on a silent chuckle. Dana is oblivious as her hazel eyes are glued to Noah.

Noah smiles. "No problem. You should try the quinoa salad on the next table. It's amazing."

Blushing, her gaze returns to her plate. "I will."

We continue down the table train. I glance over my shoulder, and Dana's gaze is following Noah's back. I smile; I can commiserate with the sisterhood-of-bedazzling-Noah. She tucks a strand of hair behind her ear, smiling in return.

Noah squeezes my hand, and I look up to see him smiling down at me.

As the afternoon passes into evening, the lanterns are switched on, creating multi-colored bubbles of light hanging from ghostly branches. As the sun descends and the mountain's shadow reaches out, the cool fall air develops a nip, and I contain a shiver. The Weres around me seem oblivious to the dropping temperatures. Dresses flutter in the breeze, shirt buttons remain open at the neck.

We settle at a table on the outskirts. We chuckle together when Aunt Mavis teeters on her heels, wine glass in one hand, her laden plate narrowly missing Uncle Joe's head. We're rolling with laughter when Tara has to rescue poor Mr. Puddles from the branches of a tree with a broomstick, her frustrated statement that Mr. Puddles does not fly carrying across the yard. Our heads practically touch as we discuss which is superior—coleslaw or potato salad. We sit up in surprise when a click and a flash bursts around us.

"Smile," Beth calls, then flits off, camera in hand.

Aunt Mavis brings over a plate of chicken pieces, sitting it on the table in front of me.

"I brought you these, dear. No need to be worrying about ruining that beautiful figure of yours yet."

I pause, looking at the cooked pieces of bird. "Thanks, Mavis."

"Aunt Mavis, we told you Eden is vegetarian."

Aunt Mavis flaps her hand. "I know, dear. That's why I brought her chicken."

Noah blinks. "Thanks, Aunt Mavis."

Aunt Mavis nods, a satisfied smile on her face as she weaves away.

Noah reaches across me. "Thoughtful woman, that Aunt Mavis," he announces as he scoops the meat onto his plate. I roll my eyes; I know it won't go to waste with his endless capacity to eat.

We look over to see Tara and Mitch talking to Mr. and Mrs. Channon. Tara is beaming her I'm-with-Mitch-beam, hanging on his arm. Mitch's face is serious as he talks to Mr. Channon. Lara stands quietly, nodding and smiling occasionally.

"Have you met Mr. Channon?"

"Yes."

Noah's gaze returns to me, holding that assessing look I'm getting to know well. But I don't want to talk about Kurt's welcome. I don't want to ruin a wonderful night. Where, despite being more different than I've ever been, I've felt the most wonderful sense of acceptance.

"Noah, Mitch." Adam's voice carries through the crowd and music like low-lying thunder. We head over to where Adam stands on the back porch, two large garbage bags at his feet.

"Can you guys take these to the trash cans? I've moved them over by Grandfather Douglas."

"Sure." Noah turns to me. "Coming?"

"Sure. Grandfather Douglas?"

"Yeah. He's pretty old."

Noah and Mitch each pick up a bag. Bottles and cans rearrange themselves within, clanging and pinging. With his free hand, Noah grasps mine and we head around the house, toward a towering spire outlined against the evening sky. My neck cranes back in an effort to see the tree's crown. The Douglas-fir is certainly ancient, his mammoth trunk wider than my arms. The lower branches have been pruned, creating a natural shelter beneath. I imagine this ancient tree has stood solidly through generations of Phelans. I can just picture a swing hanging from its powerful branches.

I turn to see Noah watching me, blue eyes glowing in the dusky air, lips parted. My breath catches in my throat as warmth trickles from behind my ear, across my cheeks and down my spine. Just as Noah kicks a trash can, the loud clang rupturing the silence.

"Weren't watching where you were going, big bro?" Mitch drops his bag on top of Noah's, the bottles clashing loudly, breaching the heated spell.

"Dad's right, you do need a Precepts refresher," Noah mutters.

Mitch laughs, teeth flashing in the dim light. He replaces the lid on the bin, dusting his hands on his slacks.

We've only taken a few steps back when Tara skips up next

to me, dragging Mitch with her. "Don't you just love this time of the night, Eden?"

"Twilight is lovely."

"It just makes me want to..." I slow my pace as I wait for her to finish. "Race!"

And Noah rolls his eyes besides me. "You haven't won against Mitch and me since you were seven."

"And you tied our shoelaces together," Mitch adds.

"This one will be much more even." Tara's eyes are wide with excitement, a look I'm getting to know means an idea's just popped into her crazy, impulsive head. "A piggy back race."

A piggy back race! Mitch looks to Noah, a challenge in the way his gaze holds Noah's for long seconds, in his cocky grin. Noah narrows his eyes at him. Surely he's not entertaining the idea.

Mitch squats down, and Tara springs on his back. He catches her, his hands just above the back of her knees. They whoop and holler as Mitch runs circles around Noah and me, goading us to race. I look over at Noah skeptically. With the size difference between Tara and me, this race is not even at all.

"I'm no fairy, y'know."

Noah arches a brow at me, and turns his back, a silent challenge. I glance over at Tara and Mitch, both grinning and Mitch stomping his feet. Images of Noah, a paraplegic in a wheelchair for the remainder of his years, flash before my eyes. Noah stands there, hands on hips, waiting for me to pick up the gauntlet. *Can I be that reckless?*

A giggle escapes my lips as I step forward. Noah doesn't need to crouch; I'm not much shorter than him.

"Ready?"

Noah makes a show of bracing his legs in a wide stance. "Locked and waiting to be loaded."

I huff in indignation and leap onto his back, and Noah pretends to stagger under my weight. He rights himself, and flashing his signature grin over his shoulder, lines up next to Mitch.

Tara calls out, "First one to the veranda. On your marks, get set, *go!*"

Noah and Mitch leap forward. Despite his earlier posturing, Noah is as agile as if he was solo. He sprints forward, but Mitch keeps pace. Tara's discovered her cowgirl alter ego, and is calling out 'giddy up' and 'yee ha!' at the top of her lungs. As we near our destination, Noah starts to make headway. Seeing the possibility of losing, Mitch suddenly swerves toward us. Tara and I squeal and shriek as we crash, bodies slamming and limbs tangling. Noah shoulders his brother back, and Mitch stumbles to the side. Laughing loudly, Noah dips his head and, with a quick burst of power, vaults onto the veranda.

As we do a victory lap, we're both laughing so hard my cheeks hurt. Tara slides off Mitch's back, laughing breathlessly, demanding a rematch.

Noah slows and, as the rush of adrenaline fades, I realize that I'm wrapped around his back like a limpet. The laughter fades from my lips as my hands flex on firm shoulders, registering the dip and rise of ridged muscles beneath heated skin, feeling my legs wrapped around his lean waist. Suddenly hyperaware that everything in between is pressed intimately against his back.

That heat is building at an alarming rate.

My breath hitches as Noah's hands tighten on my legs. *Oh my.*

I feel his chest expand as he takes a deep breath. I clear my throat, and Noah releases my legs. I slide down his back, and flames of heat explode as our bodies graze. My hands remain on his shoulders; I just can't bring myself to remove them.

Noah turns slowly. I feel the rise and fall of his chest, his breathing harder now than a few moments ago. My lips part on my own rapid breathing. Tingling awareness pulses across my body. I want to step closer.

Instead, I take a small step back, my hands falling to my sides. I smile a shaky smile. "We won."

Noah's smile is just as crooked. "Yeah. We won."

He holds his hand out and, without a second thought, I grasp it. The pulsing heat of before still lingers in the air. Tara and Mitch come up next to us and we all head back toward the party.

The moment we round the veranda, Adam signals to Noah and Mitch. He and Beth are standing at the apex of the semi-circle of tables. Noah and Mitch look at each other quizzically and head over. Something tells me to hang back, and Tara chooses to stay under the protective cover of the veranda too. Although, a short moment later, she rushes off after one of her younger sisters.

Once Noah and Mitch have joined Adam, he steps forward, clapping his hands. The sound is not loud, but it has every head turning his way. Friends, family, loved ones all go silent as they wait to see what their Alpha has to say.

"Thank you all for coming. The Phelan family barbecue is a wonderful opportunity to reconnect with our heritage, our pack." He clears his throat. "But this get-together is particularly special. As you all know, things have been...difficult for us." The crowd shuffles, murmurs of assent rolling amongst them.

Adam's blond head drops a little as he focuses on the ground ahead of him. "When things don't go the way we expect them to, the way they always have, you're left wondering why. All that sustains you is faith. And hope."

His head lifts, and a smile has lit up his face. "And then prayers are answered, hopes become reality." His smile turns a little wry. "Admittedly, sometimes in the most unexpected and unorthodox of ways."

Quiet chuckles reverberate through the crowd as I step farther back into the shadows.

Adam reaches behind him, and Beth steps up to take his hand. "And things can return to their rightful place."

Under the shadowy canopy, I still.

His tone carrying across the lawn, reverberating with pride, Adam looks to Noah. "I wish to announce that Noah will take his place as my heir, as the next Phelan Alpha."

Roars and shouts erupt from the crowd, and people rush to pump hands enthusiastically, to slap Adam and Noah on the back with fervent force. I look to Mitch, the one who this will affect the most. He's there, slapping the hardest and clapping the loudest.

Beth is a still island amongst the melee, a smiling, proud figure. A tear leaves a wet trail down her cheek. She looks up to see me watching her, her light brown eyes brimming.

Across the grassy distance she mouths two words.

Thank you.

I stand in stunned silence. What do you do with an unsolicited gift? One that seems much too expensive, far too extravagant? When its thoughtfulness touches you somewhere deep inside? Well, I just found out.

You stand there, at a loss for words.

Then Aunt Mavis is hugging Beth, rocking her from side to side. The two women laugh and cry. I take a step back. I don't feel like an outsider, but this is a family rejoicing. And I'm not family.

I take a few steps along the veranda, then notice Mr. Channon standing at the edge of the crowd. He's quite still, except for his barrel chest moving with slow breaths. No one sees young Kurt pulling down, trying to extricate his little hand from his father's frozen grip. His face cramps with the effort before a final tug finally frees him and he falls backwards. He scrambles toward the crowd. Kurt hasn't moved a muscle, except for that regulated chest moving in and out. In and out.

I quickly pull into the shadows, not wanting this disapproving man to catch me staring. In a few short steps, I'm on the grass, and I make a quick beeline for the trees. There, at the shadowy edge where the colorful lights can't quite reach, I sit down, my back against a solid pine. I watch the joy apparent in light dancing steps, in tender hands that cup faces, in arms that throw out wide before clasping anyone within reach. Where Noah is center of this blossom.

It's not long before I've lost sight of him in the moving masses, so I sit back, enjoying the sounds of laughter and celebration. I'm not in the least bit surprised when, half an hour later, I hear footsteps approaching. I had a feeling the other times Noah found me weren't coincidences. Without a word, he sits beside me against the tree, our shoulders touching. Like two magnets, our hands come together.

"Your mom and dad are so proud of you."

"They want to say 'thank you'. We wouldn't be here without you."

I continue as if he hasn't spoken. "They should be."

Noah's sigh reaches me in the dark. His gaze tracks his parents across the lawn. "Where's your father?"

Whoa, topic change. I suppose I asked for it with my blatant deflecting. I sigh myself, my outbreath leaving my shoulders a little lower than before. I pick up a pine needle, twirling in between my fingers. "No idea. He disappeared before I was born."

"What's your Mom told you about him?"

"Absolutely nothing. The topic is taboo."

Noah's brows pull down. "He must have really hurt her."

The pine needle snaps in my fingers. "Maybe. Could have been a one-night stand, for all I know."

Noah turns his head toward me. "What's it like? Growing up with a single mom?"

I wonder how much to tell him, how much to let him in. "Well, she's very successful, so I've never lacked for anything."

"I can see that. And?"

"It means she can work long hours."

In the dim light, I see a single brow quirk. "And?"

"Tenacious, aren't you?"

Noah grins, and says nothing.

I sigh again. "It means we've never been very close."

Noah nods, rubbing his finger across his bottom lip in that distracting way of his. Why do I get the feeling he's reading between the lines?

It's time for my own topic change. "Kurt is very different to your father."

"He's very...traditional."

And it's my turn to read between the lines. "Old school?"

"Yeah, old school."

"How come there's only two of you, and hundreds of them?"

Noah chuckles. "Mom had a difficult birth, so she couldn't have any more kids." He looks down at our intertwined hands. "And Kurt wanted a son."

So he kept going until he got one. I think of the little blue bundle Lara was holding. "And he just kept going until he got one?"

"Yeah." Noah sighs.

"That's a little...medieval."

Noah puffs out his chest, thumping it with his fist. "Alphas are serious business, young lady."

I sigh, unsure of where I fit in this complicated jigsaw, and rest my head on Noah's shoulder. It's only when Noah stiffens that I realize what I've done. I hold my weight, unsure.

"No, leave it there. I was just surprised." *That I was the one to touch.* "I like it."

Very quietly, I whisper. "I like it too."

We sit there and watch the Phelan crowd from our shadowy cocoon. Slowly, they begin to disperse, but unlike the usual family barbeque, they don't head for their cars. Some in pairs, the odd trio, and several solitary figures all dissolve into the woods. When the first howl breaches through the trees, I know it's time for me to leave.

As if reading my mind, Noah stands and dusts off the pine needles clinging to his pants. He holds out a hand, and I place mine in his. He pulls me up with little effort. My eyes get a fast track view up his dark slacks, across his pressed shirt, past the open top button showing that little dent between his collar-bones, across his firm chin, to stall at his lips.

My eyes trace the sharp outline of red against stubbly tan. The sculpted upper lip resting on its full bottom counterpart. Wishing I could do the same with my fingers. I realize I'm staring when they part on a sharp inhale. *As if he feels it too.* My eyes fly up to see heated blue pools watching me. My breath skips in my throat as my eyes return to his collarbone, heat riding high on my cheeks.

"One day, Eden. You'll let yourself go, follow your instinct."

"I hope so." The words squeeze out of lungs devoid of oxygen.

Noah's chin lifts, like he's smiling. "Luckily the journey is half the fun." He glances over his shoulder. "Come on, I'll walk you to your car."

Hands twined, we cross the lit area of the yard. Halfway down the tables, Adam is clearing them of paper plates and empty cups, a garbage bin beside him. He straightens when he sees us approach.

"Off home, Eden?"

"Yes, Mr.—" I'm cut off by a finger in the air, a wide smile behind it. "Adam. Thank you for having me. I had a lovely time."

"You're always welcome in our house, Eden." Adam's blue gaze holds mine for meaningful seconds.

I hope he can't see my blush in the muted light.

"I'll be back in a sec to give you a hand, Dad." Noah tows me across the yard, saving me from trying to formulate a response.

We've only traversed part of the way when Beth's voice calls out. We turn to see her beelining toward us, her skirt billowing in her haste, holding the cleaned salad bowl.

She reaches us, holding it out. Once again, meaningful eyes hold mine. "Thank you."

I know this time my blush can't be missed. "My pleasure."

"I'm just taking Eden to her car, Mom, and I'll be back."

"No problem, honey." She breezes over to Adam, her hand patting my arm as she passes. A completely unconscious gesture. But one that imprints itself on me like a brand.

Noah's shoulder brushes mine as we begin walking again. "Told you."

"The thanks really aren't necessary."

"Well, they originally wanted to buy you something."

"Oh no, I hope you told them not to."

"Of course I did."

Relief whooshes from my lungs. "Thank goodness."

Noah's lips twitch. "I told them that's my job."

We've reached my car, so I spin around to face him, my hands falling to my side. "Noah, I don't want you buying things for me. You don't owe me anything."

"No need to worry."

Thank goodness. I don't know how I'd react to a gift. I don't know what to do with all he has given me so far.

Noah takes a small step forward. "When I buy you a gift, it won't be to say 'thank you'." All of a sudden I notice we're enveloped in darkness, cloaked in intimacy. "What I feel is far more than gratitude."

Oh.

And in a split second my world narrows, my senses converge. My sight fills with cerulean pools and angled planes and sculpted lips. I breathe in intoxicating sandalwood. I hear the deep, deep breath he pulls in. And I want to touch, to get a taste of Noah up close.

My hands flex by my side, caution and desire warring along their fingertips. Wanting to know the feel of his skin. Yearning to explore his heat.

But I don't. The feeling of vulnerability, of restraint keeps my hand by my sides. For lengthy seconds we stand there. Time grows and swells along with the pulsing connection surrounding us.

My hand twitches, coming up a fraction.

"Noah. Mitch." Adam's booming voice crashes into the darkness.

With a last exhaled breath, Noah steps back, a rueful smile on his lips. I realize the battle is forfeited; I missed my chance. My hand falls slack at the loss.

Noah takes another step back. "Next garbage run. It won't be the same without you."

I take a deep steadying breath; sandalwood still lingers in the air. Noah turns and starts walking toward the lit yard. I watch the pale light outline those broad shoulders.

A few paces away he turns, that beautiful grin of his back. "You free next weekend?"

"Yes."

"Good. I want to show you something."

18

NOAH

"Mom, have you seen Dad?"

My mother pokes her head around the kitchen doorway. "Out on the thinking chair, love."

I should have guessed. I head out to the bench with the glorified name. It was one of Mitch's first creations, put together with three planks and a handful of crooked nails. Dad had been so impressed and proud he'd promptly christened it his thinking chair and placed it in the backyard facing the giant pines.

Over the years he has practically worn a butt-shaped groove in it, sometimes using it when he wanted peace and quiet from raucous twin boys. Sometimes he would sit out there with Mom, his arm around her shoulders. Other times he would seek solitude after a tough shift. Like when Stash found the young skier, his cold body crumpled around a tree. Dad had sat there, solid and unmoving, well into the night.

I approach his still back, the massive shoulders bunched. Stash sits at his feet.

I haven't come around him before he asks, "How did your presentation with Eden go?"

"Pretty good. She was really nervous." Hands wringing, her white teeth worrying away her bottom lip so much that I felt sorry for it. So much that I wanted to reach across and pull it out, give its bruised surface a break.

I sit down beside him. "But then you could have knocked my hairy socks off when she contributed." I'd taken a breath, looking back to my notes to see if I missed anything. And her clear voice had stepped in, adding a little garnish of her own. My eyes had flown to hers, astonished and impressed. Two more times it happened. My info dump, her accompaniment, our eyes meeting over a smile. By the end, we almost had a rhythm going.

"And in the end we got an A+." She'd been so happy. She had skipped a little, moving toward me. Then contained herself. I hold my breath for those small moments when she lets herself go. Lets herself out.

"Well done, son. Sounds like the two of you make a good team."

I put my hands on either side of my legs, pushing them into the timber beneath me, bracing my shoulders. "I'm taking Eden to the Glade tomorrow."

His blue eyes turn to mine, and he has his serious face on. The muscles of his forehead, eyes, and mouth taut and still. "This is highly unusual, Noah."

"I know."

"We don't always have rules for situations that we haven't come across before."

Which would be tough for a man who has lived by the law, upheld the law, enforced the law his whole life. Both human and Were. "I know."

His eyes return to the towering pines that have surrounded our house for generations. He takes a deep breath, affording this decision the time it deserves.

"This feels right, Dad." It feels more than right.

"As future Alpha, you'll have to make these decisions for your pack." His hand comes down to stroke Stash. "Decisions using not only your gut."

As future Alpha. The title, its weight, seems odd. Like stepping back into a pair of shoes you haven't worn for a while. Shoes that you put aside thinking they didn't fit anymore. Thinking they were meant for someone else. Now they feel comfortable and familiar, but a little uncomfortable and unfamiliar too. You realize it's probably going to take some time to get used to them again.

I think of Eden—the past weeks we've had together.

The girl that made this life possible. Her rapid adjustment to a new reality. To carrying the weight of a great secret. And I want to keep creating special memories.

The girl who has an amazing connection with animals. As inexplicable as the magic that turns man to wolf. That risks her own safety to care for them. And I want to be the one to protect her.

The girl that finds it so hard to touch, I suspect due to a mother that can't bring herself to say her daughter's name. And I want to be the guy that finally breaches those walls.

The girl who still looks surprised and delighted when I bring her lunch. Nothing more than leftovers from the barbeque, two veggie sausages resting on some potato salad and coleslaw, her astonishment at these little gestures squeezing my heart. And I know I want to take care of her.

For a very long time.

As I sit there—these images playing through my mind—I keep coming back to the same question.

How can this be wrong?

"This is unchartered territory, Dad. It's never happened

before. There aren't any guidelines. So I have to go by instinct. And this feels right."

Dad slaps his palms on his knees, pushing himself up. "Then for the moment, we go with that."

And he heads in. Leaving me to do what you do on the thinking chair.

19

EDEN

I climb out of my mother's car, dragging my backpack from the passenger side. I lean against its white hood, looking at my watch. I'm not meant to meet Noah for over an hour. But my mother had me running out the door early.

Her behavior has been...unsettling. The 'how's school?' inquiries getting more frequent, and occurring outside of their usual restaurant meal times. I know what she's really asking is 'How's Noah?', then her frowning eyes not liking the standard response, 'Everything's fine'. She used to welcome my silence. Suggesting I look into work at the local vet center, then ringing up herself to enquire. And the most perplexing, commenting on my clothes the days I wear my standard outfits. On the handful of days that I venture to the right side of my wardrobe, to her purchases, not saying a word.

It was enough for me to suggest the next study session at Tara's. Kurt hadn't been home, but his hunting trophies were. Dead eyes looking out from mummified heads, displayed high up on walls. I had to contain my shudder.

Noah's hand had taken mine. "Kurt runs one of the most

successful hunting businesses in the state. He sees hunting as a natural extension of our predatory nature."

The Channon horde had also been there. Even Mr. Puddles had been hanging limply by a foot, drying after a romp in the washing machine, obviously still doubling as a hanky. We hadn't stayed for dinner. An extra three mouths to feed may have broken fragile Lara. So the time spent with Noah had been loud, chaperoned by multiple red heads, and brief. Entirely unsatisfactory, but at least away from my mother's censoring eyes.

Never before has my mother been this involved in my life. Definitely unsettling. And misplaced. Because it's too late to build bridges. The distance is too wide, the other side unreachable.

I've certainly not mentioned the acceptance letter from Wyoming State I intercepted in the mail yesterday. Telling Noah has my heart skipping a happy little beat though. The white envelope tucked in my backpack representing a college full of promising possibilities.

So I left early, not knowing when she would pop by home. Not wanting to explain I'm heading out to see Noah. So here I am, with time on my hands. Time that will pass too slowly, anticipation drawing out the minutes.

My eyes fall across the parking lot to the trail mouth that led me on that fated walk. It looks innocuous. Innocent. A trail like any other. Not somewhere I narrowly missed being attacked by three hunters. Not somewhere I was saved by a giant white wolf.

Not somewhere I learned a reality-shattering truth.

My mouth twitches, considering a smile. It's a little like Alice falling down her rabbit hole. But the world she returned to was normal. Not irrevocably changed. Even more fantastical than before.

Where the mundane has elevated to extraordinary. A world where, each day, Noah drops me off to class and, often as not, is waiting for me by my classroom door at the end. Of Noah holding my hand. Where he brings me lunch. Where being with him feels more right, more possible with each passing moment.

Of that soft caress across my cheek each time we say good-bye. I frown, hands clenching on the hood of the car. I desperately want to touch him back. For fingertips to explore those angled cheekbones. To feel the heat of his chest beneath my palm. For hands to begin conveying the depth of these feelings.

But something holds me back. For the first time I'm standing outside of my defenses. And I'm not sure I'm prepared. What does one pack for this sort of journey? Like uncharted waters, there's a bright horizon, a taste of what this place will be like. It feels exciting, full of nameless possibilities, so tempting. But there's also no guarantee you'll get there. And you can never be completely prepared for the risks and unknowns. Those risks and unknowns have deterred many a traveler.

I nibble my lower lip, resting more weight on the car. But when will Noah get tired of waiting? Frustrated with my fumbling slowness?

I look at my watch again. I don't want to spend an hour on this merry-go-round, so I decide to take a short walk. Turning my back on the trail-of-life-changing-moments, I head for an alternative route. One that has tourists milling about. A safe, populated stroll through the national park. A timbered sign is stamped with *Elkhorn Flats 1 Hour Return*. I can do that in forty five minutes.

Slinging my backpack on, I head over. The walk is easy, and I overtake numerous ambling families and a handful of snap-happy couples. Everyone is with someone. I smile, knowing soon that'll be me.

The trail is mostly flat, meandering through open, green pastures. Small creeks split and divide through the meadows, supplying water like veins and capillaries for the lush vegetation and animals. The songs of willow flycatchers and yellow warblers color the air.

I round a bend to find an ample lady rushing toward me, towing her son like a flapping Mr. Puddles, her eyes wide beneath a large perm, her mouth open above her dimpled chin.

"Bear! There's a bear just around the bend, where the trail ends."

I stop in my tracks. "Are you okay?"

She flutters a plump hand in front of her flushed face. "I think so. It's just such a shock to see such a big animal, you know?"

"I imagine it was."

"She had a cub. I'm going to head back, warn anyone else coming up." She tugs on her son and waddles off, a vigilante on a mission.

A bear, with a cub. Bears are known for the protectiveness of their young. And for their unpredictability. A dangerous situation that should clearly be avoided. I turn, because although I'd love to see one, I'd prefer to keep my limbs.

I've taken two steps down the path, following the wobbling crusader, when I pause. I don't know why. But I do. I have a feeling I'm heading the wrong way. Which doesn't make sense. Away from the bear and her cub is most definitely the right way.

A pained, high-pitched groan filters through the air, from the direction of the bears, making me frown, prompting me to turn around again. The next step, I start walking toward it. Heart beating painfully, mouth dry, I follow the anguished sound.

I round the bend and stop. Because a mother bear and her cub are indeed sitting in the balloon-shaped clearing that marks the turnaround point of the trail. The hunched back, silvery coat, and massive size tell me it's a grizzly bear. The biggest of the bears in the park. Even across the clearing, her massive size is overwhelming.

They both turn at my arrival. There, with the focus of four black eyes, my heart stops. Stutters, and struggles to start again. When it does find its rhythm, the thundering pace echoes in my ears.

What am I doing here?

The cub shakes his head, pawing at his muzzle. The mother bends down, nuzzling him. She does it again, and I realize she's nudging him. To do what? The cub groans again, then gets up. He takes a few steps away from his mother and looks back. She growls, head nodding. The cub faces me and starts walking forward.

She's sending him to me?

I take a step back. My heart thumps furiously, making my chest hurt. You don't mess with a grizzly bear's cub. Ever. And one is walking toward me.

The cub approaches cautiously; he's an older cub, his gangly body filled out for his first hibernation. Another step backwards and I'm not far from the bend. I'm ready to run, and there's certainly enough adrenalin pumping through my muscles to facilitate a frenzied escape.

Then I see the cut on the baby bear's face. A jagged gash runs down his snout, reaching from just below his eye down to his nose. And the closer he gets, the more infected it looks.

The cub stops a few feet in front of me. He stands, like he can't really believe his mother sent him to me either. He looks back at his mother. I look back at his mother. She stands on all fours, head up, sniffing the air. Not making a move toward him, not calling him back.

The cub and I stare at each other. He paws his muzzle again.

And I know what I need to do.

With careful, slow movements I remove my backpack. From the front pocket, I remove my first aid kit. Both bears watch me silently.

Hoping I've reached the right conclusion, I step forward, first aid kit in hand. Unconsciously, I start to hum. The bear cub sits back, and I step up beside him. His dark eyes watch me, his body tensing beneath shaggy fur.

I step to the side, just a couple of feet away, still humming. Mother bear remains still, her panting breaths moving her massive chest in and out. I take a closer look at the cut. Ragged skin has split open to show red, angry flesh below. The edges are raised and raw, slightly puckering the skin at the edge of his eye. A small amount of opaque liquid oozes from the bottom, running down to his lip.

"That looks sore, little man."

The bear cub lets out another high-pitched moan. "Can I try and fix it?" I glance at the mother, and she sits. I hope that means yes.

From my first aid kit, I remove the saline and some cotton gauze. The humming song becomes a little raspy, scratching past my dry throat. Very carefully, I start to dab at the cut. Thankfully, the not-so-little cub holds still throughout my ministrations, because I know I don't have much time. Slowly the dirt, crusted blood, and oozing infection washes away. My heartbeat begins slowing, becoming less thunderous in my ears.

In the clearing the mother bear begins to sway from side to side, and my pulse leaps in alarm, once again sounding out a frantic tempo. I've read countless pamphlets and books and warnings about bears. But my frazzled mind can't access one piece of information as to what the swaying means. Is she enjoying the tune? Or is she a testy mother at the end of her tether, doubting the reliability of the medical help?

I've finished cleaning the cut, meaning it's time for antiseptic, and they have yet to invent one that doesn't sting. But it's the best I can do considering he really needs antibiotics. If the infection were to reach his eye, it could leave him blind. And I doubt the longevity of a half-blind bear is high. I take out the ointment, squeezing some onto more gauze. Gently, gently I dab it onto the exposed flesh.

A mewling grizzle comes from the cub, and he pulls away, his paw coming up to swipe at his muzzle. I flinch as a sharp claw catches my skin, slicing a thin track down my forearm. A bright bead of blood springs along the line. Mother bear's head comes up, and she pushes up to stand on her hind legs. My wide eyes try to take in the size of this carnivore. She rumbles a question to her cub, nose sniffing the air. *Can she smell my blood?* I look to the cub, knowing he has the power to sign my death sentence.

The cub sits, offering up his nose. Relief washes through muscles that had been ready to run. Mama bear sits on her back haunches again, but alert eyes watch me carefully. This time the cub knows what's coming, and although he flinches, he doesn't make a sound. I gently and quickly disinfect the wound.

A final swipe and I'm done. I pick up the supplies and step back. "There you go, little man."

The cub remains where he is, his dark eyes staring at me. I take two more steps back. "Okay, you really need to go now, or your mama is going to get in an argument with a very big wolf."

Because there's no doubt in my mind that Noah is coming. I know that my pounding pulse, the fear flashing across my nerves work like a homing beacon. Bringing my wolf savior to my side.

And I don't want him to meet this fellow predator.

The mother grizzly stands on all fours, bellowing. She turns her shaggy body, heading toward the trees. The bear cub stands, and takes a few steps toward her. He turns back, letting out a sort of growling woof.

I hold my hand up in a wave. "Anytime, little guy."

He trots after his mother, their rhythmic sure-footed movements taking them toward the forest edge. Neither looks back as their stubby tailed rears disappear into the undergrowth.

I sit down on a rock to tend to my cut, legs a little wobbly, not wanting an infection myself. I haven't had a chance to wipe up the congealed blood when an intimidating white wolf pounds into the clearing on my left.

Just like before, he's massive, breathtaking, and angry. His broad head pivots from side to side, scanning the clearing. When he sees me sitting on the rock, wild blue eyes instantly register the cut on my arm. A roar accompanies two more arcing steps into the clearing. Eyes scan the flat, clear ground, the solitary bushes, the unbroken tree line. And register there is no foe.

It's then that I stand, one hand covering the scratch on my arm, and start to walk over.

"They're gone."

He turns to me, chest expanding on panting breaths, ears angled toward me. "I wasn't in danger." Well, I'm pretty sure I wasn't.

A few more steps and I'm almost in front of him. Blue eyes watch me.

"I was just a bit shocked by the bear." I don't elaborate on the grizzly part. "And the cub had a cut on his face."

Those wolf eyes widen. "Yes, I know. But it was infected, and really close to his eye."

The wolf sits, his back haunches hitting the ground with a thud. His head drops down between his shoulders, shaking from side to side. Relieved? Or exasperated.

I bring myself face to face with him. He raises his head, and we're eye to eye. Intense blue eyes, so familiar, stare from a white-furred face. Rimmed in black, they're mesmerizing. His snowy white fur, fine and soft around his muzzle, fans out as it frames his square head. Just like his eyes, two furry ears are trained directly ahead, on me. I wonder if all that fur is coarse, or as soft as it looks. And just like any other times I am near him, I want to touch.

Of its own volition, my hand comes up. I scan his face, asking permission. Not a muscle moves in that massive body. I cup my hand across his cheek, the heel of my palm resting beneath his jaw. Ridged bone beneath solid muscle rests in my hand. I feel the wolf's throat work as he swallows. My other hand comes up to join it, resting in mirror image on the other side.

Without conscious thought, they move backward, sinking into the thick mantle around his head. It's warm and soft, like a pillow that just begs you to rest your head on. My fingers spear into its heat, the delicious thick undercoat. My right hand comes forward to feather across his muzzle, where the short hair feels like velvet. I trace across its ridge line, up and around the blue eyes that haven't left my face. I'm touching Noah in wolf form, in all the ways I can't bring myself to do when he is human.

A soft hum rumbles deep in his chest. Do wolves purr?

I feel a tremor run down his muscled body, his head sinking as his legs bend. Oh no, he's changing back.

"Come on, we'd better get among the trees."

He nods, and we head to the tree line. Just like before, we've only taken a few steps into the protective canopy when his white body sinks to the ground.

And once again, morphs back into human form. The change is quicker this time, the evolution of wolf to man happening in a few painful seconds. Except this time I'm far more aware of that split second of glorious naked skin. My skin flushes, but I don't look away. In that brief moment, I see Noah's ridged chest, and the mark that adorns the upper part of its left side. Imprinted into defined pectorals, over his heart. It's the fluid outline of a wolf's head, arched up in howl.

Then Noah is lying before me, dressed, eyes closed.

I squat down, hand reaching out, when he sits up in a rush, eyes instantly locking onto mine. I fall back on my behind.

"You did what to a bear cub?" His voice is not quite a shout, but certainly not far off. "With the mother there!"

His legs push him upright, and he storms two paces to the left, before coming back, long fingers pushing those unruly locks back from furious eyes.

I stay seated amongst the pine needles. Noah has recovered much quicker this time around. And this time he's really mad.

"I..." I clear my throat. "He needed help."

"Do you know how dangerous that is? No wonder you were scared."

My shoulders drop. I was really scared, which is exactly why Noah is here. But the cub needed medical attention. "I'm sorry, Noah."

Noah's pacing brings him back to stand in front of me. His knees sink onto the padded ground. Blue eyes search mine. His hands come up to cup my cheeks, blazing their pale surface with heat.

"I was scared. Scared that I wouldn't get here in time."

It takes long moments for it to dawn on me. He was worried. A splitting grin arches across my face, pressing my cheeks farther into those hot palms.

Noah blinks. And blinks again. His breath comes out in a rush, its sweet scent caressing my nose. "You've got to stop doing that to me." And I know he's not talking about the bear.

I didn't think it was possible, but my smile widens.

Another gust brushes my face. And Noah is smiling back.

"You should have seen it, my knight in white-furred armor. But no one to pull limb from limb."

Noah's hands fall to hang between us. His head cocks to the side, eyes sliding to join it. "We don't hurt humans," he mumbles.

I giggle. "Could have fooled me."

He grins. "You give meaning to the term 'you bring out the animal in me'." Noah stands up, holding his hand out to me. "Come on, I've got something to show you."

We leave the trees, hand in hand, heading back to the trail. The walk out takes longer. Because we stop to look at a lanky moose grazing amongst willow thickets, to point out a lone western meadowlark sitting atop a fence post, to try and count a herd of pronghorn grazing in the distance. As we walk, our hands reflexively pull us closer together. Shoulders brush, hips sway in tandem, smiles simultaneously spark. Making this trail the trail-of-memorable-moments.

Back at the visitors' center, Noah heads for his car. "Leave yours here. We'll pick it up afterwards."

"We aren't walking?"

Noah opens my door for me. "Not here."

Confusion tangles my brow. "Then why did you ask to meet here?"

Noah waits until we're both in the car and heading for the highway before he answers. "Where we're going there's no meeting point."

With that cryptic remark, he heads west. Away from the reserve, his house, and the Inn. In the direction of Wilmot.

"We're picking up Tara?"

Noah's eyebrows wiggle, and he says nothing. From the corner of my eye, I catalogue his strong arms, long fingers wrapped around the steering wheel. The confident manner in which he drives. I breathe in the warmth that fills the car, the sandalwood that fills my lungs. I decide I'm content to drive for a while.

Without warning he turns right, onto a barely legible track that is rapidly swallowed by shrubbery. Noah doesn't even glance at the 'Private Property Trespassers Will Be Prosecuted' sign as it sails past. He slows the truck once we're amongst the greenery, and the track rapidly turns rough. For what seems like ages, we bump and thump through potholes and over mounds. Tall trees crowd the road, their branches occasionally brushing past my window. Where are we going?

We arrive at a small grassy area, a parking lot of sorts. We get out, and I see a trail heading into the undergrowth. I step toward it, assuming that's where we're heading. I've taken one step when Noah grabs my hand.

He smiles. "Decoy." He indicates toward a thicket on our right. I keep my face blank, although there's a strong urge to grimace. I don't relish the thought of trekking through the thick, prickly brush he just pointed at. I'm glad I wore long slacks.

We head to the thick greenery. Noah reaches out, and like he's done it countless times before, reaches in and pulls back a large branch. I gasp. He reveals a hidden track, lined with grass, bordered by trees.

"Ladies first." He gestures with a flourish.

I step through and Noah follows. He lets the branch fall back into place and we're instantly cut off from the outside world. And I'm cocooned in a wonderland with Noah. An Oscar-worthy grassy carpet stretches before us. Nature's kaleidoscope surrounds it, starting with the lime green of new growth, moving through jades, emeralds, and olives, finishing with the deep, almost blue-green of aged vegetation.

He takes my hand, and we walk, deeper into Mother Nature's bosom. We've only been walking for a few minutes when the trail ends, and opens out into a clearing—a beautiful, magical glade.

Towering pines frame lush grass awash in sunlight, surrounding it like soaring alpine guardians. The mountain range dominates the left, a snowcapped mammoth so close you could almost touch its ancient walls. Stands of rocks litter the border, placed so artfully, the landscapers at the Inn would be envious. This mystical place bears the passage of time proudly, in the giant trees, the massive mountain, and the weight of the ages that hangs profoundly in the air.

"This place is incredible." My tone is hushed, reverent.

"Every pack has a place, a place of meaning. This Glade is believed to be one of the first. It's been shared by the Phelans and the Channons for as long as anyone can remember."

I walk a few steps farther in, feeling like I'm walking into nature's cathedral.

"This is where we come to bond, to change."

Where Noah didn't.

"Come." He grasps my hand, and we cross the clearing, the grass soft and lush beneath my feet. I can feel his excitement, his anticipation pulsing through his palm. At the head of the Glade, is one of the rock stands. Bigger, more prominent, than the others. A large squarish rock juts through the soil, dotted with a few smaller at its side. A mother keeping her young close.

Noah kneels down in front of it. "Look," he whispers, brushing the long grass from the base of the rock. Two words breathe out on a prayer. "The Precepts."

There, hidden by Mother Nature, carvings have been etched into the rock. I kneel beside him, my fingers tracking the words, knowing countless others have done the same before me.

YOU SHALL NOT REVEAL THE BLOODLINE
YOU SHALL NOT BOND WITH THE OPPOSITE BLOODLINE
YOU SHALL NOT ATTACK ANOTHER BLOOD MEMBER
YOU SHALL OBEY THE ALPHA

"The Precepts are our law."

I frown; so many things making sense, so many not. "Bloodlines?"

"Humans and Weres"

I look at the carvings, my eyes tracing the first line. "What happens if you break them?"

"That's up to the Alpha." Noah shrugs. "Worst-case scenario, you're cast out of the pack."

I stare at the ancient code of honor. Wolves are pack animals; they have evolved to depend on their social hierarchy. Wolves in the wild that are cast out don't always survive.

I stand, taking a step away. What is Noah trying to tell me?

"What does it mean, Noah?"

He comes to stand in front of me, his sky-blue gaze trapping mine, taking my hands in his. "It means what we have is special and unique, Eden."

I want to believe him. So badly.

Noah steps in, so close I can feel his heat radiating down the length of my body. His head tips forward, those fascinating lips coming closer to mine. My pulse skips through my body, tripping out an excited, nervous rhythm. Yearning, longing, has my lips parting. Warm breath brushes across my cheeks, making me tingle. I stand still, not moving back, not moving forward.

I want this so bad it scares me.

A ping sounds through the clearing, and I feel something tug at my jacket. Noah lands against me, a groan rupturing from his lips. Arms that had been frozen by my side a second ago, come out to brace his weight. But I can't stop his downward trajectory, and his body crumples to the ground.

"Noah?" I look at my hand, feeling something warm and sticky. Horrified eyes see a smear of blood across my palm. "Noah!"

Noah groans, rolling onto his back, both hands on his left side.

"What just happened?"

"I don't know." Noah's voice is rough, low. He brings his head up so he can look down, keeping his torso still. Two hands pull away to show crimson streaks across his fingers.

I fall to my knees beside him, mouth open, but no words coming out.

Noah's head falls back with a soft thud, eyes closing. "I think I may have just been shot."

"Shot?"

My eyes dart around the small clearing, scanning for the threat, thinking of the hunters. But there are only two people here. One lying still on the ground, blood pooling in his palms. The other equally unmoving, struggling to process what just happened. As the blood continues to pool.

"Eden?"

That single word spurs me into action. I press my hand onto his, and Noah groans an objection.

"We have to stop the bleeding," I explain. "Keep up the pressure."

I sling off my backpack, once again retrieving my first aid kit. I pull out scissors and more gauze. Kneeling beside him, Noah watches me silently as I cut away his shirt. I know I need to see the wound, but I'm scared of what I might find.

Carefully, carefully, I peel back the pieces of shirt, slowly lifting Noah's hands. Beneath is a long diagonal gash and ragged edges of skin softly oozing bright red blood, creating crimson rivulets trickling down his ribs.

My breath gusts past tense lips. "It looks like it just grazed you."

"Just?" Noah echoes.

The tightness between my shoulders eases a little. This I

know how to deal with. I place several nonstick gauzes over the wound in a neat row, and keep up the pressure. The blood eventually stops seeping out from beneath the no-longer hospital white patches. Then I get out a broad bandage. And a second.

"What else have you got in there? A gurney?"

The well-stocked kit sits by my side. "Duct tape."

"Duct tape?"

"Keeps the patients quiet."

Noah goes quiet, a light grumble rumbling through his chest. I begin wrapping the bandage around his torso. I lean in, passing the bandage from one hand to the other, my nose inches from his chest. Breathing in his warmth. Sandalwood tainted with the coppery tang of blood tingles my senses. I hear an intake of breath, and realize I've paused.

I bring the bandage around, resuming the wrapping, reminding myself I'm tending to an injured Noah. "Sorry."

"You didn't hurt me."

The soft statement only heightens my awareness. But I keep my eyes at chest level. Now is not the time to see if I have the courage to touch him, despite the expanse of naked chest before me. Despite the overwhelming desire to trace the wolf tattoo that's right before my eyes. And if those eyes are doing what I think they are doing, I suspect my crumbling caution may finally collapse.

So I keep up an efficient rhythm. Across the chest, around the side, I pass the bandage, back to the front. I don't pause. I don't stray. My patient remains still, taking shallow but even breaths.

In a few short minutes, I'm done. I sit back, eyeing the evenly spaced bands, the skin above and below, assessing I haven't wound too tightly.

Noah's chin sucks in as he looks down at my handiwork.

"Should I be concerned that you've obviously bandaged guys who have been shot before?"

"Of course I haven't."

"Well, you've done a pretty professional job here."

"I worked at a vet center back in Boston." I smile a little. "I just pretended you were a Great Dane."

Noah snorts, then grimaces when the motion hurts.

"Come on, we need to get you to a hospital."

"Home actually."

"What? Noah, that cut is going to need stitches."

Noah pushes himself up, his face contorting with the effort. I rush forward to help him, but he's upright before I get a chance. Shallow breaths move the fabric lines in and out.

"We don't go to..." Noah pauses, his hand at his side. "... hospitals unless we're at death's door. Too hard to explain the high body temps and rapid healing."

"But—"

"Dad has some paramedic training."

I huff. "Fine. Come on, let's get you home."

I slip under Noah's good side, and look up to see him gazing down, a single brow arched. "I don't want you opening up that cut again."

"I'm not complaining."

We slowly waddle back to the parking lot, although I seem to be bearing very little of his weight. Nonetheless, he keeps his arm around me as we cover the short distance back through the green tunnel. At the car I help Noah up into the passenger side, and he winces as he digs into his pocket for his keys.

The drive out is slow as I try to avoid the worst of the potholes, but the slow-moving truck does little to level out the deep ruts. Beside me Noah doesn't say a word, his lips in a firm line, making the edges a little white. Small spots of red dot across his bandage. I check him regularly, keeping an eye for signs of shock: cool and clammy skin, rapid and shallow breathing, and loss of consciousness.

I pull into the Phelan driveway, slowing to a gradual stop. I slip under Noah's arm again as we walk to the veranda. This time he leans his weight against me, and I have to brace myself as solid muscles bear their weight down.

We angle through the front door, where Beth is in the lounge room. "Ah, you're home." Her smile drops as she takes in Noah's bare chest, and the line of spotted red. "What happened?"

"A bullet," Noah says in a strained voice.

"Adam!"

Adam rushes in; he hasn't missed the urgency in her tone. "Beth?"

Blue eyes scan Noah leaning against me. He strides forward, relieving me of Noah's weight.

"Let's bring him into the kitchen."

I stand back as Adam, stooped below his son's arm, directs him to a kitchen chair. From a cupboard above the bench he pulls out a first aid kit. He opens it on the table, trays coming up to stack in diagonal shelves. It makes mine look like a My Little Nurse toy.

Noah's eyes close. "You're going to need a lot of band aids."

Adam is carefully unwrapping the bandage, the red spots getting progressively bigger. "What happened?" he asks past tight lips.

"We were in the Glade." Noah looks at me, that moment passing between us. "And the next second, I was down like a sack of Precept rocks."

Adam has unwrapped the bandages and my row of blood-soaked gauze march across Noah's side and up his chest. The blood has dried in places, sticking them to his skin. Adam pulls out some saline, flushing the crusted pieces of material off.

"Nice work, Eden."

I shift on my feet. "Thanks."

"It's not deep, just long." Adam wipes some alcohol gauze across the cut. Noah's breath sucks through his teeth, the muscles of his chest tightening. I lock my legs into place, wanting to go to him.

"Just a few more, son." I can see Noah's jaw clench as his father finishes cleaning the wound.

Beth comes over to stand behind Noah, her hands on his shoulders. Worry lines are etched across her brow, fanning from her eyes, tightening her mouth. "How could this happen, Adam?"

Adam pulls out a stack of butterfly strips and fresh bandages from the kit. "The Glade isn't too far from the reserve. Hunters ignoring the border, a ricochet bullet." He squints as he pinches the pieces of torn flesh, then tapes them together. "It's possible, but pretty unlucky."

Noah rests a weary head against his mother's arm. "Tell me about it."

With practiced speed, Adam wraps up Noah's chest. "There, all done. It should heal in a few days. But you'll have a pretty good scar."

Noah grins. "Chicks dig scars."

I roll my eyes, shaking my head. Only Noah could grin after a lengthy cut has been cleaned and bandaged.

Adam glances pointedly at Noah. "Bed and rest, young man."

Beth starts collecting the soiled bandages. "I'll put these in the bin."

"I'll go wash up."

Adam and Beth disappear, neither choosing to do their tasks in the kitchen.

I look at Noah, at his mummy-wrapped chest. I want to be near him.

"Come here."

I move forward, taking the seat beside him. He grasps my hand in his.

"I'd say thanks, but you'd probably—"

"Poke you in the ribs. The sore side."

A rueful smile tips up his lips. "In that case, can I have your number?

"My number?"

"Yeah. Mom won't be letting me go to school tomorrow."

"Oh." School without Noah. "Sure."

Noah looks around for something to write with. He rustles through his father's first aid kit, finding a marker. I rattle off the first few digits, and my eyebrows raise when I see where he's writing. Black numbers scrawl across his dad's handiwork. I finish the last few, and there's my number, across Noah's bandages. Across his chest.

"I'd better get going. You need to rest."

Noah scrunches up his nose, but doesn't object.

I start to rise, but Noah's hand tugs me down. I stay in my seat, eyes turning to Noah. And I'm instantly trapped. Cerulean intensity wraps around me. His hand comes up to graze my cheek. Just like he always does when we part. This time I tilt into his fingertips, moving my head softly from side to side, absorbing more of the heat, our eyes locked the whole time.

"I guess I'm the chauffeur?" Mitch is standing in the doorway, the car keys bouncing up and down in his hand. He spends extra seconds scanning Noah's face. Noah uses the time to give him a your-timing-is-impeccable look, and Mitch's shoulders relax.

Oh, yes. I don't have a car. I stand, the room feeling cool against my cheek. "If you don't mind?"

"No probs. It's about time I introduced you to the Phelan car rule."

A groan filters up from the chair beside me. "Oh no."

"Oh yes."

I don't think I like the glint in Mitch's eye.

Once in the car Mitch fiddles with some CDs. "So, a ricochet bullet, huh?"

"Yeah."

"You didn't see anything?"

"No." My eyes had been totally consumed by one thing. "I wish I could tell you more."

"That's okay, it was worth a try. It was just unlucky." I wonder if he realizes he just echoed his father.

The drive to the reserve parking lot is blissfully short. Mitch's music feels like it has irreversibly damaged my eardrums. And he didn't even have it up loud. As we arrive, he leans forward, wrists resting on the steering wheel.

"Eden." My hand pauses on the door handle. *Please don't let him thank me.* "Although we live alongside humans, they've never been someone we can trust. Certainly not someone we could hold a powerful connection with."

"Oh." I blush, remembering Mitch's behavior in Noah's room that day. I feel like such a fool.

"Like you and Noah do." He smiles, his handsome face softening. "You've certainly broadened my horizons."

My second 'oh' is completely different. It's softer, higher, more drawn out. Still accompanied by a blush.

His smile turns a little mischievous. "Anyway, I'm glad you liked my music."

I smile too, opening my door. "Well, then we're even. Your music has certainly been an educational experience."

Mitch waits until I'm in my car and I follow him out to the highway. I flash my lights when we eventually go our separate ways.

I'm almost home when my phone bings. I smile, knowing who it is.

Thanks.

The smile vanishes. Sitting in the driveway I type a response.

Grrrr.

In a split second I have my reply.

That's my line.

And my smile is born again.

20

NOAH

S tuck at home.

Tara and Eden are studying at hers, and I'm stuck at home.

Stupid cut.

Stupid inflated Werewolf body temperature that means I can't go to hospital and get stitches.

Stupid rapid Were healing that isn't healing fast enough.

I tried everything to convince Mom. Reasoning had proved fruitless. Begging and pleading had been met with humor. Pointing out I was the future Alpha of the pack had been met with an unimpressed eyebrow raise. And a query about whether I wanted to stomp my foot.

I was very, very tempted.

So here I am, stuck at home. Pretending to study.

I look at the stack of textbooks beside me on the bed. At my brother on the other side of them. He's watching the screen of his laptop with keen intensity, headphones in. I know he's watching something on YouTube. As if to confirm my hunch, Mitch chuckles, his shoulders shaking the bed.

Just because he managed to get an apprenticeship yesterday, with the local builder, Sam, who runs a well-respected company. Mitch was pretty nervous about approaching him, then acted like the day he was twelve and got his first power tool when Sam agreed to take him on. When he told us, I rejoiced alongside Mom and Dad. I wince just thinking about the back-thumping hug I had given him, completely forgetting about the six-inch gash down my side. My mother had noticed, just giving her more ammo for the you-aren't-going argument.

Now I'm not feeling so charitable. Because unlike him, I really do need to study.

Without Eden. I smile my own smile. The boredom only broken by our texts.

My mom just made me a sandwich, egg and lettuce.

Sounds harmless enough.

The egg objected to being boiled so long. It's retaliating.

Well, you should see Mitch's face. He just bit into a cafeteria rissole.

I'd grimaced, having been there myself, but not feeling much sympathy. *Is his lunch beating him up from the inside?*

He said don't bust a butterfly clip.

Tell him not to worry—I know an excellent nurse.

Silence, then another text. This one from Mitch.

Eden's blushing again.

Then yesterday.

Missing you.

I'm in chem!

I'm in bed. Betcha this is more boring.

Doubt it. I'm so bored, I could eat my textbook. The one I spilled copper sulphate on.

I'm so bored I could have a snoring contest with Stash.

I'm so bored I could hang out with my mom.

Ok. You win.

A slight pause, and I think she's done. Before my favorite one lights up the screen.

Missing you too.

At least I got to go to school today, with a note to get out of gym. Today I'd brought Eden a haloumi salad. She continues to look surprised, and delighted. I pointed out you learn to cook young in my mother's household. She'd exchanged it for some of Stan's awesome cookies. One of the many rhythms we've established. The smiles, the looks. The trading of food.

A knock sounds downstairs, and my father's heavy footsteps can be heard heading to the front door. Kurt Channon's voice carries up the stairs. Mitch and I look at each other. What's he doing here?

Mitch scrambles off the bed, while I gingerly throw my legs over and stand. As we head downstairs, we see Kurt talking to my parents in the lounge.

"What a wonderful surprise, Kurt. Would you like something to drink?"

"No, thank you, Beth. We don't plan on staying long."

We? Then I see Tara behind his wide form. Mitch has also seen her, judging by the way his face lights up. But I thought she was studying at Eden's?

"Come in then. Make yourself comfortable."

Mitch steps toward her, then stops. Kurt has stepped to the side as he heads for a lounge chair, and Tara's tear-streaked face comes into view. Mitch resumes his movement toward her but Tara shakes her head, eyes widening. He steps back, a frown on his face.

Kurt takes the two-seater across from my parents, Tara sitting beside him, her hunched form dwarfed by her father. That leaves Mitch and me to drag over two dining chairs. Mitch places his near Tara, but not too close. She doesn't look at either of us.

What is going on?

My father is thinking along the same lines. "How can we help you, Kurt?"

Kurt straightens in his seat. "Adam, our families have been friends and neighbors for generations. As Alphas we've always recognized the importance of maintaining our alliance."

"Indeed, valued friends and allies."

"As our packs have grown in numbers and strength, we've become aware that it would be advantageous for a match to be made between our packs."

My father frowns. Where is Kurt going with this?

"When your family's...development didn't go according to plan, the Channons were there to support you."

"Yes, you were."

"And when Tara and Mitch's friendship developed, I was happy to support your enthusiasm."

Dad strokes his chin. "My understanding is that both families were happy with the match."

Kurt crosses his arms, not bothering to acknowledge my father's statement. "But now Mitch will no longer be Alpha."

"I'm not sure why that's an issue, Kurt."

Kurt stands, his brows sinking low. "Tara will not bond with a Beta."

"Noah will take his rightful place as the Alpha heir, Kurt." From the corner of my eye, I see Tara shrink in her chair.

"As he should." Kurt fills his chest, expanding himself in the room. "And for this reason, Noah will be the one to bond with Tara."

Mitch shoots to his feet. "No!" Echoing the word screaming through my mind.

Kurt rounds on him. "I'd be mindful of who you are speaking to, beta." He spits the last word out.

"But Tara and I are to bond at the end of the year!"

Kurt turns back to my father. "It is the firstborns that will bond."

"What does it matter, Kurt? If Tara bonds with Mitch, the packs will have their alliance." This comes from Mom, her tone placating, the voice of reason.

Kurt shakes his head. "It's my duty to safeguard Tara's birthright."

Dad remains in his seat, and Mom grasps his hand.

"I feel it's important that we settle this quickly. On the next full moon."

Bond with Tara? At the next full moon? He can't be serious.

I look to Tara, seeing the misery etched in her stooped shoulders, raw eyes, wet cheeks. What about his daughter's heart?

I break my silence. "This isn't right, Kurt." It's the first time I've used his Christian name. And I do it deliberately.

He tilts his head, hazel eyes hard. "For you? Or for your pack?"

"Tara is your pack."

Kurt's eyes narrow; his nostrils flare.

My father stands, his big body cleaving through the tension. "I appreciate your perspective, Kurt." Kurt's shoulders relax a little. "You have given us a lot to think about."

Kurt heads for the door, the silent Tara by his side. "I know you'll make the right decision, Adam."

We all stand and watch as Dad shakes Kurt's hand as he leaves. Surely he can't agree with him.

"Surely you can't agree with him." The words burst from Mitch like a detonating explosive.

"It's not that simple, Mitch."

Mitch glares at my father, chest heaving. My father holds Mitch's look, as solid and steady as Grandpa Douglas in the midst of a hurricane. Mitch storms up the stairs, the slamming door echoing his rage throughout the house.

Dad flinches.

And I know.

I know that Dad's stooped shoulders hold a great weight. The weight of his sons' hearts. In hands that have always protected them. And the weight of his pack. In his obligation to our age-old neighbors.

And I know he's considering Kurt's request. His demand to uphold Tara's birthright, our pack's alliance.

I sit, the weight of its implications collapsing my legs beneath me, my head sinking into my hands.

Eden.

My heart constricts so much it hurts.

One question slams through my mind.

What have I done?

21

EDEN

I pause, my hand frozen in midair. Stomping echoes from the upstairs area of the Phelan house, reverberating footsteps setting up a heavy rhythm.

Maybe now's not a good time. The white chocolate cheesecake in my other hand wobbles uncertainly. When Tara cancelled our study session, I thought I'd surprise Noah. With midterms coming up, I thought we could review the sheet Mr. Dougherty gave us today.

A cool breeze ruffles my hair, making me shiver.

A dark, heavy mass has wormed deep in my belly, different from my usual anxiety. Now I'm being silly. I've spent so much time and energy trying to overcome the useless emotion— venturing out so much further and discovering all the wonderful things outside its walls.

Like Noah. And his warm glances. Heated touches. His enduring patience.

My hand comes up, rapping on the door.

It opens much quicker than I expected, like there was someone waiting on the other side. Noah stands in the doorway.

"Wow, you even know when I'm coming?" I joke. But the

smile falls from my lips when I see his expression: his face pale, lips faded, his blue eyes missing their usual light.

"What's wrong? Has your cut reopened?"

Noah shakes his head. "Come outside." He steps out, closing off the warmth and light that had been spilling out.

I look down at the cheesecake in my hand, but its smooth surface has no answers. I put it on the wooden seat, along with my backpack full of school books.

Noah heads to Grandfather Douglas, his hands shoved deep in his pockets.

The dark, heavy mass grows, snaking through my insides. I struggle to identify it, and where it's coming from. All I know is its presence, along with Noah's behavior, is deeply unsettling.

Underneath the tree that has witnessed countless moments, Noah turns to me. The afternoon light caresses his unsmiling face.

"What's going on, Noah?"

He pulls his hands out of his pockets. Then shoves them back in, his shoulders hunching. I've never seen Noah speechless before.

And I know it's bad. Really bad.

"Tell me." Although the statement is a direction, it comes out in a whisper.

Noah sucks in a deep breath. "Kurt just left."

I wait, knowing there's a punch line.

"He's demanded that Tara bond with the Alpha heir, as is her firstborn birthright."

And it slams into me with the force of a well-aimed wrecking ball.

I take a step back. "What?"

"He wants me to bond with Tara. To maintain the alliance between the packs."

"But..." All of a sudden I'm cold, bone chilling, achingly cold.

My arms wrap around me as I scramble for refuge, protection.

And find nothing.

I'm the one person you can trust to keep you safe.

The words, once said beneath a different canopy, whisper through the branches above us. Through the space between us. Over my chilled skin.

Noah takes a step toward me, hand stretched out. Eyes pleading. I take a step back, both hands coming up. "Please... don't."

I don't want to feel his heat. His touch. His warmth and heat against this chilling cold would be overwhelming. Much too painful.

Belatedly, I recognize the feelings that had accompanied me to this tree, realizing they were not my own. Grief. Sorrow. Regret. They multiply as they find their mates within me, cold, jagged weights that are freezing me from the inside out.

"I won't do it, Eden. It's not right."

Fragments of thought are falling through my mind. Tara. Mitch. Kurt. Adam. My eyes scan the ground, like the answers are amongst the pine needles before me.

They come up to meet his. Shocked green locks with agonized blue. "You may not have a choice."

Noah's lips part, but no sound escapes into the chilled air.

I take another stiff step backward. "I have to go."

"Eden..."

My name on his lips hurts. I have to get out of here. Before the tears start. Before I shatter along with everything else.

"There's nothing more to say." I continue to back away. *We never stood a chance.* A part of me always knew. I'm still not ready for the hail of pain lancing through me, making my eyes sting.

Because Camelot has been razed to the ground. All that

surrounds me is rubble, debris, and crushed dreams. I'm alone and in the open. Exposed and defenseless.

"Please, talk to me. We can't just walk away."

"I have to go." Because I'm too late. One betraying tear slices down my cheek, the pain overflowing. I brush it away.

"Eden." Noah's voice is tortured, choked.

I turn and run.

In the car, I reverse blindly, then head down the drive. I don't look in the rear vision mirror. The parting image of Noah, standing beneath the Douglas-fir, shoulders low, eyes haunted, is more than I can handle right now.

And the tears begin. Once the dam has broken, it's like a fury of pain has been unleashed. They flow down my cheeks, down my jaw, down my neck. Because these aren't little trickling streams that dry out shortly after their birth. These are gushing rivers of anguish that flow down my face, pooling in my neck.

They blur the road in front of me like torrential rain on a windowpane, making the world disfigured and twisted. I swipe at them and they soak my hands, making the steering wheel slick. Although I desperately want to get back, I slow down. The drive home takes a lifetime.

I pull into our driveway and head inside. Caesar greets me at the door, leaping and barking. I lean down to pat him and he's instantly quiet, sensing the change. He knows the drill. We go straight to my room, where I pull back the cover and crawl into bed. Caesar stretches his big, warm body next to mine. I curl up and bury my face in the brown fur of his neck. And cry.

Because it's over.

Although Caesar has been here before, this time is different. The tears come and come and come, as if they are surging up from a deep, bottomless ocean. And I'm drowning in their salted sorrow. Drowning, sinking, suffocating...

I don't know how much time has passed when my door opens. "I said, it's time to head to dinner."

My mother takes in my fetal form and the shuddering shoulders. "Oh, it's happened."

She comes into the room, and sits on the end of my bed. I stay, wrapped in misery, my face buried in Caesar.

Her voice, softer than I have ever heard it, flutters between us. "I know it hurts. But sooner is better than later."

Cold comfort. But I don't mind that she's here. Hers is the one comfort that I can handle right now.

She sighs, patting the comforter by my feet. "You'll need some time. I'll phone the school, say you won't be in tomorrow." Present, but not touching.

"Good boy, Caesar." And she leaves, closing the door behind her.

Short lived.

Darkness envelops me, but gives me no peace. I curl farther into my bed, but I can't get warm. Bitter, brittle words repeat in my head. Counting the passage of time.

It's over. *It's over.*

It's. Over.

Each painful shard accumulates in my body. I worry if I move I'll shatter.

So I don't move, possibly for hours. Maybe days.

Caesar's whining seeps through the wall of pain. Puffy raw eyes open to look into pleading brown eyes. He paws at the comforter. "I'm sorry, boy. I haven't taken you out."

Achy legs hit the floor; aged arms push myself up. I drag myself across the lounge room. I open the back door, and Caesar rushes out the minute it's wide enough to fit through.

For the few minutes it takes Caesar to disappear into the darkness, I don't feel the cold. The numbing, frigid weight within me is far more arctic. I stand frozen in the doorway, staring into the darkness.

Caesar comes up to me, whining. "I know. We need to go inside."

I close the door on the ghostly night, and head back through the lounge room. There I see what I missed on my way through.

My mother is curled on the lounge. The one where Noah and I sat. Her head rests on the arm, asleep. A bottle of wine stands on the coffee table, an empty glass beside it. I frown. She finished the bottle?

I walk over, and notice her tablet on her lap. My mother's face is completely relaxed, mouth parted. The dark scent of fermented grapes stings my nose. I pick up the tablet, intending on placing it on the coffee table when my thumb accidentally brushes the screen.

A document brightens the screen, and I scan it, wondering if it's an annual report or the latest marketing trends.

His hand curved around the nape of her neck, his eyes dark and hot.

"Always and forever, baby."

What the—?

My mother is reading a book. Not a cold, calculating business document, but a piece of fiction. Romantic fiction.

I tap on the screen and rows of covers assemble in a two-dimensional grid. All dominated by feminine hands caressing rippling tattoos, flowing hair framing sultry eyes, parted mouths touching ridged chests. I scroll through flowing titles including words like destiny and always and yours.

Shock has me sitting on the coffee table, head alternating between the unbelievable tablet and my mother's sleeping form. Every one of these books is known for one thing.

Happily ever after.

Why would she read these?

I don't have the energy to untangle the mystery, so I sit the tablet beside me, cover open, like it's just been placed there. I grab the throw that lies diagonally and artfully along the lounge and carefully tuck it around her. I tiptoe, Caesar at my side, back to my room.

As my door shuts, it hits me again.

It's over.

I double over, the next torrent running down my cheeks. Will they ever end?

I climb back into bed to find my pillow saturated and cold. I drop it onto the floor, pulling the spare over. Gritty eyes close, and tears fall to wet the next one.

I lie there, bleak and sobbing, hoping sleep will claim me.

22

NOAH

I pull into the school parking lot. Once again, Eden's car is nowhere to be seen.

"She'll be back," Mitch says besides me.

I sigh. Her backpack, her books within, rests on the back seat.

"Like Tara?"

Mitch pushes his palms into his eyes. "Like Tara."

We head into the building. Despite our looks being as similar as any two siblings, we wear matching twin masks. Chatting to friends, smiling, and high fiving. Like we are happy, average teenagers.

I'm at my locker when Bianca comes up. She flashes a smile, brushing her hair forward to rest on her shoulder.

"Hi, Noah."

I pretend to be looking for something in the depths of my locker. "Hey, Bianca."

She asks the question no one else has asked. "No Eden?"

"No Eden." It feels like my chest has just collapsed.

Her hand comes to rest on my arm; it feels cold. "That's too bad."

I look down at it. Bianca's smile falters, and her hand slips away. Down my arm. "I've got to get to class."

"We're heading in the same direction. I'll come with you."

"Oh." My heavy head struggles to deal with this obstacle, like a drunk guy trying to do hurdles. "I have to see Mitch about something first."

Bianca flashes another bright smile. "Okay. We should catch up sometime."

The ludicrousness of that suggestion almost makes me smile. I'm far from interested. Or apparently single. But I don't. Because the next thing I'd do is punch my locker door. So I mumble something about focusing on exams, and head down the hall.

The day passes as it did yesterday. Classes, recess, classes, lunch. No Eden. No Tara.

Although Tara is actually at school. She just spends all her time somewhere else, probably the art room. I'm almost glad. It would be too hard to disguise the pain; the mask would shatter. Besides, what do you say to the girl who is so many things? Your childhood friend. Your twin's love. Apparently your future bond mate.

Biology—last period. The class I enjoyed the most has become the one I dread the most. I'm back at my previous bench, the back bench empty. I'm once again met with Jordan's raised eyebrows, and Darlene's frown. Luckily neither asks the question, because I don't have any answers.

I enter the classroom, walking down the aisle between the rows of benches. And stop.

Eden is sitting at her back bench. But this time in the aisle seat, her books on the bench beside the window, very clearly marking it as not available. My eyes devour her—her head down in her text, mahogany hair falling over her cheeks. Those amazing green eyes tucked from sight. There's a tenseness to her curled shoulders that tells me she knows I'm here. Telling me that despite the time apart, the insurmountable obstacles, the connection hasn't faltered.

That kinda sucks.

"Hey, Noah."

Jordan has his fist up for our standard greeting. I thump the curled hand, sliding into my seat. It takes a herculean effort to keep up the mask, to not storm down that aisle.

And do what? Nothing has changed.

"Hey, Jordz. What's up?"

"Global temperatures," he quips.

Darlene rolls her eyes. "You're a comedian, Jordan."

Jordan shrugs. "It seemed fitting. Biology and all."

Mr. Dougherty stands, slowly straightening; I can see his mind consciously clicking each vertebra into place.

Just as Dale saunters into the room.

"Mr. D." He salutes old Dougherty as he strolls to the seat beside me.

"Mr. Gordon." Dougherty's eyes track the progress of the faded black. He stares at the beanie, and Dale pulls it off. He knows which battles are worth engaging in.

"Exam season is fast approaching. Tests that can decide the direction of the next few years of your life."

No pressure.

"It is for this reason that we will prepare for them. And prepare for them well. Please open your textbooks to chapter three."

Right back to the basics.

Mr. Dougherty starts reading and quizzing. But how do you concentrate when the one person you hurt the most is sitting just a few rows behind you?

"Mr. Gordon. Can you tell me what factors determine the abundance of a species?"

"Good question, Mr. D." Dale twirls his pen in his hand. "I'm guessing it depends on what's around. Is there somewhere to hang? Is there anywhere to chow down?" Dale waggles his brows. "Are there any babes?"

Dougherty cocks a grey brow. "Thank you, Mr. Gordon." He heads to the back of the room; I doubt he'll be coming up the front for a while.

"Ms. St. James. How would you sample a species abundance?"

Eden's voice carries across the room, spearing into my heart. I turn. "Total counts, sample counts, indirect counts, or mark and recapture."

Her eyes don't waver from Dougherty. "Exactly, Ms. St. James."

Then return to her book.

Dougherty's voice rambling through the text fades into the background. Eden's bent head is all that I see.

"You should talk to her, dude."

Dale's beanie is back on his head, low over smiling eyes. And say what? "It's not that simple."

"It's gotta be a start."

I look back. At the head pointedly ignoring me. Would it?

The rest of the class passes with me trying to answer that question. And coming up with zilch.

The bell goes and the room begins to empty. I remain where I am. As does Eden.

She's waiting for everyone to leave. Including me.

But my butt stays in my seat.

Dougherty looks at me, and back at Eden, wise grey eyes assessing the tension in the room. Then he stands, collects his books, and leaves. It's the fastest I've ever seen him move.

I walk down, passing each bench. Shoes crossing the lino floor.

And stop before her bench. Our bench.

"Eden." Her downcast eyes close for a brief second. Before continuing to stare at her book.

Time stretches between us. I don't think either of us knows what we are waiting for.

"I was just leaving."

But I don't want her to. "I have your bag in my car."

Her lip slips beneath her teeth, considering. I know she needs those books. "Okay."

She stands, and waits. I step to the side, knowing she'll have to go past me.

Eden pauses. Then braces her shoulders, tucking her head in, like she's about to run a gauntlet. She rushes past, and the wildflower scent that never quite left my lungs, infiltrates again. My chest expands as I suck it in, recharging. My mark heating.

She doesn't look back as she heads out of the lab. I follow her tense back, looking at the dark hair in its knot between taut shoulder blades. So many things I never got to find out.

I feel the distance between us in the walk to the car. Side by side, but not touching. I shove my hands in my pockets. They have a will of their own around this girl. And I instinctively know touching Eden will cause her more pain.

At my car I reach in and grab her bag, holding it out. Eyes locked on the bag, her hand extends and grabs it, her fingers never coming anywhere near mine. She brings it to her chest, and begins to turn away.

"Eden." She stills, arms wrapped around her bag.

"I never knew..." I try again. "It seemed so..." My shoulders slump. "I'm sorry."

Her eyes finally come up to meet mine. Their green depths are shadowed, haunted, ghostly. Tinted with pain. "I know."

And she turns, gets in her car, and leaves.

I lean against the truck, shoulders curling around my chest. I may as well have booked myself into a medieval torture chamber. It would have been less painful.

Mitch throws his bag on the back seat. "It went that well, huh?"

"Yep."

We climb in, and Mitch drives us home. In silence.

Once inside I head to the kitchen. My mom is stirring a stew over the stove. The whole room smells of oven cleaner.

"Keep it down, guys. Your father just got home from a long shift."

I open the fridge, only to have the cheesecake's round face look up at me, still whole. I'm not sure what it represents, but no one has touched it. I grab a juice and head upstairs. Mitch is already in his room, door shut; I'd say headphones are pumping screeching bass through his eardrums.

I pick up my guitar, plucking a few random chords. A tune begins to form. *Her Diamonds*. A fitting choice. I hear Rob Thomas's rich voice match my slow strumming.

Every line pierces me. The lyrics going straight to the core.

Because there is something harder than living with your own pain.

And that's seeing hers.

DARKNESS IS FALLING when the downstairs phone rings.

Mom rushes to answer it before it wakes Dad. "Hello? Oh, hi, Riley." There's a pause as she listens. "It can't wait?" Her sigh brushes over the receiver. "Okay, I'll get him."

Heavy footsteps shuffle to the phone. "Ah-ha, I see. I'll be there shortly." I don't need Were senses to hear the weariness in Dad's tone.

What would have him out of bed already?

"Noah. Front and center."

I head down the stairs, curious. "Yeah?"

Dad is pulling on a shirt, getting his keys. "Alpha duty."

"I'm coming?" Dad has never taken me. I was supposed to after I turned sixteen. But then...

"Yep. Down to Riley's. Let's go."

Mitch is standing on the stairs, also curious about the change in routine. At the door Dad turns back to him. "We'll be back shortly. Don't go anywhere."

Dad is yawning and rubbing his eyes as we drive into town. I'd been awake when the phone rang before the sun was up and heard Dad tell Stash to shush as he barked excitedly. Callouts are fun for him. For my father they are a duty and a responsibility. Undertaken with pride and integrity. And a woofing sidekick.

The Alpha callouts he has done on his own.

Until now.

"What's up at Riley's?"

"A couple of guys getting a little testy."

"Phelans?"

"One of them is."

Meaning the other is a Channon.

Streetlights illuminate the way through town. Riley's is on the outskirts at the west end, strategically placed to service the residents of Jacksonville, and the visitors from nearby Wilmot. We drive through the suburbs, avoiding the tourist-lit main drag. Quiet houses watch us from residential streets. Normal people inside, living normal lives. As we hit the edge of town, the houses become browner, the gardens barer. And Riley's comes into view.

Sitting in the middle of an asphalt parking lot, the constant pine trees not far behind, is your standard-looking bar. Awnings over large square windows, potted plants functioning as glorified ashtrays, a neon Riley's flashing across the top.

Although not even Riley himself knows that it's a frequent for Weres.

Dad heads inside, only to come out a few moments later.

"Riley said they decided to take it outside."

We head around the corner of the building, where two guys are circling, angry scowls matching their barely human growling, not far from the trees. The blond guy I recognize as Jared, a Phelan relative. His opponent is a brown-haired guy. A Channon.

From what I can see, all that's been thrown so far are words. But hands are fisted, muscles coiled. The smell of alcohol hits my nostrils, and another unique fragrance. One that can't be smelled by a human—the shimmery scent that happens just before or after a change, slightly metallic, a little mystic, with a slight taint of canine.

"That's enough!" My father's voice cracks like thunder, jolting both men.

Jared stops, his hands instantly unclenching. Both men turn, each noticeably swaying on their feet.

"You will conduct yourself as the law commands." Everyone there knows he's not speaking of human law.

"I don't have to obey you." Channon has crossed his arms.

My father's voice drops to carry on the breeze, for Were ears only. It whips through the parking lot like a tempest. "You will answer to your Alpha if you violate one of the Precepts."

The Channon guy's arms loosen, then drop.

The two Werewolves look at each other. Each waiting for the other to make the first move. Neither willing to make the step toward a truce.

"Now."

The single word spurs two sets of feet into motion. They each take a step back, then away. They split as they walk around us, and I feel like I'm standing between a Montague and a Capulet. Who said Shakespeare wasn't relevant today? They walk toward the building, keeping the other in their sight.

Dad crosses his arms, biceps resting on his broad chest. "Neither of you will be driving."

Jared hangs his head, while the Channon stiffens, turning his away. They each pull out their cells, speaking rapidly and quietly. Dad never moves from his position, legs apart, arms crossed. I stand beside him, hands by my side, a little awestruck, a lot impressed. Dad wields the steel of authority with composure, calm, and self-possession, tempered by respect expected, respect given.

This is what I haven't been learning for the past two years.

When Jared's ride arrives he walks over to Dad. "Thanks, Adam. You came at the right time." He rubs his hand over the back of his head, a head that is hanging between his shoulders.

Dad nods, but otherwise doesn't move, chin tucked in, brow low. Jared waits, but when Dad doesn't move, heads toward the red hatchback waiting in front of the pub. Jared was at the Phelan barbeque. He joined my parents at their table, chatting for a good while. But with a Channon nearby, my dad can't be seen to have favorites.

An Alpha must be fair and impartial.

Another car arrives, driven by a woman. The moment Channon opens the door, a shrill voice spills out. Most sentences starting with 'I told you not to—' He quickly climbs in, shutting the door on the ear-splitting tirade. He doesn't look back as he drives away.

Riley comes out as the last car leaves. "We need to meet less often, Adam. People are gonna start talking."

I look at Riley's tattooed sleeves, bulging muscles, his whispy goatee. I doubt anyone would be game enough to question his sexuality.

He looks over to me. "Ah, the future constabulary. Think you'll be as good as your dad?"

"I hope so, Riley."

Dad grunts. "I'm heading off, Riley. Got some zeds to catch up on."

"Come round again Adam. This time for a drink."

"That'll really get people talking, Riley."

We get in the car and head back through the streets. I think of the angry guys, their animosity pushing aside their better judgement.

"I wonder what that was about."

Dad's head falls back, resting on the seat behind him. "It doesn't have to be anything big. Nowhere else are there two big and powerful packs so close together."

I look out the window, the dark world beyond feeling smaller all of a sudden.

"It puts people on edge. And if you're a young Were, with the fuel of alcohol in your blood, it doesn't take much."

I ask the question I don't want to ask. "Would this situation have been avoided if there was an alliance?"

I get the answer I didn't want to hear. "There would certainly be less of them."

I keep my eyes out the window, voice low. "I thought you'd say that."

Dad reaches across, squeezing my shoulder.

We've been driving for a few more minutes when Dad's voice breaks the silence. "It was nice having you there, Noah."

"Anytime. Although I didn't actually do anything."

"You shared the load, just being there."

I realize Dad's been doing this alone since Grandad retired. For two years he was supposed to have been taking me, training me. Today he finally got to do what he's supposed to with his firstborn son.

"Let's go for a run, this week."

"That sounds good, Dad. Really good."

We're driving down Valley Road, an appropriately named stretch of asphalt between two swelling hills—houses on one side, a grassy park on the other—when something catches my eye.

I lean forward, eyes closer to the windshield. "Is that our...?" I quickly shut up, but it's too late.

Dad's breath pushes out his nose with emphasis. "Yes, it is."

Beside the park, our blue truck is sitting beneath a spreading spruce. And next to it is Tara's car. I scan the park. Unfortunately, I have plenty of time because Dad has slowed down.

Mitch and Tara are standing by the tree. It doesn't look like they ever went to the park. Because two sets of arms are wrapped around each other, and they are twined together like strands of rope, Tara's head buried in Mitch's shoulder.

And Dad has seen it all.

A rumbling growl vibrates next to me and I shift in my seat. That's not good.

"Get him home," says a controlled, low voice.

Dad accelerates. I get my phone out of my pocket, typing quickly.

You might want to get home.

The rest of the trip passes in silence.

We're only home for a few minutes—time spent with me sitting in a lounge chair, knee jiggling like it's on speed, Dad pacing a groove into the lounge room floor—when Mitch walks in.

He stops in the lounge entry, hands and jaw clenched. "I was already on my way back."

"I told you to stay home."

"We didn't do anything wrong."

"I told you to stay home." This time each word is drawn out through equally clenched teeth.

Mitch's hands explode outwards. "We had to talk!"

"Then you discuss it first."

"This isn't about obeying your Alpha, Dad. This is about two people being torn apart!"

"It's not just about that, Mitch."

Mitch takes two steps into the lounge. "How can you do this? Tara and I..." Mitch's hand arcs around, trying to encompass and convey everything Tara means to him.

Dad takes a deep breath. "No decisions have been made, son."

"How can you even consider it?"

I stay in my seat—Dad on my right, Mitch on the left, my head probably looking like it's at a tennis match, watching my inner battle being played out before me. In all its excruciating, gory glory.

"This isn't about what I want, Mitch." My father's shoulders cave in, a shattered leader. "I don't have the luxury of that option."

Mitch steps back out of the lounge room, a defeated warrior acknowledging this is a battle he never could have won.

"We were saying good-bye."

He heads up the stairs, heavy feet scraping from one step to the next. His last comment wafts down.

"We know the pack always comes first."

23

EDEN

"You're not going to be late for school again."

Caesar whines, burying his head into the pillows. It's nice to have someone do your talking for you.

"Get up."

My mother, wearing a dark grey jacket with black piping, stands at the end of my bed, bangled hands on hips. They match the hoop earrings peeking from beneath her hair. Apparently forty-eight hours is her accepted mourning period.

"You need to get to school. And you have an appointment at the Shoshoni Vet Center after. Don't be late for that one."

That has me sitting up. "The where?"

"We talked about it last week.

A hazy memory filters through my mind. My mother speaking, taking my silence as assent.

My head drops back to my pillow beside Caesar. I look into soulful brown eyes. It's just too hard. Seeing Noah at school had only inflamed the wound, made me realize how close to the surface it is.

I curl beneath the covers, trying to find some warmth.

My mother sits on the bed, and I peek around Caesar's

muzzle, looking for signs she's softening again.

Granite eyes look at me. "Life keeps moving. So do we."

I don't think she understands. "I have nowhere to go."

"We move away from this." She waves her arm over my curled body. "Toward something you can actually rely on."

She gets up and walks to the door. As she grips the handle, she turns. "Everything else, it's just not worth it."

By 'it' I assume she means the new world I discovered. A world composed of feelings more overwhelming and real and amazing than I ever experienced. A world which had a new sun. Where every time that sun brushed my skin, I blazed with sensation. A world where I revolved around that shining star.

Or is the 'it' the aftermath once that world implodes? A new reality where you turn around to find your defenses collapsed. A new reality that leaves you raw and alone and exposed. Where the coldness grips with icy fingers deep down, right to your marrow.

I sit up, feet falling to the floor, limp hands on the bed beside me.

Was it worth it?

I dress, blindly grabbing jeans and a thick sweater from the left-hand side of my wardrobe. I don't bother with breakfast; I'll just make it on time as it is.

School slaps me in the face with that question everywhere I turn. Like walking alone to class, where I once got to taste what it was like to have a warm hand, warm body to accompany me.

In psychology, where I once had some ability to deflect Bianca's comments.

"So, Eden. Too bad it didn't last with Noah."

Brandon frowns, leaning back in his chair.

My whole body tenses, my teeth clench, my fingers clamp onto my pen. "Change is inevitable, Bianca."

"So true. We just have to look for new opportunities,

don't we?"

She reaches out to pat my arm, but I pretend to adjust my knot, figuring hair is something Bianca can understand. She smiles a kind, insincere smile.

I want to get up and leave. Instead I put my head back into my book. And pretend I'm alone in the room.

Time crawls like a sedated snail. The moment the bell goes, I'm out of my chair and heading for the door. I've just stepped through when I hear my name. I turn, to see Brandon coming up beside me.

He leans forward, eyes narrowed with concern. "Ignore her."

"I'll try."

He gives me a small smile. "If you ever need to talk..."

I try to smile back. "Thanks." Knowing I never can.

I turn to head down the hallway, and freeze. Noah is standing by the lockers, a statue carved from misery and anguish. Brandon scowls at him.

I feel his flash of pain. I wrap my arms around myself so I don't start shivering in the climate-controlled hall.

That question follows me between classes, where I once scanned to find then intercept. Now I scan so I can avoid and run.

Biology is the worst. Where seeing him is unavoidable. Where I need my defenses the most. *The ones that no longer exist.*

I head to my back bench, concentrating fiercely on the patterned lino floor. But it doesn't make a difference. Because although I can *not* breathe as I walk past, although I can *not* look as I stare straight down...

I can't *not feel.*

I fall into my seat, emotions and nerves already raw. Wishing this was already over. I get out my books, my pens, my resolve, and stack them neatly around me. I'll focus down or up, nowhere else. I'll look at my text or Dougherty only.

Then I look, his presence a magnetic pull to my eyes. Blond hair crumpled and mussed. His shoulders hunched, muscles defined beneath his shirt. His back sculpted and chiseled. Looking both desolate and delicious.

They tense, just a miniscule shifting of his shirt. It's enough to break the spell and my gaze shoots to my book. Pain has me panting shallow breaths. The twofold pain of two people.

I won't be doing that again.

Then there's lunch, which once held laughter and chatting and touches. Now I've returned to lonely locker bays, my peanut butter sandwich repeatedly lodging in my throat. Wanting to come back up.

In math, where I got to taste what it was like to have a friend to talk to, now I have two girls, neither knowing what to say, avoiding looking at each other, awkwardly conversing.

"Have you figured out question three?"

I point to my sheet. "You need to calculate the tangent first."

Tara returns to hers. "Oh, thanks."

At the end of the day, where I once had summer eyes promising me tomorrow, a graze on my cheek filling me with heat and warmth, now I have dread, cold and hard. I no longer linger in the parking lot, but rush to my car. Inside, I pump up the heat, and leave school as quickly as is safe.

How am I going to do this day after day?

I almost forget I have the appointment at the veterinary center. Meaning I have to make a U-turn down a side street. I'm not sure why my mother would choose now to make this happen, and I don't think I have the energy to do this. But I definitely don't have the energy to deal with my mother if I don't go.

I enter a standard veterinary reception room: tiled floors, neutral colors, plastic chairs. But no receptionist. I ring the bell, the ding sounding loud in the empty room to my sensitive ears. And no one comes.

I don't want to ring it again; my raw nerves aren't up to it. So I stand and wait, taking in the posters advertising worming tablets, scientifically balanced dog food stacked on shelves and a sign saying 'please keep your pets contained at all times'.

I have my back to the door leading off to the side when I hear it open. I turn at the sound, to see a woman, probably in her twenties, enter the room. Her brown hair is up in a ponytail; she's drying her hands on some paper towel. Tanned skin and lean limbs speak of long hours outdoors.

She looks down beside me, registers no pet by my side, and raises her eyebrows. "Can I help you?"

"Ah, I believe I had an appointment to discuss a volunteer placement?"

"Oh yes, of course! Your mother rang." The woman crosses her arms. "She was very—"

"Pushy?"

She smiles. "Insistent, that I make a time to see you. Now, I'm not so good with human names..."

"Eden."

"Come on in, Eden."

Rather than entering an office, we head out the back. We enter a large room where four pens line the back wall. Two dogs rush up to the mesh doors, one a fluffy, white shih tzu, the other a dark Doberman. To my left the wall is lined by a bench, underneath are rows of drawers, above are rows of shelves. In the middle of the room is a stainless steel table, and sitting on it is a cat carrier. Hissing feline and all.

"Just be careful of Jaws. He's a little unhappy about having a urinary tract infection." Protesting yowl echoes around the surgery room. "And about being here."

The cat wails, closely followed by a round of shih tzu yapping and Doberman whining.

The woman heads to the opposite wall, and starts emptying

a box into the trays and drawers. I stand between the shelves of medical paraphernalia and the hissing table, awkward and silent.

"So, a volunteer placement, huh?"

"Yes."

"Shoshoni Vet Center services Jacksonville's domesticated animals. But we also service the Reserve, so we have wildlife coming through the doors fairly regularly."

This has my attention. Jaws lets out another spitting hissy fit, and I take a few steps toward his carrier. The vet continues emptying autoclaved scalpels and tweezers into a stainless steel drawer.

"We have countless kids ringing up, wanting to work with the baby badgers, cuddle the cute little raccoons, hand feed the pika. Do you have any experience with wildlife?"

A swan. A grizzly bear cub. I'm not sure if the cougar counts. "No."

"Right." And now I look like any other kid with a pushy mother. "I can filter out most people just by mentioning the cage cleaning."

"I volunteered four afternoons a week at a vet center in Boston, and some Saturdays. I cleaned cages, walked dogs, prepped instruments, checked vitals, monitored anaesthesia..."

The vet holds her hand up, her mouth quirking. "Anything you don't do?"

I think of the empty receptionist chair, and my mouth shoots off before I can think. "People."

"Ah, a woman after my own heart."

I'm now beside the table, and Jaws is quiet. I peer into his carrier; a great big ginger cat looks back at me, feline eyes blinking.

"And I've been accepted into early placement for Veterinary Science at Wyoming State." Not that I intend on going there.

The icy sadness that is never far away slices through me, raising goose bumps.

Jaws steps forward, rubbing his cheek against the bars of the door. I reach a finger through, scratching his chin. A low hum reverberates from within.

I realize the room is quiet, and I turn to see the vet watching me, eyebrows raised. I blush, straightening.

She angles her head to the side. "Do you mind putting Jaws in the last pen for me?"

I blink at the request. "Sure."

I open the cage door, and Jaws jumps out, onto my shoulder. His thick ginger fur curls around my neck, his tail brushing my collarbone, his eyes closing as he gently nudges my cheek. Low purring sends a vibrating warmth down my spine. It's a soft, soothing sound.

I take him to the last pen, leaving space between him and the dogs. Inside is a bed, a bowl of water, and a tray of litter. Jaws brushes his head against my chin, letting out a small meow.

I rub my chin on his orange head, whispering into the folds of his neck. "Thanks."

I extricate him and place him in the cage, missing his comforting warmth. Jaws heads for the padded place at the back, curls up, and closes his eyes.

I glance back to see what the vet is doing; her back is to me as she stacks bandages. I walk past the Doberman, my fingers brushing against his cage. He licks my hand, brown eyes big and sad. As I squat down in front of the shih tzu, he brings up a furry paw against the cage. I brush its leathery surface—touching comfort from this little dog.

The moment I'm back at the table, the vet turns, making me wonder how absorbed she really was. She smiles a warm smile.

"So, when did you want to start?"

My own eyebrows shoot up. "Anytime. Later this week?"

"I could use a hand on Thursday—that's surgery day."

"Sure. I'll head over after school."

"Excellent. Do you have any questions?"

"Um, maybe your name?"

She bursts out laughing. "Oops, see? Not so good with human names." She puts out her hand. "I'm Emily Patton."

I take her firm grip. "Nice to meet you, Emily."

"I'm looking forward to working with you, Eden."

The drive home is quick. I reflect that this will be a good thing. It gives me something to focus on, and the comfort of the animals was heartwarming. Right now I'll take any warmth I can get.

My mother is already home when I walk in. I bet her staff are thinking she's seriously ill to be taking this much time off. She's sitting in the lounge, TV on the local news, wine glass on the coffee table.

"So, how did it go?"

"Good. They actually service the national park, so I'll get to help with wildlife too."

"Great. How often?"

Apparently the frequency is more important than the work itself. "I'd say a couple of afternoons a week."

"That's a good start. We'll look at increasing it from there."

"It's fairly similar to what I did in Boston. It won't make a difference for college applications."

She turns back to the TV. "You need to keep busy."

I almost ask why. And then understanding hits me. Work is my mother's escapism, a feel good fix, enabling her to focus on something she can excel in, and she has certainly excelled. A nice controllable focus that provides a sense of accomplishment, satisfaction, positive feelings that are not dependent on anyone else.

That's why it became her everything.

"Why is this so important?"

Her eyes remain on the television; her hands tighten around the wine glass.

"You've learned the same lesson I did. They never stay." Her voice is hard, small.

And I know who she's talking about. Why her voice speaks of inevitability. I wonder what has my mother talking. I glance at the bottle, already half-empty.

"What did he look like?" My voice just as small, but far more hopeful.

My mother's eyes scan mine, brush over my hair, then sink back to her glass of wine. He looked like me?

Her eyes flicker, her mouth turning down. "I have to look over the winter advertising campaign."

She turns back to the papers on her lap, effectively closing the shutters. Disappearing into her work, her equivalent of morphine.

He looked like me!

I head to my room. Today has been long and exhausting, and just became confusing. Caesar's tail thumps out his welcome from the bed.

I sit on the bed, thinking of my mother organizing the placement at Shoshoni. Realizing she's offered to be my dealer.

But will it be enough for the brittle cold that has infiltrated my core...for the disillusioned pieces of my mind...for the shattered shards of my heart?

For the millions of questions that are battering my head, plaguing me every moment of every day.

The biggest one of all never far away.

Was it worth it?

At the end of the day, I don't have any answers.

24

NOAH

"Come on, Noah." Dad's booming voice carries up the stairs.

Mitch smiles. It's the first one I've seen in days.

I jam my trainers on. "Are you sure you don't want to come?"

"Nah. This one is all yours."

I nod. "Then it's our turn."

Mitch's smile brightens a notch. "Then it's our turn."

I jog down the stairs to see Mom come out, camera in hand.

"Really?" I practically whine.

Dad pulls me in by the shoulder. "You know the drill, son."

We paste smiles on our face.

"Say 'I'm a Werewolf,'" she chimes.

We echo the cue, using that false high tone people do for these moments, and a flash digitally immortalizes the moment. I wonder what caption she'd use for this one in a scrapbook.

We head to the car. Mitch has his hands in his pockets, shoulders a little hunched. Mom's hands are clasped beneath her chin, camera wrapped in her fingers. We climb into the car, and Mom's voice carries through the metal door.

"Have a good time."

We both lean to the side, giving a thumbs-up, and the camera flashes again. Dad reverses and turns off the driveway. We slump back in our seats, the required smiles falling away.

We're almost at the Glade when Dad speaks. "Kurt is coming by this evening."

My hand grips the seat belt at my shoulder. "He'll want to finalize details."

"This is a two-pack decision." Dad flexes his shoulders, big muscles bunching like a vice. "First we run. Then we talk."

I wonder if Dad needs this as much as I do.

We walk toward the hidden path, now so full of memories. My mark heats. My healed cut aches.

We pause at the edge of the Glade, the trees opening out with welcoming arms. With a smile Dad starts running, and shifts. And a giant, grey wolf is thundering ahead.

Show off.

I stand at the edge of the grassed clearing. I'm not sure if I'll be able to change. The two times I have up until now have both been in response to Eden's fear. But my wolf has been close to the surface. Agitated by Eden's pain. Animal instincts wanting to tear away the obstacles that are keeping us apart.

If only it were that simple.

Because that obstacle would be my family.

I start running after Dad, not really sure how this is supposed to work. As I head toward the rock, the one carved with the Precepts, I run past the ghosts of Eden and me. Standing so close, heads tilted. Her so uncertain. Me so sure.

And I'm changing, muscles severing and reconnecting. Organs shifting and relocating. Bones grating and repositioning. I don't know if it's the sound or the sensation that has a shudder ripping down my spine.

And it's done.

Once again, smells and sights hit me like a tidal wave. I can finally appreciate the adrenaline rush. Muscles that have been pulled tight with tension, stretch and lengthen. A powerful urge to head east pulls through them. But I know I can't go to her.

Instead I lower my head and follow Dad, his light grey form powering toward the trees. I push another burst of power through limbs that feel like someone put the Energizer bunny in there.

I dart around trees, bark brushing my fur, the wind stinging my face. Dad looks over his shoulder, sees me coming, and picks up his momentum. So that's how it is.

I go out wide, bounding over a fallen tree. Stepping up the pace, I shoot forward, catching up. Leap after leap I close the distance between us, until we're level, fast moving trees a blur of green and brown between us.

Looking ahead, I see a gap. With instinctive precision, I dart through the space between a determined old tree growing diagonally from a stand of rocks. I leap, push off the granite boulder, and thump into Dad's fur-covered muscle. He veers to the left, stepping around a wide trunk, a light growl rippling his muzzle. I streak forward. Dad drops his head, lengthening his stride. A bark escapes my lips, and I vault over a moss-covered rock. The hunter just became the huntee.

Time flies as we rocket through the forest. Playing chase, but neither winning. Doing it just for the thrill of running and pursuing.

We're both panting, chests heaving, when Dad stops, his head indicating it's time to turn back. We set up a loping stride back toward the Glade.

All around me are the rhythms of nature: in our loping limbs crushing the litter beneath our paws, in the trumpeting of the last sandhill cranes before they head south for the winter, and in the cooling temperatures, promising a snow-covered vista in a few short weeks.

In the deer buck standing in the meadowy opening before us, fur thickened and body fattened in anticipation of the harsh winter months.

We both stop, dropping to our haunches. Animal instincts track his antlered head, his fawny hide outlined against brown bark and green pine, his eyes alert but not alarmed. He doesn't know we're here. Our noses twitch, scenting his sex, age, health. My gums water. The predator in me takes two slow, stealthy steps forward.

The grey wolf beside me shakes his head.

I drop to the leaf litter beneath me. He's right. I'm not hungry. It would be a waste. Done purely, selfishly for the joy of the hunt.

We both stand, and the buck's head shoots up, fear blatant in his wide eyes and tense body. In a flash he leaps between the trees, and is gone.

Dad walks forward, his big body brushing past mine, his head nodding once.

We're almost back at the Glade when Dad stops. I come up beside him, wondering why. He looks at me, those matching blue eyes holding mine. He takes a deep breath in, that massive chest drawing out, filling to capacity.

And he throws back his head, a victorious howl echoing through the trees. Birds of all colors flap up into the air, joining the notes he has thrown into the sky.

I join him. The sound wells up from deep within my chest, swirling up my throat, spilling from my lips. This moment, its significance, its poignancy, thrust into the yowling notes. Because this moment, the one I've always been waiting for, now means I can't have what my heart wants most. The two sounds mingle and twine, carrying up to the heavens.

A crack echoes through the trees.

And my father drops, morphing back to human form.

As a wolf I run toward him, as a boy I kneel beside him.

And try to understand the crimson stain expanding across his shirt.

25

EDEN

I pull my notepad closer on my lap, turning the page of the text sitting on the leather lounge. Caesar rearranges himself on my other side, his heated body next to my leg. The only part of me that's warm.

Studying alone on a Wednesday, again. I don't even know why I've kept up this painful routine, with memories fluttering around like ghostly pieces of ash, drawing my attention like a car wreck. You don't want to look. But you can't look away.

I rub my pounding temples. It feels like I've been studying for hours. Not sitting in front of a blank notepad for twenty minutes.

Caesar's head shoots up, eyes and ears alert, and a knock sounds at the door. I look at him, brow furrowed. We're both wondering who's on the other side.

It can't be Jenny, Tony's wife; she already dropped off cookies earlier. I thanked her, not really sure what do with them. They ended up in the fridge, the white chocolate chunks beginning to melt in the furnace-like heating I've turned up.

And it's not Tony; he stopped by with cheesecake. I thanked him too, and put it in the fridge beside the cookies.

Caesar leaps up and heads to the door, me trailing behind. I open it, and take a step back. "Tara?"

"It's Wednesday night." She smiles, although her arms curl around herself, rubbing her upper arms.

The door stays in my hand. This is the girl who will bond with Noah. "I'm not very good company at the moment."

"I don't need to talk. Just a break." She holds up a yellow and red packet, eyes pleading. "And I brought popcorn."

I push the door open for the girl who bailed me out on my first day of school. Who accepted me, no questions asked. Who believed Noah and I were possible.

Tara lets out a breath. "Thanks."

We head into the lounge and Tara sits on the sofa she shared with Mitch. She looks at the space beside her, then slowly places her books there, her shoulders slumping even farther.

"So, how have you been?"

I almost choke on the emotions welling up. I scramble for something normal. "I've started some hours at the Shoshoni Vet Center."

"Cool. You really have a way with animals."

My pen pauses. *What has Noah told her?* "You think so?"

"Definitely. Just look at the bond you have with Caesar."

Relief relaxes my grip.

"Even humans are drawn to you."

A sliver of warmth snakes into my heart. It feels so out of place, it gives me goose bumps. "Tara, you could make the Grinch feel good."

"Just calling it the way it is." She pulls out her math text. "All ready for midterms?"

I shrug. "I don't know. I'm finding it a little hard to concentrate at the moment."

"Tell me about it."

She takes her notepad, then stares at it. Echoing my own stance from just minutes ago.

"What do you do during the day?"

"I get around." I hedge. "You?"

"Art room."

"I thought so."

We continue to skim the surface of our pain. "Life is pretty awful at the moment."

"Yes, it is."

Suddenly Tara jumps in, from the highest springboard she can find. "How do I do it, Eden?" Her hazel eyes are torn, tortured. "If you were me, what would you do?"

I sit back into the couch. What would I do? If she bonds with Noah, what sort of life would she lead? Living every day with him as her mate, his twin, the one she loves, never far away. If she doesn't, she'd be banished from her pack. Never to see the family she loves, the pack she needs.

A little voice whispers somewhere in recesses of my mind. *If she didn't, Noah would be free again.*

"Can you unbond?"

"It happens, but it's rare. The pair must stand before the pack, and their Alphas, and renounce each other." Tara's hands drop. "It would look like we're rejecting the other pack."

Leaving the alliance shaky at best.

"Not an option then."

"Not an option." Tara's echo drops like a dead weight.

I let out a quiet breath. "Is there really a choice?"

Her hands come to her face, pushing backward into her hair. "This is so messed up. Do you know what one of the worst things is?"

I look at her.

"I hate my dad for doing this to us. For breaking up so many things, just to make something else."

I think of my own mother. "I wonder if they know. What they're saying when they put something else before you."

Tara's lips tip up in a watery attempt at a smile. "I'm glad I came, Eden."

My hand rubs down Caesar's spine. "I'm not sure I should have."

Tara's brow furrows, confused. I watch her figure out what I'm saying. *If I had never come...*because I was the spark that started all of this. This chain reaction.

As realization dawns Tara starts shaking her head. "It's not your fault, Eden. Noah was meant to be Alpha. Mitch hated the idea of taking it from him."

I wish I could believe her.

Tara flops back onto the lounge. "It's next week."

My heart constricts. So soon.

"On the full moon. So clichéd. We don't even do it at night."

And I know I won't be friends with Tara anymore. Goosebumps spread across my skin like a rash. School will be unbearable.

Tara brushes her deep red hair back from her face. "We could have been besties," she says sadly.

I could have had a bestie?

"That would have been pretty cool." My tone echoes hers.

Tara straightens in her seat, reaching for her book. "We should really get our study pants on."

I like the way she thinks. I grab the matching text, gaze flicking over the tightly jammed numbers. "How do you think Pascal came up with his triangle?"

"My theory is he probably sneezed, spilled his ink well, and then his cat tracked it across his desk."

I feel my chest lighten a little. "And voila! We now have binomial coefficients to torture many generations to come."

"Exactly."

And even though we haven't found any answers, the light-hearted joking is enough to lessen the load, enough for us to focus on the study we have to do. We bend our heads over our texts, and pens begin scrawling across notepads.

I'm just wondering if I should pull out the cookies, when I freeze.

My head shoots up. "Noah."

Tara glances up at me, her face changing from confusion to concern when she registers my expression.

I throw the text on the sofa. "Something's happened. We need to go. Now."

"What? What's going on Eden?"

My stomach, abdomen, entire chest cavity is roiling and heaving, an awful mix of fear and despair churning through them. *And I know they're not mine.*

I head to the door, grabbing the car keys, a confused Tara following. She must have picked up on my panic because she jumps into the passenger seat, quiet.

I drive the fastest I've ever driven in my life. Dangerously and obnoxiously. I cut off a slow-moving van on the highway, not having time to make room. It sounds its horn long and hard.

"Go suck a duck!" Tara calls from the window, then falls back into the leather seat. "Some people have no idea."

We arrive at the Phelan house, and my seat belt is undone before the car stops, my door open before I turn off the engine. I rush up to the front door, but pause.

"What?" Tara's voice is getting panicky.

"I think they're inside." But Noah is not.

Tara opens the door, scrambling inside. "Mitch?" Her voice carries into the house.

I turn, and follow the veranda, out to the backyard.

I find Noah sitting on a timber bench, shoulders curved down, head in his hands. I walk over and stand before him. He looks up at me, eyes full of shock and fear and hurt. Without a thought to the shattering pain of the past weeks, I fall to my knees in front of him. Wordlessly, he lifts his arms and I slide between his legs, my arms moving around his waist. He pulls me against him, laying his cheek on my head.

We fit together with the inevitability of two magnets connecting. As natural as two halves reuniting, feeling like the universe has realigned to its rightful place.

An instant warmth radiates from the point where my head touches his chest. *Gosh, I missed that warmth.*

He breathes in a deep, deep sigh. "Dad and I went for a run. It was amazing."

I can almost see the images, a large, white wolf and his larger, grey counterpart, paws thundering through the Reserve. Running, leaping, howling. I feel Noah's exhilaration at finally being able to roam with his father. As a wolf. As the Alpha heir.

My arms tighten around his waist, and the warmth pulsating behind my ear becomes a throbbing furnace. Spilling its heat down my spine, through my body.

"We were heading back to the Glade. We were both done. I heard it, and then he dropped."

"Heard it?" I whisper.

"A shot, Eden. He was shot."

I pull him even closer, spurring another burst of heat through my scalp. "Another ricochet?"

"Not this time. It went straight through his chest."

"Noah."

I lean back and look up at him. At this boy who is broken and hurting. At this boy whose pain is overflowing in steady trickles down his cheeks. At this boy who has shown me more light, hope, and joy than I ever imagined.

I tuck my head back in, holding him tight. The point where my head touches his chest is generating so much heat that it's winding and spiraling around us. I feel like it should be glowing, luminescent with the energy it's producing. Tangible heat that wraps us in warm arms.

With my ear against his chest, I can hear each breath flow in and shakily out, choked by helplessness. "I wish I could have been there, Noah."

"There's nothing you could have done." Another shuddering breath rattles through his blazing chest. "There was so much blood, Eden. So much blood."

I hear everything he doesn't say. Noah would have had to carry his father out of the Glade, to the car. Then driven him out to the highway, protecting the location of the Glade, calling an ambulance as he went. As his father continued to bleed. Was he conscious and in pain? Or unconscious and silent?

"It took so long for the medics to get there," he whispers.

All I can do is hold him tighter, fueling the scorching blaze between us.

He clears his throat. "They've taken him to hospital. Mom went with him. Mitch and I are getting some stuff together and meeting her there."

"You need to go." Although I don't want to, I shuffle back, my fingers brushing across his chest, the area where his tattoo is scorching hot.

Noah takes my hand and we walk to the house. Mitch meets us on the veranda; a tear-streaked Tara is tucked into his side.

"Let's go."

Mitch nods, and heads for the truck, a duffel bag over one shoulder, Tara under the other.

Noah turns to me. His brilliant blue eyes are shining. "Thank you for coming."

"There's nowhere else I would have been."

His hand comes up to brush my cheek. Like all the times before, when so little stood between us.

Then he's jogging to the truck and climbing in. Noah reverses and, in a spray of gravel, shoots down the road. Tara waves a small hand in the window.

I hold my own up.

It's only once the truck has rounded the bend that my own legs give out.

26

NOAH

I don't really remember the drive to the hospital.

I don't remember if there were stairs, or an elevator.

I don't remember asking for directions.

I must have, because I find myself standing at the glass sliding doors, a white room on the other side.

I'll always remember finding my mother. Hunched over, arms crossed and clasping her elbows. A smear of blood on her cheek.

We walk in, and she doesn't move. I walk up to her, and she doesn't move. I stand in front of her, and I can't find my voice.

She looks up. "Noah. Mitch."

And she's in my arms. For the first time I'm taller than Mom, and her face buries in my shoulder.

"What's happening?"

She slips from me to Mitch, and they hold each other for long seconds, dark heads close. "They've taken him into surgery. I haven't heard anything else."

Mom takes a seat, and I sit on one side, Mitch on the other. Tara reattaches herself to Mitch's side. The waiting room is all white and pale blue. Someone probably thought the color scheme would be soothing. They were wrong. The white walls are a glaring reminder you're in a hospital; the pale blue lino and pastel blue chairs leave you waiting in a vast ocean, an endless sky, with very little to hold on to. I shove helpless hands into my pockets, my head falling back onto the wall behind me.

Why do they call this a waiting *game*? It's the worst thing I've ever had to endure.

Endless hours later we all turn, each shooting to attention, when the door opens. A woman enters, bronze skin in blue scrubs, her dark hair obscured by a gauze hospital cap, her dark eyes somber.

She puts out her hand, and Mom steps forward to shake it. "Good evening, I'm Dr. Martinez. I was the head surgeon operating on Mr. Phelan."

Mom's hands rise hesitantly, palms up. "How is he?"

Dr. Martinez hands fold in front of her. "I'm sorry it took so long Mrs. Phelan. Gunshot wounds are unpredictable, and require exploratory surgery to track the path of the bullet. In Mr. Phelan's case, the bullet entered the chest wall and punctured his lung, before exiting through his back. Luckily, most other organs were left relatively intact, although there was some damage to his aortic arch and trachea."

Mom's hand flies to her mouth.

"We were able to repair the collapsed lung, and we didn't find any complicating bone fragments. But with the massive blood loss and the trauma to his chest, Mr. Phelan went into cardiac arrest."

Mom collapses onto her seat. "The partial disruption in the supply of oxygen to his brain has left Mr. Phelan in a coma."

We're all silent. Maybe waiting to see if Dr. Martinez has anything else. Hoping there couldn't possibly be more.

"I know it sounds overwhelming, but remember he's young and healthy. The bullet missed most of his internal organs, and there's no structural damage to his heart. We will be providing him the best possible care."

It feels like she's parceling out the good and the bad onto a set of scales. A reality where no one really knows which side they will tip to, leaving Dad's life hanging in the balance.

Mom looks up, eyes large and face pale. "Can we see him?"

Dr. Martinez nods. "He's in the intensive care unit. At this stage visiting times are very strict: one at a time, for five minutes only. You will have to be prepared. Mr. Phelan will be unresponsive, with a lot of medical equipment keeping him stable."

After more lifts and corridors, we come to another waiting room, this color scheme earthy browns and creams. The ICU waiting room is designed for longer stays; plush chairs surround round tables in groups, magazines clustered on each one. A small kitchenette is set up in the corner. Boxes of tissues are strategically propped around the room. I've watched enough medical dramas to know that only half the time they're used for happy tears.

Mom is the first to go in. She returns short minutes later, her cheeks now wet, eyelashes glistening, arms clasped so tightly, her knuckles are white.

And it's my turn. I enter the room where Dad is the center-piece, surrounded by myriad complicated-looking machines. It looks both cluttered and barren.

I stop beside the large man, bandaged chest bare beneath a white sheet, a ventilator hanging from his mouth, tubes in his arms, wires taped everywhere.

Dad has always been big. Big in size. Big on life. Big on love.

But now he looks small. The room dwarfs him as he lays so still, surrounded by white. The damage that a projectile has left to his insides, the complex medical procedures to try and repair it, diminishes the man that has been my rock. The massive blood loss that left his brain starved for oxygen leaving behind a shell.

I take his hand and squeeze, just like the pain does in my chest. His hand doesn't move.

Machines are bleeping constantly. Sounding out Dad's heartbeats. His breathing. His life.

My knees go a little weak. Please don't let it be a countdown.

Within half an hour we've all been in. One at a time. Mom, me, Mitch. Each coming out pale and silent.

Now we're in the ICU waiting room. Waiting. Mom in one of the plastic seats, arms cradled again. Mitch, with Tara curled into his side, beside her. I'm pacing, wishing Eden was here, when a question starts to formulate.

How did we get here?

My side aches where a scar should have been. Two shots. By the Glade. This just stepped up from coincidentally unlucky to bloody suspicious. For the first time anger starts to simmer. More questions start to surface.

The door opens again to frame two uniformed police officers. We all remain where we are. I don't know why we're surprised. Cop families get to know these drills, learning about them vicariously. And Dad was shot.

I walk forward, realizing I know these two men. Geoff, the older, grizzled man whose middle age has started to expand his waist, has known Dad for years. The tall, skinny one is Stan, a more recent recruit.

Geoff ducks his head. "Beth, I'm so sorry. Everyone down at the station is praying for him." Stan shifts from one foot to the other, looking a little uncomfortable.

Mom looks up with wet eyes, a small smile tipping up her lips. But she doesn't respond. I step to the side of the room, indicating for them to follow. Mitch joins me, leaving Tara with Mom.

"How is he, Noah?"

"In a coma, but stable."

Geoff ducks his head. "We need to ask you some questions." He pulls out his little blue notepad, his pen clicking in the silence.

He clears his throat, his tone becoming businesslike. "Can you tell me what happened in the lead up to your father being shot?"

"We went for a hike, south of the national park. Not far from the hunting reserve. We were heading back when he just dropped." I manage to start with complete honesty.

"Did you see anyone, hear any strange noises?"

"Nothing. I didn't see anyone, hear anyone." Unusual in itself, given we were both in wolf form.

"What happened after he was shot?"

"I carried him to the car."

"You, carried your dad, to the car?" Geoff's tone is dubious.

"Yeah."

"Why would you do that, Noah?"

I shrug. "No phone reception." Which could be true, but the truth is slowly being stretched.

Geoff makes some notes.

"He would have been bleeding, needing immediate medical attention."

"I phoned the minute I could." Desperately hoping I had done the right thing. Knowing we need to keep the Glade a secret. As I watched my father bleed out before my eyes.

Stan clears his throat, shifting a little on the spot. "Has your dad had any altercations recently?"

I frown, thinking. "He went out to Riley's a week or so ago. I think it was a drunken argument between a couple of guys."

Geoff scribbles again.

"It sounded like pretty routine stuff."

"Has anything suspicious happened that would be relevant to this?"

A flash of heat streaks down my side. "Not that I can think of."

"Can you think of anyone that would have a vendetta against your father?"

"Geoff, he's a cop. You know there's lots of people out there that aren't happy with the calls he's made." Wife beating husbands, drug dealers, delinquent youth.

Geoff grunts. He looks at me with shrewd, grey eyes. "Is there anything else that you could tell me that would be relevant to this investigation?"

"Investigation?"

"Noah, a cop has been shot. We're going to need the location he was shot for forensics."

That could be a problem. "We were just hiking, Geoff. Dad wasn't in uniform. I'm guessing an idiot missed then didn't stick around to see what damage he'd done."

He looks at me, pen poised over the notepad. "The location?"

I rack my brain for what I've already told them. "Not far from Jensen's trail." The truth has now left the building.

Geoff takes some more notes. "Is there anything else you need to tell me?"

"No. But I'll let you know if anything else comes to mind."

"We'll be in contact once we've been out to the scene."

"Dad would be glad you're taking this so seriously."

"Adam is a good guy. We want to make sure this is done properly." I hold out my hand to shake theirs. "Tell him we'll see him when he wakes up."

"Will do, Geoff."

Once they are gone I fall into the nearest chair, hands in my hair.

Mitch flops beside me. "Nicely done, Noah. Although forensics at the location is going to be tricky."

"I didn't give it to them."

"Smart move."

Mitch gets up to go back to Tara, squeezing my shoulder as he goes. I stay in the seat, feeling alone, and a little bit dirty after all the crap I just fed Geoff. His questions start to move through my mind, burning open trails. I'm starting to get angry again.

"Dad?"

I look up then stand. Kurt has come through the door, stopping just inside. He scans the room, his gaze pausing on Tara, wrapped in Mitch's arms.

"I came as soon as I heard."

Tara stands up, Mitch following her.

"How is he?"

Mom's hunched back stays in her seat. "He had a heart attack during surgery, leaving him in a coma. The doctors are optimistic, but there's nothing to do but wait."

I come to stand by Mom, and she grasps my hand.

Kurt moves into the room, standing before her. "If there's anything you need, Beth, I'm here."

"Thank you, Kurt, your support is appreciated."

"Adam is a fine strong man. I'm sure the wait won't be long." Kurt's eyes slide to Mitch and Tara, before coming back to me. "Noah. Can I have a word?"

"Sure." I don't move from Mom's side.

I think Kurt's lips tighten, but it's hard to tell in that bushy beard. "I know this is a difficult time, but with your father... recovering, I'm conscious your pack will need an Alpha."

Someone else as the Phelan Alpha? I can't imagine it. "I doubt it will be an issue for long, Kurt."

He smiles a little. "I'm sure it won't be. But with important events coming up, it's best the pack has someone to lead it."

He means the bonding. Mom straightens in her seat. "Surely you don't mean for the bonding to go ahead?"

"Of course I do, Beth. It's very important that the alliance be formalized. Noah knows this." His chin drops, his beard brushing his chest. "So did Adam."

His hand comes up to rest on my shoulder. For some reason I want to shrug it off. Concerned eyes look at me from his lion-mane face. "We've always been there for the Phelans, and I want to do what I can to help. I'd be happy to oversee the pack until Adam is back on his feet."

My first instinct says I don't think so. Actually my tired, fried mind says "No way!" But then I pause. What would Dad want? What would he do? I could sure use an instruction book right about now. Once again I have to go with my gut, although even I'm not sure that has been right up until now.

"I think we should be fine, Kurt."

"Noah. This is a tough time for you, and you've been the Alpha heir for such a short time. And with such little training."

Each word feels like it's sucking the false bravado out of me. I'm not sure I can support the weight of the arm on my shoulder.

Mitch stands, and comes to my right. I lock my knees, my head coming up.

Kurt ignores Mitch's show of support. "You can't leave your pack without a leader at this time."

"You're right. That's why I'll do it."

Kurt steps back, arm falling down. "You'll be Alpha?" His tone shows exactly what he thinks of that idea. "Think this through, Noah."

I can feel Mitch crossing his arms behind me. I'd like to do the same, but I don't. "I'll be the Phelan Alpha, until my father recovers."

Mom stands too, and we form a triangle. With me at the apex.

Kurt smiles, taking another step back. "I understand. I'm sure it won't be for long." He turns to Tara. "We should let these guys have some space."

Tara opens her mouth, and Kurt's big chest fills with a breath. Tara's mouth shuts.

She gets up, her fingers brushing Mitch's as she goes. When she reaches me she looks up, her hazel eyes telling me she wants to stay. "Let me know if you need anything."

"Thanks."

Once they're gone I look at Mitch. Mitch looks at me. We're both asking the same question.

What just happened?

Mom squeezes my shoulder. "You did what needed to be done, Noah."

Needed to be done? I just stepped myself up to Alpha.

I don't feel the need to pace anymore, so I sit beside Mom. I wish I could talk to Dad. Ironically, the situation where I need Dad the most, is the situation that has left him unable to give the guidance I need.

Mom sits again, arms crossed, each elbow resting in the opposite palm. I suspect this is going to be her holding pattern. For the waiting game.

In that moment I realize what she's cradling.

Hope.

27

EDEN

I stop. These are the last few trees before they open out like a river mouth to the cultured lawns of the Inn. Our cottage, a lovely little island in a sea of lush grass. But I don't want to go back yet. I'm pretty sure my mother is home.

Caesar stands beside me. I feel guilty that my mood is ruining his walk. We're usually exploring the forest, wandering amongst the pines, rambling through the undergrowth—Caesar unearthing new sights, scouting out new scents and chasing after curious sounds. Even if it means a sprained leg, just like it did a couple of weeks ago. Certainly not enough to stop a curious canine.

Now he walks alongside me on the path, occasionally brushing my leg, a silent companion. I don't know why, but I don't stray from the familiar, safe track.

"Why don't we sit down for a while?"

I step to the nearest pine, sinking down into the soft bed of needles. Like a rag doll I flop backward, lying on my back. Caesar is the only one to sit, eyes searching, ears twitching. I stare up at the fractured sunlight reaching through the branches, casting dappled shadows down on us, any warmth progressively filtered out through each layer.

Leaving me cold and dark at the bottom.

Images move through the boughs: Kurt, barrel chest inflated with his ambitions for Tara, no matter the cost for his daughter, Mitch, having to sit back and watch, hands tied by an Alpha's command, and Beth, husband and mate in a coma, her two sons in pain.

Because I know Noah is hurting. Every day I can feel his burden, his regret. His sense of duty tearing him apart. At school. At home. In my short-lived, tear-filled, nightmare-riddled sleep.

His pain only compounding my own, making it over-whelming.

I wish I could run, get rid of it, shut it down. Anything to avoid the raw agony that's so close to the surface. Escape this jagged ice carving up my heart.

The leaves and branches above me blur, making them look closer and darker, obscured by the slow trickle leaking from my eyes, tracking icy trails to my temples. This is why I don't stop. An idle mind is a dangerous thing.

Maybe my mother was right. I need to talk to Emily about going to the vet center more often. I'll study harder. Blinking, I realize that in this bleak wasteland there's a path, one that's been compacted, soil surface hardened and traversed countless times. By my mother.

And I know exactly where it goes. Somewhere where people can't reach you. Because you are always slightly apart. Some-place where pain struggles to touch you. Because you pour your-self into what you can succeed in.

Caesar stiffens beside me. His ears twitch, his head turning toward the depth of trees.

"You go, boy. I'll still be here."

He looks at me, doggy eyebrows raised, body tense with the need to investigate.

I nod. *You go.*

He darts off, the slight limp not slowing him down, the prospect of pain and discomfort not holding him back from blazing a trail of his own.

I sit up straight.

When did I become my mother?

I shoot to my feet, calling out to Caesar, a second later using my voice. He comes powering through the trees, skidding to a halt before my feet.

"We need to get back."

He sprints down the path, my two-legged run not far behind.

I burst into the house, scanning for the car keys.

They're not on the hook. Or the table beneath it. My mind scrambles to think who had the car last, where they could be.

"What's the rush?" My mother has stood up from the dining table. Papers are stacked in neat piles across its glass surface.

"Where are the car keys?" Caesar is sniffing around the entryway, like he knows what I'm looking for. As if he feels my urgency.

My mother takes a step forward, eyes narrowing. "Where are you going?"

"I'll explain when I get back."

Sharp heels clack out my mother's approach. "Where are you going?"

It's tonight. She doesn't know, but that doesn't stop me from wanting to scream the words at her. I scrabble through the magazines on the hall table, looking in drawers.

"I need to tell him." It won't make a difference. But I need to tell him. Maybe make the burden a little lighter.

"You don't want to do this."

"No." I straighten, hands clenching. "You don't want me to do this."

"It's not worth it." Those words are thrown out again.

"But at what cost, Alexis?" She pulls back at the use of her name. But what do you call the mother who never uses yours? "When is enough?"

Her heels rap out her backward retreat, and my voice softens. "Will I eventually also need the wine? The longer work hours?"

My mother's fingers come up to rest in the hollow beneath her neck.

"Reading endless fiction. About the only ones who actually stay?"

She flinches. Her head drops. And she pushes her purse toward me. The leather bag tips, and the car keys spill onto the glass table top, skidding a few inches across its smooth surface with a tinkling, scraping sound.

I grab them and turn toward the door, without my mother saying another word.

My heart is pumping as I start the car and drive through the Inn grounds. It doesn't know what to do with the frustration at what I left behind, or the apprehension at what lies before.

Noah.

I drive with controlled concentration to his house. I want to push my foot down, and drive like a maniac. I want to snap the steering wheel down, and turn around and head home. Instead, I focus on the grey asphalt, keeping my foot steady on the gas, keeping my hands at ten o'clock and two o'clock.

As I turn onto the dirt road, a waft of dust blows over the Saab. Like someone has driven here recently. Not surprising really. I suspect there's a lot of commotion going on right now.

There is a bonding happening today.

I slow down, telling myself it's for the dirt road, that I'm being a safe, responsible driver. Not the nervousness that has stepped up to heart palpitating, sweaty-palmed anxiety.

I pull up in the driveway and climb out of the car. And see Noah coming out of the house, his shocked eyes registering my presence.

Oh no. *He's wearing a tux.* It makes him look taller. Broader. Devastating my senses. Disastrous for my fragile control. My palms itch to touch him. To run over the material hugging his shoulders. To feel that wild blond hair, almost tamed for the occasion. To taste his heat. The irony that I'm so, so ready.

But I can't.

Today he bonds with another.

I jam my hands into my back pockets, my thumbs clamping onto the denim for good measure.

I meet him on the pathway, where he hasn't moved a muscle. I join this Adonis statue, drinking him in, devouring everything I've missed. I can already feel his warmth thawing the endless winter that has invaded my veins.

I open my mouth. But now that I'm here, with Noah in a tux in front of me, uncertainty raises its ugly head. I don't know where to start. What to say.

Behind Noah the door opens and Tara comes out, looking breathtaking in a brilliant ivory dress, her hair up, the sweetheart neckline showing off her own wolf tattoo. The Channon mark resting within, a rectangle with a line through the middle, like a domino.

"Oh, hi, Eden. I'll come back out in a minute." She turns back inside, her skirt swishing around white heels. Something strikes me. Maybe it was her smile. Her light step. But she seemed...happy.

And although it hurts, I'm glad she is.

Noah glances over his shoulder. "We need to talk."

He heads to Grandpa Douglas, the silent witness to so many

of our moments. I follow those broad, black shoulders, thinking of how they felt beneath my hands during the piggy back. How I felt.

Beneath the spreading branches, he turns to me. His eyes are soft, caressing my face. I take a deep breath, spiced sandalwood giving me the courage I need.

"I wanted to thank you."

"I—" His mouth clamps shut. "Thank me?"

"I wanted you to know I have no regrets."

He opens his mouth.

"No, Noah. I need to say this before..." I wave my hand toward his suit. "I want you to know." My voice drops. "Every moment with you was worth everything we're going through now."

Noah is shaking his head. His hands come up, then drop again. "Eden, I'm not choosing a life without you in it. Which is why this," his hand does its own arc, "isn't happening."

Shock reduces me to a whisper. "Not happening?"

"I'm not doing it. To Mitch. To Tara." He takes a step closer. "To us."

"But—" And I can't go any further. What is he saying? What does this mean?

"I told Kurt a little while ago. The bonding will go ahead, but I won't be in it."

My eyes widen. He wouldn't have taken that well.

"Yeah. I don't think I'm on his Christmas card list. "

"That means...you're...we could be..." My hand comes up, hovering between us. "Together?"

Noah's echo flows out on a breath. "Together."

My hand rests on his chest, finally connecting. It reflexively curls over his mark, anchoring me. Because I'm drowning in blue oceans of promise. Heated promise.

Together.

Ever so slowly Noah leans in, head tilting down. His beautiful face fills my vision. My senses. My heart is climbing up on each hopeful beat, like it's trying to reach out, trying to draw him closer. And like all the other times, he stops.

Our breaths mingle on a question. A wish.

A prayer.

With no hesitation, I push up on my toes, banishing the remaining inches between us. Our lips touch, meld. And I melt. His lips feel just like I expected. Firm...soft...amazing.

And like nothing I could have imagined.

They move across mine free of tentativeness or uncertainty. But firmly, born of the knowledge that this is achingly right.

Exploring. Caressing.

Impossibly beautiful.

Simultaneously, we press closer, our bodies merging like our lips. The kiss deepening. Noah's hands wrap around my waist, hauling me against him. I feel his muscles hot and hard against me. My hands shoot through his hair, pulling him closer, and I finally feel those strands weaving through my fingers.

A feeling I've only ever sampled blazes through my body.

Desire.

It explodes across my skin, streaks through my veins. Obliterates my mind. The heat passed from cell to cell, beginning at every point we touch, burns through each atom, every fiber, through entire layers of skin, muscle and tissue. All coursing toward, converging on one point—my heart.

"Noah, where are you?"

The sound takes long moments to infiltrate my consciousness. Through the haze of desire in my mind. The haze of Noah.

Noah's hands loosen their powerful grip around my waist, and come to lie on my hips. I slip my hands from his hair, bringing them down to rest on his shoulders.

We pull away and Noah rests his forehead on mine.

And we're back where we started. Close, breaths mingling, eyes questioning.

But everything has changed. As is always the case with this amazing boy, something has irrevocably transformed. It's there in our panting breaths. Our locked eyes. Our speechless lips.

"Wow."

A soft smile tips up my lips. "Wow."

Noah grins. A softer, gentler version, but his grin nonetheless.

"Noah, where the fishsticks are you?" Tara's sweet voice is now a growl of frustration.

Noah twists his head to the house, calling out. "Coming."

He turns back to me. "We have a bonding to get to."

I look down at my jeans, jumper, sneakers. "Oh no 'we' don't. I can't go looking like this."

Noah pulls back a little, but doesn't let go. "Beautiful?"

I blush. "You know what I mean."

"No one will care."

I sigh. Noah is being an obtuse male. It only took a minute for us to have a men-are-from-Mars-women-are-from-Venus moment. "I will. I'm not going to a Were wedding in jeans and a sweater."

"But I really want you there."

"And I really want to be there."

Planetary stalemate.

"There you are, Noah." Tara is walking toward us, holding up her full, white skirt as she tiptoes across the pine needles. As she gets closer I notice her delicate bodice, the tendrils of lace curling down onto the organza skirt. It's exquisite. She doesn't blink an eye at our wrapped arms, the absence of space between us.

"We leave in ten."

"Eden won't come."

"Well, of course she won't. Look at what she's wearing."

Ah, fellow feminine understanding.

"But I can fix that. Come with me." Without waiting for permission, she grasps my hand and pulls me away. Every inch of my body instantly mourns the loss of Noah's closeness and his heat.

But Noah doesn't object as Tara drags me away, into the house. There Beth is standing, looking worried. She smiles a smile of relief when she sees Tara has me by the hand.

"Beth, we need your wardrobe."

Beth quickly realizes the issue. "Go for it, there's a lovely blue number that will probably work a treat."

I blush. Not only was I just kissing her son under the branches of the family tree, I'm now going to raid her wardrobe. "Thanks Beth," I say in a little voice.

Tara doesn't release my hand as we head up the stairs. Maybe she suspects I'm tempted to run.

In Noah's parents' room, Tara opens the walk-in wardrobe. Beth, the picture-perfect mother and housewife surprises me with a small section of bagged hangers.

"Beth has always been a bit of a social butterfly." Tara, efficient as always, quickly unzips and peeks in each bag.

"She was right." She pulls one out and opens it up.

Inside is a royal-blue dress. Pleated chiffon starts at the shoulders and falls to the floor. Cinched at the waist, the lined skirt flares and flows, thanks to the added volume of the pleats. She pushes it toward me.

I stand there, looking at it. "Come on then, I have a bonding to get to."

I duck into the bathroom, quickly undressing. Goose bumps skip across my skin as the silky lining slides down my body. Deep blue layers have just brushed my ankles when Tara bustles in.

"No time for hair. Let's just go with it down."

I blink. Bondings can really bring out the drill sergeant in people. For once I say it out loud.

Tara giggles, her shoulders hunching above her strapless dress. "Hair down," she commands.

I remove the mass from its tie and it falls in heavy waves down to my waist.

"Dang it girl, how can you hide that much hair in one knot?"

She grabs a brush and pulls it through in long strokes. From a small clutch, she removes mascara, eyeliner, and lipstick. So that's what girls carry around in their bags. Not maps, drink bottles, and dog treats.

Tara hitches her lovely dress as she comes around and, in swift minutes, has applied a light layer. She steps back to admire her art work.

"Holy Frijoles, Eden. You look amazing!"

I duck my head. "Just trying to keep up."

Tara curtsies; with her red hair up and full skirt, she looks like a queen of old. "Bonding ceremony, here we come."

Back in the bedroom Tara fishes out a pair of strappy, silver sandals. I put them on and I'm glad they don't pinch. I don't want to repay Beth's generosity with stretched shoes.

Standing in the doorway, Tara is hopping from one foot to another.

"I'll be down in a second."

Tara grins and skips out of the room.

I look in the mirror at the new girl in front of me—the change deeper than the emphasized eyes, unbound hair and flowing dress. I bring my fingertips to my glossed lips.

I took the leap.

And faith feels heavenly.

It's full of hope, trust, and a willingness to take a chance on these intangible ideals. Scary, but so, so worth it.

I take a trembling breath, filling my lungs with courage, and head for the stairs. The pleated skirt buffets and swirls with each step down. I'm so preoccupied in not tumbling that I don't see Noah until I'm almost at the bottom.

He's wide-eyed and open-mouthed.

I blush, my hand habitually coming up to rub behind my ear.

"Wow." This time he only mouths the word.

I blush brighter, hotter. I cover the last few steps, coming to stand before him. In the low heels, we're eye to eye. Green meeting darkening blue, a color I've never seen before. A color that raises my body temperature significant degrees. My hands come up to rest on his chest.

"I stopped my mother from cutting it when I was five."

Two hands slowly come up, brushing my cheeks as they travel to my hair. His fingers graze my scalp as they flow past my neck. They brush my bare shoulders, moving down to finally rest, tangled in the ends of my hair at my hip. Heat follows his fingers like the tail of a comet.

"It's kind of hot, so I've just got used to wearing it up."

He blinks once. Twice. "We're always living in cold climates."

Before his lips are on mine.

Those soft, hot lips brush against mine. Stealing my breath. Creating magic all over again. Sending my pulse skyrocketing.

"We are going, people!" Tara has the door open, ivory foot tapping impatiently. Noah grins then grabs my hand. We all head out to the Phelan truck. Not your standard wedding car. But I suppose a BMW would never make it to the Glade.

We climb in, Noah driving with Beth in the front, Tara and I in the back.

"I'm so glad you're here."

"Me too, Tara." Noah's eyes meet mine in the rearview mirror.

Tara grabs my hand in a painfully tight grasp. "Eeek!" She squeals in an ear-splitting pitch.

Noah turns onto the highway. "I'm not taking it personally that the prospect of bonding with me had you in tears."

"It's very personal. Mitch is much better looking."

"Now, Tara, both my boys are devilishly handsome." Beth turns toward me, also in a strapless number showing off her wolf tattoo, this one in pale green. "Isn't that right, Eden?"

I feel a little cornered. *Faith Eden*. "Beauty is certainly in the eye of the beholder." My gaze holds Noah's in the rearview mirror. His eyes widen, a little pleased, a lot flustered. My heart swells.

We turn onto the rutted track surrounded by green. Tara bounces three times higher than anyone else, like she's full of helium.

There are already several cars in the mini parking lot, all sturdy AWD's. Noah comes around to open the door for Tara, and she clambers out in a puff of tulle. Without warning she launches herself into his chest.

"Oomph."

"Thank you, Noah. You have no idea what this means to me. To Mitch."

"I think I have some idea."

"You've made our dreams come true."

Noah releases Tara, rubbing the back of his head and messing up the not-so-tame hairdo. Tara darts to the hidden trail, lifting the branch like it's half its size, and disappearing behind it. Looking like a fairy-tale princess disappearing into a magical forest. Off to find her prince.

"I'll see you in there, Noah." Beth rubs her hand down his arm before following Tara.

Noah comes up to me and we head into the Glade. Just like

last time, Noah moves the branch and we're back in the green cocoon. Noah squeezes my hand, and I squeeze his back.

The path opens out and the Glade stands before us. It's like I've stepped into another world, one that's even more magical than before. The giant pines, almost black in the half-light, stand imposing and silent. Their tall spires surround the Glade like a city of cathedrals. The space in the center is empty—a sacred, solemn expanse—the dusky twilight making it glow. The place is spellbinding.

There are people everywhere, all standing around the grassy center. Most are familiar faces from the barbecue, meaning there aren't any Channons here. I scan for Lara or Dana, and find neither. My hands clench. Tara deserves better.

"I have to go."

I look at Noah. He glances to the head of the Glade, where Uncle Joe is sitting next to Grandpa Ben. They both wave and I wave back. Funny-looking guitars are sitting on their laps, one leaning against a rock.

"You're looking at the band."

I don't want to let go. "Oh, okay."

With a squeeze of my hand, he heads over. Beth comes to stand next to me. She's watching Noah cross the Glade, her shoulders back and head high.

Noah picks up the guitar. Its body is a teardrop shape, multiple strings extending up the stocky arm. I realize it's not a guitar, but more like a lute. Intricate carvings extend across the timber face. I think I can see the Phelan mark etched into the corner.

Noah's head dips over the lute, and my eyes trace the strong hands that come up. Sure fingers strum the first chord and the rippling sound catches everyone's attention. Taking their cue, Grandpa Ben and Uncle Joe join the melody that Noah is now pouring out. Strummed baroque chords underscore lilting folk music, the beautiful melody cascading through the Glade. At times the three lutes play together, other times going their separate, harmonious ways, the notes tumbling, gliding and rippling over and around each other. The Glade is brimming with the sweet, romantic tune.

Tara materializes from the trees, her ivory dress glowing in the twilight. She's staring across the other side where Mitch is coming out, eyes captivated by his beautiful bride. I feel my jaw slacken, and catch it just in time. Mitch is shirtless, tanned shoulders held proud and straight over ridged abdominal muscles. His tattoo is just like Noah's, but then I notice the small mark in the bottom corner. Just like the one in Tara's painting, like a back to front *r*.

In unison they begin walking to the center of the Glade, the rhythm of the music counting out their steps. The intensity between them is palpable; it takes my breath away.

A wedding march like no one has ever seen.

And most never will.

Once they are only a foot apart, they stop. The music stops. The whole Glade stops. I don't think anyone takes a breath.

Mitch stands tall and proud. Tara looks like she could float away at any moment.

Mitch's voice carries through the clearing as he takes Tara's hand in his. "In your hands..."

Tara's eyes soften, her hands gripping his as she finishes the sentence. "I place my trust."

Her fingers come up to brush his cheek. "In your eyes..."

"I found my home." Mitch's palm lifts to rest over her heart, over her mark. "In your heart..."

"I found my love." Tara's voice has become a little choked. She leans into his hand. "In your spirit..."

Mitch's voice is firm and strong. "I found my mate."

Tara's hand comes to mirror Mitch's, over his heart. And I

realize that their marks have begun to glow. With their hands over each other's hearts, their tender gazes locked on each other, Tara and Mitch speak together. Their voices ring with the depth of their feeling, their conviction.

I GIVE YOU MY BODY, so that two become one.
  I give you my soul, till our life shall be done.

MITCH LEANS DOWN to kiss Tara—a tender, loving touch that seals their words. They hold there for long seconds. When they pull away Mitch is grinning that Phelan grin, while Tara's smile is christened by the moisture creeping down her cheeks.

I'm pretty choked myself. Beth has pulled out a tissue beside me. This must be a bittersweet moment for her. To see the son she adores bond with the girl he loves. Without her husband, her own mate, by her side. Aunt Mavis is hiccupping loudly into a handkerchief. Even a few men clear their throats.

The music starts up again, this time a clear rhythm, sounding much more like a medieval dance number. Noah's lute plays out the distinctive notes, his grandfather and uncle playing the background melody.

Tara and Mitch fold their arms behind their back and begin to move. They step back and to the side, then in. Opposite shoulders brush as they turn a half-step and step away, moving in a slow circle.

Each time their shoulders meet, their marks glow and pulse, the black etchings lit with an inner fire. The flowing lines of the wolves are now outlined in glittering detail, luminous red-gold, making them look almost three-dimensional. In, brush, turn and out. Magic lighting up their tender faces, creating a luminescent orb in the center of the Glade. I squint a little, seeing that Tara's is changing, the Channon square slowly morphing, stretching. As it slowly becomes the Phelan mark.

I look over to Noah. He's watching his brother with the same intensity as everyone else. His fingers moving unconsciously over the strings, the tune well-known. He must sense my gaze, because he turns to me. A soft smile tips his lips.

The music picks up tempo, as do Mitch and Tara, their steps now becoming a light jig, their turns a swirl. The tulle of Tara's wedding dress furls out, brushing Mitch's legs. Their marks flash each time they touch, gilding their tattoos with flaming, shining light. My eyes are wide with wonder as this spellbinding, magical moment unfolds before me.

Then Mitch grabs Tara and they are spinning. They spin faster and faster, creating their own tempo. The music swirls around them. Tara throws her arms up into the air, and delighted laughter spills from her lips.

Everyone in the Glade smiles, grins beams. The couple's happiness is contagious.

The music stops, and Tara and Mitch slow to a standstill. They are both panting, bare shoulders lifting and falling. Mitch's hand comes to brush over Tara's tattoo, tracing the Phelan mark. A wide grin splits his face. Tara throws her arms around his neck, pulling him down for an exuberant, tender kiss.

A raucous round of applause lifts up to the trees. My breath rushes out, a breath I had been entirely unaware I was holding. My hands go a little numb as I clap right along with them.

In the words of Noah Phelan, *wow*.

Now that the magical moment has slowed, reality filters in. I rub the goose bumps on my exposed upper arms, the thin, blue material of my dress fluttering in the fall breeze. The Were women around me are oblivious to the falling temperatures.

The music starts again—a new tune—more of a waltz, or a slow dance. Couples begin to filter onto the grassy dance floor.

Oh, the bridal waltz is done, and now everyone joins in. I glance from the corner of my eye. Phew, Noah is still playing. I've never danced, let alone in public. I don't think I'm up to trying it on a floor full of Werewolves.

I see some movement from the head of the Glade.

Noah has put down his lute.

And is walking toward me.

28

NOAH

"You go, son."

"Huh?" I turn from where I was watching Eden, standing on the edge of the Glade looking impossibly beautiful in that dress. That hair.

"You're needed somewhere else."

So tempting. "But—"

Uncle Joe hasn't paused in his playing. "We've been playing this long before you were born, young man. Now get going." He tries for stern. And fails.

I grin. "Twisted my arm."

With quick movements I put down the lute and stand. Uncle Joe is right, I'm not meant to be here. I'm meant to be with the girl across the Glade. There are no longer any barriers between us.

I start to thread through the few people left around the edge, some sitting on the rocks scattered around, the notes of the lutes curling between them just like I am.

Although Eden is watching the dancers, she knows I'm coming. I can feel her nervy edginess, see her shifting her weight from one foot to the other.

I see Mom, standing alone, a smile on her lips as she watches Mitch dance with Tara. The absence of her mate in her clasped hands.

Dad should be here.

But he's not. And it's not okay that she has this moment alone. I push aside my disappointment and alter my trajectory. Just as Grandpa Ben breezes past me. Very subtly, but very effectively, cutting me off.

He stands in front of Mom. She looks up at him and a moment passes between them. Her husband. His son. One arm behind his back, his other hand out, he bows a little.

"Shall we?"

"We shall." And they head to the moving masses.

My gaze goes back to Eden—that cascade of mahogany skimming her hips, her eyes brighter than I have ever seen, that blue dress hugging her curves.

I squint. Her curves look like they're shivering. I quickly cover the last few yards between us as another wave of shivers passes through her. I wrap my arms around her and she sinks into me without a second's hesitation. My heart swells.

We fit together like we'd never been apart.

"Shall we?" I repeat Grandpa Ben's offer. It seemed to work for him.

She stills. "Ah, can't we watch?"

"Ah, no."

Eden watches the slow-moving couples. She takes a deep breath. "Okay."

We move to the edge of the crowd. Her lip slips beneath her teeth. "I've never done this before."

I grasp her chin, gently removing her bottom lip from its pearly clamp. "Me neither."

She looks doubtful. "You've been to plenty of bondings. You would have danced at them."

I pull her in close, our faces inches apart, legs brushing and chest to chest. "Not like this."

"Oh." The word brushes me with a puff of wildflowers.

She doesn't move, looking for my cue. I don't bother with the standard dancing position, one hand on the waist, the other pointing out like the bow of a ship. My hands stay around her waist, fingers spreading wide so I can feel more of her. Eden's tender, tentative palms climb up the lapel of my tux, then cup my shoulders. The lilting music swirls along with that amazing sense of connection.

Together.

I'm still trying to grasp it. But the undeniable happiness that fills my chest, overflowing into the massive grin I can't wipe off, is proof enough.

My fingers tangle in the silky strands of her hair. "I'm glad you came."

Green eyes glowing, her lips tip up. "Me too."

We begin to move. I take a step backward, and the body molded to mine follows. A step to the side, and her lean form is right there with me. With a twitch of a smile, I make several choreographed steps, swaying around our little space on the grassy dance floor. Our bodies are so in tune; where one goes, the other follows. I have a feeling we could master the tango in thirty seconds flat with our phenomenal connection.

Eden smiles up at me. "That was so beautiful. The Glade, the dancing, their marks changing." A little frown crinkles her brow. "The tattoo on your chest, it doesn't have a Phelan mark."

"When did you—?" I try to figure out when she would have seen it. Oh, when I changed. I smile even wider. "Looking, huh?"

Eden's delectable blush creeps up her cheeks. I feel my chest expanding a little. "I never had one."

"Why not?"

I shrug, feeling her hands pressing in even more. "No one knows. Another of my freaky tendencies."

I take her on a little spin, using it as an excuse to pull her in a little closer. "Every pack has its own symbol. The closest we've seen is an ancient alphabet."

"So Weres go way back."

"Seems so. We don't keep a written record. It's all passed down by word of mouth." I sidestep around Aunt Mavis, who's happily swaying to the music solo. "So, we've been dancing for a solid few minutes now."

Her eyes widen. "We have."

"Toes are intact, no humiliating stumbles."

She ducks her head. "You make it easy, Noah."

"Only with you, Eden." I spin her again, her hair flowing out then falling back around the two of us.

I look down into shining green eyes, soft lips, my heart doing its own happy dance. My arms tighten around her waist. I think of how she looked when we were under Grandfather Douglas. The unbelievable things she said.

"It was worth it?"

Her hand comes up to cup my neck, fingers brushing the edges of my hair. "Every moment."

"Even though...?" I could feel her pain. Its depth. Its breadth.

"Even though."

A powerful pull to hold her close, cherish her, protect her wells up. "But you didn't know the bonding with Tara wasn't happening."

"Even then."

"Eden." I can't hold back any longer. My hands leave her hips and come up to cup her face.

Those soft lips are ready, waiting. No hint of caution.

The ultimate gift.

My lips brush hers. I want to savor this moment—so special,

so unbelievable. Her mouth, so, so soft, opens like a fragile blossom beneath mine.

Warm protectiveness comes up against heated desire, calling me to crush every inch against my body. To explore that exposed skin. To taste her heat again. My fingers tense along her jaw as I resist the hunger building in my body, firing through my veins. Eden deserves to be cherished. To know what she means to me.

But then her fingers spear into my hair. She places heated pressure on my scalp, pulling my head down, closer. Our lips crush and meld. Whoa. Desire rages like wildfire, blazing through my body, scorching through rational thought. I pull away before I stop acting like the Alpha I foolishly signed myself up for.

"Hey, we're the newlyweds here." Mitch jostles me with his shoulder.

I release Eden so I can give my brother a hug—a back-slapping, spine-crushing hug. The extra seconds that Mitch holds me tells me his thanks, both of us not needing, or wanting to say it out loud. I figure he realizes it was a win-win situation for the two of us.

An insidious little question raises its hand. Was this just a selfish decision?

I ignore it and the tension spawns in my chest. "Congrats, little bro."

Eden and Tara are doing the same. Tara steps back, and holding Eden's hands, does a few little hops. Her smile is splitting. "Hooley dooley!" She practically sings the words.

"That was amazing. You were amazing. The whole thing was amazing."

"I'm so happy, Eden."

Grandpa Ben slips in amongst us, bowing like a gentleman of old before Tara. Tara giggles, giving a little curtsy, before they dance off into the middle of the throng. Mitch looks at Eden, and her eyes widen a little.

"You don't have to look that horrified." He grins, grabbing her before she gets a chance to object. He spins her away, her hair billowing out behind her. She's smiling before they've stopped.

I hold out my arms for Mom. "Looks like it's you and me."

She smiles, stepping into my arms. We've done this countless times before, and we shuffle through the familiar steps. We stay at the edge of the crowd, the protection of the trees not far away. Mom's eyes are a poignant mix of pride and disappointment, happiness and sadness.

I hold her in close. "I wish he was here too."

That anger simmers along my veins again. He should have been here.

The hairs on the back of my neck step up to attention. Over Mom's head I look into the trees. A giant russet wolf stands in the dark, the width of an old pine obscuring most of his body, head dropped low between hunched shoulders, Kurt's eyes are glowing fury. He sees me register his presence, and his muzzle wrinkles, teeth glinting in the dark. He came!

I seek out Eden. She's dancing with Grandpa Ben, a soft happy smile on her lips. When I turn back to the trees, Kurt is gone. I double-check on Eden.

Mom misinterprets my concerned glances. "Go to her. These old legs need a rest."

I look at her, knowing she's neither old nor tired. But protectiveness has my shoulders tense. She nods again, stepping away.

"Mom, you're the best."

"Totes awesome. I believe Tara called me."

I give her a big kiss on the cheek. "She was totes right."

Another check of the trees and there's no sign of the angry, red wolf. So, Kurt came to see the bonding. He obviously didn't like what he saw then left. Still, the one person he could be a threat to is Eden. The need to be closer to her grows stronger than ever.

I head over to Eden and Grandpa Ben. He sees me coming and steps away. He holds Eden's hand up, bowing at the waist. I roll my eyes. I have no idea where he gets this stuff from; he's not that old. Eden blushes, thanking him.

And she's in my arms again, slipping in like she's meant to be there. Because she belongs there. My arms fill with her warm body; my lungs fill with wonderful wildflower scent. My heart fills until it feels like it's going to burst.

There, with the stars above us, the green grass beneath us, and the magic of the bonding, the Glade, the magic purely created by the two of us, I'm tempted to say the words. Words I've known since the day she walked into my world. Words that only begin to capture the depth of my feelings for her. Words I'm not sure she's ready to hear.

She's looking up at me, tilted green eyes luminous with emotion. Maybe she feels it too. I open my mouth, the words so close.

Grandpa Ben clears his throat, and the music comes to a finish. We all stop, to find he's standing at the head of the Glade. He indicates for Mitch and Tara to join him.

It's time for the blessing.

Grandpa Ben lowers his grey head, and we straighten to face him. Tara and Mitch are glowing in their little bubble of happiness.

Grandpa's voice carries over the Glade and through the trees, quoting the ancient Indian blessing we've used for generations.

NOW YOU WILL FEEL *no rain,*
   For each of you will be shelter for the other.

Now you will feel no cold,
For each of you will be warmth to the other.
Now there will be no loneliness,
For each of you will be companion to the other.
Now you are two persons,
but there is only one life before you.

GRANDPA HOLDS OUT HIS ARMS. "Ladies and gentlewere, I present to you, Mitch and Tara of the Phelan pack."

Mitch takes Tara in his arms, giving her a sweet kiss, as the crowd once again breaks into applause.

I squeeze Eden's hand. "And it's done."

Tara slips from Mitch's arms and they both head toward the trees. In a blink of an eye, two wolves stand there. A big, black wolf and a slightly smaller red one. Their heads tilt in, nuzzling, before they leap forward and disappear into the trees.

Slowly at first, my extended family starts following, each changing into shades of grey, brown, and red. More and more morph and leap into the trees, until I'm standing with Eden and Mom. Mom turns and heads for the path. I know she won't run without Dad.

Eden turns to me. "You should go."

I take her hand, pulling her in the same direction that Mom is heading. "Nah. I'm good."

She stops, and my arm jerks as I come to a stop too. "You should go."

I turn to face her, knowing she doesn't understand. "Eden, I don't want to run as the Alpha. That's my dad's job."

"Oh."

Instead I focus on the positives. "One day we'll join them."

"We?"

Her confusion is enough to unbalance her, and, with a quick

pull, we're heading toward the path. An idea has anticipation pulsing through my mind.

Once we're back at the parking lot, I turn to her. "So, what time are you usually up on a Saturday?"

"I'm not much for sleeping in, why?"

I grin. "I thought we might go on a date."

29

EDEN

L ight is barely touching the Inn grounds when I tiptoe out our front door. Alexis and I have barely spoken since the day I rushed to the bonding. She hasn't asked about Noah, but I suspect the dramatic change in my behavior answers any questions she may have. I generally try to avoid our brief, tense interactions defined by avoidance of eye contact, monosyllabic conversations and unsaid encyclopedias of words hanging around us.

I wait at the front gate, the cool, moist air creeping into any little gaps between my jacket and skin. Every now and then a wave of goose bumps flashes across my arms, seeking any flicker of heat they can glean. I flick my braid over my shoulder, once again treading the fine line between nervousness and anticipation, when I hear his truck. The man-made sound overpowers the gurgle of the river and the sweet tweets of the yellow warblers, blasting the concealing silence. The blue truck lumbers around the bend, with a red canoe strapped from the tray to the roof.

Canoeing! I can't help myself; I skip straight into anticipation and out of the gate.

Noah hops out of the truck, a huge, happy grin lighting up his face and his eyes. My heart feels like it could float out of my chest. He's closely followed by Stash, his tail wagging out his excitement and enthusiasm. It's times like these I wish I had a tail too.

"Hey, boy." I kneel down and he barrels into my arms. I rub his head, his chocolate-colored ears flopping from side to side.

"I figured we could bring the dogs," he states in a hushed tone. A little redundant considering his truck obliterated the dawn quiet.

"I can bring Caesar?"

Noah grins. "Only if you want to."

I spin on my heel and run up the path. I open the door and call him. In a split second Caesar leaps through the front door, and skids to a halt on the path. Stash is there, eyes alert. Caesar looks at me and I nod. A few cautious steps and he's in front of Stash. The two males reach out, noses sniffing the air, their tails straight and erect. Stash is the first to move. His tail twitches a little and pauses, waiting to see its reception. Caesar mirrors the micro tail wag. And that's all they need. They step forward, and with a quick head to toe sniff, tails are wagging and excited leaps abound.

Partway down the path, I notice Noah is rubbing his lip. "You didn't have to use your voice, did you?"

I stop. I didn't want to risk waking my mother. "No."

The corners of Noah's mouth turn down as he considers this, his bottom lip tipping out. He gives a sideways nod. "Lucky you."

I move again, heading to the truck. I don't know why I worried, Noah has always accepted me unquestioningly. But I suppose old fears don't just throw their hands up and slink off, never to be seen again. It would be nice if they would.

I open the door, tapping the red plastic shell above the cab. "So what are we doing today?"

"I thought we'd play chess."

I smile my own happy, excited smile. "Can't wait."

Noah chuckles, opening the door. The two dogs jump into the backseat, and he starts strapping in Stash. He even brought two doggy seat belts. I reach in, realizing we look a little like a married couple strapping their kids in.

As we pull out of the driveway, I glance over my shoulder. I think I see something move in the front window, but I'm not sure. I turn back to the windshield, Noah's profile in my peripheral vision. I'm not going to let it dampen my excitement.

"So, where do the board games start?"

"Well, I know a secret little spot where we can launch and then it's a matter of floating down the river."

Oooh, a private canoe trip. My feet tap an excited little ditty on the car floor.

Noah heads away from the national park, toward the Glade. We zoom past a sign saying 'Wilmot 10 Miles' and it reminds me.

"Have you heard from Kurt?"

Noah's hands tense on the steering wheel. "No. But it's done now. Let's hope he takes it gracefully."

"And your dad?"

His shoulders slump. "No change. We can't figure out why the healing is taking so long."

My hand reaches out, and finds his. He grasps it, and I can feel his heartache, with the hint of desperation shifting beneath it. I give it a squeeze, wishing I could do more.

"Do they know who?"

Those shoulders drop another inch. "No. And without front-line evidence, they're not likely to find out." Noah glances at me before turning his eyes back to the road, returning the squeeze. "Today is about us. Let's just enjoy it."

"I can do that."

We pull off the highway and onto a dirt road leading into the trees. I have a sense we're near the national park, in the vicinity of the Glade. In the back Stash gives out an excited bark. He knows where we're going. Caesar has picked up on the atmosphere, his nose smearing lines down his window as he tries to figure out what might be coming up.

The trees open out and the river is before us. Right where its massive width has divided, a smaller tributary passes before us. It's like we're standing on Mother Nature's shoulder and she's extended a curvaceous sweeping arm, the remainder of her serpentine body curving away. The jagged mountains, so majestically close, watch her lounging at their feet.

We pull up beneath a willow, its weeping branches brushing the truck. The two dogs leap out and are instantly absorbed in scenting the place out. They follow each other, seeing who's found something more interesting, more new.

Standing at the river's edge, I breathe in the cool mountain air—the scent that fast became one of my favorite smells. The sun, a gentle glowing giant concealed behind the trees, outlines the tall conifers with shimmering detail. In the muted light, the flowing water course gurgles and splashes. It's breathtaking.

Noah steps up behind me and his arms slip around my waist. I sink into his chest, its warmth instantly filtering through my layers. His cheek comes to rest against mine; his bristly skin feels delicious. My most favorite smell fills my lungs.

I turn my head a little, resting it more against Noah. "This is beautiful."

"It's the best time to see it."

At that moment the sun arches over the trees, spilling golden light over the panorama. Rays of light lance over the jagged horizon, each one brushing the scene with its Midas touch. Every pebble, blade of grass and drop of water becomes suffused with vibrant light.

I turn in Noah's arms, my hands wrapping around his shoulders, and my breath catches. With his honeyed hair touched by the sun, his blue eyes glorious and intense, he's more breathtaking than the scenery. More importantly, his lips are dipping down to meet mine.

Gently they brush mine, a butterfly breath leaving them tingling and craving. Once. Twice. So sweet, so tender. Making me feel something new, something I can't identify.

But it's not enough.

My fingers spear into those tawny, glowing locks and grip, pulling him close as I push up on my toes. Bringing his lips into direct contact with mine.

They're warm and soft and heavenly.

I want more. I tug on his silken strands, creating more pressure. More heat.

All of a sudden they're hot and strong and fierce. Noah crushes me to him, like I've unleashed something within him. Something within me. How can it blaze so hot, so quick?

Passion explodes through my tightly strung body. Noah's chest rumbles on a groan, the sound amplifying the explosive feelings. Arms tighten, bodies press. Hands begin to move.

A bark bounces around the clearing. And another. I pull away, and we turn our heads. My unfocused eyes and fuzzy brain slowly register two dogs watching us, tails wagging. My breath rushes out with a smile. Caesar barks again, giving a little hop forward.

Noah's arms loosen around my back. "Nothing like an audience."

I giggle, and then it steps up to all-out laughter. My forehead sinks to his chest, which is shaking with amusement. Caesar leaps up, two muddy paws thumping onto my hip. I rub his head, down to his shoulders. Stash is jumping like a jackrabbit, his own barks bubbling up.

I release Noah, giving Caesar his own hug. "I'm glad you approve," I whisper into his neck.

Noah ruffles Caesar's head. "Me too."

I shoot up straight, surprised. *Oh yes*. Were super-hearing.

Noah winks. "Let's get going."

In no time we have the canoe sitting at the edge of the water, efficiently lifting it, turning it, and placing it ready for launch like we've done this countless times before. Stash doesn't wait for an invite before leaping in, and Caesar takes his cue, jumping up beside him.

"Safety first." Noah passes me a red U-shaped contraption— a life vest. He helps me slip it on, tightening the straps. "If you go in, pull this." He points to a yellow toggle at the front, then quickly slips his own on.

Noah holds out his hand and helps me step into the boat, my hiking boots only touching the edge of the water. I sit on the center bench, that unidentifiable feeling bubbling up again.

"Hold on." And with practiced speed he pushes the canoe out and leaps in, a few watery droplets catching the light as they follow him into the boat. He settles himself at the back, picks up a paddle, and steers us into the river.

Caesar and Stash sit at the front, two canine captains at the bow, one fuzzy set of ears straight up, one velvety set perma- nently folded down. Four eyes darting left and right, up and down. Two tongues lolling happily.

My head follows theirs, trying to take it all in. This new perspective of the wilderness I haven't seen: the canoe a floating island in a river that is a complex patchwork of stillness, eddies and ripples, and the shore a moving buffet as the golden sunlight casts the grasses a glowing orange, darkening the conifers to a deep dark green.

I look back at Noah. I watch the way he competently steers the canoe, strong confident hands making small adjustments with the paddle. The early morning light is touching his tousled hair. He's smiling. I can see his happiness. I can feel his happiness. And it matches mine.

A breeze ruffles the water, and it feels like it's come straight down from the snowcapped mountain. I tuck my hands into the opposite sleeve.

"Come here." Noah extends his arms, and I look at the inviting space he has opened up.

"Don't we need to keep the canoe balanced?"

"I'll move forward and those two boof heads at the front will do the rest for us."

I don't need any more convincing. Noah shuffles to the next bench seat and carefully, with the canoe swaying from side to side, I creep back to him. He wads up a spare jacket and tucks it at the base of his low bench, effectively creating a little cushioned seat. I clamber between his open knees, and lean back against him. Instant warmth cocoons me.

"Better?"

"Hmmm. Much better."

I feel a few feathery brushes at my lower back. "Much better," Noah echoes, and the three strands of my braid slowly unwind. I look over my shoulder at him, and he gives me a cheeky grin.

"Look." His arm brushes my shoulder as he points toward the shore. A moose is standing in the shallows, munching on the willow leaves conveniently hanging over the water. He lifts his flattened antlers, watching us cruise past. His long, gangly legs step backward, his rotund nose sniffing the air, like he can feel I'm not a threat, but senses that something about Noah is. Noah dips the paddle in, giving the canoe a gentle push and we sail quietly past.

Farther down, a beaver lodge looms at the edge of the river, logs stripped of bark thrown together into a haystack of pick-up sticks, the homeowners nowhere to be seen. The timber hill has redirected the edge of the stream, creating a little dam, constructing a still space where two Canada geese paddle peacefully. I snuggle into the solid chest behind me, warm and content to watch the nature documentary pass by.

Within the protection of my personal heater, I twist to the side so I can dip my finger into the water. It's icy cold. Ripples of water fan out from where I break the surface. I watch the rhythmic little waves push out then dissolve. I jolt when something brushes my fingers. I peer into the water and see a fish swimming alongside my hand. I turn wide eyes to Noah.

He glances over the side. "That's a cutthroat trout. A decent-sized one too."

Hundreds of small spots cover the fish that rubs its scaly body against me, its streamlined shape so much bigger than my hand. I turn my hand over, fingers extending, feeling the cold, firm body sinking into my palm. My fingertips brush over the ridges of its silvery scales, skim the distinctive crimson stripe along its lower jaw. Its fins gently fan the water, caressing my palm. With a flick of its tail and a flash of red, it dives into the deep water.

I'm a little speechless as I lean back into the boat. "Well…"

Noah hugs me to him. "You'd be a fisherman's dream."

I snort. "There's a reason they don't go near them unless they're hungry."

Noah holds me a little tighter. "The truth is, you're everything I've ever wished for."

Warmth wells from somewhere deep inside me, bubbling up from a dormant volcano that can no longer be contained. I rub my head against his chin. "You're the dream I never let myself have," I whisper. Knowing full well he can hear me.

His arms flex, holding me as if he never wants to let me go.

Which is fine. Because I never want to leave.

We stay like that for a long time, the canoe slowly floating down the narrowing tributary. Taking in all that's around us. Taking in all that's between us.

We round a bend and Noah sits up a little straighter. I lean forward, seeing a clearing at the edge of the water. Noah starts paddling toward it. I think we've arrived at our destination.

The canoe beaches with the quiet crunch of plastic across sand. Caesar and Stash leap into the shallow water, splashing their way to land. I slide back to the center bench, collecting my backpack.

Before I can stand Noah is up and, just like the dogs, splashes into the water up to his calves. I watch horrified, as he walks around the canoe, grasps it, and hauls the front half out of the water. Then heads back into the shallows to stand beside me.

"Noah, your shoes!"

He looks down at the water lapping his ankles and shrugs. "They'll dry. And I don't feel the cold." He extends his hand, just like earlier.

I take it, and next thing I know, his other arm scoops behind my knees and lifts me into his arms. I squeal in surprise, my hands flying to his shoulders, fingers digging into solid muscle.

My eyes fly to his. "What are you doing?" Dancing blue eyes look at me with a mix of humor and tenderness. And a little splash of heat.

"Keeping your feet dry."

"Oh."

That alien feeling is creeping across my chest, making my cheeks pink. I feel...*cherished*.

Noah carries me the few feet to land. I can feel strong biceps across my back, below my legs. Ridged muscles beneath my hands. And a solid wall of heat against my shoulder. My cheeks feel warmer than they should be.

He holds me for another few seconds then very carefully, very gently, he releases me. My legs touch the ground; my body remains against his. I don't know if this day could get any better.

I step up on tippytoes. Then stop, wondering if I should, jolting back down to flat-footed safety.

"What?"

"Nothing."

His eyes narrow, giving me no quarter. "Why did you stop, Eden?"

I lift my one shoulder then drop it, unsure of how to put this into words. "I don't want to set up a false economy."

Noah snorts, his arms tightening. "I don't think demand will outstrip supply."

I look at the sincerity in his blue eyes. Can I really let myself go?

"In that case then." I push back up and press my lips to his.

The feeling of his mouth on mine is still so new, so intriguing, so intoxicating.

And with permission comes curiosity. The desire to know more. I kiss the edge of his mouth, then with fluttering lips I explore the ridge of his bottom lip, following its curve to the opposite corner. Noah's mouth parts, his breath catching then exhaling. I breathe in through my mouth, tasting his warm masculine scent. I continue my exploration, my lips moving over the bow of his top lip. Discovering the firm edge, the soft lip, the taste of Noah. Without conscious thought, the tip of my tongue slips out, hungry for more.

Noah's hands fly up to cup my head, his fingers in my hair, keeping my head still. I stop, confused. His lips come to rest at the edge of my mouth. And he begins mirroring my movements, little flutters along my bottom lip to the opposite corner. My own breath stutters. He moves over my top lip, his mouth hot but oh so light. I practically tremble, knowing what's coming next.

A hot, hot tongue slips out, and flutters across my bottom lip. Over the one that is waiting, suspended in anticipation.

And it's my turn to groan.

His mouth crushes down on my parted lips, and his tongue is inside, my own reaching out to meet it. Passion, hunger rocket through me. I angle my head, and Noah is there, moving in closer, hungrily delving deeper. Mouths move, tongues stroke, each exploring, giving and taking. My knees give out and I clamp my hands on his shoulders. His hot hands are around my waist, his scorching hard body my foundation.

I'm spiraling out of control. I pull back, breathing hard. These feelings fire so fast, burn so hot. Shouldn't there be more tentativeness, fumbling, faltering? Instead the blaze is fueled by sureness, affinity, and feelings more fierce than the sun.

Electric blue eyes look at me; Noah's breathing is just as labored as mine. A crooked smile tips up those delicious lips.

"We're gonna have to watch that."

Tell me about it...

I smile, and I know it's a small, shy smile. I haven't recovered enough to talk yet.

"I love your smile, Eden."

My lips tip up a little wider. "You could look at it all day?" I ask, letting him know the feeling is mutual.

And he grins that grin that leaves me a little breathless, mindless.

"Let's have some morning tea."

He walks over to a log and sits and starts pulling off his wet shoes and socks, placing them in the sun. He pads back, those bare feet, his tousled locks, giving him an adorable boyish look. I sigh; is there any look that doesn't have my heart constricting, swelling or beating madly?

Noah pulls a thermos and two travel mugs out of his bag. "I brought hot chocolate."

I pull out a paper bag from my own. "I brought cookies."

"A match made in heaven."

A picnic blanket closely follows and Noah spreads it beside the log. He pours the hot chocolate then leans against his makeshift backrest. I don't wait for an invite, but quickly snuggle in next to him. He passes me one of the mugs, and I wrap my hands around it. We sit back, enjoying the peace.

Peace punctuated by the occasional canine bark. Stash and Caesar periodically shoot past, at times a chocolate streak leading, the next a blur of black and brown at the head. Caesar loves this wilderness as much as I do, and now he has a companion to share it with too. During one lap he stops in front of us, barks a happy bark, before following Stash to a new unexplored area. Noah wouldn't realize the ultimate compliment Caesar has given him by leaving me alone with him.

"Mitch and I spent most summers here. The river is a bit more of a rush with all the melted ice coming down from the mountains." Noah takes a sip. "What were your summers like?"

"Depends on the city."

"Where else have you lived?"

"Chicago, Pittsburgh, Detroit. We did a short stint in New York."

"Quite the nomads, huh? We'll start with Boston. What was it like?"

I look at him, my eyes no longer masking all the pain of those two years. "I didn't really fit in."

His steady gaze holds mine. "They weren't very nice to you, were they?" His arm curves around my shoulder.

"It was my first day when I came across some kids tormenting a stray kitten."

"So you helped it."

"Yeah well, the minute Whiskers curled into my arm, one

girl went from ringleader to animal torturer. It turns out the most popular girl in the school found her next victim."

I feel the flash of anger in the body beside me, and Noah's right. It wasn't fair. But I shrug; Boston was the worst, but it was always the same. "I've never really fitted in."

Noah pulls me in, and I nestle farther into his side, head tucked beneath his chin, arms locked around his waist.

"You fit right here."

And he's right.

So I stay there, snug and warm, reveling in the perfect fit our bodies make. Our hot chocolates and cookie stash slowly dwindle as the sun progressively rises. I'm pretty sure it doesn't get any better than this.

Beside me Noah leans back and stretches. "Shall we run?"

"You want to go for a jog?"

"Not quite."

"I don't..." Noah has cocked an eyebrow, patiently waiting.

A run!

"You mean, with you as a..."

"Uh-huh."

"It would be more of stroll for you. I could never keep up."

Noah rolls his eyes. I think I'm missing the punch line. "You'd be with me."

With him? My eyes consider popping out of their sockets. *He can't mean what I think he means.*

Noah chuckles, amusement lighting his eyes to a clear azure. "Come on."

He takes my hand and pulls me toward the trees. He can't mean it, can he?

Once we're amongst the brown trunks, the pungent scent of pine spilling down on us, Noah releases my hand. He takes a few steps back.

"But—"

He starts to change—growing, his body multiplying. It's quicker and looks almost painless compared to the change I saw last time, as if it's becoming familiar. I see a flash of naked chest, his mark capturing my attention for a split second...

And a proud white wolf stands before me. I stand a little open-mouthed. Will this magical transformation always leave me awestruck?

Noah steps forward, his broad head dipping, blue eyes assessing—both striking and imposing. He takes another two steps forward, passing me until his chest is alongside me then stops. He looks over his shoulder, jerking his broad head.

He is serious.

I look at the white body before me: the shoulders just a little lower than mine, curving down to powerful back haunches and the thick, snowy tail. I can't help myself; my hand reaches out to brush the animal before me, sinking into warm, white fur. That lush tail wags just a smidgen, his body stepping a little closer.

Really serious.

Caesar and Stash rush up. Stash barks madly, his excited tail wagging out of control. Caesar's brown eyes are wide, entirely unsure of the massive wolf in front of him—an animal that should be a threat, but one that is standing calmly beside me. Noah's head brushes against me, and I turn back to find soft blue eyes looking into mine. His velvety face grazes mine. My hands come up to touch fuzzy cheeks as I bring my forehead to rest against his.

"What do you think, Caesar?"

I turn my head to gauge his response, letting my cheek rest against Noah. Stash is jumping from side to side, doing a canine Mexican hat dance. Caesar looks at him, then at Noah.

"Woof!" And he's leaping around the same sombrero, tail high, eyes excited.

"Well, I believe majority wins."

The wolf beside me does a little excited hop of his own. He lines up before me. I bite my lip, unsure of how to execute this. Noah in wolf form, although not the size of a horse, would give a pony healthy competition. Do I take a run up?

Before I give myself too much time to think, which could be just enough time to change my mind, I leap.

Hands grasp and legs clench around a huge, furry body. It's almost like I'm practiced at it, even though I've never ridden so much as a rocking horse, I land squarely on his back. To my delighted surprise, I don't bounce straight back down, or fall straight over the other side. Instead, I find myself right in the middle, a saddle of white fur beneath me. I shift a little from side to side, finding the perfect balance.

Noah's broad head swings to look over his shoulder, and his lips pull back, his tongue lolling. I smile right back.

"So, shouldn't we be moving or something?"

And that's all the prompt he needs. He starts walking forward, heading to the trees. I grip a little tighter, my legs cinching around his ribs, my hands grasping his fur. I can feel muscles bunch and release beneath thick padding. A few feet off the ground, my heart has started to pick up an accelerated rhythm, spurred on by equal parts nervousness and excitement. *Please don't let me fall off.* Caesar and Stash leap around down at ground level, barking.

I look at the slow-moving scenery from my elevated vantage point, humbled by the power that is beneath me, for the moment feeling like it's part of me. Is this what a queen feels like? Although I doubt even royalty has ridden on something so magnificent. What a surreal, exciting feeling. And Noah has chosen to share this with me. I lean forward, my mouth near his ear, white fur tickling my nose.

"Thank you."

Those glittering blue eyes look back at me, snowy eyebrows raised.

He steps up to a loping gait, his paws setting up a rhythmic cadence. My eyes open a little wider at the increase in speed. My hands grip tighter, and I hope my fingers aren't digging in. Noah doesn't seem to mind because trees are passing us with increased momentum. Caesar and Stash step up to a run. The cool air brushes my cheeks, making wide eyes blink a little more rapidly.

Noah agilely steps through the trees, like he's so much smaller than he is, but with the power inherent of an animal his size. I find myself swaying with each sidestep, dipping with each overhead branch, lifting with each obstacle he steps over. We move deeper into the secluded forest, swallowed by nature, absorbed by the magic of the moment.

Up ahead the trees open out to a sunlit meadow, an expanse of swaying grass brushed gold by the sun. A growl trembles through the body beneath me, and Noah leaps forward. My hands grasp his snowy fur, my legs pulling up to hold more tightly as he accelerates. His ears tip back while his head arches forward. His whole body stretches out to become a streamlined speed machine.

The world becomes a blur of greens and browns and yellows. The wind whips my hair behind me like a sail. Powerful paws thunder out a reverberating rhythm. Unrestrained power is bunching and releasing beneath me. Noah lets out another wild, excited growl.

And I can feel him—everything a little wilder, more raw than before. His own exhilaration, excitement. And another emotion. One that calls to me at a deeper level.

The feelings whip through me, and instead of holding even tighter, I throw my arms wide, arch my back, and tilt my face to the sun. Cool air rushes past me, stinging my face, flowing over my arms and ripping at my clothes. But I don't feel the cold. Instead I feel pure emotion rising, ascending and erupting from a brimming volcano. Happiness. Joy.

And freedom.

Freedom coursing through my unbound hair and my over-flowing heart. The freedom of this day spilling from my lips in delighted laughter. The sound is caught by the wind and whips around us before being snatched by the turbulent wind. Noah throws back his head and howls, his notes joining mine. The privilege, the liberty, the freedom of being with Noah allowing me to do what I thought was almost impossible.

The freedom to touch. The freedom to feel.

The freedom to love.

I BLINK, surprised but impressed. "But how?"

We've come back to the canoe, and the Phelan truck has been parked beneath a tree, a spruce this time.

"Mitch and Tara. Believe me, I've done it for them plenty of times. It was time they returned the favor."

"Oh."

Caesar and Stash have collapsed by the car, panting heavily. They had to run like the wind, even then not keeping up with Noah's stride which was so much longer than theirs and so much more powerful. Caesar will sleep well tonight.

We pack up the canoe with the same efficiency we unpacked it, and it's strapped down to the roof of the truck in a few short minutes. I can't help but watch strong muscles bunch as Noah lifts, his T-shirt hitching up to show me a flash of abdomen. When I turn from clipping Caesar in, I find Noah's warm eyes on mine.

We drive back in companionable silence. For the short

length down the highway, Noah grasps my hand, his thumb stroking rhythmically over my knuckles. A soft smile is permanently imprinted on my face.

It's lunchtime when we arrive back at the Inn. Noah pulls up and we unbuckle the dogs. We come around the front of the truck, meeting face to face. I look up into those sculptured features and soft eyes the color of a clear sky, his mouth matching my gently tilted smile.

I take his hand. "Today is unequivocally awarded the best-day-of-my-life."

Noah's smile tips up to a dazzling grin. The one that sucks all the air from my lungs. "I was going to give it most-unforgettable-day-of-my-life."

"Multi-award winning then."

He steps in so our bodies are flush. "Definitely."

My hand comes up to stroke his cheek. Finally I can return our good-bye gesture. Noah's hand comes up to spear into the hair at the base of my neck.

My chin tilts up as he leans down. I love that we're establishing such a strong, rich economy. His mouth gently brushes mine.

"Have fun studying."

"I'll try. Tell Mitch and Tara I said thanks for bringing the car around."

"Will do."

We both stand there, hands touching, bodies brushing, lips close. Neither willing our time together to end.

But I know he has to go back to the hospital. To sit beside his silent, unmoving father. The sad knowledge provides closure for the day's beautiful start.

I step back, cool air replacing his warm heat. "Bye."

Noah leans back against the truck, arms folded across his front. "Bye."

I head for the house, Caesar by my side. At the door I give Noah a small wave, cataloguing his muscled frame, tousled hair and gentle smile, as the perfect ending for the unforgettable memories we've created, then enter the house.

"Where have you been?" My mother's voice startles me, and I spin. She's standing in the lounge, arms crossed. Not in Noah's relaxed, soft way, but in an angled defensive pose.

I'm not going to let her ruin this. "On my first date."

Her chin sucks in. "What first date starts at dawn?"

I pause, alternating between angry words on the tip of my tongue, and the urge to ignore the question. "The best ones."

I walk out of the room, not bothering to see what she thinks of that.

In my room Caesar jumps up onto the bed, does two circles, and collapses with a groan. It appears that trying to keep up with a humungous wolf has exhausted him. I flop down beside him, consciously pushing my mother out of my mind. Her jaded tongue is not going to diminish the wonderful, memorable day I've had.

I smile as I remember the rush of those moments when we raced through the clearing, Noah slowing down, doing a semi-circle at the end of the clearing, and turning around. Me falling forwards to bury my head in his thick white fur, wrapping my arms around his broad chest. Feeling those powerful shoulder blades move beneath my cheek. The whirling mix of emotions slowing down, teasing apart, until I could almost differentiate them. I'd felt grateful, exhilarated, special, stunned.

But most of all I'd felt the freedom.

The love.

I stare up at the ceiling. Knowing it's time to acknowledge the truth of my feelings for Noah.

Because I know it's true.

It's deep.

And eternal.

It's a beautiful feeling, a liberating admission.

I frown. It's also dangerous, making me feel vulnerable. I know Noah cares for me, but the L-word? He's a Were, and Alpha heir; I'm an ordinary human. Dark thoughts of old nip at the edges of my mind—whispering, hissing, undermining. Reminding me I'm insignificant. That maybe, just maybe, this unexceptional girl is not good enough.

I roll over, facing Caesar, turning away from the voices, just like I did my mother's. Instead I focus on the words that have sunshine singing through my veins.

I'm in love with Noah Phelan.

30

NOAH

I roll over and look at the alarm clock. Red digital numbers tell me it's eight-thirty.

I shoot upright; I've slept in. It would seem running as a wolf can take it out of you. Maybe it was all that time sprinting as if I was about to break the sound barrier. Or maybe it was the rush of doing it with Eden. I smile, pretty sure I'm doing a fairly impressive Goofy impersonation. Either way, I slept the mindless sleep of the exhausted.

Padding to the toilet in nothing but sweats, I pass the bathroom mirror, a tousled sleepy head passing through at the same time. The minute he's gone, I stop and reverse. He comes back into view, and wide eyes are staring back at me. He sees it too.

My mark has changed.

The wolf is still there, head thrown back, mouth curved in a silent howl. I step closer, and I can see the whites of my eyes expanding. Below, where the Phelan mark should have been is a star—a five-pointed star formed by intersecting lines and surrounded by a circle. I see a hand come up, and I feel my palm pass over it. Then I rub a little harder, the skin pulling and twisting. When my hand drops to my side, it's still there.

I don't recognize the symbol; it's not one I've seen anywhere associated with Weres. Where in the heck did it come from?

My mind immediately turns to Eden—how my tattoo has always heated around her. Until recently. Just when I thought my eyes couldn't get any bigger, I feel their muscles straining. In all the drama I hadn't noticed that it stopped getting warm. But when? And what does it have to do with her? I've never seen something like this before, and Eden has never mentioned having a mark of her own.

I shake my head, my fingers tangling through my messy hair.

"Noah, we've got to get going shortly. Dr. Martinez is meeting with us at nine." My mother's voice flows up the stairs.

"Just getting changed." I call back down, my voice surprisingly steady.

With a last rub across my chest, just to make sure, I head back to my room. The mystery will have to wait.

I change and am downstairs in fifteen minutes, a shirt now covering the inexplicable new addition.

"You'll have to eat breakfast in the car." Mom passes me four pieces of blackened toast. Mitch grins at me as he munches on the slices he cooked himself. I guess that's karma for running late.

In the car Mom sighs. "Dr. Martinez wants to talk about Dad's progress."

"There hasn't been any."

"Hence the discussion."

I clench my hands. Dad has been the same for a week now. No worse, but no better. As a Were he should have been running laps around Stash by now. None of us have said it out loud, but that's scary.

At the hospital, the route through white corridors, up a stainless steel elevator, and through silent sliding doors is now familiar. We're all here every day, now allowed unlimited time with Dad, but only one or two at a time. Those short couple of hours spent with Dad after school I use to tell him everything that's happening. Desperately wishing he would wake.

Because I'm not the only one struggling to stay strong, and the cracks are starting to show.

You can see it in the strain around Mom's eyes. The stoop in Mitch's shoulders. By Stash waiting by the door day after day. I can't escape my uncertainty about whether I'm making the right decisions. We need him. We need our Alpha.

Dr. Martinez greets us at the entry to the ICU, and whisks us to a meeting room.

Mom's hands clench on the table. "How is he?"

She shakes her head slowly. "There's no change, Beth."

Mom's hands come to rub at her eyes, her elbows on the table. "He should be healing more rapidly."

Dr. Martinez arches a quizzical brow at Mom's choice of words. "Yes, we expected to see more progress by now. We are concerned there may be some complications."

I lean forward. "Complications?"

Dr. Martinez turns to me. Mom's hands stay holding her head, brown eyes focused on the table. "Yes. Your father maintains a consistently high temperature which is concerning. We have had to increase the antipyretic medication to address this, but it doesn't seem to be making a difference."

"You've been medicating him for it?"

"Of course. Fever, particularly one that is resistant to medication, can indicate an infection. We're worried the bullet may have fragmented and not all pieces were removed during the initial surgery."

Mitch looks at me before turning to Dr. Martinez. "Does that happen?"

She shrugs. "It can. Like I said, gunshot wounds can be complex and are often unpredictable."

I sit back. We all run at high body temperatures, it's as much a part of being a Were as our rapid healing. I've never considered if the two could be linked. Are they? Meaning the medication is messing with his ability to heal. Or does Dad really have an infection? Which would need potentially lifesaving surgery.

I sit forward. "What if I told you his high body temp is normal?" I feel Mom stiffen, but I have to know.

"Hyperpyrexia is not a normal body temperature."

"But what if it is for Dad?"

Dr. Martinez looks thoughtful. "Well then, we wouldn't need to treat it, I suppose."

I take a deep breath, once again not knowing if I'm doing the right thing, but doing it anyway. It seems to be the trend for the past couple of weeks. "We have a family trait of running hot."

Which is pretty much the truth.

"A genetic predisposition? I've never heard of it."

"I know, but everyone from my Dad's side has it. Look." I lean my head forward.

Dr. Martinez's cool hand comes up, the back of her hand resting on my forehead. Her eyes widen as she registers the warm surface.

"That's highly unusual."

"I know. But all us Phelan men have it." Also the truth—just don't check Mom.

Dr. Martinez's lips purse. "Why didn't you mention this at the intake interview?"

That's a valid question. I fumble for an answer, but thankfully Mitch is thinking on his feet. "It's something we take for granted." He gives her a rueful grin. "Just means we don't need as many layers in winter. I guess we forgot with all the drama and shock."

Dr. Martinez looks down at Dad's chart, flipping through several of the pages. "It's difficult to differentiate the origins of the fever then. We now have a choice to stop the antipyretic medication, or treat this as an infection and prep the surgical team."

She looks up at the three of us.

I turn to Mom, to find she's looking at me.

Through a throat full of uncertainty I say, "I think we stop the medication, and give it some time to see what happens."

Mom's hand grips mine beneath the table. "I think so too."

"Very well."

I don't sag, although I want to. These decisions are weighing heavily on my shoulders. On my conscience. I wonder if this is how Dad felt being Alpha. He was always so strong, so...stoic, making everyone else around him feel like he was in control, giving them a sense of reassurance. Which is about all I can give Mom right now. So I remain upright, jamming another shot of false bravado down my spine.

Mom stands. "I'd like to go see him now." Her arms are once again crossed in front of her, elbows in palms.

Dr. Martinez shuffles her papers together and stands. "Go ahead, Beth. I'll need to speak to the nursing staff."

She opens the door, only to take a step back. Geoff and Stan are standing on the other side, light blue shirts sporting shiny badges. Her clipboard flies to her chest. "Oh."

Geoff tips his hat. "Apologies ma'am. We need to speak to the Phelan family."

"We'd just finished."

Mom's shoulders dip a little. I'm pretty sure she was keen to see Dad. Sometimes you need that physical touch to give you the reassurance they are not slipping away from you.

"You go, Mom. It's me they need to speak to."

Mom looks at Dad's co-workers. Geoff nods. "We'll call you if we need you, Beth."

The men enter, Geoff taking the seat left by Dr. Martinez and

Stan looking a little tall and awkward beside him. Geoff clears his throat. "Noah, the coordinates you gave us came up with nothing. No tracks, no fibers, no blood splatters."

I frown. "We didn't stick to the track, Geoff. I must have got confused."

Geoff's little notebook comes out, and Stan copies him. "Talk me through it again."

I sigh. "I don't know anything more than what I've told you. The whole thing is a blur. Dad was bleeding out. I got him to the nearest point to get help."

Geoff sighs; I sense his patience is as thin as the hair on his head. "The trail is getting cold, Noah. Rain has probably cleared most of the evidence as it is."

I clench my fists. "I want to know who did this just as much as you, Geoff. Probably even more."

Geoff's notebook shuts. "I know. Sorry, Adam is a good cop."

"And an even better dad."

"We'll take another look." Rain would have certainly washed away the remnants of those long minutes when I carried Dad to the highway. Far quicker and farther than a seventeen-year-old boy should be able to. And about a mile east of where I sent Geoff and Stan. "But it looks like it will go down as a hunting accident."

I shake their hands again, thanking them for their help. For the millionth time, hoping I've done the right thing.

Mitch stands. "Let's get a coffee before we head in, give Mom some time."

"Sounds good."

We head to the ICU waiting room. Tara is waiting there, hands slowly annihilating a tissue. Mitch grabs her in a hug.

"They've been treating him for a fever."

"Oh. But…"

Mitch heads to the coffee machine, grabbing a mug from the

cupboard above. It's a worry when this place is as familiar as your own kitchen. "We know. We're going to try taking him off the medication."

"To see if that's why he's not healing?"

"Yeah."

I sit at one of the tables. Unless it's an infection.

I feel as old as Dougherty right now. So many decisions. I wish Dad would hurry up and wake up.

If whispers through my mind.

I stomp on it, jamming its pointed 'I' and hissing 'F' back into a soundproof, titanium coffin, one that I'm sending to the center of the earth.

I pick up the magazine in front of me. A parenting magazine. I absentmindedly flip through the pages. When several glossy photos of happy families sail past, I put it back down.

Just as Kurt comes through the door.

Tara's cup stops on its way to her mouth. Although she's spoken to her father, things have been strained. She hasn't been home, having moved into Mitch's room. We've kept the whole thing a secret at school. They were supposed to bond after graduation. Instead they had a bonding where Tara's mother, sisters, even Mr. Puddles weren't present. Then they would have moved into the house Mom and Dad had planned to build them on Phelan land. But Kurt's demands had pressed fast forward on all that.

I stand, and consciously have to unclench my hands.

Kurt takes a few more steps in. "How is he?"

Tara is silent; Mitch's arm around her. I cross my arms. "We're taking him off some medication they were giving him for high body temperature. We're confident this will be the turning point."

Kurt looks thoughtful. "That's great news."

I wait. Last time Kurt came, it wasn't just to check on Dad.

"Noah, we need to discuss your decision."

I know this was inevitable. But I still don't relish what's coming. I wonder if I should offer to take this somewhere else, but this affects Mitch and Tara just as much as me.

Kurt stands there, arms by his side. There's no outward sign of anger, but for some reason I sense a storm is brewing beneath that calm exterior. He tilts his head down ever so slightly. "You made the wrong choice."

My voice is soft, but steady. "Quite a few people disagree with you."

"You're too young, too inexperienced to know what you've done." He takes a step forward, getting into my space. "You've compromised the alliance."

I shake my head. "A bonding between its members can only strengthen it."

Hazel eyes flare, telling me a fire had been banked in there all along. "It should have been the firstborns!" He pulls back a little, his tone quieting. "The Channons and Phelans, united, have the potential to become the most powerful pack ever known."

"That's why you demanded your own daughter bond with her love's twin?"

Kurt waves his arm, like it's inconsequential. I have to move back a little as his branch-sized limb sails past. "You humiliated me. You humiliated the Channons."

"I'm the Phelan Alpha. I made the best choice for my pack."

Kurt's nostrils flare, and he throws his shoulders back as his chest expands.

Is he trying to intimidate me?

"You did this because you've become attached to a human."

The words fan my guilt like a hot breeze. I don't respond, because I don't know if denying it would be a lie.

I don't get a chance because Kurt's chest is expanding again.

"I'm going to give you an opportunity to redeem your mistake. You will step down and announce me Alpha while your father is incapacitated."

The ramifications of what he's asking flash through my mind. "I don't think so."

"I will restore my pride." The words are growled through clenched teeth.

Or what? I narrow my eyes. "What are you threatening me with, Kurt?"

"Or I will challenge you to a Claiming."

Mitch gasps. Tara steps forward. "No Daddy!"

Kurt's hot eyes remain zeroed on me.

A Claiming? They're the stuff of fables. He can't be serious.

His tense shoulders, clenched hands, and ferocious frown all spell serious. Dead serious.

My crossed arms tighten, over a stomach that is feeling sick. "So be it."

Those tense lips in the depth of his beard part a little. The low brow hikes up a quarter of an inch. "That's not a smart move, Noah. It's a rash, immature move."

Is it? But I don't have another choice. "You made the call, Kurt."

"Very well." His tone says 'you just signed your death warrant'. "We will not wait for the full moon. It will happen..." He pauses, eyes narrowing. "...in three days' time."

"That's a break from tradition, Kurt." Which is very un-Kurt. "What's the rush?"

Kurt's lip curls. I don't think he's used to being questioned. He certainly doesn't like it. But I would never have stepped up to Alpha if it wasn't for him, so he can deal with it.

"We will settle this quickly. In the manner that custom demands."

Kurt appears to be waiting. He stands there, breathing loudly.

I nod once. There's nothing else to say.

Kurt's gaze moves to Tara. "You've been away long enough. Come, we're leaving."

Tara looks shocked then bewildered before settling on resolute. Kurt watches his own pride, his own determination blossom in his daughter. Just not in the way he would have wanted. "Dad, I'm a Phelan now."

Kurt's face twists with something I haven't seen before. "Very well." The words come out in the same tone as just a moment ago. He spins on his heel and strides from the room, taking all the tension with him.

I sag. Responsibility, duty, and my heritage are all weighing down on my shoulders. Any pretense I know what I'm doing crashes to the floor. How did that just happen?

Mitch curses. Then curses again. Tara has collapsed into the seat next to her. The seriousness of what just happened hits us.

A Claiming.

I just agreed to a Claiming.

I walk to the nearest table, my hands coming out to grasp it. My head sinks between my shoulders. All the decisions I've made, the ones that seemed so right, have led to this.

I hear Mitch come over, feel his hand rest on my shoulder. I wonder how much my twin can sense.

"He chose this, not you."

Okay, he's got a pretty good handle on the situation.

And then Mom comes in. She takes in Tara sitting in the corner, me straightening up from the table, Mitch beside me. Her arms cross again. "What's going on?"

No one answers. We all look at anywhere but her.

"What's? Going? On?" Clenched teeth bite off each word. I know she's not angry. She's bracing herself.

Tara stands. "Dad just came by…"

"He just challenged Noah…" Mitch falters.

"To a Claiming." I finish the inescapable sentence.

Mom's mouth opens then shuts. She frowns, anger tightening her mouth. Turning, her narrowed eyes glare at the door that Kurt stormed through not long ago. Her mouth opens again.

Then she sits in the chair beside her with a thump, devastation slumping her shoulders and clamping her mouth shut.

Suddenly all the confusion, the unanswered questions, the hospital walls get too much. I head to the door, needing air and needing out. I brush Mom's shoulder on the way; she gives my hand an understanding pat.

I'm heading home.

The drive is a blur of thoughts and emotions. Little else has room to register in my overflowing brain. I pull into the driveway, knuckles white on the steering wheel, teeth gripping all the things I wish I'd said to Kurt.

And she's there, hair wisping in the breeze, tilted green eyes anxious, full of questions.

I get out of the car and stride toward her.

And she's around me. Her scent surrounding me.

Being with Eden is the best place in the world.

31

EDEN

Grandfather Douglas is my silent companion as I wait. Low, grey clouds loom heavy on the horizon, casting distant shadows and turning the world ashen. A gust of wind catches my hair, throwing a few strands across my face. I tuck the coiling pieces back over my shoulder, only to have them flip right back. I can smell the moist promise in the air. A storm is coming.

I know something big has happened.

I automatically think of Adam. But these feelings aren't grief. They are darker, more complex. I can feel the tense anger simmering. But there's something else, clenching my stomach. It's like he's rattled, shocked...scared.

Add that to my own anxiety, knotting everything from my shoulders to my toes, and I'm a tightly wound coil. I take a deep breath, trying to make room for it all. I want to pace, stretch taut muscles. But my entire being is centered on the road. My eyes and ears wait for the physical proof. Noah is coming.

I hear the low rumble, and a blue metal nose rounds the bend. He roars up, gravel crunching when he brakes.

Then he's out of the truck, not bothering to shut the door.

Long, strong legs are powering toward me, sky blue eyes carrying their own grey clouds. I stand, just as rooted to the ground as the tree beside me.

And strong arms are around me, crushing me to him. His palm cups my head, fingers tangling in my flyaway hair, tucking my face against his chest. Warmth and tenderness fill me, and I don't know if the feeling starts with me or with him. I feel his lips brush my hair as he takes a deep, deep breath. As we stand there, the feelings ebb and flow, then slowly subside.

"What's happened, Noah?"

Another deep, expanding breath enters and leaves. "Kurt wasn't happy with the call I made."

"The right choice by his daughter?"

Noah rubs his cheek against the top of my head. "He says it should have been the firstborns, and that I humiliated him. He wanted me to appoint him the Phelan Alpha."

"No." I breathe.

"Exactly. So he challenged me to a Claiming."

A Claiming. The name and Noah's tone have an ominous sound. I don't even want to repeat it. So I wait.

"A Claiming is his way of getting...restitution."

"Sounds like an excuse to me."

Noah shrugs. "Maybe. Either way, it's a fight at the Glade."

A sick, awful feeling is creeping up my throat. My voice is a hoarse whisper as it tries to scrape past it. I pull away, looking up into stormy-blue eyes. "But the third Precept..."

THY SHALL NOT ATTACK ANOTHER BLOOD MEMBER.

"A Claiming is the only place you can." Noah shifts a little. And I know there's more. "Only one can walk away. It must be a complete victory."

Each word slowly sinks in. They have to pass denial. Then they hit anger. Before tumbling into a deep pit of fear.

"But...." *But what?* What do I have to say to that? Noah is going to have to fight for his life, because of Kurt's injured pride? "How did this happen?" My whisper is now ragged.

Noah steps away, pacing a few steps beneath the branches, his hands clenching and unclenching. "I couldn't let him step up as the Alpha, Eden. What if Dad doesn't...?"

He doesn't need to finish the sentence. Noah doesn't have a choice. He has to fight for his pack, because if Adam never wakes, and Kurt was the head of the pack...Kurt could become the Phelan Alpha.

"Your hands are tied."

"They're set in freaking concrete."

I lean against Grandfather Douglas, rubbing my upper arms. The cold has started to sink in. "When?"

"In three days."

Three days! "What about the whole full moon thing?"

"He wants to settle it quickly."

"That doesn't make sense. He's breaking tradition so he can settle this traditionally?"

Noah shrugs.

"He's not playing fair."

"Nothing about this is fair. I don't think that's Kurt's first priority."

Choked words slip past frozen lips. "I don't want to lose you."

And I'm back in his arms. Strong, protective, warm arms. "You're not going to, Eden. We've only just started, and I want a whole lot more time with you yet."

If Noah could win based on the fierceness and determination in his voice, then Kurt would never stand a chance.

But this fight depends on far more than that.

"You haven't trained for this for two years."

He pulls back to look at me, and that glint is trying to break free in his turbulent eyes. "Just think *David and Goliath...Rocky...Kung Fu Panda*."

I smile. Noah's unfailing faith and optimism are one of the many things I love about him. But when my cheeks push up, they tip the tears that have pooled along my lower lids. Cold trails streak down my cheeks.

Warm thumbs come up to rub them away. "Eden." His voice is choked, pained.

I tuck my head back under his chin, sinking into his warm, hard chest. Wishing I could crawl in there.

Another rumble, this one more high-pitched, comes from the road, and Mitch and Tara drive up in her little silver hatchback. The dark clouds have sunk closer to frame their car, the two pale faces within. They climb out and Tara is instantly in Mitch's arms; her hair whips around in the gusty wind.

"Mom stayed for a bit longer with Dad."

Noah nods. "Fair enough. Let's get inside before the storm hits."

We shuffle into the house, where Stash greets us with the simple affection of a canine. He scans each person's face, judging the somber mood. He comes to stand by Noah, whining.

Noah leans down to ruffle his neck. "I know, bud."

We enter the lounge room, then stand there. My head is so full of what Noah has told me, overflowing with dread and crawling with fear. I'm trying desperately to get it under control; Noah doesn't need to deal with these awful emotions too. No one speaks; no one really moves. *Now what?*

"Why don't we watch a movie?" Tara says brightly, artificially.

Noah looks down at me, and I offer a small smile. It would be practically normal, two couples hanging together. Normality might be good right now. "Sure, why not?"

Mitch heads to the TV cabinet, rifling through the DVDs. What does one watch on an occasion like this?

He pulls out Kung Fu Panda. *Uncanny.*

While he puts it in, Noah and I settle ourselves on one of the lounges. He lifts his arm, and I curl in, both of us adjusting and nestling into each other, maximizing any point of contact we can get. My head sinks into his shoulder, I breathe in his sandalwood scent, and I begin to calm. Mitch turns the lights off and joins Tara on the adjoining two-seater just as the heavens open up. Rain pummels the roof, creating a muted, steady drumroll. The wind whips angrily against the house, slamming the waterfall against the windows. I curl tighter into Noah, and his arm fastens around me, binding me to his side.

The TV lights up, and I really try to focus on the overweight panda that looks like he's meant to be the unlikely hero. But the movie passes in a blur of flashing, bright colors and unheard sound.

I can't concentrate. This isn't two teenage couples watching a movie together. This is two bonded Weres that have to hide in his childhood bedroom, her father demanding a fight, his twin threatened. This is an unwilling Alpha heir having to protect his pack's heritage, with his life.

This is a powerless human girl having to watch it all happen.

There's nothing normal about that.

Noah's hand is rubbing up and down my arm, his fingers grazing my skin. It sends tingles skipping along my nerve endings. I look up, and his pensive eyes are on the TV, his finger rubbing his bottom lip in that way of his. I don't think he's aware he's stroking me. Or the effect it has.

I give up on the movie. All I feel, all I want to feel is Noah—my senses memorizing his smell, his powerful arms around me, his heat seeping into my side...the sensation of his breath pulling in and pushing out.

All of a sudden Tara pushes herself out of her seat. Mitch jumps back a little, surprised. "How can he do this?"

We all look at her, no one saying anything. In the background an angry snow leopard is demanding that he should be the Dragon Warrior.

Mitch gets up and turns on the light. "We need a plan."

Noah and I both turn to him, Noah retrieving his arm so he can sit forward. "I'm open to suggestions."

Tara slaps her palm with her fist. "I'll kill him myself!"

"We'll put that down as Plan B, maybe Y or Z," says Noah. His index finger returns to his bottom lip. "Let's look at the facts. I don't think Kurt expected me to pick up this gauntlet."

Tara nods. "He did looked surprised."

Mitch is thinking hard. "He's going to depend on your inexperience."

My heart is a crushing weight in my chest, bruising me from the inside.

Mitch sits forward. "Yes, he has experience and size. But you have speed and youth." He grins ruefully. "Dad did say you were fast."

The heavy weight in my chest lightens, ever so slightly. Hope needs so little to feed it.

Noah sits up a little straighter. "If I learn some moves, do some training, we're starting to even it out."

Noah and Mitch look at each other and twin mouths speak in unison. "Uncle Joe and Grandpa Ben!"

32

NOAH

I've managed to jam a whole lot of living into three days. Training has taken up most of my time. Mom rang school to say I wouldn't be in. Then each day has been spent in the back-yard—Mitch my training partner, Grandpa Ben and Uncle Joe my coaches. Eden, Tara and Mom make up my cheerleading squad.

Initially I struggled to find the drive to attack my own twin. But Mitch knows how to push my buttons. He reminds me that Kurt is the one who attended countless family barbeques, called himself my father's friend, and was the one who offered support and help with Dad in the hospital. It gets me angry, aggravated and agitated. It stirs the Alpha blood in my veins.

Grandpa stands in the middle of our yard, trying to prepare me. "The neck is the most vulnerable part, the tool of submission. You must protect yours, while aiming for his."

That doesn't even sound easy. But Mitch is a boulder of black fur coming at me, so I duck my head and lunge at him. He hits me like a semi, knocking me over, meaning he's on top, with the upper hand. I struggle and shove, knocking him off balance then jump up and leap at him, doing my own impersonation of a truck. We clash and roll through the soft grass. When we pull away, we're both breathing heavily.

I smile at Mitch, thinking this could be fun...if my life didn't depend on it. He responds with a black grin of his own. Then I run at him. For a brief moment I see wide surprised eyes, hear Eden's gasp, and I'm on him. This time we're sucking in lungfuls of air when we disentangle.

Uncle Joe grunts. "Adam was right, he is fast."

Grandpa Ben has his arms crossed, one hand stroking his grey stubbled chin. "He'll depend on your inexperience, but your speed will be your advantage. If you do this right, he'll never see you coming."

So I try harder, go faster. By day two I've taken Mitch down twice. Which makes him angry. No Were likes to be beaten. So we step it up, get rougher, get tougher.

When we break, I transform like I've been doing this all my life as we head back to Eden and Tara. Eden slips beneath my arm, and I hold her close. I don't need to ask how they're feeling. I can feel Eden's fear; Tara's is stamped on her pale skin and wide hazel eyes.

I wipe the sweat from my face, passing a towel to Mitch. "Tara, you don't need to be there."

Her hands come up to her hips, eyes turning into hazel slits. "Noah, I'm going to stand by my mate, stand up for what's right." She has a just-try-and-stop-me tone that I know is pointless arguing with.

I look at Mitch—he knows what I'm thinking.

Tara's compact body steps between us, cheeks now matching her hair. "Oh no you don't, there will be no secret twin planning to keep me out of the action."

Mitch rubs the back of his head, knowing we've been caught out. I don't care; this is her father I have to fight. Tara will not be there if this gets unpleasant. I almost snort, 'if'...Unpleasant is unavoidable, ugly is highly probable.

"Let's go, peoples, I mean wolves." Grandpa chuckles at his own joke. "Now we're looking at maiming your opponent, a good little trick for slowing them down."

Uncle Joe steps up beside him. "Not literally of course, but the knack is to get a swipe or a nip into the front or back legs. Mitch, I want you here. Noah, you're going to be on the defensive."

I sigh, the sound sucked in as a human, released as a wolf. Defense again. We all know Kurt is going to be single-minded and aggressive. I'm going to need a good defense. I manage to barge Mitch, moving fast enough to take him by surprise. He rolls and gouges through the dirt. I stop, thinking he needs a break. But he pushes up onto his feet, shakes himself, and runs at me again. He knows this is too important, that we don't have time to take it easy. That this is what he can do to help. Exhaustion and bruises are just collateral damage. I'd be grateful if he wasn't the one giving me the bruises.

We're eyeing each other off again, planning our next offensive, when Grandpa steps up. "Let's call it a day."

I look up to see the sun low over the trees. It seems time flies when you're madly, desperately trying to jam two years of Alpha-training-that-includes-necessary-life-saving-moves into two short days.

"Good job, guys. We've covered a lot of ground." I wonder if he's making another grandad joke, because Mom's lawn is trashed.

Mitch morphs back to human, but I stay as a wolf, and head over to Eden. She's on the thinking chair with Mom. I lean in, head tipping down to her, and she smiles a little smile, her hand coming up to rest on my cheek. I jerk my head toward the trees.

Her eyes light up like Vegas. "Again?"

I nod. She doesn't need any more encouragement. She leaps on my back like I'm no bigger than a standard wolf, and we're off. Heading straight for the trees. Eden twists around and waves to the others, and they wave back, their broad smiles echoing hers.

For half an hour or so there is no fear, no Claiming, no Kurt. It's just me and Eden, flying through the forest. Like nothing can stop us, nothing could slow us down. Because no matter how close the trees are, how low the branches, what comes at us, I sidestep, she ducks, we work as one. Shy, timid Eden is gone. She squeals with delight each time I go a little faster.

Up ahead I see a big rock, getting bigger and bigger as we power toward it. I line it up, gain some speed, and hear her intake of breath. Her legs grip my ribs as I push off the ground and we're sailing over. My heart does its own aeronautic gymnastics when I feel Eden let go. I know she has her arms out again, doing her *Titanic* impersonation. Her laughter spills out when we land on the other side. Our joy and freedom is so strong, so limitless, I doubt it could be contained within the boundaries of the forest.

She falls forward when I turn, head nuzzling into my shoulder. With a deep breath she relaxes into me, her lean body molded to my back. An emotion so strong, so powerful, fills my chest. Reaching out to her. Connecting with her.

We come back to Grandfather Douglas and Eden slips off. I pretend to be some magician as I circle his wide trunk. Walking behind a wolf, coming out a guy. I hold my arms out. "Ta da!"

Eden claps, smiling. Never seeing that my mark has changed.

Just like last night, we curl up beneath the branches. Yesterday we asked countless questions. I got to watch the way she still bites her lips as she considers whether a person can live on cheesecake, how she seems to be drawn to touching me as much as I'm her, how I'm still bowled over whenever she smiles. It's like we were cramming a hundred dates into one short night.

Tonight we are silent, watching the sun go down. This time I'm absorbed in the way the fiery oranges light up her face, the twilight blends into her hair, the golden yellows reflect in her happy-sad eyes.

Then we head up to my room, and I prove that I can, indeed, play the guitar while lying down. My head is in her lap as I play *Magic* from her favorite band, Coldplay. Because it's true, being with Eden is magic. Her fingers run through my hair as I play Snow Patrol's *Chasing Cars*, as we lay there and forget the world. Strumming *Wonderwall*, because there are so many things I want to say, and just like Oasis, I don't know how.

Then it's time for Eden to go home. We're at her car; she's leaning back against it, my shoulder beside her as I face her. "It almost seems silly—you leaving, considering you'll just be back in the morning."

Her eyes widen, showing more white, more green. "I couldn't...stay."

I grin; she looks so flustered and still shy. "I know. Just saying..."

She nudges my chest with her shoulder and smiles. "You could tempt a dedicated vegetarian, Noah Phelan."

And my grin widens. She's tempted? She turns so her shoulder is against the car too, facing me. "I should go. You need to rest."

Looking down on her, I lose myself in the beauty of Eden at twilight. My fingers come up to tangle in her hair, and I hear her breath hitch—that small intake of air pulling me in. All the times our hands brushed during lunch, the times she slipped into my arms during breaks, the amazing sense of connection during the run has amped up my awareness and kindled the heat.

Our lips touch and that fire is unleashed.

Ignited by touch. Fueled by desire. Driven by desperation. Eden's hands grip my waist as my fingers clutch the back of her head. Blazing mouths meld, gasping lips merge, hungry tongues mingle as the heat intensifies, until all I can do is feel. Feel the heat, the sensations, feel her desire echoing mine. Because there's no greater fuel for these flames than knowing Eden is right there with me.

We pull away at the same time, before we spontaneously combust.

"I should go..." Eden has that breathless, panting breathing that keeps my pulse dialed up to crazy. I uselessly try to get my own mad gasps under control. Neither one of us releases the strong grip we have on each other.

I think we're trying to hold on to this moment—trying to freeze time.

But the chirping of the crickets counts down the seconds. The hoot of an owl is like the chime of a clock. Each of our breaths, gradually slowing down, are the sounds of inevitability.

"Okay, I'm really going now. I'll be back in the morning." Eden pulls away, and I unwillingly let her go. I stay under the great tree until her taillights disappear around the bend, until I can no longer hear the hum of the engine.

With my hands in my pockets, I head inside. I didn't have the guts to ask her if she thought it was worth it now.

Mom is in the kitchen, although thankfully nothing's cooking. I can hear Mitch's music softly screeching in his room.

"I'm gonna head up to bed now, Mom. I'll see you in the morning."

She puts down the cloth she'd been using to wipe the bench and comes up to me. "Try and get some sleep."

"Sure." She's kidding right?

She smiles, her worn features lifting, lighting up for the first time in ages. Her hands come to rest on my cheeks. "Noah, I want you to know how proud I am. During this whole mess, you've stepped up to every challenge with the courage and the honor of a Phelan. You make a fine Alpha. Your dad would be so proud." Her brown eyes shimmer, fear making them waver.

"Mom, you and Dad have been..." I struggle to find the words; they have been the ones that prepared me for this—made me strong, kept me strong. My mouth twitches. "Totes awesome."

Her own soft lips tip up. "You made it totes easy."

We hug, and she feels so small. "See you in the morning."

I head up the stairs, knowing I need to sleep.

But probably won't.

33

EDEN

I arrive at Noah's house with the first light of dawn. Sleep was elusive as peace of mind. A silent, solemn car trip brought me to his house. There's no music appropriate for a day like this.

Noah is already sitting underneath Grandfather Douglas. I wonder how long he's been there.

The dawn light is a soft glow, his silhouette an outline as he leans back against the rough trunk, legs bent up, forearms resting against his knees, blue eyes gazing toward a sky that is being slowly suffused with light. Idle clouds linger—a glowing apricot beneath, dove grey above—waiting, knowing it's just a matter of time before it all changes.

The opalescent colors outline his solitary form. I see his shoulders lift and fall, a deep breath filling his chest. As I approach, his head falls back as he lifts his arm. I slide in, curling up beside him.

"I wish this didn't have to happen."

"Believe me, if I could find a way out, I would have kicked that door down by now."

"How's your mom?"

"She looks like she's aged fifty years over the past week."

My side, pressed against his, feels the flash of heat—the anger that has been brewing beneath the surface since Kurt made the ultimatum. I squeeze that warm, strong hand.

A light comes on in the lounge room, spilling pale color onto the front garden. A second later Mitch's bedroom window goes from black to yellow. They're all waking up. Nobody would have slept well last night.

These will be my last few moments alone with Noah.

I turn, to find him gazing down on me—blue eyes mirroring the soft heavens behind him.

Capturing me, mesmerizing me.

I meet him halfway, this kiss a gentle brushing of lips. My fingers come to rest on his jaw as his tender mouth connects with mine. He presses closer, increasing the pressure; I pull down, amplifying the sensation. Warmth spikes and blossoms. My senses, heightened by the tension of the past three days, glory in every movement and every feeling. It's all a dizzying mix of flushed cheeks, heated sandalwood, yearning mouths, caught breaths, delving fingers, and pounding hearts. Subtly under-scored with a hint of desperation. It takes my breath away.

With his forehead against mine, our panting breaths mingling and mixing, Noah pulls back a little.

"Eden..."

There's a depth of emotion in those electric blue eyes that once again leaves me breathless, wordless.

"I want to tell you I love you."

I feel my chest swelling and my eyes pricking.

"But what I feel for you is so much bigger...deeper... stronger...than that one little word." He stretches an arm out, as if he's trying to encompass his feelings.

My hand comes up to cup his cheek. My heart sits in my throat; all I'm feeling must show in my eyes. "I know. What I feel is far more, so much more."

His shuddering breath flows over my lips, and he's kissing me again—the depth, strength, and breadth of his feelings flowing from his mouth. I'm cocooned, caressed, cherished by them. I push up on my knees, wanting him to know they are living and breathing within me too. Wanting to convey my adoration and devotion for this courageous, patient, beautiful boy who's putting his life on the line.

Telling him that, despite the threat hanging over our heads, although the relationship with my mother is more fractured than it has ever been, and even though the future is so unpredictable and uncertain and unknown...

These have been the best three days of my life.

Doors open and feet thump from within the house. We pull away again—breaths uneven, gazes steady.

Ben and Joe arrive, their Phelan truck a deep, dark red. We all head into the house to have breakfast. Beth, looking so tense, pinched...diminished, pulls out a frying pan. "I'll do eggs and toast."

Joe gently grasps her, leading her to a stool by the kitchen bench. "I'll cook, love."

I'd say Joe has offered to cook to take the strain off Beth's shoulders, but also because I doubt anyone's stomachs could handle the smell of burnt egg this morning. Tara and I barely touch the beautifully cooked meal.

After some last minute training and a meal of hearty sandwiches, again prepared by Joe, and it's time for them to leave. Time had felt like it was crawling, dragging us to this moment. It felt like it passed in a heartbeat.

I'm not sure how, but we find ourselves under Grandfather Douglas again, pulling aside for a last moment of privacy. We stand there, arms around each other, my head against his chest. A powerful urge surges through my arms, telling me to never let him go.

Noah's warm fingers slip under my chin, lifting my face to meet his. A tide of emotion is ebbing and flowing in those eyes. Pulling me in, letting me go.

There are no words.

Until Noah finds one. "More."

Effectively, efficiently condensing everything we feel and mean to each other.

"More," I echo in a whisper.

Please let us have more.

I don't cry. I know he can already feel my pain. He doesn't need to see it too.

And then he is gone.

34

NOAH

I don't think I ever would have been prepared for this. But I'd say two days of training with Grandpa Ben and Uncle Joe, with Mitch as my sparring partner, would define 'totally and inadequately prepared'. Two years of missed Alpha training and the title is complete.

Now I stand at the edge of the Glade, the Phelan pack spread out behind me—Mom to my right, Mitch to my left, and Tara beside him. Everyone is tense. I think of Mom having to watch this while her mate is in hospital. I think of Mitch, knowing how hard it would be for me to see him in this position. And Tara, although she's bonded with this pack, her family of origin on the other side.

Now anger is no longer simmering. It's a burning, heated blaze coiling through my muscles. Kurt has been the cause, the root of all these troubles. It's time to dig up the mass that is poisoning everything around him.

I hope I'm the one that can do it.

I have to be the one to do it.

My senses are on high alert. The Glade is quiet, any animals in the vicinity long gone. This many Weres are just too great a threat. The hint of metallic scent in the air shows our wolves are moving restlessly beneath our human veneer. I can practically taste the tension in the air. And through all this I can feel Eden's fear. It's so powerful, so strong, making me think she's close. But I push it aside; we agreed she'd stay in town, and I need to stay focused.

Because Kurt has just stepped from the trees on the other side of the Glade.

He's shirtless, as tradition dictates. His massive chest, covered with the same bristly red hair as his beard, is bloated and pushed out, his Channon tattoo black and prominent. My shirt remains on. Most people know my tattoo; the one that has now changed, was never complete, so I decided not to rob them of this assumption until I figured out what in the world it means. I bristle, because it makes me look like a novice.

He struts to the center of the Glade, and I meet him there.

His arms spread out—a welcome or a challenge. "Noah Phelan." His voice booms. "In recompense for overruling, for humiliating an Alpha, I challenge you to a Claiming."

I take a deep breath but it doesn't slow my thumping heart. I want to give this one last try. "Kurt. Let's settle this in a less... archaic form. No one wins if someone gets hurt."

His eyes light up. "You're refusing?"

"No. I'm trying to avoid bloodshed."

Hazel eyes harden, and I can see his biceps flex as his hands clench. "Coward. Do you accept or not?"

Resignation pulls everything down as I surrender to the inevitable.

"This is wrong, Kurt." Grandpa has stepped up beside me, arms crossed, grey eyebrows pulled low. Surprise, shock, and confusion spear through me. I manage to keep my eyebrows where they are.

"He's right." Uncle Joe is now on my other side.

Mitch steps up too with his arms crossed. Then Tara is there on his right. Mom comes to stand beside my grandfather, and her hand slips in his—a sign of strength and solidarity.

The core Phelan pack, lined up before him, inflames Kurt. His mustached lip curls, a glint of teeth showing. The fact that his daughter is amongst them would just be tinder for the flames.

"A Claiming is between Alphas only." He snarls.

"This should never have come to that," Grandpa calls loudly.

"Would the Phelans defy tradition, and obstruct my right to retribution?"

The Channon crowd behind Kurt shift and growl.

"A Claiming is a primitive and violent form of retribution." Grandpa's tone shows exactly what he thinks of the term 'retribution'.

Kurt's anger has him leaning forward, as if it's a strain to hold himself back. "Do you forget your roots? We are Weres! Ultimate predators—animals that have the strength, the power, and the right to decide life or death."

I shake my head. But it's Uncle Joe's voice that carries over the Glade. "We've come a long way from that." A murmur of assent rumbles through my pack, gaining momentum as it moves through the ranks.

Pride has my chest filling, despite the tightness that grips my ribs. This is my father's legacy—the knowledge that Weres are more than this. That we stand for integrity, equality, and honor.

"You've gone soft." Contempt twists Kurt's mouth, lacing his voice with disgust. "Phelans do not deserve to stand alongside the Channons."

The Channons shout their agreement, thrusting their fists up, punching through the metallic veil that hangs over the Glade. Then they are changing. Humans morphing to Weres like a Mexican wave. From one side of the Glade to the other, pale skin become grey, red, brown fur. Upright forms become four-legged masses of muscle. Frowns become snarling muzzles.

Behind me the threat is changing the Phelan pack. In the flash of an eye, my own family stands as a mass of predatory animals behind me—ready to protect what we stand for. Ready to protect me.

Oh no.

This just stepped up to something much bigger and much more dangerous.

Kurt remains human before me, his barrel chest filled with satisfaction. He wants this. He dips his head slowly, his burning eyes looking up from beneath thick brows.

My stomach sinks as my shoulders straighten. There cannot be any more blood spilled than necessary. "I accept. But this is between you and me only." My voice carries through the clearing, and rumbles carry through the two packs. Beneath it all, I hear Mom's quiet whine.

A small smile twists Kurt's mouth. "Very well."

35

EDEN

"*Y*ou can't be there, Eden."

Noah had been so intense when he'd said those words three days ago. I remember his handsome face pulled taut with concern, his blue eyes serious, arms wrapped around me tightly; he'd voiced what I already knew. As a fragile human, I'm nothing but a liability. The cowardly part of me had been relieved, the part that still wants to run away from all of this. Pretend it isn't happening.

But in the end I knew I couldn't stay away.

Not knowing was unbearable. Intolerable.

With my mind whirling about how I could be close, but not a distraction, I'd driven off after they'd all left, for the second time in a few short weeks driving like a maniac. I'd parked off the highway, creeping the sporty sedan through the trees. My black tires crawled over the leaf litter, and I cringed when a branch scraped down the white paint. When I couldn't go any farther because the trees were too close together, I parked it amongst the shadowy conifers.

Now, my nervous legs stride through the forest, rough bark brushing my arms and pine needles sticking to my shirt. I skirt the Glade, heading for higher ground, my heart thumping and my breath rasping in my throat. And it's not because of the sloping terrain. For three days there has been one word that can instantly spike my pulse, one word that is never far away. A *Claiming*.

Kurt claiming his right to restitution.

Claiming his lost pride.

By claiming a life.

Images of Noah training flash through my mind—him leaping at Mitch with their teeth snapping and mouths snarling. Black versus white. The duality of yin and yang crashing together—twisting, blending, then separating, pulling apart, and pushing away. Breathing heavily, weighing the other's strengths and weaknesses, preparing to do it all over again and again. And again.

The intimidating show of power had left me awed, and scared. And that was only a practice. Not a drop of blood had been spilled.

For the first time, since I arrived in Jacksonville, the tranquil calm doesn't soothe me. I start to notice the untamed wildness around me. A kaleidoscope of colors assails my sensitive eyes. Rustling, nervous, unnamed sounds hit my skittish ears. Scents that I can't distinguish are filling my lungs. Today this natural world feels unpredictable. Outside of my control. Oblivious to my most heartfelt wish.

Please let Noah be okay.

A small clearing, a bare ledge of rock a short way up the mountain catches my eye. It's a place where I could be close and watch, but away from the danger that two fighting Weres could pose. The size of the parking lot outside the Inn, the clearing's uneven ground is all whites and greys. Trees frame it on either side, the mountain making up the back wall, looking like a colossal seat for a giant. A throne overlooking the arena.

I walk across the unforgiving rock, my hiking boots crunching over the sharp shards that have been cleaved by erosion and frost. At the edge, where the rock falls away to the trees below, I stop. The Glade sits like a stadium—an emerald clearing framed by trees—my silent, fellow witnesses. The sun is shining down, lighting the stage. I have a clear, unobstructed view of the train wreck that time is bringing inevitably closer.

Because there will be no winners.

For Noah to win he must kill another.

Or die.

Fear peaks through my body again, scorching my mouth dry and cramping my stomach. Restless, I begin to pace. I've only taken two steps when movement catches my attention, bringing me back to the bare, rocky patch. People are entering the Glade. My lungs struggle to suck in air as the two families filter through on each side—the Channons below me, the Phelans before me. About twenty-five on each side.

Kurt steps forward, chest naked, and Noah is there, his shirt still on. I briefly wonder at his choice. They're talking, and even from here, my human eyes can see Kurt is angry. He's rigid, tense, hard. Determined. They talk, the passing of time stretching my nerves taut. My head pulls back when I see Ben step up beside Noah, followed by Joe, Mitch, Tara, and Beth.

I don't think this is normal. What is going on?

I hear more talking with the odd voice wafting up, but the words are indecipherable. I think I hear Grandpa Ben and maybe Kurt's angry tones. I don't know why, but dread is sinking heavily in my stomach.

Then the Channons are changing. My heart is in my throat, my eyes like giant saucers; I see the Phelans transform too.

Please. No.

Fifty odd Werewolves are facing off with yards between them. What was going to be a deadly duel is about to become a blood bath. Hot bile is searing up my throat. It contrasts against the shivers racking my body. My arms wrap around my waist.

Kurt transforms, and a split second later, Noah does too.

No. No. No. Beth. Tara. Mitch. Grandpa Ben. Uncle Joe. How do I watch this?

Call them.

The whispered words brush through my mind.

I whip around, swinging my head frantically from side to side. But no one is there. A gentle breeze brushes my hair across my face, and I impatiently throw it over my shoulder. I turn back, my gaze drawn to the horrible sight being played out before me.

Call them.

This time the whisper is more insistent. An urgent exhale compels me to do something…but what?

Who is in my head? And what are they trying to tell me?

This time I turn and spend precious seconds scanning the empty clearing—the tree line. And I see him—a tall man is stepping from between the trees, grey flowing robes rippling in the breeze. Steady steps bring him closer.

I see the long mahogany hair and the evergreen eyes tilted up at the corners.

He says it again. *Call them.* Without moving his lips.

Shock has frozen my entire body. Now is not the time to be trying to absorb features I'd never thought I'd see.

I drag my gaze away to look back down on the Glade. The wolves are fanning out, taking up offensive positions, Kurt and Noah at the front and the others waiting to see who will make the first move. It's only a matter of time before Kurt snaps.

I turn back, to find him beside me. He's looking at me like I should know what he's talking about. Call who?

An idea morphs in my mind. Something that might just tip the balance.

"But how?"

He nods, a small smile curling up the corners of his mouth. He comes to stand beside me. He's taller than I am, his hair longer; his fair skin makes it impossible to tell how old he is. Woven gold threads circle his head—a fragile, intricate crown. He raises his arms, tipping his head back; his eyes drift closed.

I take a deep breath, dragging in calming, soothing air. I pull the air deep down, everything opening up. Flowing around, making room for the dark mass of fear wedged in my stomach.

I copy the crowned, robed man. My arms lift open, and I feel the sun kissing my face and my skin. Behind closed eyes, the words form. My desperate plea moves through my mind, pushing out to the trees—a desperate frantic prayer.

Please come…

Please come.

"Look," a melodic masculine voice says beside me.

My eyes open and fall to the Glade.

Big bodies are emerging from the trees, behind the Phelan pack. I gasp and my eyes widen. The first to come out into the open is a grizzly bear with an adolescent cub by her side. There's no way I can tell from here, but I suspect he has a scar across his muzzle. Farther down, a cougar slinks from the tree line, coming to stand just feet away from a Were. *They came?*

But there's more. Like a dam has been breached, more grizzlies, mountain lions, even black bears materialize from the trees. They line up behind the massive wolves, some stepping between them, ready to fight.

The giant profound breath whooshes from my lungs. My arms drop limply to my side.

The scales have just tipped.

36

NOAH

The rust-colored wolf before me stretches up as his head drops down. Kurt's muzzle ripples, lips lifting to show white teeth glinting with moisture. I brace myself, my own mouth feeling like the Sahara.

My ears snap back and I hear the scuffing of countless paws, heavy uneven breathing, and stormy, raw growls. My pack shifts forward again, and more of the same comes from the Channons. How do I avoid a massacre?

Kurt's head comes up, his eyes flaring open and glowing with a fierce, determined light.

It's about to start.

A breeze rockets through the Glade, gusting over my fur and rushing up the trees. Uneasy growls rumble from both sides of the Glade. I glance quickly left and right, never taking my eyes off Kurt for more than a split second. I don't see anything. Kurt's gaze never wavers—a hazel laser zeroed in on me.

His lips tip up, a rabid distortion of a grin.

Anger once again flares inside me—outrage at his abuse of power, desecration of all we stand for, violation of our law.

So be it.

I bend my knees slightly, like a lightly coiled spring, just like Grandpa Ben taught me. I tilt my head, protecting my throat.

And I see her. Eden is standing at the edge of a rocky clearing up above the Channons, arms raised to the heavens in a wide V. And a man stands beside her. Light-colored robes flow in the breeze while his identically colored hair streams in the wind, and his arms also reach for the sky. They look like two deities beseeching, petitioning some higher power.

What is she doing here? Actually, what is she doing, period?

Sucking in startled breaths, I see Uncle Joe and Mitch straighten, their heads turning. But it's only when I see Kurt's eyes widen, maybe even his jaw slacken, that I allow myself to turn.

Animals are coming out from the trees. Not just any animals. Grizzly bears, black bears, cougars. Big, angry ferocious animals. One big grizzly is standing on its hind legs, huffing and snorting. A smaller, but still intimidating cub by its side. Farther to the left, a cougar is stalking from the trees. It walks straight past the back ranks, feral eyes gleaming, coming to a stop not far from Grandpa Ben. It hisses, never taking its yellow glare off the Channons.

More and more come out, until they line up behind us, amongst us, doubling our numbers.

What the—?

I don't have time to figure this out because Kurt growls a deep, low, vicious sound, as if something is twisting and snapping in his throat. Saying very clearly that, even though we now have these wild animals on our side, outnumbering them, Kurt is not planning on backing down.

My fast beating heart sinks.

A smaller, grey wolf at the back of the Channon lines moves. From the corner of my eye I see it disappear back into the trees.

And another. Two more follow, melding between the brown trunks.

I hear a Phelan give a low, excited bark.

The Channons are steadily reabsorbed by the forest. Their lowered heads admit defeat—a silent unobtrusive retreat.

As each footstep leaves the grassy Glade, Kurt stiffens. Until he's standing, stark and straight, with only two wolves beside him—Lara, a pale blond wolf, and Dana, a lighter shade than her father.

They face off against the Phelan pack and their wild counterparts.

I morph back to human and feel Mitch stepping in closer, his big, black body practically on top of me.

I take a small step forward. "It's over, Kurt."

Something violent and vicious passes through him. I see it shift in his eyes, ripple down his back, tremble in his paws. Mitch is back at my side, and Grandpa flanks my right. Lara whines besides Kurt; she steps closer, but doesn't touch his motionless form.

"There were no losers today. No blood was spilled."

His shoulders flex and his lip curls ever so slightly. Lara whines again.

I hear, feel the Phelans shift behind me, closing in, contracting like a heart.

Kurt takes one, then two steps back. His eyes scan the numbers before him—hazel eyes that are no longer glowing, but are now a dark, ashen grey. With another twist of his lip, he turns and stalks to the trees, Lara and Dana behind him, their tails low. A few steps away from the tree line, he pauses, shoulders contracting, head lifting. I tense, but he continues walking, swallowed by the shadowy darkness.

There's a ripple of sighs from all around. I feel Mitch relax beside me. I sag, like a hot air balloon that just ran out of gas.

I turn, in awe of the animals around me—a family that had stood by me and defended me. And the wild animals that were willing to put their lives on the line. They begin to quietly and quickly retreat. The cougar glances at me, and with a twitch of its tawny tail, leaps between the wolves, disappearing into the trees. The mother grizzly looks a little disappointed, furred shoulders low as she escorts her cub back into the woods.

My gaze returns to Eden, high up on her ledge. She's alone, a small smile on her beautiful face. I wish I could be there to tell her what this means to me. What she means to me. My heart swells, pressing against my chest.

But my family is jostling me, now a mix of human and Were, relieved and rejoicing. Tara and Mitch, still wolves, nuzzle. For the millionth time, over the past two weeks, I wish Dad was here.

From the corner of my eye, I see something move across the Glade, in the trees. I frown, my shoulders bunching as I peer closer. I shoot my head back, and my eyebrows spike up.

And I'm changing, then running.

Because Kurt is racing up the hill.

Toward Eden.

37

EDEN

When I turn back, the man is gone.

I whip around, searching. The clearing is empty, the trees still. Gone.

He looked like me!

My mind stutters, struggling to process what that means.

From my vantage point, I can see the Phelans below are celebrating and hugging, a couple even doing a little jig. Ben and Joe are on either side of Noah, their arms around his shoulders. Relief has tears stinging my eyes. Noah looks up, eyes that I know are a shining blue, even though I can't see them at this distance. I give him a small smile. I have a pretty good idea what his look is trying to convey.

I turn back, heading to the granite wall. I'm going to have to sit down for a moment and get my heart under control, slow my breathing, and find strength in my limbs so I can start the hike back down.

I hear someone step through the trees behind me. I turn, thinking the man, the one that looks like me, has returned. But it's not him.

It's Kurt.

Too late, I realize the grey, robed man never made a noise. Kurt's boots crunch over the gravelly ground as he moves into the clearing. My smile fades. Kurt looks angry—a barely controlled, feral anger that has his fists clenched and his mouth in a grim, depressed line.

"You." The heated word explodes like fire. "You did this. I don't know how...but I know it was you."

I step farther back, my heart hammering. "I don't know what you're talking about, Kurt."

Kurt moves forward, over the uneven ground, with slow predatory steps . My wary eyes track his approach. They register when he stops, several unthreatening feet away. They catalogue the hands that clench and unclench by his sides.

"I had plans, a destiny to be something more than just an Alpha."

More than an Alpha? I don't say anything, wondering what he's talking about, unsure why he has chosen now for confessional. Why me?

"But you ruined everything."

He straightens, and a small smile plays on his lips.

The change, the incongruous smile, escalates my nervousness. I take a small step to the side, moving inches closer to the trees. The move is not missed by Kurt, and his body mirrors my own. That subtle shift of muscles tells me I'm trapped.

His smile grows a little, and he continues like our little dance didn't just happen. "It all started with Noah and a stray bullet..."

I frown. How does he know about the bullet that injured Noah? I suck in a shallow breath. "It was you."

"Actually, that one was an accident. Somehow I missed the elk. But it wasn't totally wasted. It gave me an idea."

"An idea?"

"A new plan."

And I'm rocked by understanding. "You shot Adam."

"Of course I did. He was taking too long to decide. He was always too soft." He says the final word quietly, full of scorn and contempt.

"You could have killed him!"

Kurt crosses his arms, smirking—an ugly twist of his mouth. "That was the idea."

I don't, can't, reply. There are no words in my shocked, scared brain. No muscles that can work in my tight, agonized throat.

He takes a step forward, eyes blazing. "But you, a weak human, was all it took." He shakes his head then looks at me. "Showing Noah is as soft as his father."

"The bonding." I breathe.

"Yes." Kurt hisses the word. "The bonding."

My hand comes up to my head, pushing in on my temple as connections are made and implications are grasped. "You didn't expect Noah to make a different choice."

"To overrule me." The second word seethes out on a growl.

"He made the right choice for his pack. And for Tara." *Your daughter!*

"And I had to resort to that." His finger stabs the air, pointing past the ledge, to the Glade. "At every step I was able to respond and keep moving forward. It was you that kept getting in the way."

And now I'm getting angry. A nervous anger fueled by fear, but anger nonetheless. It makes me reckless. "You wanted this all along."

"I was meant to rule them both. Them all!"

I drop my voice, knowing he can hear me. "Noah's twice the Alpha you'll ever be."

Kurt inflates and expands, rage distending his body and his face. "You will learn the superior power of a Were!" He roars, a drop of spittle catching on his beard. His big body trembles, fury rippling up and down.

A funny smell wafts over, a slightly metallic scent weighing on the breeze. Kurt is close to snapping.

What do I do?

I need Noah. But if he's here, the fight that was just averted will become a reality.

But the barely controlled fear spiking through my nerves is not optional.

He will come.

Kurt begins to change, but it's not the fast magical shifts I've seen up until now. He does it slowly, agonizingly. His face lengthens to form a muzzle, the skin stretching and twisting. His arms drop to the ground, bones grinding as they shorten and thicken. His back arches as russet fur pushes through. It's drawn out and grotesque. Caustic bile leaves an acrid taste in my mouth. I don't have any saliva to wash it away.

An angry, red wolf stands before me. He stretches his neck, head tilting from side to side— adjusting to his new predator body. A growl ripples across his serrated muzzle. Hatred shines from his hazel eyes.

He throws his head back and falls forward on a roar, spittle flying through the air in a stringy arc. And I know why he has chosen to tell me the truth. He doesn't plan on me living long enough to tell the story.

This is a wolf with nothing to lose.

Then he's powering toward me, thundering paws counting down his approach, eyes getting closer, teeth getting bigger. I'm frozen, fear congealed in my throat, no longer letting me breathe.

Just a few yards away, he pushes into the air, into a leap that will bring him crashing down on me. His mouth opens, two rows of teeth preparing to sink into my flesh. I bring my arms up in front of me—useless fragile protection against the snarling mass of fury and hatred that is bearing down.

In a sudden blur of movement, dazzling white streaks through the space before me, crashing into Kurt midair, pushing him off course and slamming his body into the ground. Kurt's wolf form gouges through the dirt and gravel, leaving behind a shallow groove.

Noah stumbles, then rights himself, instantly turning and coming to stand in front of me. My knees go weak, relief and fear robbing them of strength.

Kurt heaves his russet body up and walks toward us, growling menacingly, his head low and shoulder blades jutting to the sky. He weaves from one side of the clearing to the other. Noah stands still, only his head tracking Kurt's zig-zagging approach.

Without warning Kurt leaps again, jaws open, straight for Noah. I feel my own body brace for the impact. Noah rears on his hind legs, meeting him mid-flight. They crash together, teeth flashing, mighty growls bouncing off the rock wall behind me. Kurt's momentum pushes Noah back; Noah twists slightly, preventing him from falling over. Kurt pushes his head forward, trying to get to Noah's throat. Noah twists again, snapping inches from Kurt's face. It's enough for Kurt to pull back and take a few steps away. He stands there, taking stock.

Kurt moves forward, another stealthily measured approach. Noah takes three steps forward, intending on meeting his attack. Kurt's gaze flicks over to me, seeing the opened space around me. He sidesteps, looking to get around. I take two frightened steps backward, my back crashing into the wall. Noah registers his intent, a roar ripping through his chest, and in a flash, he steps to the side and pushes his front paws off the ground, and moves to deflect the attack.

Kurt locks his massive body, ready for the white Were that is coming at him. Canines glint as his mouth, wide open, spears for Noah's throat. Again the massive bodies collide, and broad heads snap, biting at throats, shoulders—anything they can get a grip on. A yelp rises from the writhing mass of fur, and my heart stops.

Kurt has managed to push Noah to the ground, his fast-moving head snapping, pulling back, and snapping again. Noah uses his powerful back legs to push Kurt off him, and he stumbles back a few steps. Noah instantly rights himself, skidding back to his place before me. I feel something tear in my chest when I see a dark, dirty-red gash down his left shoulder. *Noah's been hurt.*

Kurt sees the seeping blood, garish against snowy-white fur, and an evil, satisfied smile lifts up his lips. He bows his head again as he moves forward once more. He's sensed a weakness and he comes in, looking to exploit it.

This time Noah doesn't move from his position in front of me.

Kurt moves forward, and the agonizing fight is played out once more. Noah rears, and once more, there's a clash of coppery red and silvery white, of sharp teeth and colliding bodies, of angry attacks and desperate defenses. Kurt's onslaught is powered by violent, mindless fury. I'm his target, and Noah is in the way. Noah pushes him away again and again. Kurt comes again and again. Each time they collide, my wide, frightened eyes can barely register what's happening, who is gaining in this battle.

I dig my hands into the wall behind me to hold me up as I realize that in this fight, a fight that was never fair to start with, Noah is at a disadvantage. He's the proverbial sitting duck; all he can do is wait for Kurt to come at him again and again. At a disadvantage because he's protecting me.

Unable to use the speed that could have given him the upper hand.

I need to do *something*, but what? I look at the great big wolf before me, the older, more experienced russet wolf that is getting ready to attack again. And an idea forms. But it's going to need two of us.

As Kurt accelerates, his body gaining momentum as his stride extends, I take two steps back. Please let him hear me.

Don't move, Noah.

Noah freezes, his ears turning back. And I leap onto his back. I feel his body halt, tense beneath me.

Jump!

Without hesitation, with split second timing, Noah arches into the air. I duck low over his shoulders, my hands sinking, gripping into his fur, my left hand becoming slick with Noah's blood.

And we're sailing through the air, straight over an astounded Kurt.

Noah lands a few feet past him and instantly spins to face his adversary. The moment he's still, I slip from his back.

I'm okay. I run for the edge of the trees, finally giving Noah the room and freedom he needs.

With my assurance, Noah doesn't need to turn back. He keeps his eyes trained on Kurt, who has skidded to a halt, surprise, astonishment slowing him down. Which is all Noah needs.

He runs at him, his powerful, white body lancing across the clearing, at a speed I've never seen before.

Kurt never has a chance to completely turn around. Noah is on him within a split second, and with unerring accuracy, his mouth goes for Kurt's throat. His momentum crushes Kurt to the ground, Noah's muzzle never leaving the soft, exposed flesh it has attached to.

It's then that I feel them. I turn to see two packs of wolves surrounding me. The Phelans and the Channons have arrived, fanned out through the trees.

Just in time to see Kurt's defeat.

Noah's massive head pins Kurt to the ground. Kurt struggles, his russet body scraping over the dusty, rocky ground then stops when the movement puts more pressure on his throat. Noah growls, his muzzle wrinkling, body heaving with exertion, the dark red blood now extending down his leg.

Kurt goes limp, his head falling to the hard ground, eyes closing. He is incapacitated and completely submissive, waiting for Noah to finish him.

Noah's lips tip up, showing the razor-sharp teeth that are digging into thick fur. He growls again, jaws clamping down just a little bit more. Kurt doesn't move.

I hold my breath, wanting to tear my eyes away from the gruesome, humiliating sight, but they stay trained on the two Weres.

The Phelans are silent as they watch the victory, the Channons among them watching this voiceless loss.

Noah releases and he steps back. He pushes his proud, dirty body upright, expanding on a breath. His neck arches up, his eyes trained on Kurt. Despite the dirt, the blood, and the barely concealed exhaustion, he looks striking, imposing. Magnificently alive.

Kurt lies there for another moment, taking long seconds to register what has happened. Hazel eyes open and his head comes up, seeing Noah then registering the two packs behind him. As he pushes himself up, his head drops.

Noah transforms to human form.

"Kurt Channon." His voice carries through the clearing, ringing with the authority of an Alpha. "You have broken the Precepts, dishonored all that Weres stand for. You shall never again hold the title of Alpha, and are banished from the Channon pack."

I feel rather than see the flash of anger that spears through Kurt. His body never moves; his eyes remain downcast. I tense, knowing Noah is painfully vulnerable in human form. He has put far more trust in Kurt than he deserves.

But Kurt merely turns toward the opposite side of the clearing, and with his head hanging low, his tail brushing the dirt, heads for the trees. He doesn't look back at the pack he has to leave.

The silence is absolute. Birds are mute. No one moves. Even the breeze has been curbed.

Noah slowly turns to face me, the trees, and the two packs. His handsome face is a jumble of shock, regret, pride, relief.

And a roar lifts up from the trees. I turn to find the Phelans as humans too, and they are clapping, cheering, their arms lifted in victory. They rush at Noah, whose eyes go wide at the tidal wave of family coming at him. They engulf him, Beth taking him into her arms, Mitch wrapping both of them in a hug of his own. The others revel and whoop around them like a carousel.

I smile, and it makes my eyes sting. Relief is washing through me, making every exhausted muscle and every trembling joint go weak. *He's okay. He's okay.* I squeeze my eyes shut, trying to contain these emotions, but a small tear manages to slip down my cheek.

I open them to see Noah peeling himself from the mass of people, and they part as he takes a few steps forward. Then he is striding toward me—electric blue eyes holding me captive. Their intensity steals my breath.

His hand comes up to cup my face, his palms along my jaw, his fingers spearing into my hair. And he is kissing me with fervent emotion. His lips fasten to mine. He tastes of dust, of the sun, of Noah. The best taste in the world.

His lips and his hand don't let go. Our connection is physical, emotional, visceral. Reassuring me, reassuring him. An affirmation of life. A testament to our love.

"I love you," he murmurs against my lips.

"Oh, Noah, I love you too."

38

NOAH

Our whole journey, we've been like two magnets drawing closer and closer, the pull becoming stronger and stronger. Nature taking its course to bring them together... Eventually coming to a point where nothing can keep them apart. Only at peace when they are united, aligned, and balanced. And if you try to separate them, that magical connection will blaze, the two halves will pull, tremble, strain in their drive to return to the other.

One of the most powerful, undeniable, impenetrable forces known to man.

I pull Eden in closer, her warm, delicate hand in mine, her lush green eyes soft with tenderness. And there, in the ICU waiting room, I kiss those rose-red lips. It's a kiss full of heat, affection, and potential. It doesn't take long before it's a kiss full of fire and promise and need. And I have to remind myself where I am. I pull back, sucking in lungfuls of unforgettable wildflowers.

With foreheads touching, hands caressing, we smile. We have so much to talk about, but there's been no time, no privacy. We've barely discussed the Claiming, who her identical male alter-ego was, Kurt, calling the animals...does she have a favorite cheesecake recipe.

But we have plenty of time for that. Because the invisible, persistent force that pulled us through has never been stronger. I can feel the warmth of her happiness, the intensity of our passion, the gentle glow of love. The twinge of helplessness that the final piece of the puzzle, my father, remains unconscious down the hall. Each of her emotions mirroring mine.

A beep fills the room, and Eden sits forward, retrieving her phone out of her bag. Tara, across the room, covers her mouth with her hand, quickly tucking her own phone between her and Mitch. Bored Tara is always a worry—an unpredictable, some-times hazardous force. I can't imagine she can get up to much in a hospital waiting room, but I've had an entire childhood learning not to underestimate my brother's mate.

Eden's hair shifts over her shoulder, the hair she always wears down now. I can't help myself, I lean forward to tuck it behind her ear. My fingers brush those silken strands.

Then stop.

And fall away.

Behind Eden's ear, partially covered by her hair line, is a mark. That place she always used to rub. A perfect circle...with a five-pointed star inside it. My hand smacks over my own tattoo.

Eden turns toward me, and her face furrows. I'm pretty sure my face has the lax, wide-eyed expression of shock.

"Noah, what is it?"

But my slack-jawed mouth hasn't recovered the ability to speak. Eden and I...we're...

"Noah, Mitch!" My mother's voice, urgent and high, carries across the ICU.

Grabbing Eden's hand, I rush into Dad's room, hot on the heels of two nurses. Another is already bustling by the machines, one hand on his pulse. Mom is holding the other, tears raining down on her cheeks. Mitch is holding Tara. Everyone is looking at Dad.

Groggy blue eyes are blinking back.

With a croaky voice and a crooked smile he asks, "So, what have I missed?"

THE END

Ready for the next installment in the Prime Prophecy series?
Check out PROPHECY ACCEPTED!

PROPHECY ACCEPTED

Their connection is binding, their love undeniable.

However, Noah and Eden are about to discover that even a love prophesied through the ages must be founded on one thing.

As Noah carries the secret he's too afraid to share, Eden desperately wishes for a destiny that's already come to pass. But as the Prime Prophecy reveals itself so does the greed for what it promises.

As tensions between the packs grow, as the existence of Weres is threatened to be exposed...as Eden finally learns the truth about her inexplicable gift with animals, the two will face their greatest challenge.

Because ultimately the Prime Prophecy will ask for the one thing they have yet to grasp hold of...

Faith.

Continue the epic story of a love that defies boundaries
CLICK HERE

http://mybook.to/LegacyAccepted

Keep reading for a taste of Prophecy Accepted (Chapter 1) - Book
2 in the Prime Prophecy Series!

CHAPTER 1: NOAH

My heart slams my chest with the same thundering beat as my paws pounding the soil. Claws dig into the ground, chewing out clods of dirt as I propel myself forward. Lungs fill like bellows, stretching to capacity then rapidly deflating, keen to do it all over again. The trees become a blur, a camouflage of green on green, the scent of pine hitting me so hard I can taste it.

My head dips, dividing the wind that rushes at us.

Faster.

My whole body smiles as the legs gripping my ribs tighten. Who knew this quiet, shy girl of mine had an inner-adrenalin-junkie just waiting for the right Were to unleash it? Not that I'm complaining—there's no bigger, better rush than running with Eden.

She leans down, her head brushing close to my ear, breath tickling my fur. "Faster," she breathes, this time out loud.

I heard you the first time.

I glance back, at the reddish-brown wolf and larger black wolf who are already falling behind. Tara slows, having the competitive spirit of a sloth. Mitch, on the other hand, dips his head, black brows coming low.

Bring it on little bro.

I stretch eager muscles, suck in my essential fuel—Eden and oxygen—and run. I run like gravity is optional, like the sound barrier is just ahead; I run like this will never end.

Mitch slows, and although I can't hear my twin's growl of defeat, my victorious mind imagines it. Eden's laughter bubbles out, a natural sound of joy and freedom, the magical sound that has progressively lost its rough, unused edge.

But I don't stop; I can't help myself. Without slowing, I angle to the left, forging a new track past the trees. With Eden, I always feel like I can gain a little more speed, a little more strength, a little...well...more.

Because when we're running, nothing matters. It doesn't matter what time it is. As if four months haven't passed since I banished Kurt, that it's only weeks since the icy snow of winter melted. That graduation isn't looming on a very near horizon.

It doesn't matter who we are. Me, the Alpha heir; her, a human. Well, mostly human. Because it was Eden who called the bears and mountain lions—a surprising, unimaginable act that prevented a blood bath. And the average human certainly can't do that. But that guy, her male alter-ego, the one who appeared on the rock ledge, has never shown up again. The very same dude Eden won't mention, let alone discuss.

I head west, knowing exactly where I want to go. Eden leans forward a little more, like it will help us get there a little faster.

Yes.

I smile, feeling canines push into my bottom lip, the wind whipping up the exhilaration. It's just Eden and me and the miles falling behind us. The sun smiling down on us. Our feelings flowing freely between us. Bigger, more real, more doggone incredible than anything I could have imagined.

Because here, alone and together, it doesn't matter that I've carried a secret for four long months. That I've concealed the small circle with a five-pointed star within it, undeniably imprinted on my chest. A little mark with huge implications, implications that make my conflicted heart soar and sink, depending on which way my thoughts take me.

Because no one knows, not one person or Were, that we've bonded. An impossible, confusing dream come true. Not even the one it affects the most–Eden.

Impossible because it's never happened before, impossible because our laws say it can't be.

A dream come true because, well, because it's Eden. The heart-tripping, mind-blowing, soul-grabbing girl that already owns my heart.

But ultimately confusing because I have no idea what it means. I don't know how to tell her. How she's going to take it. Shoot, if she wants this. I don't doubt her feelings for me; I feel them every single day, but a never-heard-of-before-bonding to a future Alpha? That's big. Irreversible, life-changing, how-do-you-even-bring-that-up big.

A stand of rocks crests on the horizon, at the top of a rise, breaking the skyline with their stoic harshness. Every time we run, I find something to jump. First fallen trees, then rocks, eventually the odd monolith. Each jump a little bigger, a bit more of a challenge. I see the rock we jumped last time, all rounded greys and angled whites. But those six feet of granite no longer pose a challenge. My head tilts up, and I angle slightly to the left. The boulder's bigger brother next door does.

Or maybe it's a daddy, because it's almost twice the size.

Now that's a challenge.

Through the wind blasting my ears I hear Eden's intake of breath, sense the jump in her heart rate. I certainly feel her hands clench my fur. The smile grows to a grin as I scan the rock getting closer and bigger.

Paws concertina in and out, over and over, devouring the

distance, bringing us closer. Eden presses her front to my back, hands deep in my fur.

With precision timing, I leap, hit its cold hard surface, and push. My front paws have barely landed when they're replaced by my back legs, and I push up again. A powerful thrust and we're on the top. Now comes the awesome bit. I compress down as I land, coiling the spring, loading the gun. And bam! All that potential energy is propelled into the sky. Eden lets go, leans back, and arches to the sun.

The air that was rushing past slows, lifting us, holding us in suspended animation as we defy the laws of physics, stalling the passage of time. There's just a white wolf, stretched and taut, and his gorgeous girl, arched and open. I can just imagine that mane of hers flowing behind like a mahogany sail. It's a beautiful, breathtaking image.

But all things that go up and over a boulder must come down and honor gravity. A breathless moment later I hit the ground, elbows and knees bending, absorbing the impact. Eden's body crashes into mine, for a split second blending us into one.

Making our landings equally as awesome.

Neither of us needs to say a thing; everything we feel is overflowing between us. Two bodies, even one as big as mine, can't contain such a whirlwind. I gallop over grass and gravel, giving us a bit of time, a little to get our breaths under control, but mostly to bask in the wild feelings our runs unleash.

Because I know. I know it's the freedom that Eden loves, that makes this so special. She's had so little choice in her life, so few opportunities to decide. Which is why I'm not landing the bonding in her lap. She deserves to choose, in her own time.

And that's fine; I really don't mind.

I've waited this long.

Eden's legs tensing around my ribs bring me back to the

present. Her thoughts tickling through my mind suggest we should turn around before we end up in Canada. I slow, making a big arc. A rhythmic lope takes us back to the Glade.

Tara and Mitch are sitting in the middle of the grassy clearing. The pine trees that surround it like protective parents glisten with melted winter snow. Back in human form, they're both leaning back, propped on bent arms, chests sucking in lungsful of air.

Eden slips off, her hand running down my shoulder, making me shiver.

Thanks.

Anytime, I reply, my response as sincere as her gratitude.

I head over to the Precept rock, the mini mono-lith that has our four laws carved into it.

YOU SHALL NOT REVEAL THE BLOODLINE
YOU SHALL NOT BOND WITH THE OPPOSITE BLOODLINE
YOU SHALL NOT ATTACK ANOTHER BLOOD MEMBER
YOU SHALL OBEY THE ALPHA

I don't look at the reminder of everything I've just pushed out of my mind. I slip around the back, doing my usual transformation away from the green eyes I can feel following me. I hate hiding, pretending, but the alternative stirs an uncomfortable feeling I've yet to name.

As I return, Mitch grabs a handful of wet grass and tosses it at me.

The green blades are caught in the breeze and swept toward us. I leap in front of Eden. "Hey, that could have hit my girl!"

Eden's forest green eyes peep up at me as she slips beneath my arm. That sense of connection that never leaves gives me a jolt. I love it. It keeps me anchored. It keeps me high.

"My hero."

Tara snorts. "Thank Galactus you were there. Eden, you're going to have to gain some weight. We need to slow this Were down."

"I won't if we keep doing this every week."

I squeeze her hand. "Although if Tony keeps making those cheesecakes..."

Eden's eyes light up at the mention of the chef who works at her mother's Inn. A chef that seems intent on spoiling her more than me. "A cheesecake challenge."

My girl's version of heaven.

"As your bestie, I should help."

Eden nods sagely. "Proving there is no such thing as the selfish gene."

Tara shrugs dainty shoulders, tilting her head in an unsuccessful show of modesty. "I'm a team player."

Eden's eyes squint as she stares ahead, her lips puckering just a little, just enough to focus my eyes on them. "We'll start with the raspberry white chocolate swirl."

"Or the triple-choc cheesecake with the salted peanut caramel."

"We don't want to leave out the baked cherry and hazelnut praline."

Mitch sits up a little straighter. "It couldn't be a pizza challenge?"

Both girls turn to him, shocked, a little stunned, looking a bit like Eden did after she witnessed the first time I changed. Come to think of it, I looked like that, too. I shake my head. Mitch has been with Tara long enough; they're bonded, for heaven's sake, to know better.

"Of course not!" Tara punches his arm. "They don't even start with the same letter."

Eden and Tara laugh as Mitch mumbles something about cheese fitting the bill.

Just as I plonk myself on the grass, bringing Eden down with me so I can rest my head in her lap, Tara decides silence is over-rated. "So, guys, we have a double birthday coming up, and it's a significant one. I've already spoken to your mom about initial preparations."

I feel Eden tense in the legs cradling my head, but more so deep within. "How big is this thing going to be?"

"I'm defs keeping it low key this time. Some peeps, some dancing..."

I hear Mitch shift in the grass. "Can I do the music?"

"No!" Three voices chorus their horror.

Mitch grins as the girls laugh, and I look up to the sky, seeing the weak spring sun doing its best to warm us. It's all I need to expand my chest in a deep breath and squeeze out any residual doubts that I'm doing the right thing.

Sitting there, in this place where time seems to stand still, I look to the girl I want to spend the rest of my life with, a girl I'm not supposed to be able to. I suck in another deep breath, a breath full of hope, her wildflower scent...and patience.

I can wait.

CONTINUE THE STORY OF A LOVE THAT
DEFIES BOUNDARIES HERE

HAVE YOU READ THE PRIME PROPHECY PREQUEL?

As an exclusive for my subscribers,
you can download it for free!!

Tara grew up playing and laughing with her two best friends. Life is uncomplicated and carefree...until she falls for one of them. The wrong one.

Because Tara is the first born of her pack, and with the title comes responsibility - the expectation that she will bond with an Alpha heir to strengthen her pack's standing...and Mitch was born seven minutes too late.

Tara's heart is torn when a deep connection with Mitch is awakened and she discovers the potential for so much more than friendship. But her mind knows what she must choose.

When the impossible strikes Mitch's family, when their

sacred Glade is threatened, Tara is forced to decide — her heart or her pack?

USA Today Best-Selling author, Tamar Sloan, brings you the prequel of the breathtaking and best-selling Prime Prophecy series. Discover where a love destined to leave a legacy all began!

CLICK HERE TO DOWNLOAD FOR FREE!

ALSO BY TAMAR SLOAN

KEEPERS OF THE GRAIL

The legendary Holy Grail is real.

Yet everything known about it is a lie.

KEEPERS OF THE CHALICE

A vampire. A huntress.

A cure that will change everything.

KEEPERS OF THE LIGHT

Angels and demons have battled for millennia.

Their inevitable war has begun.

KEEPERS OF EXCALIBUR

A fated love. A cursed wolf.

A supernatural war only they can stop.

DESTINED DEMIGODS

Love that defies the gods.

Powers that define destiny.

ELEMENTAL GAMES

Elemental powers. Deadly Games.

No escape.

THE SOVEREIGN CODE

Humans saved bees from extinction...and created the deadliest threat we've seen yet.

THE THAW CHRONICLES

Only the chosen shall breed.

ZODIAC GUARDIANS

Twelve teens. One task.

Save the Universe.

ABOUT THE AUTHOR

Tamar hasn't decided whether she's primarily a psychologist who loves writing, or a writer with a lifelong drive to make a difference. She must have been someone pretty awesome in a previous life (past life regression indicates a Care Bear), because she gets to do both. She divides her time between helping families and writing emotion driven YA stories set in amazing imaginary worlds that surprise even her.

The driving force for all of Tamar's writing is sharing and connecting. In truth, connecting with others is why she writes. She loves to hear from readers. Find her on all the usual social media channels or her website, www.tamarsloan.com where can download one of her books for free.

(Seriously, I LOVE hearing from you guys!)